FIFTH
GIRL

THE FIFTH GIRL

Georgia Fancett

PENGUIN BOOKS

PENGUIN BOOKS

UK | USA | Canada | Ireland | Australia
India | New Zealand | South Africa

Penguin Books is part of the Penguin Random House group of companies
whose addresses can be found at global.penguinrandomhouse.com

Penguin
Random House
UK

First published by Penguin Books 2021
001

Typeset in 11.75/15.7 pt Times New Roman PS Std
by Integra Software Services Pvt. Ltd, Pondhicherry

Printed and bound in Great Britain by Clays Ltd, Elcograf S.p.A.

The authorised representative in the EEA is Penguin Random House Ireland,
Morrison Chambers, 32 Nassau Street, Dublin D02 YH68

A CIP catalogue record for this book is available from the British Library

ISBN: 978–1–787–46344–8

www.greenpenguin.co.uk

For my husband Ben, my children: Calico, Hero and Hardy, and my mum and dad. Thank you for your support, suggestions and love.

Chapter 1

Detective Sergeant Peter Rawls had not shaved for more than a week and it was starting to get on his nerves. It wasn't that he had been meticulous about shaving before – far from it, in fact – but he did find, as the days went by, that he resented not having a reason to. It had been more than two months since he had last needed to shave because it had been more than two months since he had last been at work, and somehow, without work, he had seen little point in making the effort.

Rawls was clipping his bonsai. He was in his happy place, or at least, the place where he was as happy as he could be, under the circumstances.

The two days of leave that his DI had first suggested had turned into two weeks, the two weeks had turned into two months. He hadn't asked for the time off. He hadn't wanted the time off, but God knew, and Rawls did too, that he had needed it. The trouble was that Rawls didn't like having time off. He didn't like his own company; it gave him time to brood, and wasn't that the reason he had needed time off in the first place? Because he had spent too much time in his own head?

He dragged his palm across his cheek, irritated by the noisy stubble, then picked up his pruning shears and forced his fingers into the delicate handles.

Rawls didn't exactly fit the profile of a person interested in bonsai. He was tall and broad-shouldered and, at more than six foot by the time he was fifteen, he had developed first a slouch and then a shambling stoop that had stayed with him ever since. He stood in that manner now, his shoulders hunched as he snipped rapidly at a stunted Chinese Elm with the dexterity of a trained hand working from muscle memory.

It had been DI Washington who had pulled him to one side. He had pressed his skinny fingers into Rawls's considerable bicep and whispered into his ear that he should get his arse into his office, right then and there, if he knew what was good for him. Rawls had not resisted, and they had moved together through the open-plan office with the air of a couple of ballet dancers in a well-rehearsed scene.

'This has got to stop,' Washington had said as the door closed behind them. 'Right now, right here, it has to stop.'

Rawls had nodded. Washington was right; he had gone too close to the edge, and he did have to stop before he tipped himself right over.

'You know that I can't let this carry on, don't you?' Washington continued.

Rawls had nodded again but kept his eyes on his shoes, his head low, his brain racing.

'Peter,' Washington's face had the look of someone in pain as he spoke, 'you have to move on, you can't let it eat at you like this.'

Rawls had known that he couldn't, that he shouldn't, but he had tried anyway, and every day, instead of feeling better, he had felt a little worse. First his patience had grown thin, his temper a red line as tight and narrow as a cotton thread, or perhaps more accurately, a fuse in a stick of dynamite, and then he had stopped sleeping. To be fair, he had stopped trying to sleep because, when he did, his mind had shown him pictures that he had not wanted to see; pictures of his past, of his future, of his mistakes. His mistake.

'I just need a bit more time,' he said. 'Maybe a couple of weeks off, just to get my head straight.' He'd hoped that a couple of weeks would be enough – truth be told, he'd hoped a couple of days would be enough – but he'd been wrong. He'd needed time to recover, to recharge, but the realisation had not come easy. He wasn't the kind of guy who liked to spend too much time in his own head.

Washington had fiddled with a book on his desk. 'How long do you think you'll need?'

Rawls had had no idea. A week? Two weeks? Who knew? Now, more than two months later, he felt rested but not healed, and, if he was being honest with himself, he wasn't

3

entirely certain that one ever really did heal from this sort of thing. It was like an open wound, almost healing over before tearing itself open again.

He put the shears down. He needed to get out of the house, to clear his head.

Rawls glanced at the time – it was a little after six; he'd been out all day. He closed the door, shook off his wet jacket and hung it over the stairs.

'Hello?' he called, his voice too bright, like a drunk trying to fool a traffic officer. 'Anyone home?'

'In the kitchen,' Eileen called back, and he thought her voice had a similar quality to his own.

The kitchen was steamy and hot, and Eileen was at the sink in what Rawls thought of as her home uniform: baggy trousers and a tight black T-shirt.

'Where have you been?' she asked without turning round, absorbed in pouring boiling water into a large pan of potatoes.

Rawls could tell from the tone of her voice that she wasn't happy. 'I was pruning all morning and needed some air so I popped out to get some milk.' He held a bag up as if to demonstrate, but he needn't have bothered because Eileen still hadn't turned round. 'I bumped into Mike from Waterloo Road, you know? The guy who had the heart attack. Anyway, you know what he's like – can't stop him talking once he gets started. I had to listen to every detail of his life since we last—'

She cut him off, turning to face him, her face drawn, her eyes a warning. 'Really? For the entire afternoon?'

Rawls bristled. 'I didn't know that I needed permission to go outside; I'll remember to fill in a slip next time. I am allowed to leave the house, you know? I'm on garden leave, not house arrest.'

He tried to smile, to let Eileen know it was joke, but she ignored him and reached for a bottle of wine which was open on top of the microwave. She filled a glass before offering the bottle to Rawls who studied the label briefly.

'Merlot.' He screwed his nose up. 'No thanks, I'll grab a beer.'

'Suit yourself,' she said. 'I've been trying to call you – don't you check your phone these days?'

Rawls reached into his pocket. His phone was on silent. In fact, he had felt the light vibrations of incoming calls, but had chosen to ignore them. He had been lost, not literally but figuratively, lost in his own head, considering his options. How long he had walked, he couldn't have sworn to, not even in a court of law, but his tired legs attested to the fact that it had been further than he might usually have gone. He had found himself outside of St James's cemetery. He had always loved the place with its smooth finished limestone chapels and their Gothic stone traced windows. The chapels were joined together at the centre by an ornate gateway where once a magnificent spire had reached up towards heaven and carried with it the aspirations of so many who had passed beneath it. The spire had gone now, removed some time back in the Eighties for fear that it might topple on someone and hasten their own journey through the glorious porte cochère and into the consecrated ground beyond. Rawls often wished that he had taken time to admire it before it had gone. It was funny, he thought, just how true the old saying was – you really didn't know what you had until it had gone.

He swiped his phone's screen now: eight missed calls, six from Eileen, and the other two from Tess McGovern, DI at Bath Constabulary.

'Shit, sorry,' he said. 'Did something happen?'

Eileen took a moment to answer. 'I had another call from school. Our daughter has been AWOL again.' She sipped at her glass then turned to check the pot on the stove.

'Shit's sake, what's she playing at?' He glanced towards the stairs then back to his wife.

Eileen shrugged. 'I had to endure that bloody pastoral woman lecturing me on the importance of school attendance; she makes me want to scream.'

'Have you spoken to her yet?'

'Who?'

'Carmen,' he said, looking again towards the stairs.

'She's not here, Peter,' Eileen said. 'She called me earlier to remind me that she had a piano lesson after school,' she made little speech marks in the air over the word school and swallowed another mouthful of wine as if to wash away her frustration. 'I don't know what to do with her.'

Rawls shook his head. 'Me neither.' He paused, considering before he spoke, planning his words carefully, 'Have you given any more thought to going part-time?'

Eileen put the glass down and turned her back to him, poking with a fork at the pot on the stove. 'Are you honestly still going down this path?'

'It's not a path,' he said. 'I just think she would benefit from seeing more of her parents, that's all.'

'Oh, of course, but by parents I assume you mean her mother. I am her mother after all, aren't I?'

'I didn't mean that,' he said, 'I just meant that you work long hours.'

'I work long hours when I should be home. Is that it? Never mind that you're never home and, when you are, it's only because you've been forced to take time off.'

'That's not fair,' Rawls protested, but he knew it was.

Eileen reached for the colander. 'While we're on the subject, you do realise that one of us is still working, don't you?'

The words caught him by surprise; it wasn't like he didn't want to be working. 'I know you're busy,' he said.

'And yet,' she turned to face him, 'here I am cooking dinner while you've been out walking all day. A little help might be nice.'

Rawls flushed. He thought about the washing-up that he'd left beside the sink, his plate from lunch, his coffee cups. 'I was going to do the washing-up,' he started to say but Eileen gave him a look that stopped him.

'The washing-up, eh? Not the washing, the vacuuming, hanging the clothes on the line. Just the washing-up.'

He glanced around the room, at the post he'd opened and left scattered across the counter, the washing machine still

7

full of damp clothes that Eileen had put on before she'd left. She had a point. 'You're right,' he said.

Eileen nodded as if her being right had never been in any doubt. 'And,' she smiled at him briefly, 'I'm not sure that I understand why you can't spend more time with Carmen.' She paused but he knew not to say anything. 'Or is that simply her mother's job?'

He shook his head, defeated. 'I'm sorry,' he said, and she sighed loudly.

'Sorry,' she said under her breath, 'yeah, that'll get the washing dried.'

He stood where he was, unsure of the correct behaviour or what he could do to make it right.

The front door opened and Eileen turned, listening. 'Carmen?'

'What?'

'Carmen, can you come here, please? We need to speak to you.'

'I'm all wet, can we talk when I've changed?'

'No, just pop in for a minute now, hon, please.'

Carmen came into the room and gave Rawls a brief hug. She smelled of rain and cigarettes, and Rawls hoped that his wife wouldn't notice. That, he thought, was a battle for another day.

Carmen was tall for her age, her long, slim legs protruding from beneath a tight black skirt that was so short that Rawls had found himself, just that morning, joking that she might have forgotten it altogether.

'God,' said Carmen, 'did someone die or something? It's so depressing in here.'

Rawls looked at Eileen, who was drying her hands on a tea towel. She kept her eyes down and said nothing, and he guessed that left it to him to open the proceedings. 'Carmen,' he said, 'your mother had a phone call from school today.'

Carmen looked at the floor, her arms folded, her long, wet hair obscuring her face. 'And?'

'And, you didn't go in.'

Carmen looked at him for a moment. 'I didn't feel well.'

'You looked OK this morning.'

'You wouldn't understand,' she said.

'Try me.'

'Mum,' Carmen said, 'explain to Dad about lady stuff, would you?'

Eileen turned round, her glasses steamed from the pot. She took them off and wiped them as she spoke, 'Carmen, I don't know if you think this is all a big joke, but I'm just about at the end of my tether with your behaviour.'

Carmen folded her arms but said nothing.

'I don't know what to do with you,' Eileen said. 'I don't know what to say any more to make you listen to me.'

'Listen to you?' Carmen looked up, pushing her hair behind her ears. 'Listen to you, Mum, that's all I do. I listen while you tell me about all the things that I'm doing wrong, how I need to get it together, like it's all so easy, like you have it all sorted and I'm some kind of failure because I haven't.'

'Oh, for heaven's sake.' Eileen threw her hands up.

'God forbid I defend myself.'

Eileen folded her arms, too; they were like mirror images of each other from across the room. 'Will you just stop with the bloody woe-is-me routine,' she said. 'Honestly, sometimes I wonder what I have to do to get through to you.'

'Perhaps you should try a whistle,' Carmen said. 'Maybe that would make me jump through hoops, or sit up and beg on your command.'

'Carmen,' Rawls interrupted, striving to sound in control, rational, parent-like. 'That is no way to speak to your mother. Honest to God, do you not think we have enough on our plates without you acting like this?'

'Like what?' Carmen asked him. 'Like what, Dad? Like someone who isn't perfect? God, imagine someone not living up to your expectations.'

'That's not fair,' Eileen said.

Carmen turned to her. 'Really, Mum? You don't think that I'm under any fucking pressure of my own?'

Rawls shouted. 'Don't you swear at your mother!'

Carmen swung round to him, her face a mask of fury. 'Oh, because you never do? What is this? "Do as I say, not as I do" day? Sorry, I must have missed the poster.'

'Carmen,' Eileen's voice was shrill with anger, 'while you live under this roof, our roof, you will show us some respect, do you understand? Do you?'

Carmen took a step backwards, pressing herself against the door. 'Of course I understand, it's not like you don't remind me every single day.' Her lip trembled as it had done when she was a child, and she started to cry, covering her face as though the emotion was somehow shameful.

Eileen studied her briefly. 'Don't turn on the bloody water-works,' she said, but she turned the stove off and crossed the room.

'I'm sorry,' Carmen whispered through her fingers and Eileen wrapped her arms around her.

'I'm sorry too.'

Rawls stood motionless; he was never very good in this type of situation. It made him feel like an outsider.

Eileen pushed her daughter gently away from her so that she could see her face. She brushed at a piece of fluff on Carmen's jumper, then leaned forward and kissed her on her forehead. 'We have to sort this out,' she said.

Carmen nodded. 'I'm sorry,' she whispered, her voice muffled. 'I just felt so ill this morning,' she glanced at Rawls, 'I had a migraine. I came on, and I just couldn't face going to school.'

Eileen held her gaze for a moment, and Rawls could see her weighing the conversation. 'Why didn't you say that before?'

Carmen shrugged. 'I felt stupid.'

Eileen hugged her again. 'You're not stupid, but you should have gone in, or at least you should have called and let me know what you were doing.'

'I came back home, you were at work and Dad wasn't in.'

Eileen glanced at Rawls, pursing her lips. He raised his eyebrows at her – why did it matter where he was?

Carmen was saying, 'So I went to bed. I felt better later on and I went to piano and I just didn't know how to tell you, that's all.' She held Eileen's gaze, her face puffy from tears and impossible to read; she was like a tiger one minute, a sparrow the next.

'OK,' Eileen said at last, 'but listen, you can't do it again. One more time and they're talking about an exclusion. We can't go down that road, babe, we just can't.'

Carmen smiled thinly. 'I know. I'm sorry.'

'OK.' Eileen picked up one of Carmen's cold hands and Rawls knew that she was doubting herself, doubting Carmen, doubting him probably, although he wasn't entirely sure why.

'How are you feeling now?' she asked Carmen, and Rawls knew that Carmen had won. Eileen had accepted defeat; it was easier that way, easier than the banging and shouting and crying that would ensue if she hadn't.

'I feel OK now, just cold. Can I go get changed?'

Eileen kissed her daughter's forehead. 'Alright, but dinner won't be long.'

'OK,' Carmen said.

'Do you believe her?' Eileen asked Rawls when they heard the shower go on.

'Nope, not a bloody word,' said Rawls. 'Do you?'

Eileen shrugged. 'I don't know. What are we going to do with her?'

'I was hoping you'd know,' Rawls said.

Eileen handed him the pot. 'Drain these, would you, then give them a mash. I'm going to have another quick chat with her.'

'Don't,' Rawls said. 'Just leave her be, it's not the end of the world.'

Eileen shrugged. 'I just hate leaving it like this.'

'We're not leaving it; we're waiting for the right time.' Rawls wasn't sure when the right time might be but, for now, he needed some breathing space. He always felt exhausted after an argument, washed out and flat. 'Can we just have dinner and talk about it later?'

Eileen sighed. 'You're right.' She paused for a moment then said, 'Where were you?'

'When?'

'When Carmen came home, she said you weren't in.'

'I already told you – I went out to get some milk but I got waylaid by Mike. That is permitted, isn't it?'

Eileen offered him a thin smile and rubbed at her forehead. 'Sorry, I don't know why I even asked.'

'You'd make a good cop,' Rawls said, and laughed.

The evening passed without further event, Carmen quiet and pale, and Eileen stopping occasionally to lay her hand on her daughter's brow as if taking her temperature. Rawls watched them, his two girls, their interactions somehow tentative, like strangers, as though the earlier argument had left a veil between them, unseen but ever present, an energy built in equal measures of distrust and mutual love; it was a strange thing to witness. Later, as he lay in bed next to Eileen, the room lit by a bedside lamp and the blue light of Rawls's phone screen, he hoped that the storm had passed. He rolled on to his back, his phone perched on his chest, and scrolled through the latest bonsai vlogs while Eileen stretched out beside him reading a book.

Eileen sighed and shifted beside him and he glanced at her briefly. 'You alright?' he asked.

'Fine,' she said, 'just thinking.'

He put his phone down. 'Thinking, eh? That's a worry. What are you thinking about?'

'Nothing,' she rolled over and propped her book against him, 'nothing at all.'

'Uh-huh, nothing at all – that's even more worrying than just thinking.'

'OK.' She pushed herself up on to her elbow. She smiled, but it did little more than crease the corners of her mouth. 'I tried ringing you a million times today – why didn't you answer? Were you ignoring me on purpose?'

Rawls closed his eyes. 'I wasn't ignoring you. I promise, I just—' He just what? He didn't know what – he had just needed some time on his own. Had he ignored her, or had he just not known what to say to her? He didn't know that either, all he knew was that he had walked the way people did when they had things on their minds. He had peered through fences into other people's gardens, he had stopped to talk to cats, he had smiled at old ladies, he had walked around a cemetery – he imagined Eileen would have a field day with that one. He had walked and nothing more, but he couldn't tell Eileen that. She would know, no matter how much he might protest to the contrary, that Rawls walking was a bad sign. Walking was not his strong point. If he was walking, Eileen would know that he had something on his mind, and if she knew that, Rawls was sure that Eileen would want to know what it was. The truth was, he wasn't certain that he had the right words to explain it to her.

Eileen laid her head back down and Rawls was struck, as he often was, by how beautiful she was. He bent to kiss her neck.

'Don't,' she said, pulling away from him. 'Please.'

He rolled on to his back and sighed up at the ceiling. 'Sorry,' he said. 'I didn't mean to offend you.'

'For fuck's sake, Peter, can't we just talk?'

You can talk, Rawls thought, *I'll listen*. 'Fine,' he said, 'what do you want to talk about?'

'Where you bloody well were this afternoon,' she said, 'that would do for a start. Oh and you could also tell me what you were up to.'

'I wasn't "up to" anything,' he said. 'I just had my phone on silent, that's all, and, for your information, you rang six times, not a million. Six.'

'Either way, you didn't pick up.'

Rawls sighed again, 'I'm sorry,' he said. 'I just lost track of time. I won't do it again.'

'Yes, you will,' she said, 'and you still haven't answered my question.' She waited a moment, then went on, resigned, 'By the way, did DI McGovern get hold of you?'

Rawls turned to her. 'She called here?'

Eileen sat up and pulled her knees under her chin, wrapping her arms around them. 'Yes, she did. Sorry, I totally forgot to tell you, what with all the hoo-ha with Car and the bloody school calling. Anyway, I guessed from the tone in her voice that she'd also been trying to get hold of you for a while. I also guessed that might have explained why you weren't picking up your phone.'

Rawls made a snorting noise. 'Something like that,' he said. 'Is she the new DI?'

Rawls nodded. 'She's taken over at Bath.'

'Have you met her?'

'A couple of times.' He thought for a minute. 'She's one of those people that you can't quite make out. She's fine one minute, off with you the next.'

'Perhaps it's difficult for a woman in your world.'

Rawls glanced at his wife. 'It's not that, she's just stand-offish.'

'Stand-offish can be down to insecurity, you know.'

'I guess, but I can't imagine her being insecure about anything.'

Eileen smiled at him. 'Sometimes I wonder if you go to work in a car made out of stone.'

He cocked an eyebrow. 'Eh?'

'Like Fred Flintstone.'

He laughed. 'Am I that bad?'

'Maybe not that bad.'

'She's just hard to read, and she has a reputation as a bit of a hard arse.'

'You could just talk to her and get it over with.' Her face clouded for a moment. 'Speaking of DI McGovern, you don't think she could be calling about the missing girl, do you?'

Rawls froze. 'Why?' he asked. 'What have you heard?'

'I don't know,' Eileen said, fiddling with her book. 'Just the stuff on the news ...' She sighed. 'It's just a bit scary, that's all. They're comparing the latest girl to others – you know, older cases. Girls who have gone missing over the past ten years or so. I mean, it just seems to me that you'd be the right person for the job, don't you think?'

Rawls took a moment to choose his words. 'I do know what you mean, but it seems unlikely. I'm off work, I'm out of the loop and, let's be honest, they weren't exactly supportive of my handling of my last ... situation.'

'Ha, not exactly supportive – I think that might just be the understatement of the year.'

Rawls closed his eyes. He didn't want to go there, didn't want to relive it. 'It is what it is.'

'Yeah,' said Eileen, 'and what it is, is just a bit shit.'

'Eileen, can we leave it alone for now?'

She glanced at him. 'They're saying on the news that there might be as many as six girls missing, maybe more.'

'The press do tend to spin things,' Rawls said, 'that's what they're paid to do.'

'Well, what do you think?'

'I think that girls go missing,' Rawls said.

It was true, there was nothing unusual about teenage girls going missing. Girls left home after rows, they ran off to be with boys they had met on the internet, they left to find a better life, they ran away from home; it happened all the time. But Rawls remembered each of the cases, and each time he'd had a feeling that there was something not right about the circumstances. These girls had vanished – no confirmed sightings, no crime scenes, nothing; it was as if they had never been there at all. The first girl had disappeared ten years earlier, two more in the years that followed and finally, only a few days ago, the fourth girl had gone missing. Until then the three girls had not been linked, not officially anyway, but now, with a fourth disappearance, people were starting to join the dots. They were talking, blaming, accusing. People were looking at the police and asking how they had not seen what was blatantly obvious. In hindsight, Rawls thought, it probably *was* obvious, but at the time, perhaps it had been less so. Perhaps – although Rawls had always wondered; he had never quite accepted the official line.

Eileen was evidently not finished.

'Did you know that they're all from Bath? Apparently, they may have joined that cult. The one in Coleford or somewhere, maybe Leigh-on-Mendip, somewhere like that – out in the middle of nowhere. I don't know, but that's what they're saying.'

'Who's saying?' Rawls asked.

'They are,' said Eileen. 'I don't know who, just people.' She looked at him. 'They're saying that your lot, the police, can't get their act together, that everyone knows that something bad is happening up there but no one is doing anything about it. I thought you might have heard.'

Rawls sighed. 'Tell you what, I'll call the office tomorrow and see if I can get the low-down.'

He would be calling the office in the morning, that much was true, but not to get the low-down. He would need to give them an answer. Tess wouldn't wait long, and what she was offering was a way out of the mess he was in. It should have been an easy decision, but still he wasn't sure. This was Tess after all, and he didn't want to jump out of the fire and into what may well be a blazing inferno.

He felt his wife watching him, studying him. 'Anything else?' he asked.

She watched him a moment longer, her eyes searching his. 'No,' she said, 'just call her in the morning and tell me what you can, OK?'

'OK,' he said, and he turned to kiss her, but she had turned her back on him already. He kissed her shoulder instead. 'Night,' he said.

'Night,' she said, 'love you.'

'You too,' Rawls whispered, and he closed his eyes.

It was a little after eight when the clock radio woke Rawls. He turned it off and listened to the sounds of the street for a few minutes: cars and buses, children and dogs, the sounds of the outside world. Inside, in his world, everything was quiet. Eileen and Carmen would have left half an hour ago.

He still hadn't got used to being at home on his own during the day. It felt strange for him to be there. It always seemed too quiet, too empty; it made him feel jumpy as if he were an intruder. When he went downstairs, his footsteps echoed in the hallway, the final floorboard shouting indignantly up at him, as it always did, when he stood on it. He made his usual mental note to fix it. At the end of the hallway was the lounge, a mess of sofa cushions and throws, and he collected his keys from amidst the newspapers spread on the coffee table. He looked around at the room, contemplated tidying it, thought better of it and left, clicking his keys against the palm of his hand.

He looked at the keys for a moment. There between his car key and house key was another, the key to a pristine Ford Focus RS with one careful previous owner. He stared it at for a moment. *Buy in haste, repent at leisure.* He laughed, although he wasn't sure why. The car had cost too much to buy, it had cost too much to insure, and Rawls had palpitations at the thought of anything going wrong with it; the tyres alone would cost more than a month's Tesco bill. Eileen had gone ballistic when he had finally plucked up the courage to tell her. She had accused him of having a mid-life crisis, and he couldn't say that he entirely disagreed with her. Still, the car was the only thing that got him feeling remotely excited at the moment.

Not that excitement had been his goal. He had developed a habit of making poor choices since that first panic attack when his body had broken out in a cold sweat, his heart had raced so fast that he was almost certain he was going to have a heart attack, and his hands had trembled like someone coming down from a night of heavy drinking. He'd bought the car without really thinking and it had seemed like a good idea at the time. To be fair, it still did, to Rawls anyway; it made him happy. The deep shine on the paintwork, the purr of the engine at idle, the way it hunkered down and gripped a bend in the road, all of it, from the look to the smell, made Rawls smile. And wasn't that what it was all about? Smiling, finding your happy place? Wasn't that what you needed when you were in a crisis? *Had* he been in a crisis?

It had come as these things so often do, like a thief in the night. It wasn't something you talked about in his position – certainly it wasn't something *he* talked about, anyway. He knew that people did talk about these things, about their feelings, how they couldn't leave the house, or how they found themselves unable to cope. And he had sympathised with them too, of course he had – who wouldn't? But he hadn't been depressed; he wasn't having panic attacks; he simply needed to pull himself together, to get on with it. Put his big girl pants on, as the saying went. He laughed at that now. If only it had been that easy.

His first inkling had been a sudden, morose sense of his own mortality, which had been followed by the sad conviction that he was of little consequence and had achieved nothing of any worth. He had found himself in bed at night, Eileen asleep beside him, wondering what people would say at his funeral were he to die at that very moment. What would they point to as the essence of what he stood for, or as an example of who he was? Nothing, he thought; he had nothing that said, 'This life belongs to Peter Rawls.'

And so, he had bought the car. He had seen it on the AutoTrader site. It had been something to do during a long, and incredibly boring, stake-out. He was scrolling absently through his phone: first Facebook, then Instagram, then Twitter, then Gumtree and finally, AutoTrader. And there it was, glorious and inviting, and so tantalising that, looking back, he seemed to recall actually licking his lips at the thought of it. He knew that he should have spoken to his wife first, but he had sent off the enquiry and the rest had all been a bit of blur. He had wanted to tell Eileen before he bought it, had been aware that he should discuss it with her, to explain his reasons and make sure that she was alright about it. Truth be told, he couldn't imagine how he would have felt if the tables had been turned – if it had been Eileen who had come home with a new car. Maybe he would have reacted in exactly the same way. The trouble was, the moment had simply not presented itself. They seldom talked any more, not properly anyway. He wasn't sure when they had last talked about anything other than work, the house, Carmen, the news.

Perhaps the reason he was so reluctant to come to terms with this sad realisation was that it would mean admitting that his mother had been right about him and Eileen all along. He could see her now, holding his hand in hers, smiling at him the way she did when she was convinced that she was right. 'You two are from different worlds,' she had said.

He never denied that they were, but he didn't think that it mattered. Besides, it was Eileen who had made the effort to change, and Rawls knew that she had done it for him, for Carmen, for everyone but herself.

Rawls had what he wanted out of life. A beautiful home, a beautiful wife and daughter, a steady income, a decent pension. Eileen had never wanted a conventional life, but she had married him and taken a nine-to-five job that helped pay for their nice house in Bath, and provide her daughter with all of the things that she had never had herself. In the beginning maybe he hadn't fully understood the sacrifice that Eileen had made, but as the years went by Rawls had seen the weight of the compromise. He would occasionally see flashes of the free-spirited girl that he had once known, the woman who had wanted to be a Reiki healer and spend her life travelling around in a camper van. However, these glimpses were fleeting, and to dwell on them sent a wave of pain through him, a pain that felt a lot like guilt.

The phone rang in his pocket and he pulled it out, considered the screen for a moment and then swiped to answer. 'Rawls.'

'Rawls, it's Tess, DI McGovern.'

Rawls screwed his face up and mouthed 'DI McGovern' to the empty room. He just wasn't sure how he felt about Tess. The thing was, she was everything that he resented in the force. Brought in from the outside with nothing but managerial experience to her name, she had been fast-tracked through the ranks, promoted to DI in less than a couple of years, and was about as difficult to read as *The Rime of the Ancient Mariner*.

'Hi Tess, I was just about to call you.'

'Have you come to a decision?'

It occurred to Rawls that at least she hadn't asked if he had come to his senses.

'Yes,' he lied.

'Good,' she said. 'Today, eleven hundred hours. I'll see you then.' She put the phone down without saying goodbye.

'Bye,' Rawls said into the silent phone.

He stood still for a moment, thinking. He would need to have a shave.

Chapter 2

Tess had left him waiting; he imagined that she always did – it would be part of her routine. A fine spray of sweat had broken out on his upper lip and forehead and he fidgeted with his collar. He stood up and headed to the bookshelf, scanning the titles for any that he recognised, just for something to do. The office was pristine and there were almost no personal effects, except for a framed photo on her desk, turned away from his prying gaze. He thought about turning it around but somehow that seemed an invasion of her privacy, not to mention the risk of being caught with the photo in his hand. He turned away instead and let his eyes settle on the neat pile of folders stacked at the edge of her desk. Rawls considered briefly the possibility that they might all contain information about him, then dismissed the idea. It couldn't be, surely – not a pile that big.

He understood that this was all part of her game, letting people stew while they waited. He had done it himself on more than one occasion, but this did nothing to quiet his nerves. He had just reached the point where he was examining his reflection in the glass cabinet against the far wall, his head tilted back as he checked for any errant nostril hairs that might be hiding there, when the door burst open.

'Rawls,' Tess said, extending a perfectly manicured hand as she stepped into the office, 'so glad you've come in.'

'It's good to see you again,' he said, extending a gigantic hand of his own.

She smiled but Rawls suspected that it was merely because it was the polite thing to do.

'Yes, well, you too,' she said. 'You're ...' she cleared her throat, 'you're well?'

'Yes, thank you.'

She frowned. 'I mean, you're OK now?'

He smiled. 'As OK as I can be.'

Her frown deepened. 'Are you still seeing someone?'

'A counsellor, you mean?'

She nodded. 'Yes.'

Rawls ran a hand over his smooth cheek. 'I think I'll be seeing him for a while.'

'But you *are* OK?'

'I'm OK,' he said.

'Fabulous,' she said, giving Rawls a tight smile.

Fabulous? Rawls wasn't sure that was how he'd describe the situation.

'Shall we start?' she went on.

'Let's,' said Rawls.

Tess wasn't doing anything to endear herself to him. He had known her previously, although not very well, in her role as a detective sergeant. Her promotion to detective inspector had come at around the same time that he had been signed off, when she had taken over from the previous DI who had moved somewhere up north. It felt strange to Rawls to picture returning to work and reporting to someone who had less experience than he did. He tried to tell himself that he didn't mind, not exactly; that it was just going to take a bit of getting used to. They had spoken once, he remembered, at a conference, and he recalled her telling a group of long-standing officers that she had joined the force because she had wanted to help. This had led to many a titter around the table, but Rawls had not been one of them. He understood this desire to make a change; it had become her one redeeming feature in his opinion. From what he had been told, she had left a job as Director of Customer Experience at Consideration Life, an insurance provider. It had been a position she had held for almost ten years, and, in joining the police, she had taken a considerable pay cut. Not that Rawls was saying the money was bad. It wasn't great but it wasn't terrible, and if you kept your nose clean and your slate wiped, you would retire in your fifties with a gold-plated pension – not everyone could say that. He knew that she was married and wondered if her wife had objected to the decision. The hours were bonkers, the workload insane, the shifts erratic; in Rawls's opinion, it took a special kind of woman to put up with that kind of shit.

Tess patted a folder on top of the pile in front of her and passed it to him. 'We've been trying to keep this out of the press, but we're coming under increasing pressure.'

'From the press?'

She sighed. 'From the press, from the families, from just about everyone.'

'Well, I think you know my thoughts already,' Rawls said.

Tess opened a folder, rifled through it for a moment and pulled out a typed form. She spread it out on the desk in front of her and smoothed the dog-eared corners. 'Yes,' she said, 'I've read your report.'

Rawls leaned forward. 'We should never have shelved those early cases.'

She took her glasses off and rubbed at her eyes. 'I can't comment on what went on before.'

'Can't comment?' Rawls said. 'This isn't an interview.'

'Alright,' she said. 'I think you're right and the investigations were too hasty, cursory at best.'

He nodded. 'I didn't want to let them go.'

'I heard.'

'The trouble was,' Rawls went on, 'there was just too much evidence pointing towards them running away – fighting, truancy, outbursts at school, terrible home lives. Those are the ones that fall through the cracks.'

She ran a hand through her short-cropped hair. 'I know that, you know that; it doesn't make it any easier.'

'I should have done more,' Rawls said.

'No,' Tess shook her head. 'You did what you could under the circumstances.'

Rawls looked away, a thread of panic trying to wind its way into his stomach. 'We never found them, *I* never found them. I have to live with that every day.'

'We can only do what we can do,' Tess said, 'and there was no sign of foul play, no bodies, nothing sinister. The truth was that it did look like they had just upped and left.'

'But you don't think so?'

'I don't,' she said.

'Me neither,' Rawls agreed. 'I never did, but …'

'But you can only do what you can do,' she reiterated. 'Rawls …' she paused, waiting for him to look up, 'you have to put that behind you if you're on board with me. I don't want you, you know …'

'You don't want me wallowing in self-pity?' Rawls offered.

'I was going to repeat my point. I don't want you going around blaming yourself,' she said.

Rawls clenched his teeth. 'Fair shout.'

Tess pulled a handful of sheets of paper from the folder, each with a photo paper-clipped to the corner, and spread them in front of her. 'But they look so similar. How did we miss that?'

Rawls raised an eyebrow. 'You don't have children, do you?' he asked.

'I'm not sure that matters,' she said. 'Why do you ask?'

Rawls held a hand up. 'Only because I do have one, similar age, similar look: tall, slim, long hair.' He looked at Tess then back at the photos. 'But they all look like that. Ripped blue jeans so tight that it must cut off their circulation and tops to freeze your arse off, long hair tied back in a low ponytail. It's their uniform, their identity. I bet if you had a close-up, they'd all have those long fake nails as well. I don't think the look changes much over the years.'

'No, but the similarities are quite striking.' She looked up at him, her face earnest. 'What do you think, Peter? Are you on board? You know you're best placed for this. You're a bloody good detective and you get results; you know the cases better than anyone.'

Rawls considered for a moment. He had worked on two of the three cases: Melody Lockyer and then, later, Yvette Solderton. He had been aware of the Harriet DiAngelo case as well and had brought it to DI Washington's attention while he had been looking into Yvette's disappearance. Three missing girls, all of a similar age, all vanished without a trace. He had not believed them to be a coincidence, not then and not now. The question was though, did he want to drag this up again? Did he want to relive the guilt of the past ten years? Did he want to go back to those days? He wasn't sure that he did.

He leaned forward in his seat, his decision uncertain even to himself until the words came out of his mouth, 'Shall we go over what we have so far?' he asked, opening the file.

She gave him a half smile acknowledging his decision. 'Four girls,' she said. She unclipped each of the photos and sorted them into a rough stack, then tapped them on the desk as though they were the world's saddest deck of cards. 'Melody Lockyer,' she said, handing him the uppermost picture. 'Sixteen years old, five foot seven. She was nearly seventy kilos in this picture, but her father tells us that she had lost a little weight after it was taken, last confirmed sighting out the front of Jolly's in the city centre.'

Rawls turned it over and read what was written on the back: '20 July 2009' – the day she had last been seen. He remembered the first time he had seen the picture and couldn't believe that it had been more than a decade ago.

Tess leaned across with another. 'Harriet DiAngelo.' She set the photo down and a scowling girl with long brown hair stared up at them. 'Five foot eight, last seen by her parents as she left the house following an argument with them; she was seventeen at the time of her disappearance. That was in …'

Rawls helped her out, '2012.'

'The seventeenth of May, 2012,' she agreed.

Rawls picked the photo up and considered it. 'Do you know,' he said sadly, 'it took them two days before they reported her missing? They said they thought she had gone off in a huff and would come home when she calmed down.'

Tess sighed as she set the last two pictures down. 'Yvette Solderton – sixteen, five foot six, fifty-eight kilos, disappeared on the third of February, 2015. Then there's Tanya Hickock, I imagine you've been keeping up with events relating to her disappearance on the news.'

Rawls nodded.

'So you probably already know, she's seventeen, five foot seven.' She leaned back in her chair and stared at Rawls as though she were trying to bore a hole into his head. 'What do you think?' she said at last.

Rawls kept his eyes on the photos. 'About what?'

'About this,' she said, nodding at the photos.

Rawls looked at the girls, then back at Tess. 'I have always believed that they were linked,' he said.

'Despite the lack of evidence?' Tess asked him.

'Because of the lack of evidence,' he said. 'I think it's the reason that they were chosen. I think they were selected because of their backgrounds, because they'd go unnoticed.'

'*You* noticed the first three,' she said.

He nodded. 'Fat lot of good it did them.'

'Well, you've never given up.'

In his time Rawls had seen his fair share of death and destruction but, no matter how many bodies he saw, or broken families he visited, none tore him up as much as visiting the families of missing people. If there was a hell, Rawls thought, it would be remarkably similar to the experience that people went through every single day where a loved one remained missing. The not knowing would eat at them every waking moment. It would rob them of laughter, of fun, of dreams, of aspirations, of anything other than the gnawing certainty that their lives were on hold till their child, mother, father, wife, husband, was returned to them.

'I still look for those girls every day,' he admitted. 'Everywhere I go – the supermarket, the doctor's ...' He rubbed his eyes. 'I know it sounds stupid, but I can't even drive down the road without looking at passers-by and wondering if they might be them. It's been ten years since Melody Lockyer went missing and I've never stopped looking, not completely.'

'Well, now is your second chance to find ...' Tess paused, choosing her words carefully, 'find out what happened to them.' Rawls guessed that she, like him, knew there was little hope that they would find any of the girls alive.

'I'm supposed to be on sick leave,' Rawls said, tapping his head with his forefinger in case she had any doubt as to the sickness that plagued him.

'I know,' she said.

'I wasn't exactly given the option to carry on,' he added.

'I know that too,' she said.

'But on the other hand, it has only been classed as leave.'

She nodded.

'So, there's nothing to stop me coming back?'

'Think of it as a trial, see how you feel,' Tess said, smiling at him.

'A test, you mean?'

'Something like that.'

'You think you can work with me?'

She shook her head. 'The question is, can you work for me?'

Her point was not lost on Rawls and he grinned at her. 'No,' he said, 'I doubt it, but I'm willing to give it a go.'

Tess eyed him over the top of her glasses for a moment, then pushed the photos apart so that they were spread across the desk, each one staring up at them with an accusing gaze. 'Hunch or no hunch, we do have to stay grounded.' She folded her arms. 'I mean, just because they didn't run away, doesn't mean they were taken. Wherever they went, they could have gone willingly.'

'Agreed,' he said, 'troubled children are easy targets for coercion.'

Tess leaned back and closed her eyes. 'We're going to have to explore this cult angle.'

Rawls nodded.

'If we're right, if they're all linked and we missed the link, the press will demand someone to hang out to dry,' she said.

'I know that,' Rawls said.

'It could get ugly,' she warned.

'Then I'm in the right place.'

Tess tilted her head as she considered him. 'They're going to bring up every other unclosed incident of missing people since the Nineties.'

'How many are there?'

'Eleven.'

'Including our girls?'

She nodded. 'But the others are different – drug addicts, an elderly lady with Alzheimer's, a couple of middle-aged men.' She looked at him solemnly. 'I'll leave you the files, but our girls, as you call them, stand out. They're younger than the rest, all still at school, vulnerable young adults.'

'How does someone just vanish?' Rawls said, more to himself than to Tess.

She shook her head. 'Perhaps the question should be, *why* do they just vanish?'

'Maybe.' He leaned forward, smoothing the creases in his trousers. 'Who else is on the team?'

Tess shifted in her seat. 'You know how this works, Rawls. Tanya's case is already a multi-agency collaboration. I'd like you heading up the local investigation but I haven't spoken with the team yet. I wanted to make sure that you were on board first.'

'So you've got MCIT involved already?' Rawls said knowing that they would; he knew too that they would already have utilised the Multi Agency Safeguarding Hub known as MASH and that CEOP, the Child Exploitation and Online Protection Centre, would be assisting, making sure that the incident was being properly managed.

Tess offered a quick nod in response to his question. 'MCIT are involved but for now, I want you to keep a low profile. I've got a young detective, Natalie Parkinson for you to work with initially. She's a good detective and she's discreet, which is good. I don't want to cause a public panic by jumping the gun on these older cases until you've had a chance to go over them again.'

'May I ask why you want me?'

She smiled. 'I think you know the answer to that, you've had solid results in the past and you get the job done.'

Rawls tried to return her smile, to convey that he was grateful for the compliment. It was true, he did get results, particularly in missing persons cases. His results had seen him move into MCIT working under DI Washington about four years previously. The role of MCIT, or the Major Crime Investigation Team, was to respond primarily to homicides and cases of missing persons across Wiltshire and Avon and Somerset. They assisted local constabularies by freeing them up for day-to-day policing.

'Let me get this straight, the team is all up and running but only on the latest case, you want me to take lead of the local team but only once I determine whether there is or is not a link to the past three cases? Is that about right?'

'That pretty much sums it up, I'll still be SIO of course.'

Rawls nodded, it went without saying that Tess would be Senior Investigating Officer but he still wasn't sure where he fitted in. 'And the rest of the local team are happy with this?'

She shook her head. 'Like I said, I haven't mentioned you yet, I wanted to give you a chance to get yourself caught up with everything and—'

'And you wanted to make sure that I was alright?'

'Look, here's the thing,' she said, 'I need your expertise but only if you feel you are up to it. I'll need you to look after yourself, keep up with the counsellor, check in with me every day,' she held a hand up as he opened his mouth to argue, 'every day without fail. Nat will do your leg-work. She can fill in paperwork, drive the car, fetch your lunch if you like but, and I can't stress enough, I need you to look after yourself, OK?

'OK.'

'Good and, one last thing. This is big, I know I don't need to tell you of all people but I need you to be honest with me and with yourself. If you feel like it's all too much and it's getting on top of you, you need to let me know.'

Rawls bristled. He didn't like all this hand-holding. He felt his face flush but he nodded at her.

'I've arranged for Nat to meet you in an hour. I thought, till I've finalised everything, that it might be better for you two to meet in town.'

He frowned but she ignored him.

'At the tea shop near Waitrose, do you know it?'

Twenty minutes later, Rawls found himself walking beneath the famous arch over Bath's York Street. Lost in thought, he barely noticed the Victorian carved statues of Roman emperors who turned their backs on the outside world and stared thoughtfully into the warm green waters of the Roman Baths below.

His hands in his pockets and his collar up against the wind, Rawls was feeling conflicted. He had argued for so long that these girls had not run off to carve out a desperate living for themselves on the streets of Bristol or London, or any other town for that matter, that he had started to feel like a creationist at an evolutionary conference, and now that it seemed as though the rest of the Police Service was finally in agreement with him, he found himself doubting his ability to drive the case forward.

He had seen the chatter on the news claiming that the links between the missing girls were unmistakable, but they weren't really substantiated. It was the other side of the coin. You could believe that they were taken or they weren't, but either way there was no real proof, and it was hard to summon faith that they would get answers a second time round. A part of him hoped that they would prove him wrong, and disappoint the media by discovering that the girls had simply run off, because the alternative was the stuff of nightmares – young girls being taken from their streets, plucked like roses from a bush.

He wondered if young Natalie Parkinson had any idea of what she had let herself in for.

It was a short walk to the tea shop and he used the time to chew a piece of gum. The coffee he had drunk at the office still hung in his mouth like a burial shroud, and he hoped that the gum would freshen his breath. The smell of sugar-free peppermint made him think about Carmen and he wondered if she had actually made it into school today. He checked his messages one last time: no missed calls, no frantic texts. For now, anyway, all seemed quiet on the home front. He jammed the phone back into his coat pocket and walked into the little shop with its boxes of open tea and overpriced teapots hanging like bunting from the top shelves.

The young woman behind the till was singing quietly along to a crackly Billie Holiday recording. She smiled and pointed to a little door which led, presumably, to a tea shop above. Rawls gave her a thumbs up and headed for it, feeling a little like Alice in Wonderland as she went through the tiny door. He grunted his way up the steep steps and was sweating a little as he reached the top. He thought, not for the first time, that he might need to address his middle-aged paunch with something other than his purchase of a car – perhaps he should join a gym.

'DS Rawls,' a voice called to him as he lumbered breathlessly over the finish line.

The woman waving at him was the exact opposite of what he had expected. She was petite with long dark hair and doll-like features. She smiled widely at him and Rawls found himself wishing, even more than he had before, that he had not had to lurch up the stairs like a trained bear at an old-fashioned circus. He rubbed his cold, clammy hand on his trousers before extending it to shake her perfectly pale and warm one.

'Natalie Parkinson,' she said, still smiling, but he noticed that her hand shook slightly when he took it; perhaps she was nervous.

'Rawls,' he said, then laughed, 'but you know that already.'

They sat down, Nat crossing one Converse sneakered foot over the other. Rawls felt suddenly very old and very out of shape and he was glad of the interruption as the waitress, clad almost entirely in black save for the tea, coffee and cake stains down her front, slouched across the room towards them.

'Can I take your order?' she asked with the air of one who cared little for either them or their culinary requirements.

'Tea, please,' said Nat, effortlessly chipper, 'builder's.'

The waitress turned her attention, or at least some of it, to Rawls.

'Do you do a flat white?' he asked, wondering why he had, as he hated them and really wanted a latte.

The girl nodded, scribbling on her pad which was rested on her ample bosom. 'Anything to eat?'

'Not for me,' said Nat, and Rawls, who had been looking forward to a scone with clotted cream and jam, shook his head.

'I'm fine, thank you,' he said, wondering instantly if it would be silly to change his mind.

Natalie *was* nervous, he saw that now that the waitress had gone. She fiddled with a napkin until she knocked over the menu and sent the pot containing a selection of sugar and sugar substitutes clattering to the floor.

'Oops,' she said, bending down to pick up the packets. She sat back up, bumped her head briefly on the table and knocked the menu over again. 'Sorry, gosh, I'm useless.'

'Well that's reassuring,' Rawls said, but he was smiling in what he hoped was a disarming manner.

'Well, you know, not useless, just a bit ...' she paused, searching for the right word, 'rubbish,' she said at last.

'Do you mean nervous?' Rawls asked, and she nodded.

'Sorry, yes, nervous, I suppose. Did DI McGovern tell you? This is my first assignment as a detective. It's hard, you know? I mean, everyone seems to object to us, but the thing is it's not our fault. We've worked as hard as we can to get here and it seems unfair.'

Her voice was fading as she spoke, as though she was losing faith in what she was saying. Either that or she was regretting it, Rawls couldn't tell. He felt a little guilty and slightly angry with Tess. He knew why he had been partnered with Detective Natalie Parkinson, and it was for exactly that reason that she was so stressed. He had been one of the primary opponents to the scheme when it was first put to them, and he had continued to rail against it with angry vehemence. According to Rawls, and many more like him, CID would not benefit from these fast-tracked graduates who came into the force with nothing but a degree and two years of experience on the beat. In fact, it would do the opposite: their introduction to CID would undermine it. CID was a badge of honour, not a school trip out. He believed then, and he still did now, that they could not do the job properly and that, although they might fill a gap, it was like plugging the proverbial dyke with sea-sand.

'Don't be daft,' he said, smiling the smile of one who is about to completely deny his true feelings, 'I'm sure you'll do an excellent job.'

She gave him an awkward smile. 'Thanks,' she said, taking the tray from the waitress who had arrived with neither a smile nor a sunny disposition. The contents rattled a little as Nat put them down and she rubbed her hands as though she might be able to physically stop them from shaking.

'Listen,' Rawls said, his voice sombre, 'this is going to be a tough gig. You know that, don't you?'

She nodded. 'Tess has filled me in.'

'That's good, but we'll need to go through it all again, from the beginning.'

'Starting with Melody?' she asked, and he held a hand up.

'Let's have a chat first, OK? I'm glad Tess suggested meeting here, but it's not exactly the kind of place that I would have picked to go through evidence.'

She nodded. 'And there does seem a lot to go through.'

Rawls gestured at her teapot. 'Shall I pour? Avoid you having to be taken to RUH for third-degree burns from scalding yourself.'

Nat flushed. 'Might be a good idea.' She pulled the napkin out from beneath the tray, making the contents wobble enough for Rawls's coffee to fill his saucer.

He smiled at her again; he found that he liked her despite himself.

'They'd be second-degree burns,' she said, sipping at her tea.

'Eh?'

'The burns. Second, not third. You'd need prolonged contact to make them third-degree.'

'Oh, I see,' he said, grinning, 'I hadn't realised I was joining the pedantic society.'

She laughed. 'Oh yes,' she said, 'didn't you see the sign above the door?'

There was a running joke in the Bath Constabulary that if you wanted to get locked up for the night, you would need to go to Keynsham. It was a fairly good example of the truth being spoken in jest. Bath did not have a proper police station, or at least it didn't have one that you could go into. In fact, if you wanted to report a crime face-to-face in Bath, you had to visit the 'One Stop Shop' on Manvers Street, directly opposite the old police station, and it would be wise to do so within working hours. If you were held in custody for the night, you had to bank on a trip out of town to Keynsham, and if you wanted to see where all the Bath police were hiding, you would need to pop around the back of the Kia garage and knock timidly on an unmarked door.

It was here that Tess had assigned them a grim little office at the very edge of an otherwise open-plan workspace, Rawls discovered when he arrived the following morning. There were windows all around and he thought it a little like being inside a fish tank. If Tess had been worried that there would be talk about Rawls being on the case, she needn't have. The entire floor seemed all but empty except for a couple of uniforms, who had wandered in, faffed for a few moments, their faces pale beneath the harsh lights, then wandered out again. They had nodded and Nat and Rawls had nodded back and that had been that. For now, they were looking into three cold cases, of little interest to anyone. Rawls suspected that that was about to change. Rawls was convinced not only that the three were linked but that the latest case, Tanya Hickock, was as well. For now the focus was on finding Tanya. No one knew who he was, no one knew why he was there but, if he was right, if they had some kind of serial killer on their hands, that quiet would change soon enough.

It hadn't taken the two of them long to cover the small space with boxes that had been retrieved from archives. The boxes had been covered with layers of sticky dust and they had needed to wipe them down before pulling them open. Inside, the notes, some typed, some hand-written, were piled in neat little groups held together with elastic bands, paper clips and staples.

Rawls felt a knot in the pit of his stomach – not fear, exactly, maybe doubt. These weren't just files containing bits of paper; they were the lives, in black and white, of three young girls. He pulled briefly at his shirt collar, a film of sweat developing on his upper lip. The room was cool, but he felt hot, too hot. His hands betrayed a slight tremble as he lifted the first package of information, and he realised that he was nervous. What if his time off had dulled his senses? What if he got it wrong? What if he couldn't do it? He had failed before, he had failed on two of these exact cases. The information either hadn't been there or he, along with his colleagues, had missed it. They hadn't been able to find them. They had let them down, the girls and their families. Could he be about to do it a second time?

His stomach twisted and for a moment he felt physically sick.

'DC Rawls?' Nat looked concerned. 'Are you OK?'

Rawls imagined his face, pinched and tight, white around his mouth, red in the cheeks, sweat running along the creases of his forehead and around his eyes.

He ran a palm across his face and tried to smile. 'Yeah, just a bit hot.' He felt dizzy, light-headed, his heart racing. He knew the signs; his counsellor had gone through them with him, given him advice on what to do, how to handle the panic, but there was a ringing in his ears and his hands were tingling – he couldn't concentrate. 'I, I think I'll just pop to the men's room,' he said. If he was going to have a panic attack it was not going to be in front of Nat before they'd even had a chance to open all the boxes. Tess would never allow him to come back to work again.

Smiling but concerned, Nat stood up so that he could pass. His mind tried to tell him that it was too soon, he wasn't ready, he needed to give himself more time, but his heart over-ruled it. He had to do this; he had to get himself back under control and pull it together, for the girls, for their families, for their friends, for himself. *Breathe*, he told himself as he rushed from the room, *just breathe, like the counsellor said*.

Splashing cold water into his face, he stared at his reflection. He looked tired, the shirt he was wearing almost as wrinkled as his face. He stared for a moment at the way that his jawbone made up the shape of his face, how he looked perpetually like someone who needed a shave, and it struck him that the last few months had not been kind to him. He looked as rough as a badger's arse, as the old saying went.

He could walk away now, just tell them it was too much, that he wasn't ready, or he could suck it up. He chose the latter and he did what he had been shown to do. He took one breath at a time: in, one, two, three; out, one, two, three. And repeat. He tapped at his collar bone and closed his eyes, acknowledging his feelings before letting them slip away, acknowledging and slipping, acknowledging, slipping.

There was a knock on the door, 'DC Rawls?' It was Nat. 'Um, sorry to disturb you. I just thought I'd let you know that, well, um, that DI McGovern is on her way up.'

Rawls imagined Nat leaning forward, her face pressed to the door, her voice low, making certain that Tess wouldn't hear. He let his head fall back, eyes closed, as a lungful of air escaped through his nose. 'Thanks, Nat, be there in a sec.' He smiled weakly at his face in the mirror. Nat hadn't needed to give him the heads-up, but she had, and that was a good start, a really good start.

Tess rounded the corner as he closed the toilet door behind him. She was rubbing hand sanitiser into her hands and she waited for him to open the office door for her before going in. 'How's it going?' she asked without bothering to greet either of them.

'We've just started,' Rawls said. 'It took a while to get everything we needed.'

'You have all the files now?'

'We do.' Rawls looked at Nat and she nodded. She had been in since six thirty and had most of them in the office by the time he had come in, another good sign.

'Where are you starting?'

'At the beginning,' Rawls said, smiling.

'With Melody? What's that – 2009?'

'The twentieth of July,' Nat said.

Tess glanced at her then looked back at Rawls. 'And you're OK?'

Rawls felt his stomach clench. 'I'm fine.'

'Is he?' Tess asked Nat with a smile that was unmistakably loaded.

Nat's eyebrows knitted together, but she nodded and looked away.

'I'll let you know,' Rawls said. 'You don't need to make Nat your spy.'

'You're being paranoid,' Tess said before turning to Nat. 'Let me have a report by the end of the day on what you two come up with. I need a timeline and key witnesses, who you need to speak to again.' She had her hand on the doorknob as she spoke, 'I'll leave you two to it.'

Rawls watched her walking along the corridor; her mobile was ringing, and she tilted her head to answer it as she turned to head down the stairs.

Nat pulled a rubber band from the first pile in front of her, 'Here are Melody's notes. How do you want to go through them – together or one girl at a time?'

'Let's go through them together.' He took a notebook from the pile, recognising the writing. 'You take this one,' he said, passing it to her.

'Is it yours?'

He nodded. 'Better that you go through it, fresh eyes.' He reached for a couple of witness statements. 'I'll go through these.'

They spent the day that way, putting together a timeline, going over key witnesses. Nat had found a flipchart from somewhere and they were bullet pointing each case.

'So,' Rawls said, 'we've got Melody Lockyer, sixteen when she went missing. Where was she last seen?'

'Outside Jolly's at the top of town.' Nat was writing as she spoke.

'Her friend Alice was interviewed back at the time; she would be – what? Twenty-six, twenty-seven by now?'

Nat wrote the name down.

'I'll want to speak to her parents again, and her siblings – she came from a big family. I think we interviewed her sister at the time.'

Nat pulled out an A4 sheet of printed notes and handed them to Rawls. The time and date were given as the 2 August 2009, about a week after she had gone missing.

Rawls scanned the page, found what he was looking for, and read out loud, 'I was with my sister the morning before she went missing. We had not gone to school that day although our parents thought that we had. We sometimes did this because both of us hated school and we both had double science to start with, so we decided to go to town and see if anyone was around that we knew. Mel had a new boyfriend but none of us had met him yet. She was looking for a new top to wear because she was going to see him either that day or the next. I did not stay with her because I saw one of my friends who wanted me to go with her to buy some stuff from Boots, like hair dye and that sort of thing, so I went with her and Mel went off because she was going to meet her friend Alice. That was the last time that I saw my sister.'

'Did the boyfriend ever materialise?'

Rawls rubbed his neck. 'The sister seemed to have been confused about the boyfriend point. We interviewed a few boys but none of them said that they were her boyfriend. They were either just friends or had a sort of relationship with her at some point or another, but nothing serious. We need to get hold of the sister again, see if she can remember anything else, maybe try to speak to Alice again, see what she can tell us. Do we have her interview?'

'Still looking,' Nat said, 'it must be in here somewhere.'

Rawls clapped his hands together; he was feeling better, more together, more himself. 'Who's next?'

'Harriet, Harriet DiAngelo.' Nat reached across the desk and touched another pile.

'OK.' Rawls leaned back in his chair. 'I remember this one. She was,' he paused, 'she was the same age as Melody, seventeen, if I remember correctly?'

'She was, but that was a few years after Melody went missing, 2012.'

Rawls thought about his own daughter at home, nearly the same age as these girls. It sent a wave of adrenaline through him and he bit down on his tongue to suppress it; this was not the time to let his mind play tricks on him.

'Shall I get us both a coffee?' Nat said suddenly, standing up. 'I could do with a loo break.'

Rawls was leafing through Harriet's file. 'That sounds great.' He was struck by how thin the file was. There were no statements other than the ones by her parents and a couple of the neighbours. It was as if she had been ignored; no one had really bothered. He pulled out a newspaper clipping, from the *Bath Herald*.

Dated 16 June 2012, the headline read: 'Bath Parents Desperate for Word on Missing Daughter.' Rawls scanned the article.

Ray and Laura DiAngelo last saw their beloved daughter, Harriet, nearly a month ago today. The couple, residents of Lattice Road, Bath, say that police have expressed what they see as little concern for their missing daughter.

'It's like they don't care,' Mrs DiAngelo told us during an interview at her home on Friday. Sitting in their front room, holding a bear that she tells us was her daughter's favourite, Mrs DiAngelo cries as she speaks. 'The police think she ran off but we don't. We think that someone took her and no one seems to care.'

Harriet DiAngelo is aged 17 and is 5 foot 8 inches tall, with long brown hair and brown eyes. She was last seen wearing skinny blue jeans and a black puffer jacket. She left her parents' home on her way to school saying goodbye as she usually did and has not been heard from since. Her parents are desperate for any news on her whereabouts.

Rawls put the article down. He didn't need to read the rest; it had told him all he needed. The DiAngelos were right: it had seemed as if no one had cared – even the paper had reported it as little more than a page filler – but they were wrong. He had cared. It might seem as if their daughter's disappearance had touched no one, but it had touched him.

He pulled at a sheet at random; it had the brittle feel of a document long forgotten. It had been typed up, a brief report from the original investigating officer, a man whose name Rawls had forgotten but whose funeral he had attended about five years previously, or perhaps it had been longer? He couldn't remember.

The report informed him that the second girl – Harriet, he reminded himself, not just the second girl – had experienced a number of behavioural issues at both home and school. She had very few friends and showed little desire to apply herself at school. She had been reported missing twice before, having run away from home on both occasions. Her parents, in the opinion of the report's author, should have faced charges of neglect. Which tallied with the fact that they had taken two days to report her missing. Rawls sighed. The first forty-eight hours were vital if they were to stand any chance of finding a missing person alive.

He rifled through Harriet's little pile of papers again, as Nat came back in with the coffees. 'Did Harriet have a boy-friend, do you know?'

Nat shook her head. 'I couldn't see anything in the file. But, if there was, I can't imagine she would have spoken to her parents about him.'

'Would you see what you can find out?'

Nat flipped a small notepad open and wrote something down. 'On it.'

'OK, who's next?'

'Yvette Solderton, the third of February, 2015.'

Rawls pulled at his lower lip. 'So that's 2009, 2012, 2015 – three years between each one, give or take a few months. Do you think there's anything in that?'

'Could be, I suppose. Some kind of cycle?'

'But our latest girl wouldn't fit the pattern. It's been nearly five years.'

Nat glanced at something on the desk in front of her, 'Yup, Tanya went missing on the fourteenth of November.'

'So, either the three years is just coincidence, or presuming it's a single person, something stopped them for more than a year and a half.'

'Maybe they were in prison, or the right girl just didn't come along.'

'Or part of the game is in the fantasy, or the planning, or maybe it's just coincidence.'

'Or a different guy?' Nat looked embarrassed for suggesting it. 'Maybe the first three were one person, and the fourth is an unrelated incident?'

'Maybe,' Rawls said, unconvinced, 'but they're the same age and living in the same area, so let's assume it's the same guy for now, OK?'

She nodded and he could tell that she wasn't sure if he was reprimanding her. 'Just for the sake of argument,' he said, trying to make amends.

'OK,' she smiled.

'But we will explore all options.'

She smiled again.

'Where were we?'

'Yvette,' Nat said, and she pushed another pile to the centre of the desk, like a croupier at the roulette table. 'The wild card.'

'I remember,' Rawls said. 'Her parents were wealthy, she went to a private school and even looked a little different from the first two. Her parents were divorced, weren't they?'

'They were,' Nat confirmed, 'and by all accounts it was a pretty messy affair.'

'I only vaguely remember her mother,' Rawls said. It seemed like such a long time ago. Had so much happened in those brief years that he could barely recall the parents of a missing child? 'Yvette went off after a family argument, is that right?'

'A row with her mum,' Nat said. 'She sounded like a bit of a handful and she used the family situation to get what she wanted from her parents.'

'Trying one against the other, yeah, I remember now. The case was big in the news for a while. We carried out a reconstruction and the parents were on the news as much as they could be. It was a nightmare because they hated each other.'

'Even their missing daughter wasn't enough to pull them together?'

Rawls shook his head. 'They could hardly stand being in the same room with each other.' He paused for a moment. 'They agreed on one thing, though, neither of them liked her boyfriend.'

'Oh yes, he had a bit of a drug problem, didn't he? Not exactly the kind of suitor that any parent would have chosen for their daughter.'

'He did have a drug problem,' Rawls agreed, 'but it was more than that; he was the kind of jumped-up little rich boy who thought the rest of the world was beneath him. Have you got his name there? I can't remember it.'

'Jacob, Jacob Spengler.'

'That's it. Good old Jacob. We had him in a couple of times about it all, but I seem to remember he had a fairly strong alibi.'

Nat nodded. 'He was with a mate, wasn't he?'

'Yeah, if you believe the two of them – but if they were lying they never slipped up.' Rawls rubbed his eyes. 'I think we should see him again, though, make it a priority.'

'I thought you might say that.' Nat smiled at him. 'I have his address, he's on parole.'

'Of course he is. What was he done for, possession? If I remember rightly, he had a habit of dealing right back in his school days. He'd been at it for a while but got cocky; we pulled him in for it and he found himself expelled.'

Nat scanned the report on Spengler and laughed. 'Why do they do it? You'd think they would know they're going to get caught eventually. This time he was caught with something like ten cannabis plants in his house along with a bag of MDMA. Get this, the only reason it was called in was because he was smoking the profits – the neighbours reported an "overpowering and constant smell" coming out of his windows.'

Rawls smiled. 'Sounds about right. I imagine his brains are like goo by now with all the shit he's done. I'd like to see him as soon as we can, after that we can have another word with Yvette's parents.' He stretched his arms above his head. His back ached and he had a headache coming on. 'That leaves Tanya.'

'Tanya Hickock,' Nat said. 'She fits the victim profile perfectly: tall, slim, age seventeen, long dark hair, comes from an underprivileged background with little parental supervision. She went missing after saying goodbye to a mate. They'd been shopping although her friend says that neither of them actually bought anything; they'd just walked about going into shops for something to do.'

There was a tap on the door and Rawls looked up to see a young police community support officer standing there. 'DI McGovern sent me up,' she said apologetically. 'She wants to have a chat with you both before the press conference.'

Rawls checked his watch: nearly four thirty. 'I hadn't realised how late it was.'

He stood up and Nat followed, the PCSO jogging along in front of them.

Chapter 3

Tess had pushed ahead with the press conference despite Rawls's protestations that it was too soon. He had wanted to talk to Tanya's father first, to introduce himself. He wanted to meet the team, let them all know what was going on, to establish the link, share his findings but she had been determined. He wondered if this was part of her powerplay, keeping everyone, not just him, off balance, letting them know that ultimately she was the one in charge. Now, as he hurried along the hallway behind her, he tried to reassure himself that it would be alright, either way, it wasn't his place to argue, she was the SIO after all. It was more than that, though. He didn't like to admit it, not even to himself, perhaps especially not to himself, but he was nervous. Things were happening too fast, he felt out of control and, if there was one thing that he had learned about himself over the past couple of months, it was that he needed to be in control.

Raucous voices came from the room ahead. 'Nothing like show business,' Rawls whispered, and Tess shot him a warning glance.

No funny business, the look said.

Me? Perish the thought, he hoped to convey with his return smile. He wished he felt as confident as the smile might suggest.

They paused at the door before going in. Rawls could see the desk set up at the far end of the room. Only one chair, he noted: he and Nat would be standing, then. A cluster of wires snaked their way across the room, terminating in a bank of microphones that had been set up in the middle. Behind the desk someone had erected the Avon and Somerset pop-up banner, the same one they used when visiting schools, and he thought how stark it all looked.

'Low-key,' Tess was saying, and he nodded. 'We're not here to scare them, just to give them the information they need to keep them happy.'

'Feed the animals,' Rawls whispered to Nat.

Nat smiled but she was trembling, and her jaw was clenched so tight that Rawls thought it would probably hurt her later. This was Nat's first press conference. Her job was to supply anything that Tess might need, whilst his was to field questions after the announcement. Tess's rationale for the conference was that they would use it as an opportunity to invite friends, neighbours or witnesses to provide information that they thought relevant. They would ask anyone with phone or dashcam footage from the time of Tanya's disappearance to come forward, or anyone who had noticed anything suspicious on the day to call in. They would assure the public that anything they offered would be in complete confidence and that all information was important, no matter how insignificant it might seem.

Rawls knew from bitter experience that they would receive more information than they could possibly deal with, and despite the list of criteria that he and Nat had worked on that afternoon, he doubted that they had enough people to sift through it all and come up with the evidence they needed to pin the guy down.

Nat had shivered, then asked him why he thought it was a guy, and he had paused to consider. 'You're right,' he'd said, 'I shouldn't assume.'

'I didn't say you were assuming,' Nat had argued, but he had held his hand up.

'I had assumed, and I shouldn't have,' he'd said, but here he was again, assuming that it was a bloke, assuming that only a man would abduct and hide or kill the four missing girls – or whatever this bastard was doing with them. That wasn't to say that women didn't abduct children, just that it wasn't the norm.

'Ready?' Tess asked, and Rawls ran his hands through his hair, preparing himself.

'Ready,' he said, and Tess clicked her way into the room, the rapping of her shoes echoing against the cold tiles like a call to attention. The invited audience had fallen silent by the time she reached the other side of the desk.

Rawls couldn't help but marvel at her. He adjusted the crumpled tie that he had pulled out of his jacket pocket and tied around his neck a few minutes earlier. Both Tess and Nat were in full uniform and he was beginning to regret his decision to remain in civvies; Tess had agreed with his reasons although he had been able to tell that she was not happy. 'Low-key,' he had reminded her.

The press conference had been anything but.

Tess held a hand up, and it threw a shadow on the banner behind her as if it was pointing to the words 'Serve, Protect, Respect'. On her shoulders and lapels, the silver insignias of her rank caught the light and somehow added to the solemnity of the occasion. She glanced briefly towards Rawls then cleared her throat.

'We are here today,' she began, 'to provide an update into our investigations into the missing schoolgirl, Tanya Hickock. Before we go any further, however, I would like to extend my heartfelt thoughts to her family, friends and the wider community for what we know is an incredibly difficult time for them.' She paused, coughed, cleared her throat again.

'Avon and Somerset Police were advised on November the fourteenth that Tanya had not returned from a shopping trip to Bath. Currently our last sighting of her is walking across the traffic lights at the bus station at a little after fifteen hundred hours on that day. She was headed south, towards the river, and we are keen to speak with any member of the public who may have seen her, or even spoken with her, after this time. Perhaps someone offered her a lift, or saw her speaking with someone; perhaps she was getting into a car, or walking on her own from the direction of the river.'

Rawls scanned the room as she spoke. It had been set up with chairs, packed so tightly together that people sat arm to arm, thigh to thigh. Their faces held an air of blank expectancy, as though they were prepared to be unimpressed, and Rawls suspected that their agendas had been written long before Tess had even opened her mouth. To Rawls they had the look of a jury rather than journalists; it was as if what Tess said would be taken down and used against her, not in a court of law but the court of public opinion, which they, the guardians of thought, would decide. He listened to Tess as she spoke, her delivery short and to the point but caring and thoughtful. He was impressed, even if the press were not.

As she finished speaking, she looked at Rawls. 'I'd like to introduce my colleague,' she said. 'This is Detective Sergeant Rawls, and he will be happy to take any questions that you might have.'

Rawls nodded a thank you and turned to the pack in front of him. Happy would not have been the word that he would have used. He nodded to the first hand that came up, a middle-aged man with a haircut that made him look like someone trying a little too hard to hold on to his youth.

The man stood when he spoke. 'DS Rawls, do you give any credence to the rumours that Tanya's disappearance is connected in any way to that of Yvette Solderton or, for that matter, to the two older cases of Melody Lockyer and Harriet DiAngelo?'

A low murmur filled the room, and Rawls fought off an urge to loosen his tie, the room suddenly feeling very hot. 'At this moment we remain open to all lines of enquiry,' he said, 'but we will, of course, release all relevant information where appropriate.'

'But you agree that they could be connected?'

Rawls took a moment to look at his notes, giving himself a chance to catch his breath and steady his hands, 'I don't wish to be drawn on this now. Speculation at this early stage of an investigation is never wise.'

He looked around. Several hands were up and he chose a young woman with straight black hair and a stare that could have stopped a bus. 'Can you tell us anything about the other girls? Are their cases still being investigated?'

Rawls coughed, glanced at Tess, saw her purse her lips and turned back to the woman. 'We are here today to discuss, um, this specific case,' he said. 'The information that I have is pertinent to this case only, not to any other cases.'

She kept her eyes on him. 'In that case, could you perhaps give us an idea of a scenario where you might do your jobs properly and look into the similarities between the cases?'

Rawls folded his arms in front of him, his hands still shaking, sweat trickling down his back and beneath his armpits. He was what they called an 'old sweat'; he'd been around the block and back again more times than he could remember, but he still hated press conferences. The young woman was glaring at him; her face wore a calm expression but she was tapping at the side of her face with her pen, and Rawls knew that she too was nervous.

'We fully intend,' he said, holding her gaze as best he could, 'to look into all lines of enquiry.' The woman went to speak but he held a hand up. 'All lines,' he reiterated, 'however, we need to be allowed to carry out our enquiries without intrusion from the press.'

'With all due respect,' she said curtly, 'you have had time – nearly ten years, in fact – in which to carry out your enquiries, and yet you still seem to have nothing.' She spoke with a thick Somerset accent and Rawls suspected that she must work for one of the village papers, perhaps Radstock or Midsomer Norton.

He looked at his notes again. He had intended to count to ten but only made it to three before he responded, 'As I said, we will be looking into all lines of enquiry.' His lips trembled slightly as he spoke.

'In that case,' she wouldn't be hushed, 'can you give an indication of why these older cases have remained unsolved for so long?'

Rawls swallowed hard. 'Any response at this time would be pure conjecture and I am unwilling to be forced into speculation which may jeopardise our investigation.' He glanced around the room for the next question.

A burly man with small glasses raised his hand and spoke simultaneously. 'So you have nothing to add to what we already know?' he asked, and the room erupted in noises of approval.

Rawls waited for the chatter to settle before he spoke. 'My role is to investigate a case that is complex and fast-moving, and our primary wish is to return Tanya safely to the arms of her loved ones. We will work closely with her family and are grateful for all the support that we have received so far.'

The man in the glasses pointed at Rawls with his pen and it had the effect of silencing the entire room. 'Have you personally met with Tanya's family yet?'

Rawls felt a surge of adrenaline, and his hand shook as though he had overloaded on caffeine. 'Not yet,' he said. 'I have only just been brought in to assist in this matter, but her family have been made aware and I will be visiting them later today.'

'What about the other families?' another voice called; it was a free-for-all now. 'Have you bothered to notify them?'

Rawls glanced at his notes. He knew that they hadn't, and Tess knew that he had not been happy about it. 'I will be speaking to everyone concerned with this enquiry in due course.'

'Due course?' a voice cried from the doorway, shrill and hysterical. 'Due fucking course – you've had more'n ten years to find Melody Lockyer; are you going to do the same with my Tanya?'

Rawls recognised the man immediately and he stepped from behind the desk even as a uniformed officer took the man's elbow. 'Mr Hickock,' Rawls said, but Paul Hickock was lost to them for the time being, overcome by emotion.

Rawls walked across and took Hickock's arm, gentle but firm despite his own stress, and nodded to the officer who stepped back. 'Come with me,' he said, and behind him, he heard Tess trying to bring the conference to a close. He didn't envy her; this was a nightmare and he suspected that it was only just the start. He walked quickly, his shaking hand pressed firmly into the man's back. He felt responsible for the mess – he should have shut the reporter down, stopped her pushing before it had turned into chaos; it was his fault that Tess was in there trying to bring things back under control. Perhaps he wasn't ready yet? Perhaps he should have waited, let them find someone else, someone who didn't have so much baggage.

He glanced back at the room, Tess flushed but professional, her hands by her sides, palms open, calm despite the commotion. He felt a sense of relief as he turned away; he didn't think that he could have dealt with it the way that she had, he wasn't sure that he could trust himself yet. He could feel his grip on Hickock's arm tightening, and he forced himself to relax. A few more seconds, he thought, and who knew what might have happened. Shit, he had to get it together.

'How the hell did he get in?' Tess asked as Rawls shut the door to her office.

Rawls held one hand up, pushing his tie back into his pocket with the other. 'Don't ask me, ma'am, I was as surprised as you were.'

She glared at him, veins standing out like ropes in her thin neck. 'What a bloody mess,' she said, pulling her hands through her hair.

'Total screw-up,' Rawls offered.

'A mess,' she corrected him, 'but not one that we can't deal with.' She turned her attention to Nat who was tapping against the glass door. 'Is he still here?' she asked, beckoning Nat in.

'Yes, ma'am.'

Tess snorted. 'Rawls, it's your case. You happy to speak to him?'

He stared at her. It was *his* case now? He suppressed an urge to point out that he had not wanted to be part of the press conference in the first place: this was her mess, not his. She had not wanted the parents involved, not yet; she'd been worried that it would turn the entire thing into a three-ring circus. Rawls thought back to the moment that the poor man had burst into the room, his hands shaking, his voice booming with nerves and anger. Now they really did have a three-ring circus, and this poor man had been the highlight of the show. He had been like the circus high diver falling from the top of the tent into a tiny bucket of water below. The press had turned to face him with a rush of clicking cameras and startled whispers. They had clamoured to ask him questions even as Rawls had led him shouting from the room.

Rawls had thought that, in Hickock's position, he might well have done the same thing. He, like this poor distraught father, might well have shouted that the press conference was a farce, that they knew there was a serial killer on the loose and that they were doing nothing about it. He too would have held his hands up and declared himself incensed. He thought again about the press conference, how he had allowed Tess to push him into it without listening to his thoughts, without allowing him to prepare properly. He shouldn't have let her do it. In the old days he would have stuck to his guns, but he had let her do it her way and he had simply gone along with it. Why?

He paused for a moment at the interview room door and collected his thoughts, then knocked lightly before going in. He hadn't needed to, but it felt polite under the circumstances.

'Mr Hickock?'

The man looked up, his face was swollen from crying. 'You know who I am, you put me in here, for heaven's sake,' he said then looked back down. He was the kind of man who breathed through his mouth and banged his fists when he was angry, and Rawls suspected that he was angry a lot of the time. Now, though, beneath the sharp white lights of the interview room, his strength seemed to have left him and he looked deflated, like a football left out in the rain for too long. The man was crumpled and dishevelled and he smelled as though he had not washed since his daughter had gone missing, but Rawls suspected that it might have been longer.

'Can I get you a drink?'

'I don't want a fucking drink,' he said. 'I want you to find my Tanya.'

Rawls nodded. 'Mind if I sit down?' He pointed to the metal chair on the opposite side of the plastic table.

'Do what you like,' the man said, leaning back in his own chair and folding his arms so that Rawls could see the dirt beneath his fingernails.

Rawls sat down but said nothing. He knew from Nat's notes that this man, like Harriet DiAngelo's family, had waited nearly two days to file a missing person's report on his daughter. According to school reports, the Hickocks had shown little to no interest in their daughter for her entire academic life, and she had been reported to local authorities on more than one occasion by school staff. Reports showed that she had frequently come to school dirty, poorly dressed for weather conditions, and without food or the means to obtain it. She had been on the 'at risk' register for several months during her last year at primary school following a broken hand which she had explained away to her teacher as having been the result of her 'tripping' over her daddy's foot just after she broke the television remote. Rawls had wondered how many trips she had taken during her childhood; it hurt his heart to imagine.

Studying the man in front of him, Rawls took in the web of red that covered Hickock's nose, the veins that shot through his yellowing eyes, and the smell of alcohol and decay that hung in the air when he spoke. Two things were immediately clear: first that the man was an alcoholic – his shaking hands alone attested to that – and second, and perhaps more importantly, he had a temper.

Nonetheless, Rawls couldn't see the man as being responsible for the disappearance of his daughter – not directly, anyway. Looking across the table at him with his dirty hands folded across his equally dirty T-shirt, Rawls thought that, whilst he did look like a man with less than conventional views on child-rearing, he did not look like the type to have harmed his daughter then hijacked a press conference in a shrewd attempt to deflect suspicion. This left Rawls with two alternatives: the girl had run away or she had been taken, and regardless of which scenario turned out to be true, the dirty little man wiping his nose with the back of his hand seemed quite genuinely distraught.

'I'll get you a coffee,' Rawls said to him and stood up.

Tanya Hickock's father started to cry again; long, heaving sobs that were somehow repulsive and heart-breaking in equal measure. Rawls crossed the room to a cabinet in the corner and pulled a few tissues from a box that rested on top. He handed them to the man then tapped on the door for Nat to open up. 'Grab him a coffee would you?' he said. 'Plenty of sugar.'

Nat nodded and Rawls braced himself before closing the door. They had so little time and he hadn't anticipated starting his interviews this way. He rubbed his hands together briefly, leaned back in his chair and folded his arms. 'OK,' he said gently, 'I want you to take your time, Mr Hickock. Just start where it feels right, and we'll take it from there.'

There was a brief tap on the door and Nat came in with two coffees, one of which she gave to Mr Hickock and the other she put in front of Rawls. He smiled at her and she went to leave but he stopped her. 'This is Detective Parkinson,' he said. 'She'll be joining us if that's OK with you, Mr Hickock.'

The man nodded and took a sip of the coffee. 'Thanks.'

Rawls took a sip of his own. 'You were about to tell us about Tanya.'

Her father stared into his cup then sighed. When he spoke, his voice was high-pitched and strained. 'I knew,' he said, keeping his eyes down, 'I knew from the moment that I came in that something was wrong.' He picked up his tissue but didn't wipe his face, instead screwing it into a tight ball and pulling pieces from it. 'She would never have left Mikey.'

'Mikey?'

'The dog,' he said. 'She just wouldn't. She loves that dog. Anyone who knows her would tell you, she never went nowhere without that dog, and if she did, she would have made sure that we had a long list of things to do: remember to let him out, take him for a walk, how much to feed him, that sort of thing, but when I got home, there was Mikey, at the window on the back of the chair, and no sign of Tanya.' He put his cup down and reached a hand into the pocket of his jacket. 'I'll show you,' he said, pressing his thumb on to his phone and swiping it open. He showed them a photo of a little black dog with a wiry coat and front teeth that stuck out too far so that he looked like some sort of mythical creature. Behind the dog, smiling with pride, was Tanya Hickock, her long brown hair tied back at the nape of her neck. Mr Hickock touched the image. 'Bloody thing will only eat chicken since she went – wife says 'e's pining for her or somefing.'

'And there was no note?' Rawls asked him. 'No instructions?'

'Nothing at all.'

'But you took two days to report her missing?' Rawls said gently.

The man looked at him, his round eyes made larger somehow by grief. 'I thought …' He looked at Nat then back to Rawls, 'I thought that you had to wait forty-eight hours, something like that, and,' he tore off another piece of tissue and rolled it between his fingers, 'she could be a bit of a bugger sometimes, so I thought …' His words trailed off and he sat in silence for a moment. 'I thought I'd give 'er a chance to come back on 'er own, you know? Give her the benefit of the doubt or whatever. I mean,' he looked down at his hands, 'you lot, you're not exactly part of our community. The only time we see the police usually is because someone's driving without insurance or they're being searched for a knife.'

Rawls understood; he'd been a copper long enough to know that some people didn't exactly see the police as an ally. 'OK,' he said, 'but you haven't seen her since she left that day?'

Hickock shook his head.

'And none of her friends have heard from her?'

'None,' he said. 'I've been checking 'er account, on Facebook and stuff, and 'er friends say she 'an't even been on that Snapchat thing neither. And we tried callin' but it goes straight to voicemail, and she 'an't responded to no texts and she 'an't been on that WhatsApp so, I don't know, she was always on 'er phone, always, always. She must be in some kind of trouble.' As he spoke his accent grew thicker, his words closer together, and his pitch lower.

Rawls handed him another tissue which he took and began pulling apart.

'Last person what seen 'er,' he said, 'was 'er mate, Rona. She said they walked up to the top of town, by the bus stop, and she walked off.'

'Rona didn't catch a bus?'

'Yes,' he looked down at the shredded bits of tissue in front of him, 'Rona caught the bus but not Tanya.'

'Tanya was going to walk? Do you know where she was going?'

'Up by Wells Road.'

'Up the hill? Did she walk a lot?'

He shook his head again, then rubbed his eyes. 'Not if she could help it. Rona said she were getting a lift from someone.'

Rawls looked at Nat before turning back to Tanya's father, 'A lift? There was no mention of this in your initial statement.'

'I never knew,' he said. 'I found out though, I spoke to Rona. You lot haven't spoke to 'er yet, so I had to.' He glared at Rawls defiantly. 'Your lot won't do nothing because you think she just run off. You look at me, at people like me, and you just see scum. You think if you were my daughter you'd run off too. But I know my daughter. She 'an't run off, not without 'er Mikey, and even then ...'

Rawls looked at Nat. 'Has Rona been spoken to?'

Nat flushed. 'I, I don't know.'

Rawls turned back to Mr Hickock. 'Can we have Rona's details?'

The man opened his phone again and navigated to his call history, then pointed to a number. 'That's all I got,' he said.

Nat wrote the number down as Rawls asked, 'Do you have any idea where she was going that day?'

'Home, I should've thought,' he said. 'She had the day off.'

'From school? Was it an inset day?' Rawls asked and the man looked sheepish.

'I should've thought,' he said.

'You don't know?'

'Why would I know?' he asked angrily. 'She's seventeen, she 'an't no child.'

Rawls felt an urge to correct him: she was a child, a missing child.

'She had a little job as well,' he said. 'I didn't like to say before. It was cash in hand like, I didn't want no one getting in trouble or nothing.'

Rawls stared at him. 'You didn't like to say?'

'It weren't nothing, not really.'

'Where did she work?'

Tanya Hickock's father stared down again at his pile of shredded tissue. 'I'm not sure.' He looked up at Rawls who bit down an urge to shout at the man. 'It was something to do with some church or fancy hotel or spa, something like that. I dunno, they just paid her to clean once a week. It were something to do with 'er drama stuff, I think, maybe like a hall.'

'But you don't know where?'

He shook his head, looking as though he might start crying again. 'My wife might,' he said, 'but she's in hospital at the moment.'

'I'm sorry to hear that,' Rawls said. 'Is she well enough to speak to us?'

'I don't think so,' he said without looking up. 'She fell over. They say it were a stroke, from 'er smoking. It were a couple of weeks ago, before,' he sniffed loudly, 'before our Tanya went, you know, went missing.'

Rawls passed the man another tissue while Nat reached for his hand. 'I didn't know,' he said, 'I'm sorry.' He cringed, he should have known, he felt like he couldn't get anything right at the moment.

Hickock dabbed at his eyes with the new tissue before wiping his nose. 'It's been a bit tough,' he said, in what Rawls considered the understatement of the year.

Tess had been watching the interview and she was waiting for him when he came back out. 'What do you think?' she said.

'About Hickock?' It was late, and he wanted another coffee.

She steered him into her office, signalling for Nat to join them. 'Yes,' she said, 'about Hickock.'

Rawls crossed the room and stood with his back to the radiator, feeling tired and cold. 'I don't think he's involved, if that's what you're asking.'

'I'm not,' Tess folded her arms and frowned, 'I'm asking if you think she ran away.'

'You know I don't.'

'Where do you want to start, then?' Tess asked.

'I'm thinking we need to speak to the other families again and to Yvette's boyfriend – he definitely warrants a second look.'

'Agreed. Anyone else you think you'll need to see straight away?'

Nat said, 'Rona, Tanya's friend.'

Rawls looked at Nat. 'That's priority number one for you, Nat. Speak to Rona first, see if she knows anything about this cash in hand job.'

Nat's face clouded for a moment.

'You alright with that?' Rawls asked.

She nodded. 'Yes, it's just …'

Rawls didn't let her finish. He knew she was worried – it was a big deal and she wouldn't want to be the one to miss anything important. 'You'll be fine,' he said, 'and I think you'll be more likely to put her at ease than I would.'

'I'll call her first thing in the morning,' Nat said. She checked her watch, 'It's a bit late now.'

'Arrange to meet her,' Rawls said. 'You'll find it easier face-to-face. While you're there, I'll get over to see the boyfriend. After that I'll head over to speak with Mr and Mrs Lockyer, Melody's parents. I could do with seeing the Soldertons, Yvette's family, as well, but I think that'll have to wait.' Rawls sighed. 'I think we should also get a move on and look into the place where all these cult rumours are coming from, if only to rule them out. The press have been playing the bloody cult angle for weeks – it's been implanted into the public psyche now. The retreat is becoming our equivalent of a haunted house.'

'A posh one,' Nat said. She turned her laptop screen so that they could see it. 'This is their website. I wouldn't mind staying there, it looks amazing.'

Rawls glanced at the screen. The retreat did indeed look like the sort of place that you might want to stay at, if you had the money. 'Dig up as much as you can on that, would you, Nat?'

She smiled. 'Will do.'

Rawls looked at Tess. 'Have we been getting tips about the retreat, from armchair detectives or the like?'

Tess shook her head. 'Not exactly. We've had mentions on our Facebook posts – you know, the ones we do automatically.'

Rawls nodded. He knew; they posted pictures of police horses and dogs and missing people and appeals for witnesses.

'Each time we posted an appeal or a reminder about the older cases, the same person would get in touch and urge us to visit the retreat. Then others would add their tuppenny-worth. You know – the usual.'

'The usual?' Rawls asked. He wasn't a Facebook kind of guy.

'Everyone jumping on the bandwagon – "yeah, check them out" or "something weird about that place". One nutter even suggested that the staff were being held there against their will. He said they'd been brainwashed so that they worked for free.'

'That's one way to keep costs down,' Rawls said.

'There've been several posts on the socials, all started by the same individual, calls herself Eve Burgess.'

'And it's always this Eve woman who posts first?' Rawls asked.

Tess was checking her notes, she nodded. 'Every time.'

'She could be a disgruntled ex-employee, I suppose.'

'Could be, except we spoke to the retreat,' Tess said, 'and get this, they told us that they've only had one member of staff leave since it opened and they didn't have anyone on their records going by the name Eve Burgess.'

'Oh, come on, you're telling me that no one leaves this place? What is it, Hotel California?' Rawls asked.

Tess managed a tight little smile. 'I know what you mean, and that was my first thought, but they've sent over their records. They have only had one person leave, unless you count the gentleman who died.' She saw Rawls raise an eyebrow and stopped him. 'Not like that,' she said. 'He had an illness – I forget what it was but it's in the notes. Anyway, he died in hospital, nothing mysterious.'

'Has anyone spoken with this individual yet?' he asked. 'The one doing the posting?'

Tess pulled a face. 'No, we haven't been able to. The trouble is, it isn't a normal profile. It looks as though it's only been used to contact us – there are no other posts or friends or likes or personal information. This person logs on, comments on our posts, then goes offline again. It's made it impossible for us to make contact. To make it worse, there are a number of Eve Burgesses online but none in Bath, or even in Somerset.'

'So you think it's an alias?'

She nodded.

'Have you sent one of those Facebook message things to the online account?' He glanced at Nat. 'I don't use it,' he offered by way of explanation.

Tess shook her head. 'We haven't been able to. Apparently the user takes the account offline after each comment, so there's no one to get back to.'

Rawls considered this. 'OK, let's look at what the comments actually said. They refer to the place? Not the people, not the residents or the staff, the place.'

Nat rifled through the transcripts and pulled one out, and Tess nodded at her to read it to them. 'Her exact words on her last post were, "You should have looked more closely at Stoney Barrow View."'

Rawls raised an eyebrow. 'That's it?'

Nat nodded. 'That's it, she says the same thing every time.'

So why would someone bother to comment without good reason? Rawls supposed this individual could just be another internet troll, but Nat said that the IT Department had said that the account had not made any other comments at all. Not one. From what Rawls understood, these internet troll types were prolific, not discreet, not careful with their words; they were the sort of people who liked the sound of their own voices, or keyboards, but this person certainly wasn't behaving like that. 'Can we get, what's it called? An IP address?' he asked.

'They're trying at the moment,' Nat said, 'but they told me not to hold my breath. Apparently it could take a while.'

Rawls rolled his eyes and turned to Tess. 'Can't you have them prioritise it?'

Tess sighed. 'They *are* prioritising it, Peter, but these things take time.'

Rawls had another headache coming on. 'I'm not sure that we have much of that,' he said.

Tess pressed her fingers to her temples and closed her eyes. 'I'll let you two get home,' she said. 'Just keep me up to date, won't you?'

They left together, like two children dismissed by a headmistress. 'Best get started,' Rawls said. 'I'm going to head over to see this Jacob character first thing in the morning, see if I can wake him up. Afterwards, providing I have time, I'll pop in and see the Lockyers. You hotfoot it over to meet with our girl Rona.'

Nat didn't look convinced, but she nodded, and Rawls grinned.

'You'll be fine,' he said.

Chapter 4

It was a little after 8 a.m. when Rawls pulled up in front of the house and killed the engine. He waited for a few minutes, his heart racing, his head pressed into the headrest. He closed his eyes and counted to ten.

When he opened them, Jacob Spengler was at the door. To Rawls it looked as though Spengler hadn't changed his clothes in the last four years. He wore a black T-shirt and grey joggers, sagging at the arse, so that the guy looked as much like a moron now as he had back then. Money, it seemed, didn't make you less of a twat. Rawls remembered not liking the man when he had interviewed him some four years previously, right after Jacob's on-off girlfriend, Yvette Solderton, had gone missing. He found that time had done little to improve his feelings towards him now.

Spengler had led what his mother would have called a wasted life. He had been afforded pretty much every opportunity the world could offer: wealthy parents who had doted on him, a nanny to wipe his arse, the best education that money could buy, a brand-new car on the day that he passed his test. He had taken these abundances and quite literally shoved them up his nose. Cocaine, alcohol, uppers, downers – you name them, and Jacob Spengler had tried them. He was a living example of how not to live your life.

'Are you here to see me?' Jacob called out. 'You the police?'

Rawls climbed out of the car, smiling, his warrant card held aloft. 'Could you spare me a few minutes?'

Jacob glanced at the card. 'As luck would have it, I have nothing else on my social diary,' he said, turning towards the house. Rawls followed him inside and then into a cramped and grubby living room. Perhaps his parents had cut the little darling loose, tough love and all that. The smell was almost bad enough to make his eyes water. Jacob waved a hand across the room, gesturing for him to take a seat, and Rawls did so, reminding himself to say no if the guy offered him a drink.

The chair was made of plastic and shaped like a half-gallon drum. It was green and covered in dirt, much of which Rawls suspected even a forensic scientist might struggle to identify. The room was hot and airless and smelled like old food and sweat.

Opposite him, Jacob lounged in a white garden chair with the air of one who didn't give a toss.

Rawls could still recall with some clarity the last time they had spoken; he had been struggling already by that stage. He had felt the familiar frustration at the guy's refusal to cooperate. He remembered still the feelings of anger prickling at him like heat rash, a heat rash that radiated from within. Back then Rawls had wanted to grab him by his designer T-shirt and shake him. Not to hurt him – that was what he had told himself, anyway – but to make him listen, to make him appreciate the severity of the situation.

Now, looking across the rubbish-strewn room at Jacob, Rawls had a whole new struggle to contend with. He should have brought Nat along but hadn't; perhaps that had been a mistake. Speaking to Jacob would be one of his first interviews with a young person since his time off and it was something that he had needed to do alone, if only to prove to himself that he could.

Jacob watched him for a moment, one leg draped casually over the arm of the chair as though he were on a photo shoot. He smiled at Rawls with improbably white teeth, then said, 'What brings you here, Detective Rawls? Same old, same old?'

Rawls gritted his teeth. Same old, same old? Was the guy kidding? This was a girl that he had dated, missing for nearly four years, and he was referring to it as 'same old, same old'. He forced himself to smile. 'You might have seen on the TV, we're looking into some old cases.'

'Those missing girls?'

Rawls nodded. 'One of those girls, Yvette Solderton, was your girlfriend at the time.'

Jacob laughed. 'I thought you might say that. I seem to recall that I told you back then, but I'm happy to repeat myself for the sake of clarity, Yvette was not my girlfriend. I grant you, she wanted to be my girlfriend, but she was,' he winked at Rawls, as though life was one big joke, 'well, just, you know?'

'I don't know,' Rawls said. 'Enlighten me.'

'She was that kind of girl, come on now, don't make me say it.'

'Easy?'

Jacob's lip curled into a smile. 'Gosh, I wouldn't say *that*,' he flashed his impossible smile at Rawls, 'but then a gentleman should never kiss and tell.' He leaned forward, letting his leg slide off the chair. 'Anyway, I had an alibi, you know that, for when she went missing, so I find myself wondering what on earth might bring you back here? To my humble abode.' He grinned as he spoke, pursing his lips. 'And to be fair, my life hasn't exactly gone the way I might have hoped; things have been quite tough recently.'

'I'll be honest,' Rawls said, 'I don't exactly care about your life at the moment.'

Jacob laughed again. 'Ah, well, of course you don't – why would you? I'm just the poor little rich boy. No one ever really cares about them, do they?' He scratched at his bare arms with dirty fingernails. 'I honestly can't remember much from back in those days.'

'Do you remember if you ever hurt Yvette? Physically, I mean.'

Jacob shook his head. 'We really are going round in circles. What do you want me to say? That she ran away from home with me and I lost my temper and killed her, is that it?'

'Did you?'

'Detective Rawls, you are so funny, but no, I didn't.'

Rawls changed the subject. 'How old are you? Twenty-six, twenty-seven?'

'Twenty-seven.'

'So, you were what, twenty-three when you were seeing Yvette, a sixteen-year-old girl, a minor.'

Jacob closed his eyes and shook his head as though Rawls was a naughty toddler. 'I'm sure we've been over this. Yvette was not my girlfriend,' he was spacing his words as if he thought Rawls might be struggling to hear him, 'I was not seeing her.'

'What about Tanya Hickock?'

'Who?'

'Tanya, she was last seen on November the fourteenth; it was a Thursday.' He held up a photo of Tanya. 'Have a look at this photo, will you? Does she look familiar?'

Spengler lifted his head slowly, reluctantly, squinted at the photo, said, 'I don't think so.'

Rawls showed him a photo of Melody, then Harriet. 'These two girls would have been closer to your age. Melody went missing in 2009. You would have been seventeen or eighteen at the time, maybe you saw her about.'

Spengler stared at him for a moment. 'Do you know what? This is starting to feel like an interrogation. I think I would like you to leave, Detective Sergeant Rawls. Please feel free to let me know if you would like me to come to your offices for a more formal conversation, that way I can arrange to have my mother's solicitor with me.'

Rawls sighed and pushed himself to his feet. Clearly Jacob hadn't had the apron strings cut after all. 'We'll be in touch shortly,' he said.

Fifteen minutes later Rawls filtered on to the A36 and skirted around the edge of Bath towards the Lockyers' home. He had put the address into the navigation, more to avoid traffic than to find his way; he knew where the house was. A light rain misted the windscreen and the wipers moved lazily across the glass. He was feeling better; the interview with Spengler had gone well. He had been fine – his old self, one might say – and that felt good. Great, in fact. Rawls felt better than he had since, well, since things had come to a head. He didn't like to label things – he was old school, always would be – but even he knew that it had been touch and go for a while and he had been lucky that things had worked out the way they had. It could have been a great deal worse.

He took the first exit at the roundabout and headed up towards Bear Flat. His journey to Southdown would not take long, ten minutes at most, enough time to gather his thoughts anyway. It had been a long time since he had met with Mr and Mrs Lockyer, Melody's parents. Melody had gone missing back in 2009 and he had kept them up to date for the next twelve months or so, but, as leads had dried up and his workload had increased, the updates had grown less and less frequent and the investigation had found itself lost amidst the cold archives of the not yet fully resolved.

The rain had petered off by the time he parked up and walked the short path to the semi-detached home. He knocked twice and the door was opened almost immediately by a tall man with a receding hairline and a skeletal face upon which skin seemed to hang like sagging curtains. He ushered Rawls inside and held a hand towards an open door. The house smelled of dogs and cherries and, as he walked into the lounge, Rawls understood why. On the sofa, a blanket over her legs and an e-cigarette in her hand, sat a small woman surrounded by Staffordshire bull terriers. Mrs Lockyer, Melody's mother, had changed precious little since her daughter had gone missing back in 2009. Then Melody had been just another runaway. They had investigated, of course they had, but they had other cases, other priorities, it had been all too easy to let this one slip. This one, Rawls thought, and how many others? Three others, his mind told him – four missing girls and poor Melody was the first.

'Hello, again,' she said, 'an't seen you in a while.' Cherry-scented vapour drifted from her mouth as she spoke, and to Rawls it looked as though her words were encapsulated in speech bubbles. Her West Country accent was broad and accentuated by a voice so gravelly that Rawls imagined the e-cigarettes must be on doctors' orders to get her away from a long-term heavy smoking habit.

The dog closest to her stood up, his hackles raised, as Rawls drew close. Rawls stopped in his tracks and the woman laughed. 'Don't mind 'e,' she said, using the masculine to describe what was clearly a bitch, "e won't bite you, not 'less you get too close.'

Rawls smiled. 'I'll stay here then,' he said. Behind him, the tall thin man laughed but said nothing.

'What you want then?' the woman asked him. 'Come to talk to us about our Melody?'

Rawls nodded. 'I imagine you saw the press conference.'

She laughed again, revealing a number of missing teeth. 'I seen it, we both seen it – what a mess. You lot couldn't organise a piss-up at a brewery.'

Rawls smiled. 'I'm inclined to agree.'

'Inclined to agree,' she squawked with laughter, 'inclined to agree? I'll tell you what, I'm inclined to agree with anyone what says that you and your lot are a bunch of idiots, how about that?' She glanced at her husband who still waited at the door. 'Inclined to agree, 'ave you ever 'eard anything like that before?'

Her husband shook his head.

'Well, what do you want from us now?' she asked Rawls.

'I just wanted to go back over some things with you, Mrs Lockyer.'

She glared at him, her face pale except for a pink spot high up on each cheek. 'You wanna go over it all with me, eh? Go through all the things you missed before?' She turned to her husband again. 'Do you "ear 'im? Wants to go through it all with us. Can you believe 'im?

'Mrs Lockyer.'

She held a hand up. 'Don't you Mrs Lockyer me,' she said. 'You never bothered before, did you? You saw us and you looked around at all my children and you thought we was just benefit scroungers, didn't you?'

Rawls felt a terrible sense of guilt. Had he thought that? Could he say for definite that he had not inadvertently experienced some kind of bias against this family? Had it clouded his ability to investigate their missing daughter? He hoped not, but hope wasn't enough, this woman would see through his hope. 'I don't know,' he said. 'If I did, I shouldn't have and I'm ashamed to imagine that I made you feel that way.'

She glanced at her husband. 'Well,' she said, 'we're not. We love every single one of our kids – they're not angels but they're good at heart, in't they?' She looked at her husband who nodded the affirmative.

'I've never stopped looking at the files,' Rawls said.

'Looking at the files? What good is that gonna do? Looking at the files weren't never gonna find our girl.' She covered her face as tears came. 'I s'pect she's dead now,' she said. The tall man crossed the room and kissed the top of his wife's head; beneath him a dog growled a low warning.

Rawls looked around the room, giving the two of them a moment. On the wall a 70-inch smart TV was showing a shopping channel with the sound down. A woman on the screen was soundlessly laughing at a man who was demonstrating the ease with which a hand-held vacuum cleaner could suck up cat litter from a carpet.

'I might get one of those for our Sandra,' Mrs Lockyer said, and Rawls turned his attention to her.

'Sandra is one of your children?'

The woman nodded. 'She were a couple of years younger than our Melody. She's, what, twenty-four, twenty-five now,' she said, counting on her fingers. 'You 'ave as many as us and you lose count, don't you, Bill?'

Her husband had resumed his place at the doorway, and he nodded once more.

'She misses 'er big sister,' she said, 'we all do.'

'I imagine it's been a terrible time.'

She ignored him, staring down at her hand smoothing the dog's velveteen head. 'If only you had tried back then,' she said, and the dogs looked up in unison, sensing her distress, 'if only you had bothered then.' The dogs crowded her, each one clamouring for the best position, to be closest to her; they licked at her face and hands and she pushed them away gently. 'You should've done more,' she said.

Rawls leaned forward. 'I know,' he said, 'and I'm sorry.'

She sniffed loudly as if his apology was too little, too late.

Rawls pushed on. 'Are you aware that there are some parallels being drawn between Melody's case and that of some other similar incidents?'

'Course I am, everyone is.'

'We have a number of lines of enquiry at the moment,' Rawls said.

'You going to ask me if she run off with that cult? Is that it? Is that your line of enquiry?'

'It's a starting point,' Rawls said.

'It's a starting point for someone going backward,' Mrs Lockyer said.

'You don't see it?'

She shook her head. 'I don't. She were a perfectly normal girl with a normal life. Why would she want to run off to join some cult? That's just plain crazy.'

'Do you know if she had friends in the group or even went there? I mean, there must have been a reason that people are saying that she ran off to be with them.'

She thought for a moment. 'Don't you think we wondered that ourselves? But we can't think of anything. She really wasn't like that and she had us, 'er family and 'er friends.'

'And to your knowledge she had no involvement with anyone who might have been a member?'

The old lady shook her head. 'No way. Like I said, I think it's just a load of nonsense that the newspapers made up to sell more. I don't know why you and your lot is wasting time on it.'

Rawls smiled. 'I tend to agree,' he said, 'and I know this must feel like old ground, but I have to ask again, to get things clear in my own mind. Is that OK?'

The woman took a long suck on her vape and the room filled briefly with a sickly sweet aroma. She pursed her lips and sighed loudly as though she wanted to protest, or to swear at him, or tell him to get out of her house, but she nodded instead.

'Do you remember Melody perhaps getting into anything different just before she disappeared? Perhaps she took up yoga or joined a church group, maybe she found God or just took up a new hobby, anything like that.'

The woman looked at her husband and they shook their heads slowly as though they were communicating telepathically. 'Nope,' she said, 'not that we can think of.'

Rawls glanced at her husband. 'She weren't that kind of girl,' he said, his voice soft but firm. 'We ain't a churchy family.'

'She couldn't have gone with a friend, a boyfriend perhaps?'

Mr Lockyer shook his head, but his wife shrugged and closed her eyes as though the question was stupid. 'Suppose she might of, but she were a teenager. They don't tell their parents if they're off trying to impress a boyfriend.'

Rawls smiled, he had to agree. 'What about meditation?'

This time the woman laughed, and the dogs all lifted their heads and looked up at her. 'Meditation! Do we look like the kind of people who meditate? Do you see my kids with pitta bread and houmous in their lunchboxes? Detective Sergeant Rawls, do you really think this is the sort of house that kids meditate in? Her brothers and sisters would have had a field day with her!' She gave a dry cackle.

Rawls flushed slightly. 'I have to explore every avenue.'

Now her eyes flashed with anger. 'Every avenue,' she repeated. 'You're going to explore every avenue now that the press is sniffing around you again. You didn't explore no avenues back when she went missing, did you, Mr Rawls? Seemed to me that you and your lot didn't care a bit back when she first went missing.'

Rawls felt the guilt as though she had slapped him. He remembered caring, of course he had, but had he cared enough? Had he really done all he could? He remembered arguing with his DI at the time, pointing out that the girl had shown no signs previously that she might run away, reminding him that she had not taken her purse, her friends had not heard from her since her disappearance. His DI had agreed but countered that there was no sign of foul play, the girl was known to be a trouble-maker, her family were well known to them and they had been out to them for a litany of complaints so typical that they were almost straight from the Police Handbook: harassment, drunkenness in public places, possession of Class A drugs, criminal damage and even arson. Rawls remembered pointing out, almost meekly, that the one thing that they had never been accused of was neglect or cruelty to any of their children and his DI had shrugged. 'They're trouble,' he'd said, 'and we just don't have the resources right now.'

He had been right about the lack of resources. This was one year after the 2008 financial crash that had seen the collapse of some of the world's largest financial institutions. The cuts had been fast and savage, leaving the police budget 18 percent worse off and demoralising the service as they had struggled to pick up the slack. Cases had been put to one side, not because they didn't care but because they simply couldn't do a damn thing about it.

Rawls felt the muscles in his face twitch. 'I'm so sorry that you feel that way, Mrs Lockyer, I really am.'

She waved her hand at him again, the dogs all following it as though it might hold a ball or a packet of dog treats. Her eyes had lost their glow; now they were flat, tired, broken. 'It don't matter now,' she said. 'We know she's gone. She'd 'ave been in touch if not, we know that.'

Rawls tugged at his shirt collar. The room felt too hot, he felt too hot. He wanted to tell her that it wasn't necessarily the case, that they might still find their daughter, she might still be alive. But he found that he couldn't, and anyway, even if they did find her, who knew what she might have been through? What were the other options – living on the streets, people-trafficking, being held captive by a madman? Were those options better? Rawls didn't think so. He tried to smile at Mrs Lockyer. 'Do you still have Melody's stuff? In her old bedroom perhaps? I would just like to have a quick look through them, if possible, see if there was anything we missed last time around.'

She shook her head again, emphatically this time. 'It's all in a lock-up, in't it, Bill?' He nodded in agreement and she went on, 'Don't know where, before you ask. The kids moved it all, said it made them sad.'

Rawls felt his heart sink. His experience of going through lock-ups was that they took an awful long time and required additional headcounts; right then he had neither. 'Is it possible for us to gain access to the lock-up?' he asked.

'I 'spect you can,' she said, 'but we'll need a couple of days.'

Rawls nodded. 'If you could make it any sooner,' he said, 'it might be important.' He stood up. 'I've taken up too much of your time already.'

On the far wall, adjacent to the enormous television, was a wall covered in photos. They were all framed and hung in neat rows, and above them, in big mirrored letters, were the words, 'Family Rogue Gallery'.

'Is Melody up there?' he asked, and the woman beamed toothlessly at him.

'Course she is.' She turned to her husband. 'Get him the one with our Melody in her uniform.'

The man did as he was bid, returning wordlessly with a photo in a shiny silver frame. One of the dogs grumbled a warning at him as he passed it to his wife. She shushed the dog and smiled at the photo.

The face looking out at them seemed happy enough: Melody, in her school uniform, knee-high socks and clean white blouse; she wore a half smile, one that might have been forced for the camera.

Mrs Lockyer touched the glass with one gnarled finger. 'She weren't a bad girl, Detective Rawls, not really. My kids is all a bit wild; there was so many of them, you see.'

Rawls shifted uncomfortably.

'She were a good girl really.' She looked at her husband, who took the photo from her and put it back in its place in the rogue gallery. 'I miss 'er,' the woman said almost to herself. 'It don't get no easier, do it, Bill?'

Bill Lockyer shook his head, his back to the wall of photos. 'No,' he said, 'it don't.'

'People judged us,' she said, looking at Rawls. 'You lot thought we 'ad something to do with 'er going missing. Your lot, they thought it might've been us, interviewed Bill for hours.'

'Did we?' Rawls was not aware of this.

'I think you'd gone off on another case. Some other guy, fat 'e was, and nasty, kept trying to trick us, you know? 'e'd say one thing to me and another one to Bill, didn't 'e, Bill?'

Bill nodded. 'He did.'

Rawls made a note to check the files. How had he missed this? He wondered if it had been Chivers – the description fitted and it sounded very much like him – but on the other hand, there was probably more than one fat and unpleasant person in the service.

'I don't think you're like 'im, are you, Detective?'

Rawls smiled. 'I hope not.'

'Sorry I gived you a 'ard time when you first comed in.' She offered a weak smile. 'It's just difficult, you know what I mean, not knowing like, it ain't easy.'

Rawls nodded. 'I don't imagine it is. Look,' he took his keys out of his jacket pocket, Thanks so much for your time; you've been really helpful.'

Mrs Lockyer scratched the upturned belly of a Staffie. 'Yeah, well, you come again if you need anything else and I'll see what I can do about sorting the key for the lock-up.'

Rawls turned to leave but she stopped him. 'Detective Rawls?'

Rawls paused.

'If you find 'er, if you find our girl, our Melody, you will tell us first, won't you? Not the press.'

'I will,' he promised. He left the house feeling an immense sense of sadness. They had failed these people, *he* had failed these people, failed them from the start. It hurt him to think it, but it was true. More than ever now, he wanted to find out what had happened to their daughter, for himself as much as for them. He had to put this right.

Chapter 5

Carmen rolled over on her bed at the knock on her door. It was too late to pretend that she was doing homework, but she had enough time to close WhatsApp and the phone was on silent anyway.

Eileen poked her head into the room. 'What are you up to?'

Carmen managed a half-hearted smile. 'Nothing really.'

'Wanna come to Zumba?'

'Ooh, Zumba eh, how can I resist?' Carmen laughed.

Eileen grinned back. 'Yeah, alright, I have to pop to Tesco after and I didn't want to leave you all on your lonesome.'

'Still, Zumba. I'm not an old lady.'

'We're not all old ladies, I'll have you know, madam,' Eileen said laughing, then added, 'well some of us are – OK, most of us are.'

Carmen looked at her phone, then back at her mother. 'Anyway,' she said, 'I can't come, I've got rehearsals in an hour.'

Eileen looked at her watch. 'Oh yes, it's Saturday.'

Carmen sat up and pulled her knees to her chin, scooching her phone into her lap as she did. It was ringing, and she didn't want Eileen to see who the caller was. 'You needed your watch to tell you the day?' she laughed.

'Well yes, er no.' Eileen laughed too. 'Can't help it. Like you said, I'm getting old.'

'No, you're not,' Carmen said, and she let the phone drop beside her, covering it with a pillow as she climbed off the bed.

'Love you,' she said, and Eileen looked back.

'Love you too, hon.'

'Sorry about all the – well, you know, basically all the stuff at school.'

Eileen paused for a moment then said, 'We just worry about you, love. You know that, don't you?'

'I know, Mum, and I'm sorry, I really am.'

Eileen smiled. 'I know.' She nodded towards the bed. 'Your phone's vibrating under that pillow.'

Carmen flushed but didn't move. 'Mum, I really am sorry.'

Eileen wrapped her arms around her. 'You've nothing to be sorry for,' she said into Carmen's neck. 'I just want you to sort it out, not for me,' she pushed Carmen away from her so that she could look into her face, 'for you. You understand that, don't you? You need to sort this shit out, for your own sake.'

Carmen nodded, her lip trembling, her jaws clenched, 'I will, Mum, I promise.'

Eileen pursed her lips into a tight smile. 'Love you, my little loaf of bread,' she said, and Carmen laughed tearily.

Carmen had always loved this little nickname; she was the loaf and her mother the oven. She had loved the story that came with it too; the one that her mum had shared when she'd been lying in bed with a fever. She'd been no more than three, maybe four. Her mum had told her how the midwife had handed her this little bundle; all wrapped up and warm, just like a loaf of bread. She told Carmen how she had wanted to peek inside but had been too afraid to open the swaddling, afraid to break the spell, afraid of disturbing this tiny, sleeping, loaf-sized miracle. And so she had simply held the sleeping bundle in exactly the same position that the midwife had left her in; she had kept her arms crooked to support her tiny head until they ached. Her mother had told her that she could not recall how long it might have been, but eventually a nurse had come in and, laughing, had taken Carmen from her. The nurse had placed Carmen in the cot beside her mother and told her to get some rest. Eileen would laugh whenever Carmen made her retell the story; she would say how right the nurse had been, how much she had needed that rest, because from that moment on, she had never really managed to sleep properly again.

'Love you too,' Carmen said, and the words hung in the air between them like two little white flags. It made Carmen want to run to her mother and smother her with kisses as she had done as a child.

The phone was vibrating frantically on the bed and she turned reluctantly to silence it.

When she looked back her mother had gone.

Rawls hit the missed call from Eileen and dialled her back; she answered on the second ring. 'Peter?'

'Sorry, love,' he said, 'I was in an interview. Everything OK? Is it Carmen again?'

'What? Oh no, just a silly thing,' her tone suggested that it was not silly at all, 'my card declined in Tesco.'

His stomach turned. 'Oh,' he said, 'which one?'

'Debit card. What made it worse was that I didn't have my purse with me. I'd just taken my card and the shopping bags so I couldn't even use another card. I had to leave the whole bloody lot at the till; they'll hold it till I go back later and pay. I have never been so embarrassed in my life.'

'Oh, hon,' Rawls said, 'I'm so sorry.'

'I haven't had a chance to check the account yet but there should have been money in it. You haven't moved it all into the savings account, have you? You know it drives me mad when you don't tell me.'

Rawls was silent for longer than he should have been, long enough, he knew, for Eileen to detect his weakness and prepare an attack.

'The car insurance went out,' he said.

'The car insurance?' Her voice was incredulous. 'What car insurance?'

'On the Focus.'

'Oh, dear God in heaven, how much is the insurance on that damn car?'

'I had to pay a year up front.'

'What? Why? No, actually, don't answer that. It has to go, Pete, that bloody thing has to go.'

Rawls nodded as though she could see him. 'I know,' he said. 'I'll get an ad on AutoTrader.'

'Today.'

'Today,' he agreed. It had not been a question.

'Shit,' she said, 'I should make you go back and get the bloody shopping. You could explain where all our money was.'

'I'll be stuck here for a while longer,' he said.

She sighed. 'I wasn't really going to make you go, I'll go in a bit.'

'Thank you,' he said, 'and I am sorry, I should have said.'

'Yeah, you should,' she said, then, her voice softer, 'Pete?'

'I'm here.'

'Are you OK? Being back, I mean. Is everything alright?'

'It's OK so far.'

She was silent for a moment, then said, 'Peter, you are sure that you're ready for this, aren't you?'

He stared out at the rain. 'I'm sure.'

'You know this could set you back?' She sounded worried.

'I'm OK,' he repeated.

She sighed, 'I know you think you that you are, but I just worry that it's too soon.'

'I'll be fine. I will, and if I feel the old ...' he searched for the right word, 'the old, well, you know, stuff, coming back, I'll tell you. I'll tell you straight away.'

She made a puffing sound at the other end of the line and Rawls could see her in his mind's eye; her lips pursed, the sinew in her neck strained; it was a warning sign that he had learned long before was not to be ignored. He changed the subject. 'We're treating them all as being linked.'

'Those poor missing girls?'

'Yup, we're treating it as one investigation.'

'Well, that's good, and it's about time,' she said. 'Who's on the team?'

'I've been working with a brand-new fast-track detective but I'll be heading up the local team. Tess will be doing the introductions tomorrow.'

He heard Eileen laugh. 'So it's just you and the newbie at the moment. Poor thing, send my condolences, won't you?'

'Whatever do you mean?' he said, pretending to sound offended.

'Well,' she said, 'I can't imagine being stuck with you for my first proper assignment.'

'Honestly,' he said, 'I'm a dream to work with.'

'Uh-huh,' his wife said, 'and what's this poor chap's name?'

'Natalie.'

'Natalie?' Eileen's voice sounded brittle.

'She's very young and green,' he offered.

'Young and green,' Eileen repeated. 'Pretty?'

'I don't know,' Rawls said.

'You can't tell if someone's pretty?'

'She's too young to look at in that way.'

'Huh,' said Eileen, 'well, it's none of my business, I suppose.'

'Of course it's your business,' he tried, 'but I can't help who they put me with.'

'It's just funny, that's all.'

'What's funny?' Rawls asked, genuinely perplexed.

'Well, you've been adamant that you wouldn't go back to work for the past few weeks, now suddenly you're back with some big old case and a pretty new detective and you don't even manage to find the time to tell me that you've spent all our money.'

'That's not fair,' Rawls tried to protest.

'Not fair?' she said. 'Ha, I'll tell you what's not fair – not fair is me standing in Tesco's finding my card has declined because my husband didn't think he needed to mention that his car insurance, which cost as much as your average mortgage repayment, had gone out that day and left our account empty. That's not fair, don't you think?'

Rawls swore under his breath. 'I'm sorry,' he said. 'I didn't realise it had gone out today. I would have told you if I had.'

'Look, Pete, let's leave it here,' her voice was cold, 'we'll talk about it later.'

He sighed, 'I'm sorry, and I really do feel OK.'

'Well, so long as you're OK,' she said, 'that's all that matters.'

Rawls sighed. 'Please don't be like that,' but the line already had the dead quality to it that told him that she'd hung up.

Chapter 6

Rawls and Nat were on their way to visit Stoney Barrow View, North East Somerset's most exclusive wellness retreat, or cult, depending on which way you looked at it. Currently a centre for wellbeing, the retreat boasted a heated outdoor pool, a yoga sanctuary, nature walks, organic food, a sauna and a host of other restorative splendours. It was exactly the sort of place that made Rawls feel as far out of his comfort zone as it was possible to get – and exactly the sort of place that Eileen would have loved. Set in idyllic rolling green pastures, it was a picture-perfect example of Somerset countryside. It hadn't always been so impressive and Rawls remembered well its earlier incarnation.

'Did you know that the house was owned by a cult back in the day?' Rawls asked.

Nat laughed. 'I had heard but only the gossip. Did you?'

'I did. It was sold a few years back, but before that it had quite the reputation.' Rawls went on to explain how the cult had been the brainchild of a man named Berkeley Wolf, a marketing consultant who had given up his worldly goods and convinced another couple of hundred or so other people to do the same.

Wolf had used what he called 'the tithes of the righteous' to work on the rejuvenation of a dilapidated manor house, with a little over one hundred hectares of land attached, on the outskirts of Bath. His followers had toiled night and day to transform the land and the house so that they could run it as a hotel. At the same time, Berkeley Wolf had made himself into a minor local celebrity by preaching his gospel to anyone and everyone willing to listen.

'The Stoney Path' was Wolf's take on a social contract, and he had ensured that his followers were well aware that their part of the contract was to provide the means with which he would build his Utopia, the Stoney Path.

'Not my idea of Utopia,' Rawls said, as he finished giving Nat the background.

'So, you went there?' she asked.

'A long time ago,' he replied, 'before they had finished the work. Back then it was a muddy hell-hole. They lived in appalling conditions while they were working on the place.'

'What took you up there?'

'Funnily enough, a similar reason to our trip today. A young man had gone missing and his parents – well, his father anyway – was pretty sure that he'd run off to join the group.'

'Had he?' Nat asked.

'We thought so,' Rawls said, 'but he was eighteen and old enough to make his own decisions. There wasn't much we could do except ask.'

'Did people seem happy there? Even though it was, what did you call it?'

'A muddy hell-hole,' Rawls said, then he frowned. 'As to whether they were happy or not, honestly, who can tell? The place was a mess. They were all living in tents and outbuildings on one side of the property while they were renovating the place. It was filthy, genuinely filthy, and I didn't exactly spend much time with them, but the people there,' he laughed at the memory, 'well, let's just say they weren't exactly the kind of people who invited the police in. They believed they knew the truth, and the rest of the world, especially the police, were all outsiders.'

Nat frowned. 'I'm always amazed at how people get sucked into that sort of thing.'

'Wolf was clever. He had created a kind of scarcity of spaces, a one-in, one-out sort of thing. He had people queuing up to join him, literally offering everything to him just to be part of the group. That's why we weren't surprised that this young man would simply have taken off to join them – loads of them did, it was all the rage back then.'

'Yeah, there were a fair few cults around in the Seventies and Eighties,' Nat said and Rawls gave her a quizzical look.

She laughed. 'I'm fascinated by cults. There was a guy arrested recently, 2013, 2014, but his cult had been going since 1977. The Workers' Institute of Marxism, I think they were called.'

Rawls thought for a moment. 'I remember, he was the guy who held all those women against their will – where was that? London?'

She nodded. 'Lambeth, I think. I only remember because they called the case the "Lambeth Slavery Case". He had them all working for him, beat them up when they did anything wrong, raped them, that sort of thing.'

'Sounds like a lovely guy,' Rawls said.

'There was an American cult over here back in the Eighties as well. They were supposed to be all about love but really, they were a sex cult. Called themselves the Children of God.'

Rawls was astounded. 'I've heard about them, but I thought they were in the US.'

'They had a branch in Scotland,' Nat told him, 'but they were all over the world. Someone famous was a member.'

'Rose McGowan,' Rawls said, nodding. 'I remember now, I watched a documentary about it. Anyway, we were talking about our very own spiritual leader, the one and only Berkeley Wolf.'

'Oh yes, you were about to tell me how you visited them, back in the olden days?'

'Cheeky,' Rawls grinned at her, 'but yes, back in the olden days, I was sent there after we'd met with the guy's parents. It turned out to be one of those things that stay in your memory forever.'

Nat smiled at him. 'The suspense is killing me.'

Rawls thought back. What had it been – fifteen, twenty years ago? Must be. God, he was getting old. He had locked the single crew panda car, hopped over the five-bar gate with the hand-painted sign that read, 'The Stoney Path, All Trespassers Will Be Prosecuted', and made his way along the muddy path towards a squat row of outbuildings in a dreary copse of trees. He had heard voices when he had first climbed out, but now they were silent save for the occasional giggle or expletive.

Rawls remembered pausing for a moment, the bottom of his trousers covered in mud, his newly polished shoes all but invisible. He had called out into the gloom, 'Hello?'

'What you want, copper?' a voice, Rawls had gauged it to be little more than a child, eleven, maybe twelve, had called back, closely followed by another.

'Grace, hush, this gentleman is our guest.'

'Hello?' Rawls had said again because he couldn't think of anything else.

'Well hello,' another voice joined in, and this time, a face appeared from inside a mud-caked shack. The man behind the voice was in his late forties, perhaps older. He had a long grey beard which he had plaited almost to his navel, his hair was tied up in a large bun and long, yellowing wisps of matted tendrils clung to his neck like the snakes of Medusa. He had not extended a hand and Rawls had been relieved.

'Mr Wolf?' Rawls asked, and the man laughed.

'They call me Father Berkeley; how can I help?'

'I'm looking for a young man,' Rawls said, 'he seems to have run off and his parents suspect he might have come to join you, your, your ...'

'Our commune,' Wolf finished for Rawls, dismissing the photo that Rawls was holding up with a wave of his hand. Behind him the voices had grown louder, and Rawls was unsettled by the fact that apart from the odd toddler crawling or wobbling its way through the mud, he could not see anyone at all. If they were hiding from him, they were doing a bloody good job of it.

'I'm sorry,' Berkeley Wolf said, smiling at him with large, yellow teeth. 'I'm not willing to divulge who lives here with me and who doesn't. It's none of your business and, before you argue the point, we do know our rights.'

Rawls straightened, feeling his face flush a little, and he had to bite his lip before he spoke. 'This particular young man is only just eighteen and his parents have reported him as missing, Mr Wolf, and that makes it our business.'

The man glanced briefly at the photo. 'And if he's eighteen, I must reiterate my point that it is none of your business. It's not yet illegal for someone to go off on their own, is it?' He stared at Rawls for what felt like hours before smiling into his dirty beard. 'I didn't think so,' he said and, still smiling, he turned his back and walked back into the shed, which Rawls now saw was an old barn. Built in the usual style of the area, the barn walls were solid Blue Lias limestone and the roof was made of rusted tin. Four arched entrances suggested an old milking parlour, and these had been closed up with a mixture of different styles of reclaimed brick. There was no door as such, but instead a thick blanket hung across a small doorway that Rawls imagined had once been the storage area. It was through this that Berkeley Wolf had disappeared, like a priest into the vestry.

The voices in the woods broke into simultaneous laughter and Rawls waited a moment longer before another figure emerged from the barn, 'Father Berkeley would like you to leave now. He says to come back with a search warrant or not to come back at all.'

The crowd voiced their agreement and he turned to leave, aware that from behind him people were coming out of the trees and following him along the mud-covered path. He paused at the gate and turned around: behind him a group of perhaps twenty women and children stared back at him. He held the photo out again. 'Do any of you recognise this young man? His name is ...'

'Get out, pig!' a woman shouted, and she hurled what he first took to be a stone at him. The missile caught him on the shoulder and exploded. It wasn't a stone but a ball of mud – mud and something that smelled suspiciously like excrement; he could only hope it wasn't human. Trying in vain to duck as the rest of the group, cheering and laughing, joined in with the game, Rawls made a dash for the car.

'Don't come back, little piggy,' someone shouted as he reached the car, and Rawls paused long enough only to take his jacket off and drop it, inside out, into the passenger foot-well before throwing himself inside.

He had driven back to Bath, freezing cold but with the windows open in a desperate effort to blow the smell out.

They had laughed when he had gone through the events back at the Bath nick and he'd had to endure jokes about being given all the 'shit jobs' for a few weeks after that, but, to his knowledge, no one had ever gone back to the Stoney Path again, with or without, a warrant.

'Oh my God,' Nat said as he finished the tale, 'that really does sound awful.'

'It was,' Rawls laughed, 'but I'll never forget it.'

'Did you find the guy?'

Rawls thought for a moment. 'Not to my knowledge, but the guy was right, he was an adult, old enough to leave home if he wanted to.'

'And you've never been back?'

'Nope, although, to be fair, I never went to the main house in the first place; I don't think I even saw it.'

'Have you seen it now? Since the new people took over?' Nat asked. 'It looks amazing.'

'I had a quick look at the website,' Rawls said. 'Funnily enough, there was no mention of old Berkeley Wolf. I assume they want to put all of that behind them.'

'What a name,' Nat said, and Rawls laughed.

'I don't think that was his real name. It was something pretty bland like Frank or John or Paul, something like that.'

'So, he changed it to Berkeley Wolf because that was better?'

'People are funny. Probably seemed like a good idea at the time,' Rawls said.

'Do you think they're somehow involved?'

Rawls shrugged. 'I don't think so. Looking at their website, I'd say that the last thing they want is to have their name linked to that lot. I seem to recall that they made a big deal in the local papers when they took over, adverts stating that they were under new management, that sort of thing.' He flicked the indicator ready to turn right. The country lane ahead of them was as stark as a scene from a post-apocalyptic movie: a watery winter sun hung low in the sky and cast a flat light across a damp curtain of mist. Trees, stripped of their leaves, lined the edges of the road like wizened old crones, and fields, barren for the winter, fell away into the distance until they disappeared into the bruised grey skyline beyond. Above them, in groups of threes and fours, crows lifted and fell on glossy black wings.

Rawls glanced at Nat. 'How'd it go with Tanya's friend Rona?'

'She was hard work, to be honest,' Nat said. 'Reluctant, I think is the technical term, but it was like pulling hen's teeth. You'd have thought that I'd threatened to waterboard her or something – she just didn't want to speak to me.'

'Did you get anything worthwhile?'

Nat scanned her notepad. 'Not really.'

'What about the job Tanya's dad mentioned? Did she know any more than we did already?'

Nat shook her head. 'She knew about it, but only what we knew already, cash in hand cleaning job, that was pretty much it. It was a couple of hours a week cleaning, at a hotel, she thought, but then she said it might have been offices or even cleaning student accommodation.'

'That wouldn't be cash in hand, would it? Student accommodation? That would be more formal, surely?'

'You'd like to think,' Nat said.

'God,' Rawls said, 'I feel like we're going around in circles, her father thought it was a bloody hall. Anything else?'

She sighed. 'What really struck me was how scared she was.'

'Of us? Talking to you?'

'No, scared of going out on her own, scared that there's some crazy out there, kidnapping young girls and killing them.'

'That's all we need, a bloody panic on our hands.'

'I can understand it, though,' Nat said. 'Have you spoken to your daughter about it all?'

Rawls nodded. 'Eileen has, but she wasn't interested, you know what teenagers are like.'

'I can imagine,' she said. 'At least mine is too young yet for me to worry on that front.'

Rawls felt like he had come into a conversation halfway through. He hadn't known she had a child but didn't want to admit his ignorance. 'So yours is how old?'

Nat smiled. 'She's nearly four. Poppy, her name is. A total monkey. She starts school in September and I can't wait.'

'Can't be easy managing. You're not married, are you?' Rawls heard himself ask the question and wondered if he could sound more like a middle-aged prude if he tried.

'I'm not and it's not,' Nat said, 'but my parents are great. They have her while I'm at work.'

'Handy,' said Rawls. He glanced at the navigation. 'I think we're pretty much here.' He slowed the car a little, peering into the hedgerows. 'I don't see any signs or anything, do you?'

Nat pointed to a tree-lined gateway further up the lane. 'I imagine that's it, don't you?'

He grinned. 'Yes, I imagine you're correct.'

They pulled up at the wrought-iron gates. They had a galvanised look to them, expensive and tasteful, designed to look like vines, each stem terminating in either a leaf or a human face, Rawls couldn't say for sure. Either way they were unsettling. Alongside the gate a sign, in the same galvanised metal, read: 'Welcome to Stoney Barrow View. Open your heart and free your mind.'

'Here we go,' said Rawls as he pressed the intercom buzzer.

A metallic voice asked them how he could help, listened as Rawls announced that they had a meeting with Sebastian, then opened the gate with a metallic clunk that matched his voice. He asked them to drive in before adding, 'Please give me a few minutes before leaving your car while I put the geese away.'

'Geese?' Rawls mouthed to Nat. 'What's that all about?'

Nat laughed. 'I believe they make good guard dogs.'

'Oh,' Rawls grinned back, 'guard geese, how nice.'

They were directed by a series of jaunty hand-carved wooden arrows through an immaculate landscape that ended in a gravel car park. There, a sign welcomed visitors whilst politely reminding them that this was a place of quiet contemplation. The sign asked them also to turn off all mobile phones and to refrain from loud or sudden outbursts. The management thanked them for their kind understanding.

'Passive aggression,' Rawls said, reading the sign. 'How much do you want to bet me that this Sebastian fella talks in an insipid, patronising voice? I'll give you fifty to one.'

Nat laughed. 'I'm sure he's very nice.'

They waited for what they considered enough time to clear the area of geese security guards before leaving the car park which was discreetly screened from the main house by a wall of trees. The main residence was what a brochure might describe as a 'Georgian retreat'. Like most of the larger homes in the area, it was built using the golden stone that gave Bath its chocolate box appeal to visitors. Austere from the outside with two great pillars at the door and a general feel of the Palladian revival that dominated Georgian Bath, the building loomed anachronistically out of the misty air.

Symbols had been carved into one of the door pillars and Rawls all but cringed when he spotted them. The most prominent was an ornate Om symbol, and Rawls arched an eyebrow at Nat.

'It's a sacred sound,' she whispered. 'It's ancient and spiritual, particularly important in mystical religions and religious retreats.'

'I do know what an Om symbol is,' he said, a little indignantly, 'I just don't like graffiti.'

Nat opened her mouth and he suspected that she was about to protest that it was hardly graffiti when the door opened and a tall man with a blond beard, long blond hair and long blond fingernails to match, extended a limp hand to them both. He announced that he was Sebastian and asked how he could help in a voice so soft that it was barely a whisper.

Rawls winked at Nat. 'Told you,' he whispered as they followed Sebastian through a grand lobby and into a cavernous lounge.

'Please,' Sebastian said, waving one pale hand at a couple of velvet beanbags.

'Thank you,' Rawls said, and Nat smiled.

Rawls folded his arms and looked around at the décor which he thought was slightly less annoying than the Om symbol but a long way away from what he might have chosen. Tall windows dressed in velvet curtains, wallpaper that made your head spin: burnt orange, or ochre, or whatever the buzz term was, covered with exotic birds and brightly coloured flowers. The look was Victoriana at its most steam punk.

'Tea?' Sebastian asked and before they could respond he turned to a vaporous gentleman who had wafted, unheard, into the room. 'Do the honours, Sash, would you?'

Sash floated back out and Sebastian turned his attention to Rawls, who had picked up a leaflet from the coffee table and was wriggling uncomfortably as he attempted to get himself upright. He fidgeted for a few seconds longer before looking at Sebastian with the air of one in extreme discomfort. 'Could I ask for a proper chair? It's just that my back is killing me.'

'Oh, of course, of course,' Sebastian said, gesturing to his ghostly minion who had returned with the tea as though he had produced it from behind a magic curtain. 'Sasha, would you fetch a chair for our guest?' He pronounced 'chair' as though it were an unclean object.

Rawls raised an eyebrow at Nat then heaved himself uncomfortably, and quite noisily, out of his beanbag. He stretched, pressing his hand to the small of his back, and his shirt pulled out a little in the front, exposing a crescent of the pale flesh beneath.

Sebastian favoured Rawls with a smile. 'Have you ever considered our retreat? We offer a weekend package. Complete detox for mind and body: no phones, no iPads, no TV, and the digital freedom is further enhanced by a deep inner cleansing: no meat, no starch, no sugar. People say they feel a million times better when they leave.'

'I'm sure they do,' said Rawls, scowling, 'but I think I'll pass. Not really my cup of tea,' he added, looking suspiciously down at the cup of green water that Sebastian had passed him.

Sasha had drifted in again, silent as a ghost, and placed a tall wooden chair behind Rawls. It looked as uninviting as the tea. Rawls sat down nonetheless, not wanting to be impolite. He smiled a thank you at Sasha who took up position like a sentinel behind Sebastian. 'Is it alright if we have a little wander about and chat with your staff before we leave?' he asked, and Sebastian rewarded him with another smile, this one displaying a set of perfectly white teeth.

'*Mi casa es su casa*,' Sebastian said, then turning to Sasha, he added, 'Sasha will escort you if you like, but you are, of course, more than welcome to talk to our staff without us if you prefer.'

'Either way is fine. Also,' Rawls looked out at the gardens, 'I noticed some plant machinery as we came up the drive. Is that all part of the grounds?'

Sebastian's face clouded. 'No, it most certainly is not.'

'You don't like it?' Rawls asked.

'It's an eyesore and one of the first things that people see when they pull up. Apparently, our neighbours are putting in a lake. The work has been going on since we bought the place and that's nearly five years ago now. Sometimes it feels like they'll have those bloody machines there indefinitely.'

Rawls nodded. 'I can see why you don't like it. I assumed it was part of the retreat. You could do with a screen, trees or hedges or something.'

Sebastian pursed his lips. 'Yes, well, thank you for your insight. It is on our list of things to address; they really are very ugly, those diggers.' He glanced briefly out of the window, as if he expected to see one of them parked on the front lawn. 'But you're not here to discuss my neighbours, are you? I understand you want to talk to me about these missing young ladies. I hear the locals think we're running a cult up here.'

'Are you?' Rawls asked.

Sebastian pulled his lips into a coquettish smile. 'My dear Detective Sergeant, do you honestly think that we would tell you if we were? What kind of a cult would that be?' He waved a hand around and Sasha mirrored the gesture like a magician's assistant. 'Our guests pay a great deal of money to stay with us, and, whilst we prefer them to spend their time in quiet contemplation without outside interference, they are, nonetheless, free to come and go as they see fit. We don't hold anyone prisoner.' He smiled to show that the last was a joke.

Rawls offered him a coy smile of his own. 'And the staff?'

Sebastian frowned. 'The staff? I'm not sure that I understand.'

'Are they free to come and go as they see fit?'

'I'm not sure that I appreciate your implication, but yes, the staff are free to come and go as they please. However, we pride ourselves on our team; they have all been with us since the start. We look after our staff, Detective Sergeant; our philosophy is that a happy team makes for a happy place.'

'Are most of your staff local residents?'

There was the sound of a commotion from somewhere beyond the room, plates or glasses being dropped. Sebastian turned to Sasha. 'Be a love, would you, see what that's all about? I'll shout if I need you.'

Sasha's face clouded briefly and then he smiled warmly and left the room.

'Sorry,' Sebastian said, watching as Sasha closed the door, 'our work never really stops. You were asking about the staff?'

Rawls nodded. 'They're all local?'

'Well no, not really, not exactly. Many of them, no, most of them were here already; they'd been part of, well, you know, the place before.'

'The Stoney Path?'

Sebastian nodded and, when he spoke, his voice was even softer than before. 'We had to retrain them all, that goes without saying, but they had lived here for twenty years or so and we felt we couldn't throw them all out, so we made them an offer to stay on and work for us.'

'Did they all stay?'

'Most of them. We offered a really good package and we run the place as a kind of a cooperative – that way everybody shares in the profits. It promotes loyalty and we ensure that the time and money spent on staff training is put to good use, because people don't leave and take their skills elsewhere.'

'Sounds great,' Rawls said, 'and business is good?'

'Touch wood,' Sebastian tapped his head, 'and we have bookings right through summer.' His face clouded and he looked at Rawls. 'But these rumours, they'll be bad for us if they persist; people won't want to come with them hanging over the place.' He looked down at his hands. 'I really don't understand why anyone would do this to us, and having the police on our doorstep, well, I'm sure you won't mind my saying that that is the last thing we need.'

'We've had a couple of tips,' Rawls said, 'that's all, just tips on our social media accounts. I'm sure you must understand that we have to investigate every single lead?'

'Of course,' Sebastian said. 'It just feels so unfair. We've put so much hard work into the place and to have something like this hanging over us, well, it's just horrible.'

Rawls nodded, he did understand. 'It goes without saying that if the tips are unfounded you have nothing to worry about,' he said.

'Detective Sergeant Rawls, I'm fairly certain that you know full well that that is not how these things work,' Sebastian said, 'and I've heard the rumours. People saying that we're some kind of sick sex cult up here, taking money from our followers and marrying young women off to old men or using forced labour, using people like slaves – it's preposterous.'

Rawls nodded. 'Any idea why anyone would want to drag your business into the spotlight this way?'

Sebastian shook his head. 'We've asked ourselves that a million times. We've been lucky so far, our guests have been darlings about it all, but the truth is that could change in a heartbeat. We just want to get this cleared up and move on from it.'

'In that case,' Rawls said, 'we would appreciate your help with a couple of things. First off, do you still have records from before you took over?'

Sebastian frowned. 'I honestly don't know. Hang on, I'll get Sash back in, he takes care of admin.' He went to the door and called out briefly and Sasha appeared again as though he had been conjured up on the spot. Rawls thought they made a fabulous double act.

'We have a list of the dates in question,' Rawls said, glancing at Nat who pulled a sheet of paper from her notepad and handed it to Sasha.

'What are these for?' Sebastian seemed confused.

'These are the days that the four young girls went missing – the earliest is from 2009. What we need is a list of staff on duty that day, also anyone who might have taken the day off unexpectedly or called in sick either before, on or after the dates in question. Do you think that you could provide us with that?'

The two men exchanged worried glances like two old ladies at a poker table.

'Is there a problem?' Rawls asked.

Sasha was looking at the list. 'I can definitely help with the most recent two – we had taken over by then – but the first two might be difficult. The Stoney Path didn't keep computerised records, so I'd have to see if the information was in any of the boxes left behind.'

'Anything you could give us would be helpful,' Rawls smiled, 'anything at all. And if I could have a list of your staff details, especially the ones that were here before, that would be great.'

Sasha smiled. 'I have sent our staff records over to your office already.'

Rawls nodded. 'And we appreciate the help you have given us so far, it's the older details that we are hoping you can help with.' He turned to Sebastian before Sasha could complain. 'One of the things that we wanted to talk to your staff about, especially those who were here before you took over, is whether anyone ran away and hid here, you know? Joined the cult without telling anyone where they were.'

Sasha had crossed the room with his usual silent grace but now he paused with a hand on the door. 'They might not wish to discuss that with you, Detective Sergeant. We are a very private group.'

Sebastian was nodding. 'And we really don't wish to be associated with the history of the place. I'm sure you understand that – this is a sanctuary now, it's nothing like it was before.'

'Absolutely,' Rawls said, 'the two of you have done a wonderful job by the looks of it. I should imagine people love spending time here.'

Sebastian smiled. 'Thank you, we do our best.'

'I think that will do for now,' Rawls said. 'You don't mind if we have a little wander around, do you? Just to have a chat with your staff and perhaps a couple of your guests.'

Sebastian looked solemn. 'By all means speak to the staff, Detective Rawls, but please, our guests have spent an awful lot of money to spend time here and get away from their normal busy lives. You will be discreet, won't you?'

Rawls nodded. 'You have my word.'

'I'll get Sasha to come and find you once he has those records for you.'

'I appreciate that, thank you for your time.'

Sebastian pushed himself up from his beanbag with a broad smile. 'Our pleasure. We really will be glad to see this all cleared up.' He turned to Sasha who had remained by the door, 'won't we, Sash?'

Sasha nodded. 'We really will.'

Chapter 7

Have you been practising?
Yes
How much?
As much as I can.
Will I be impressed?
Yes
How do you know?
B coz
How?
B coz u always r
What are you wearing?
Jeans
And?
A T-shirt

> *And?*
> *And*
> *Tell me!*
> *Tell me!*
> *OK, if you won't tell me, show me.*
> *My mum's just come in.*
> *So?*
> *So ...*
> *OK, I'll let you off – for now ...* ☺

'Carmen,' Eileen called from downstairs.

> *Omgggggg mums callin.*
> *Xxx*

'Carmen!'

'Coming, oh my God, you don't have to shout.'

'I just need a hand with the shopping.'

'Mum, it's raining.'

'No shit, Sherlock.' Eileen handed her a raincoat. 'And take your phone out of your back pocket, you'll be devastated if you drop that in a puddle.'

Carmen pulled the coat on and moved her phone into a waterproofed pocket. 'God, I hope no one sees me.'

'It's not a fashion show, love, I just need a hand with some bags.'

Carmen grimaced and headed to the car, shielding her face in case the rain made her make-up run.

They unpacked in silence and Carmen suspected her mother had something on her mind.

'You alright, Mum?' she asked after a bit.

Eileen was stacking fruit in the fridge. 'I'm fine thanks, babe, just got a bit of a headache.'

Carmen handed her a block of Lurpak, Rawls's favourite, then held up a packet of Ibuprofen. 'Do you want a headache tablet before I put them away?'

Eileen looked over her shoulder. 'You're being awfully thoughtful all of a sudden. What have you done?'

'Mum,' Carmen protested, and Eileen took out a block of cheese big enough to use as a house-brick, another of Rawls's culinary delights, and shoved it beneath the butter.

'Mum nothing,' said Eileen. 'What are you up to?'

'I'm not up to anything,' Carmen leaned on the counter, her chin resting in her hands, 'but I do want something.'

Eileen stood up, groaned, looked around at the bags that still needed to be unpacked and groaned again. She opened a cupboard and took out a wine glass.

'Mum, it's only three o'clock,' Carmen protested.

'And?' Eileen responded. She wafted a theatrical hand across the shopping. 'How else am I supposed to manage this lot? And it'll help with my headache – they say wine has more health benefits than painkillers.'

Carmen giggled. 'No, they don't.' She peeled herself off the counter. 'Can I go to see a film on Friday night?'

Eileen eyed her over her headache cure. 'With whom?'

Carmen pushed a pack of beans into the cupboard. 'Does it matter?'

'Of course it does, babe.'

'Mum,' Carmen said, as though the single word was an explanation of its own.

Eileen watched her for a moment before looking away. She supposed Carmen had to have some secrets – hadn't she had a few when she was her age? 'OK,' she said, 'but could you at least tell me where you're going to meet this person? I assume they're not coming here as I'm not allowed to know who they are.'

'It's not that you're not allowed, it's just, you know, a bit embarrassing, that's all, but I'm meeting *this person* at the Odeon, at seven thirty. The film starts at about eight, I think.'

'What are you going to see?'

'It's one of those Avenger films,' Carmen laughed, 'I pretended I'd seen the others, but I haven't.'

'Carmen, that's no way to start a relationship,' Eileen protested.

'Mum, it's not a relationship.'

'Not a relationship? Whatever next? In my day, a person would have had to meet my father before that person took me out.'

'No, they wouldn't, would they?'

Eileen laughed. 'No, but still, how do I know this person is nice?'

'Because he is.'

'Aha, so it is a boy?'

'Mum, stop it. But it is a boy and he is nice.'

'How do you know?'

'Because I do.' Carmen opened the freezer and dropped a bag of frozen fish pie mix into it. 'Yuck,' she said, then added, 'Mum, I'm not a baby, you know. You don't have to arrange my play dates any more.'

Eileen fixed her gaze on Carmen for a moment, her head cocked to one side like a dog listening for danger. Carmen stared coolly back at her, refusing to buckle under the scrutiny.

'OK, fine,' Eileen said at last, 'but make sure that you tell him that your dad's a copper.'

'Oh, Mother,' said Carmen but she resumed unpacking and they fell back into a thoughtful silence.

'Pass me that bottle, would you, babe?' Eileen said as they packed away the last bag. 'Think I'll treat myself to one more glass, for medicinal purposes, you understand?'

'When's Dad home?' Carmen said, changing the subject.

Eileen looked at the clock. 'Good question.'

'I take it he's back at work full-time now?'

Eileen swallowed from her glass. 'As far as I know.'

'He hasn't told you?'

'Oh,' she said, 'you know your father.'

Chapter 8

Nat passed Rawls a cup of coffee and then sat down across the desk from him.

'Thanks,' Rawls said. 'So, tell me. How do you know so much about cults?'

She shrugged. 'I don't know really, I just find them interesting. I always have done ever since I was quite young, and I remember reading a book called something like *The World's Scariest Cults*.' She laughed. 'Of course nowadays there's loads of information about them: documentaries, books, podcasts.'

He nodded. 'I've never listened to a podcast.'

'Really? You should. Did you know that a couple have been made about our first two missing girls?'

'Really? Have you listened to them?'

Nat blushed. 'I have. They were quite good, you should give them a listen. I could dig out the details for you if you like.'

'I'll bear it in mind,' Rawls said. 'In the meantime, though, what did you think about the retreat, about your man there, Sebastian?'

'He's not my man,' she said, 'but I felt a little sorry for them both, to tell you the truth, Sebastian and Sasha.'

'Sorry for them, how's that?'

She stared into her coffee for a moment. 'I don't know, it can't be easy, running a place like that knowing that the locals are all against you.'

'Yeah, it can't be easy, I'll give you that. What about the rest of the staff? How did you feel about them?'

Nat thought for a moment. 'I liked them. I mean, don't get me wrong, I felt they were all toeing a company line and it was obvious that they weren't willing to talk about the past; it was like they had all agreed that it didn't happen.'

'Yeah, I got that too,' Rawls said, 'but I suppose you would feel that way. The place is doing well now, and they have a stake in making it work.'

'I suppose they could be embarrassed by the past – perhaps they feel silly for being part of the place, following old Berkeley Wolf.'

Rawls nodded, remembering his own run-in with them, wondering whether any of them had been there on that day, hurling mud at him and calling him a piggy. 'Maybe, and we are the police – perhaps they're afraid of incriminating themselves by association with the place when it really was a cult.'

'It's not illegal, you know, to join a cult. In the UK you are free to choose to follow your own faith.'

'Even if the guy preaching the faith is a complete nut job?'

Nat laughed. 'Freedom of religion means that you can choose to worship as you see fit, even if the leader of your faith is a nut job.'

'You are an expert,' he said, grinning at her, 'I knew it.'

'Well,' Nat began, 'I'm not sure that I count as an expert, but here's what I do know. There are different types of cults; they're not all religious maniacs, not on the outside anyway. They lure people in, I guess that's how you would describe it, and they do it with promises that you can find nirvana or achieve better results in life or work or make more money. There are a couple of cults still around today who run successful restaurants, or teach people how to perform better under pressure, that sort of thing. And then there are the more crazy ones, the doomsday guys, the ones who are waiting for the world to end or for their masters to come and collect them in their spaceship. Some of them come across, I don't know, not just as harmless, but actually helpful, as though they really are going to make the world a better place. Jim Jones started off that way.' She paused. 'Do you know who Jim Jones was?'

Rawls frowned. 'The guy who took his followers to Guyana, then got them all to drink cyanide, back in the Seventies?'

'That's the guy, but did you know that he preached equality before he went off the rails? He was a civil rights activist. A good one by all accounts.'

'No, I didn't know that.'

'Most people don't. He was an actual minister at first, an ordained minister of the faith. I think that he really did try to do good, he genuinely believed in racial integration and he worked incredibly hard for the cause. But something changed, he lost his mind, perhaps the power went to his head. Whatever the reason, a thousand or so people died at his command. Can you imagine that? A thousand people, entire families, small children, even babies.'

'They drank Kool Aid, didn't they?' Rawls said.

'Not Kool Aid, just a flavoured drink, but it was full of potassium cyanide, and those that wouldn't drink it were injected with it. It was a terrible, terrible tragedy.'

'The guy was clearly off his trolley.'

'I suppose he must have been,' Nat said, 'but that seems to be the way that many cult leaders work; that passion for their cause turns into an obsession and the cause takes a back seat to their need for power. It tips people over the edge, I think, drives them mad.'

Rawls nodded at the door to the office. 'Got a few of those right here.'

She laughed.

'But I'm not sure that our man Berkeley Wolf was on quite the same scale as Jim Jones,' Rawls added.

'No, but there is something about that kind of guy. They know how to manipulate people, to drag them in and not let them go.'

'The kind of place that young men and women are drawn to?'

Nat nodded. 'They're such charismatic people, but he's dead, and the place clearly isn't a cult now.'

Rawls thought for a moment. 'You're right. I'm just chasing the hypothesis, but it doesn't fit.'

'Even so, do you think there's any chance that one or more of the girls is there? Perhaps hiding amongst the staff?'

Rawls considered the question. 'Hard to say. It's been ten years since Melody vanished and nearly eight years since Harriet. We'd need an age progression done, but I think we'd have recognised them. I just don't see it.'

'Where does that leave us?' Nat asked. 'Do we rule the retreat out?'

Rawls sighed and leaned back in his chair. 'Not yet, there are still too many questions in my head.' He reached for a pen and notepad. Tearing off a sheet, he drew a circle in the middle and wrote the words 'Stoney Path' in its centre, added a question mark then circled it again. 'Let's see what we have so far,' he said, drawing circles around the first like moons orbiting a planet. He wrote a name in each one: Melody, Harriet, Yvette, Tanya. Beneath these he wrote the date each girl was last seen. 'What else do we know?' he asked Nat.

She leaned forward. 'Their ages,' she said and called them out so that he could write them down. He filled in names and places: Jacob Spengler, Yvette's boyfriend; Sebastian; Sasha; the parents of the missing girls. They discussed the where, when, who and the what, but it felt like they were going nowhere. Rawls tapped the white spaces. 'These are the bits that we need to fill in,' he said, 'the unknowns. This is like doing a crossword puzzle with some of the clues missing: our job is to work out what the clues are from what we have so far then find the answers once we have them.'

Nat touched the page with her pen. 'Do you think all roads are going to lead us back to the Stoney Path?'

'I honestly can't say, but we need to know more about the place. When was it sold? Who sold it? When did old Berkeley Wolf die?' Rawls added another three circles to his diagram as he spoke and put a question mark in each.

He ran a hand through his hair and closed his eyes. They had one lead and that seemed to be slipping through their fingers; it just didn't seem right. He was frustrated by how little they had achieved. He looked at Nat and stifled a yawn. 'I don't know about you,' he said, 'but I've had it. Let's call it a night.'

Chapter 9

The local team could have been selected by a computer, one programmed to search out the exact mix of characters required for a problem-solving and decision-making exercise. Rawls knew two of them already because Tess had somehow managed to strong-arm them out of MCIT; the other two were wooden-tops, uniformed officers purloined from usual duty to assist. He wasn't immediately impressed.

'I think we'll need more bods,' he said when Tess gave him the low-down, 'just keeping up with the tip-line since the Press Conference has been a full time job for two people.'

Tess had looked at him coolly. 'we are currently providing almost wrap-around shifts on this, Rawls, I don't have any more people to give you.'

'I know that,' Rawls was trying to be patient, 'but I need more local guys, guys who know the lay of the land, I need guys familiar with Bath.'

'Leave it with me, I'll see what I can do,' said Tess. She swiftly changed the subject. 'In the meantime, though, how'd it go on your retreat?'

Rawls folded his arms and sighed. 'I honestly don't know,' he said, 'and just for your info, Tess, I wouldn't retreat there if a couple of ghost legions of Roman soldiers rose up out of the earth and chased me in that direction.'

This made Tess laugh, really laugh, which caught him by surprise. It hadn't been that funny.

After a couple of seconds, she dabbed at her eyes, still smiling, then stood up and pushed her chair in. 'Right, shall we address the troops? You can be Caesar and I'll be Boudicca.' She laughed again, louder this time.

Her mood changed the moment they stepped into the incident room. One minute she was a stand-up comedian's dream audience and the next she was as po-faced as a maiden aunt at a brothel; it was almost as though someone had turned a tap off.

'Morning all,' she said and waited for the obligatory, 'morning ma'ams' that followed. 'I'm sorry to get you all in on a Sunday, but DS Rawls didn't want to wait.'

Oh yes, that's right, thought Rawls, *blame it all on me.*

'As you know,' Tess went on, 'DS Rawls will be consulting on this, he will be reporting directly to me, I will still be SIO but I felt that Rawls's past knowledge of these incidents would be invaluable. I don't think any introductions are necessary, are they?' She glanced at Rawls and he shook his head.

He said, 'I apologise to anyone who had today off, I know you have all been flat out on this one. No one wishes more than me that we didn't have to.' The group mumbled but Rawls thought it mostly good-humoured.

'DI McGovern is going to catch us all up to where we are so far, afterwards we'll get our heads together.'

They settled into their self-identified pairs: Detective Constables Craig Chivers and Linda Greenhill from MCIT and the two that Tess had introduced to him earlier from uniform: Police Constables Stefan Iles and Barry Coccia. Given the choice, Rawls would have preferred pretty much anyone to Chivers. They had disliked each other when they had first met, and the feeling had grown to a kind of mutual loathing since.

They had greeted each other warmly, though, like two old friends.

'I hear you got yourself a get out of jail free card here,' Chivers said, scratching at the stubble on his chin.

Rawls thought, as he always did, that Chivers was the kind of person who always managed to look grubby and in need of a bath, or a hose-down.

'Don't get me wrong though, mate,' Chivers offered by way of explanation, 'I don't think you did anything wrong, none of us do, we're all right behind you. Good to have you back in charge.' There was a mixture of self-importance and contempt in his voice.

Rawls smiled at him in much the same way that a pool hustler might smile at his opponent. 'Well,' he said, 'my understanding is that I'm more of a consultant than lead detective – that's still Tess.'

Chivers tapped his nose and winked. 'Consultant? What's that all about? Have they told you one way or another yet?'

Rawls sighed. 'About?'

Chivers dropped his voice, 'Come on, mate, we all know they were talking about writing you up on a misconduct charge.' He knitted his brows together so tight that they became one black line. 'They can't just keep stringing you along – they have to say one way or another. Either they're going to take action against you, or they're not.'

'Well, so far they haven't said either way.'

'Shocking,' Chivers said. 'No way to treat you, not after what you've been through. I mean it can't be easy since your little meltdown.'

Rawls felt himself tense and for a moment he thought about having it out with the man, but in the end he simply thanked him for his consideration. Sometimes it just wasn't worth the bother. He knew as well as the next copper that Chivers would love to see him prosecuted under the Police Conduct Regulations, not because Chivers had anything in particular against Rawls but because he simply enjoyed the drama; he was just that kind of a guy.

'I'm just happy to be back,' Rawls said.

Chivers clapped him on the back. 'That's the spirit, mate. If you need anything, anything at all, you know I'm here to help. You don't need this crap.'

'Thanks, really appreciate it,' Rawls said.

'Just don't make the same mistake twice,' Chivers said with the air of one who wishes nothing more than to provide the friendliest of advice.

Rawls made an effort not to wince. He had known it was coming but the remark hit its target, nonetheless. He had worked with Chivers a couple of times in the past, most recently along with Linda Greenhill when they had all been assigned to the Charlie Ambers case. They had closed that in less than a week, and the result had been a good one. Rawls assumed that had been the reason Tess had asked for them. Linda was meticulous but there was something more than that, she cared. Chivers, on the other hand, had the air of an obstreperous schoolboy, but he was sharp, and he missed nothing. The trouble was that he was unpleasant and sarcastic with it. He also had a habit of being single-minded in his approach to suspects and Rawls knew, from bitter experience, the dangers that could bring.

He turned to Tess who was speaking in her usual clipped voice. He liked it; she was clear and concise and left nothing unsaid, which put everyone at ease. The uniforms had briefed her earlier on the tip-line so far, and Coccia had put together a list of the best.

Tess went through them all then said, 'So we've got a couple of things to kick us off. Firstly, the retreat – Rawls can give us the low-down on that in a second – and then there's the potential sighting of Tanya in Frome.' She glanced at Chivers. 'You're taking that, aren't you?'

Chivers nodded. Frome was about a forty-minute drive from Bath and not far from where he lived, so he had been the logical choice for the job.

'We also have this local guy whose name has come up more than once,' Tess continued. 'He's an estate agent, isn't he?'

Linda nodded.

'And,' Tess looked at her notes, 'there's this van that two independent witnesses say they saw parked up on the Wells Road on the day that Tanya was last seen.' She glanced at Rawls. 'We're working on finding out the company name. Lastly, there's Yvette's ex-boyfriend, his name has come up a number of times.' She looked at Rawls again. 'You've already spoken to him, though, haven't you?'

'The ex-boyfriend? Yes, but I want him in for a formal statement, Linda's going to arrange that.'

Linda nodded. 'And we're working on the other two, I'll get them in as soon as possible. You want me to do the interviews or do you want to do it?'

'I'd like to be involved,' Rawls said.

Linda nodded and Tess said, 'Refresh our collective memories on the tips, would you, Linda?'

'The first guy's come up more than once on the tip-line,' Linda began. 'He's an estate agent, a couple of the tips mention him. We know that he knew Harriet; she did her work experience at his agency.'

'And the others?'

'Not sure yet, but I'll see what I can dig up on his work history, see if we can see anything there.'

'Brilliant, thanks, Lin. In the meantime, let's get him in for a chat,' Rawls said. 'What about the van?'

Linda made a face. 'Like I said, the two callers hadn't made a note of the reg or the name on the van. It was sign-written, so we're checking the cameras for that day, see if anything comes up. Both callers mentioned the van being on double yellows so it might have been issued with a ticket.'

'You'll let me know as soon as you have something?' Rawls asked her.

She nodded. 'Absolutely.'

'OK, great,' Tess said. 'What about this place out in Wellow, do you want to fill us in on that?'

Rawls stood up. 'Yes, Nat and I have been out there. It's a nice enough place, as retreats go. It's not as far out as Wellow – closer to Odd Down – it's called Stoney Barrow View. The new owners are keen to disassociate themselves from the history of the place. Some of you will have heard of it from its previous incarnation when it was called the Stoney Path. They were mixed up in some child endangerment issues back in the late Nineties but the place was sold around five years ago.'

There was a murmur of agreement from Chivers and Greenhill, but the two PCs looked at him blankly and he elaborated for them. 'The place was a sort of commune. The guy operated a one-in, one-out sort of system; he had wealthy kids queuing up to join him and hand over the family inheritance. This was all well and good at first until it came to light that part of his doctrine was that he was to be "married" to all of the girls in the group. There were a great many of them at the time and the ones that he seemed especially keen on were all young, very young.'

'Was he done for it?'

Rawls shook his head. 'Nope, insufficient evidence.'

'The guy was a creep,' Linda said. 'I met him once, he made my blood curdle.'

'Is he still around?' Iles asked.

'He died, didn't he?' Chivers asked.

Rawls nodded. 'Yes, he did.'

'Recently?'

'That's not clear yet,' Rawls said, 'but Nat's looking into the details.'

Nat looked up and smiled.

Rawls went on. 'Our initial thoughts were that the older cases, Melody Lockyer and Harriet DiAngelo, could have joined the group at some point.' He saw Chivers frown. 'In the same way that young girls joined in the Nineties,' he said, 'but there's nothing there to back that up. We spoke to the staff – most of them have never worked anywhere else. They were there when it was the Stoney Path and the new owner kept them on.'

'What were they like?' Chivers asked. 'Hippies in baggy pants, that sort of thing?'

Rawls shook his head. 'No, the place is pretty professional. They cater to a high-end clientele; we assumed that was the reason that they were so reluctant to talk about the past.'

Chivers grinned. 'But in the past, when they were this hippy commune, they recruited staff by bringing them into the fold, is that it?'

Rawls nodded. 'That way you have a team of like-minded people working towards a common goal, I suppose.'

Linda asked, 'So you're thinking that it's possible that they may have continued to recruit people to work for them by indoctrinating them into their belief system, even today, in spite of the new owners?'

'No, not exactly.' Rawls frowned a little, he really didn't know what he was thinking. 'I just want us to keep our minds open to all possibilities. You guys know the score, nothing is ruled out till it's ruled out.' He stared at his hands for a moment then added, 'We've no crime scenes, no sign of struggles, no bodies, nothing. What we have to do now is start again. Without evidence we have to hope that our witnesses will hold the answers; we have to treat every angle as if it were the right one. It's the only way to get to the bottom of this. We have to remain open-minded.'

He thought he heard Chivers mumble something about pots and kettles. 'Sorry?' he asked. 'I missed that.'

Chivers smiled and his eyes disappeared into his cheeks. 'I was clearing my throat.'

'So you don't think this new owner is anything to do with the old place?' Linda persisted. 'He's not some new cult leader, just taking over from the old one?'

'I'll let Nat answer that one,' Rawls said. 'Turns out she's a bit of a guru on cults.'

Nat flushed a little as she spoke. 'We didn't think so. He's just dedicated to making the place work; he certainly doesn't fit the bill of a cult leader. The people there are all on board with making the place the best that it can be and there was no weird vibe, no indication that anything untoward was going on. No one looked pale or desperate or emaciated, all signs of people being held under duress.'

'In your opinion as our resident cult guru?' Chivers said.

'In my opinion, yes,' Nat said, and although her voice was firm, Rawls noticed a tiny shake in her hand.

'Well, we are lucky to have you,' Chivers said, and Rawls saw his eyes slide across the room to Tess.

The guy was a first-class prick, Rawls thought, he had to give him that.

The team spent the rest of the afternoon, and much of the evening, going over what they had so far, which they all agreed amounted to precious little. They ended up in a small coffee bar, the only one open at that time on a Sunday evening, and the conversation became more relaxed. Rawls felt good to be part of a team again, to be doing what he loved best, but he worried about Chivers. The man had a way of rubbing people the wrong way – he knew that a couple of his jibes had upset Nat and he knew that he would need to speak to him about it. In the meantime, though, he wanted to reassure her, let her know that she was doing a good job, and he allowed the others to drift away until just the two of them remained.

'Don't let Chivers get to you,' he said. 'He's a pompous prick sometimes.'

Nat rolled her eyes. 'I think I'll have to get used to him,' she said, 'but I was surprised that he was so funny with you. I heard you two were mates – the DI told me that you worked together on the case of the missing boy, the one with the weird story.'

'Charlie Ambers,' Rawls said. 'We did,' he broke a piece off his half-eaten iced bun and swallowed it before continuing, 'but the investigation only lasted three days. That much of him I can stand.'

'Three days? I thought it was longer than that. The boy was OK, right?'

Rawls nodded and peeled off another strip of his bun. 'Good bun,' he said. 'Do you want a bit?'

Nat shook her head; she still had the remnants of a chai latte in front of her. 'Got my calories for the rest of the week right here,' she said.

Rawls wiped at his mouth and looked at her earnestly. 'Charlie was terribly neglected, but he'd slipped through the net. His mother was charming, beautiful, hard-working, single; she was vegan, lived in an immaculate home and earned good money. Charlie was undernourished, but the school and health workers believed his mum when she assured them that it was just because he was a picky eater. They were vegan and his choices were sometimes limited, she said, so he didn't always eat as much as she would have liked.' He ran a tired hand across his unshaven face. 'No one, and I mean no one, pushed her on it – can you believe it? No one even questioned her, even though many had their doubts; they just kept quiet.' He sighed as though the weight of it still hurt him. 'She had been starving him, well, not starving, but restricting his food, using it as punishment, holding it back for every minor misdemeanour: not making his bed, not brushing his hair, not dusting beneath a bowl of fruit, you name it, she punished him for it. And do you know what the worst part was?'

Nat shook her head.

'He was only five years old. She never laid a hand on him, mind, but locking him in his room without food, well, that was alright.' Rawls shook his head. 'Chivers has a kid of a similar age, and his boy was ill at the time. I don't recall what it was, but he was in and out of hospital for a while and I think it affected Chivers. He went at it like a dog with a bone. We interviewed everyone that woman knew; we interviewed every neighbour, every person who walked down their road, every teacher at his school.'

A tear had made its way down Nat's cheek, and this time when he paused to offer her a piece of his bun, she took it, folding it into her mouth as though she was taking communion. 'How did you find him?' she asked.

'A woman was hiding him, a cleaner from his school, said she couldn't bear to see him wasting away. She said he was cold most days, often poorly, always hungry. He screamed blue murder when we took him away from her.' Rawls paused, swallowed, collected himself. 'She stood there wailing and

Charlie was holding on to her cardigan pleading with her to let him stay. It was the worst thing that either one of us has ever had to do.'

'Was she done for it?' Nat was aghast, her face pale. 'The cleaner lady, I mean.'

'Not in the end, no. He was taken into care and last I heard she was fostering him and applying to adopt.'

'Oh, thank goodness.' Nat stared out of the window at the car park beyond. A woman was kneeling beside her son, pointing her finger at him and telling him off for something; he would have been around the same age as little Charlie Ambers. 'What happened to the mother?' she said without taking her eyes off the woman outside.

'She was done, thankfully. Wilful neglect, endangerment of a minor and child cruelty. She'll only be in for a few years, I should imagine, but prison has a way of meting out its own kind of justice.'

Nat wiped at her face with the edge of her fingers. 'Well, thanks for that, I wish I hadn't asked.'

'Surely you've seen worse?' Rawls asked. 'Two years on the beat must have included a couple of family incidents.'

She shook her head. 'None like that.'

Rawls swallowed the last of his coffee and looked at his watch. 'It's late, best get a move on.'

She nodded. 'Thanks, Sarge. And thanks for the tea.'

'Pleasure. And listen, you really are doing a great job, I'm glad to have you with me.'

She smiled at him. 'I'm glad to be on the team.'

They headed outside and Rawls paused at his car. 'Can I give you a lift?'

She shook her head. 'I only live about a ten-minute walk from here, but thanks anyway.'

'Go careful,' Rawls said, 'don't talk to any strangers.'

She laughed, then paused, her face solemn. 'Do you think we can do this, Sarge?'

Rawls was quiet for a moment, 'I hope so,' he said, and she nodded as if that was good enough for her.

Rawls watched her walk away before he climbed into his car. 'We have to do it,' he said to the cold air. 'If not us, then who?'

The rain had given way to a clear, cold night sky by the time Rawls opened the gate and headed up his garden path. The front door was open, and he paused for a moment looking around. At the front of the house was a low walled flowerbed and Rawls was not surprised to see Eileen, wrapped in a coat and scarf, perched on the wall now, bathed in the cold white light of an outdoor lamp. It was her spot, where she found solace, surrounded by her beloved garden and hidden from neighbouring homes by a large arched trellis that, in the summer, would be heavy with both the weight and scent of an enormous climbing rose. Rawls would not have cared to try to count how many times he had found Eileen sitting out here, silently contemplating life, and he had often thought that he should buy her a little plaque, perhaps carved into wood, that proclaimed it as 'Eileen's Place'. Eileen would sit there in all seasons, a mug of tea – always from a pot, Peter, we're not heathens – in one hand and a book or her phone in the other. Tonight, she had her eyes closed and legs crossed, yoga style. She rested her hands on her knees in the lotus position. Beside her was an empty glass, stained red with a tiny puddle of maroon liquid in the bottom. In the bright light it looked to Rawls like blood. Next to the glass was a bottle of wine and he looked at his watch: it was nearly seven, too early to be pissed, he hoped.

'Hey you,' he called out and Eileen opened her eyes with a start.

'Shit, Peter, you nearly gave me a heart attack.'

He crossed the damp grass to join her. She tapped a space on the wall beside her, inviting him to sit down, but he shook his head. 'It's all wet, you'll get piles.'

Eileen laughed. 'I've got my big pants on,' she said.

Her breath reached him in an alcoholic cloud, and her smile seemed a little too eager, too chirpy; she was already two sheets to the wind, and he thought the final sheet was at the bottom of the bottle, waiting to be released.

'You coming in?' he asked and she shook her head, reaching for the bottle.

'Not yet,' she said, 'I'm considering the meaning of life.'

'Forty-two,' he said, quoting *The Hitchhiker's Guide to the Galaxy* as he was certain that she would have known he would.

'Well,' she winked, 'at least it's not sixty-nine.'

'My dear,' Rawls said, 'how very rude you are.'

She grinned at him with wine-stained teeth; it made her look like a vampire under the white light.

'Got any thoughts about dinner?' Rawls asked and she shook her head slowly.

'I have a confession,' she said, holding her finger to her lips. 'I might be a little bit pissed,' she pursed her lips and fluttered her eyelids. 'Sorry,' she said and giggled.

Rawls hovered for a moment, unsure of what to say or do; he wasn't very good with her when she was like this. He didn't like drunk people when he was sober, especially his wife. It irritated him, he couldn't help it; it was like talking to a child. 'I'll go and see what I can rustle up. Is Carmen in?'

'No, she's at rehearsals.' Eileen looked up at the cloudless night sky and Rawls felt another pang of guilt when she added, 'No one here but me, just little old me, and the stars, of course.'

He turned and headed for the front door and she called after him, 'Pete, I know I'm pissed and pissing you off.' She paused for a moment, considering her words, then laughed. 'Pissed and pissing you off, that's funny.' She laughed again but only briefly before her face clouded and she looked at him earnestly. 'Do you still love me?'

They had been married for nearly thirteen years and Rawls thought that if he had demanded a pound from her every time she had asked him this question, he might not be a rich man exactly but he would certainly have accumulated an extremely tall pile of pound coins. He turned to look at her, her long red hair held back by about a million clips that she would later leave around the house as one by one they either hurt or irritated her, her gaunt face red with a merlot blush, her long neck as pale as the moonlight. 'Who wouldn't love you?' he said, and he hurried inside before she could say anything else. The day had been too intense for drunken philosophy; what he needed right at that moment was something to eat, a cup of coffee, and perhaps an hour with his bonsai. What he didn't need was a discussion about how much he loved his wife and why he never told her she was beautiful any more or why he didn't put his arm around her in public.

He put his keys on the side table and was about to head upstairs when he stopped and sighed. He turned around, headed for the front door and leaned out. 'Love you to bits, by the way,' he said.

From the garden he heard his wife laugh. 'Course you do,' she muttered, 'course you do.'

Chapter 10

Rawls was impressed. Chivers and Iles had spoken with Warminster already; they must have left at the crack of dawn. Later that day, while DS Linda Greenhill and PC Barry Coccia were going to visit a couple of people who had come up more than once on the tip-line, Rawls and Nat had arranged to visit Harriet DiAngelo's parents. It felt as though they had momentum, they had the bit between their collective teeth, and they were ready to go. Rawls had always liked this feeling, of getting on with the job. This was why he had joined the service in the first place, to balance the scales, to put the pieces of a puzzle together and find the whole picture; it was what he was meant to do. For Rawls, it was all about justice. He couldn't help but smile as he looked around at the group. Perhaps it was going to be OK, perhaps Chivers wasn't as bad as he thought after all, perhaps he could keep it together, perhaps the past would stay in the past. He leaned back and crossed his legs as Chivers briefed them all on the trip to Warminster.

'Apparently two people reported seeing Tanya, or someone who looked like Tanya, on the train station in Frome,' Chivers was saying. 'We've got the CCTV to show to the girl's family.'

'Tanya,' Nat said.

Chivers stared at her for a moment and then he actually winked before saying, 'Sorry, Tanya's family.'

Nat flushed and looked down at the table and Rawls reminded himself that he had to have a word with Chivers after the meeting.

Chivers went on. 'The images are a bit shit, to be honest – cameras are dirty and there was water on the lens, double trouble. The officer who took the shout was a bit of a prick. I've not come across him before, but I wasn't all that impressed with his efforts. He was pretty certain that it wasn't our girl, though, said the witnesses both said she was with a group of girls.'

'A group?' Rawls said. 'Have you spoken to any of her friends?'

Chivers favoured him with an 'of course we have' kind of smile then said, 'Iles spoke with a number of her friends and none of them have been on a train trip with her; none of them even knew where Frome was.' He glanced at Iles, who nodded agreement.

'Have you got the stills?' Rawls asked, and Chivers nodded to Iles who clicked a mouse on his laptop so that a grainy image of a girl in jeans and a black jacket filled the screen set up at the front of the room.

'Not much to go by,' Iles offered, and Chivers nodded like a proud father agreeing with a doting son.

Rawls had to smile. It was the first time that Iles and Chivers had worked together but already they were like a double act – Pinky and Perky or Laurel and Hardy – although, unlike the charming comedy duo, both of these men were big: Chivers from his love of what he called 'true ale' and Iles from spending way too much time pumping iron and, Rawls suspected, drinking a great many protein shakes or raw eggs or whatever it was that bodybuilders did.

'Did our beat officer talk to anyone on the station?' Rawls asked.

'He did indeed,' Chivers said, his piggy eyes narrowing to slits, 'but I got the feeling that he didn't try too hard. He spoke with a girl on the coffee kiosk and the ticket desk.'

'Any joy?'

'No, he said she was as helpful as a chocolate fireguard.'

'He's a comedian too,' Rawls mused.

'Yeah,' said Chivers, 'he was a regular Michael McIntyre. When he wasn't being a shit-stick.'

'Is that a technical term?' Rawls asked.

'It describes him,' Chivers said. 'It seems to me that he did little to nothing on this one.'

Although Rawls agreed to a degree, he couldn't help but suspect that Chivers had said it for the benefit of Tess who had just come into the room.

'I know what you're saying,' Rawls said, choosing his words carefully, 'but I'm not sure that's entirely fair. There wasn't a whole lot for him to look into.'

'Just calling it as I see it,' Chivers said, and Rawls noticed his quick glance towards Tess, who nodded. Obviously he'd spoken to her already – he really was sly. Rawls liked him less by the minute.

'OK,' Rawls said, flushing a little – he hated the blame game and he hated show-boating and he suddenly realised that Chivers was doing both with the grace of a bull elephant in a very small china shop – 'let's assume that he hasn't done his job properly.'

'Which he hasn't,' Chivers said, and his voice had taken on a churlish tone, one that irritated Rawls even more than it had before, if that was possible; Rawls decided it was.

'As I said, let's assume …' Rawls held up a hand to silence Chivers. 'Do you want to take a trip to Frome to talk to the witnesses yourself?'

'Already booked,' Chivers said to Rawls but it was Tess that he was looking at. 'Iles and me are going to see them at twelve.'

Iles and I, Rawls considered correcting him but managed to resist. 'Can you see if you can talk to a couple more of her friends as well? See if there's anything they can add?'

Chivers raised his eyebrows in another 'obviously we're going to do that' gesture. 'Of course, in an ideal world,' he said, his coffin-nail eyes still locked on Tess, 'we would have done the job properly from the start, swept the area in ever increasing circles, looked in every house, wheelie bin, shed and outbuilding in case she was close by.' He sighed deeply, as though with enormous regret that he had not had the opportunity to deal with the case in the first place, and shook his head sadly. 'Too late now, I suppose.'

The insinuation that Rawls had somehow dropped the ball in the initial investigations was not lost on him and he felt an incredibly strong urge to cross the room and push the fat twat off the stool that he was perching on. He might get lucky and knock him out.

Instead, he said, 'Great work, you two, thanks for that. So good to have your expertise, Craig.'

Tess smiled, and Rawls grinned at Chivers; two could play this game.

They pulled up in front of the little red-brick house on Valley Rise and he was reminded immediately why Harriet's disappearance, like Melody's and, more recently, Tanya's, had initially not been red-flagged. Like the other two, Harriet, who had been missing since 2012, had lived in an area where young girls could slip through the net and plummet to the very bottom of the pond without anyone really doing much to try to pull them back out. That was the trouble with all these bloody cuts, Rawls thought to himself. The youth workers were swamped, the social workers were overworked and the police service was stretched to the limit; there was no one there to deal with the early tell-tale signs. It was a shame on all of them.

By the time they had taken their safety belts off a small crowd had gathered on the pavement opposite.

'Here we go,' said Nat. 'They're all out already and up for a fight and we haven't even opened the doors.'

Rawls said nothing, just opened the car door and climbed out, ignoring the audience as he stretched his back. It emitted several loud popping noises and he grinned at Nat. 'Did you hear that?' he said, as though he had just elevated himself off the ground rather than cleared a few tight knots in his vertebrae. He turned to scan his audience, looking for the highest rank – usually an elderly lady. He spotted her quickly, fag hanging out of the corner of her mouth, a chihuahua clutched tightly to her bosom. 'Morning,' he said amiably, and then, looking back at the house he asked, 'is this Mr and Mrs DiAngelo's home?' He looked directly at the smoking lady, forcing her to respond, singling her out from the crowd.

She nodded. 'Yeah,' she said. 'You here about their Harriet?'

'We are,' Rawls said.

''Bout time you lot did somefink about it, you should be ashamed of yourselves.'

Rawls nodded, locking the car doors with an elaborate wave of his hand. 'If anyone has any information that might help us, we'd be grateful for it.' He pulled a couple of crumpled cards from his wallet and headed across the road to the woman. 'Would you mind taking these for me? Any information would help, anything at all.'

She stared at him for a moment and those around her looked down at their collective trainers. She made no effort to take the cards and Rawls reached his hand out to stroke the dog. It tilted its head as he did, closing its eyes as he scratched the top of its head. The old woman took her cigarette out of her mouth and smiled, revealing an almost entirely empty set of gums.

'He don't usually let strangers smooth him,' she said, and she took the cards as though the dog had somehow given her permission. 'Might give you a ring meself,' she said, and she winked with all the flair that Rawls had used to lock the car.

He scratched the dog's head. 'That'd be great,' he said. 'Thanks so much, really appreciate it.' He jogged back over the road and the crowd dispersed as quickly as it had appeared.

'Wish I'd learned that while I was on the beat. What are you, a dog whisperer or something?' Nat asked, pressing the doorbell.

'I like dogs,' Rawls said. He took in the front garden as they waited. An old toy pram decorated the lawn – covered in moss and dirt, it seemed somehow to have grown out of the long scraggly grass rather than having been left amongst it. Along the fence an old sofa formed the base of a pile of household debris: a toilet seat, a washing machine drum, a couple of broken recycling bins, a black bin bag, a rabbit hutch complete with ancient straw bedding. Rawls wondered if the poor rabbit was still inside, long dead and now reduced to nothing but a pelt covering its yellowed bones. He shook his head to clear the image.

The door opened and a woman in her fifties looked out at them. Clad entirely in denim with her dyed black hair dragged tightly back into a high ponytail. The woman, who Rawls assumed to be Harriet's mother, smiled weakly.

'Mrs DiAngelo?' he asked, holding his warrant card out for her to see.

She nodded, glancing at his card, and stared at them both for a few seconds as though she was trying to get their measure, then she turned and walked into the house. 'I s'pose you better come in,' she said over her shoulder, her broad West Country accent sounding almost melodic.

The house was dark and smelled of takeaways and onions and sweat and grease; it was the kind of smell that would stay with you long after you had left the place. Along the corridor, a flurry of mail, mostly in unopened envelopes, lined the edges of a dirty red carpet like a snowdrift. It opened into a small dining room and lounge, and here too, post, junk mail and catalogues seemed to fill every available space, dirty cups, plates and bowls sitting on each pile like gargoyles on top of a church.

'Mrs DiAngelo,' Rawls said, 'is your husband home?'

'Ray,' the woman shouted out towards the open back door, 'police is here.' She turned to them, her eyes wild, the colour of old dishwater, her face ashen pale. 'She didn't run away,' she said, 'she would never.'

Nat took her hand. At first the woman tried to pull away but Nat held it tight, then she pulled the woman towards her and, without saying a word, hugged her. Rawls watched, both surprised and touched as the woman's fist first clenched stiffly then relaxed and grabbed hold of Nat as though they were old friends. She cried into Nat's shoulder until her husband appeared in the kitchen door leaning heavily on a stick. She pulled away from Nat, wiping at her face with the palm of her hand. 'They've come about Harriet,' she said, gesturing towards the table. 'Do you wanna sit down?'

'That would probably be easier,' Nat said, 'thank you.'

'Too bloody late,' Ray DiAngelo said. 'She aint comin' home now, your lot didn't give a monkey's. We said she didn't run away and she didn't, she wouldn't.' He looked at his wife who sat at the table, her head in her hands. 'She wouldn't, love, would she?' he appealed.

Mrs DiAngelo shook her head. 'She was a happy girl,' she said. 'Bit naughty at school sometimes, you know? But they all is at times, in't they?' She looked at her husband who had pushed a pile of paperwork on to the floor so that he could sit down.

'They all is,' he agreed, 'but she never did nothing terrible, she smoked a bit of weed but nothing bad, not like real drugs or drinking or nothing like that. We 'ad our differences like but she was a good girl most of the time. We told them that, but they said ...'

His wife looked up at him, her face almost a warning. 'I told them it weren't true,' she said, looking at Nat. 'They said she might of gone off with a man or a boy from the internet, from one of those chat rooms that the kids did back then. But I told them she didn't. I, I ...' She ran a hand across her face. 'I go online every day, searching for her name, checking profile pictures on Facebook, just in case one of them looks like our Harriet. Sometimes I find myself on websites that I really wish I hadn't found – you know the ones I mean, the ones where girls have to sell themselves?' She glanced at Nat who nodded.

Mrs DiAngelo drew in a long, shuddering breath. 'I stare at those poor desperate faces, trying to see if they could be my girl, our girl, trying to see if that's what it's come to.'

Nat leaned forward, her brow furrowed, the look of pain on her face almost mirroring that of the woman in front of her. 'I can't imagine how stressful the past few years must have been.'

'Stressful?' For a moment a look of anger flashed across the woman's features. 'You don't know the 'alf of it. They blamed us at first, didn't they, Ray? Made us feel like a couple of criminals or perverts or something. They searched the house, tried to make us admit to hurting our girl, making 'er leave, maybe, or worse, killin' 'er and hiding her. They had 'im,' she nodded towards her husband who sat with his head down, ''bout four times at least. Put him right through it. Did you ever touch your daughter, Ray? Did you ever hurt her? Maybe it was a mistake, Ray? Maybe you just lost your temper.' She glanced again at Ray DiAngelo and he looked up and smiled weakly. 'They nearly drove him crazy. He comed home and he would just cry and cry. Not enough that we lost our girl, no, they,' she looked first at Nat and then at Rawls, 'you people, you had to make it worse by blaming us. Then, out of the blue, they says they think she run away. Just like that, one minute we're criminals and the next she just run away.'

Nat took the woman's hand. 'I am so sorry,' she said, and Mrs DiAngelo looked surprised, as though she had expected Nat to tell her what an awful parent she was or how dirty her house was.

Mrs DiAngelo stood up abruptly. 'I'll go get us all something to drink.' She left the room, returning seconds later with three tins of Coke and a can of Monster Energy which she handed to her husband. He took it wordlessly and pulled the ring pull so that the drink hissed as though a snake had been trapped inside.

He swallowed loudly, said, 'She never did run away.'

Rawls said, 'She had run away previously though, hadn't she?'

The man shook his head. 'Not like that, she went off in a huff, but she always came back the next day.'

'But you were concerned enough to file a missing person's report.'

DiAngelo looked down at his hands. 'To give 'er a fright, that's all. We told the officers that before, this was different.'

'Can you tell us what you remember about when you last saw her? You had an argument hadn't you?' Rawls asked.

The woman handed Rawls a Coke and sat down next to Nat, who touched her hand gently and smiled at her. 'Not a proper row, it was the night before, she were cross because she wanted some new trainers,' she glanced at her husband, 'we couldn't afford the ones she wanted. It wasn't like some big show down, she knew we couldn't get them, she was just sounding off but it was all over by the time she went to bed. She got herself off to school in the morning just like she always did.' A flash of guilt passed over her face like the shadow of a cloud. 'She always was good at getting herself organised. I, we, well, we stay up late sometimes, you know? And then we're, well, tired in the morning so she, well, she always sorted herself out.' She looked briefly at Nat who smiled at her and squeezed her hand. 'She shouted goodbye, like she always did, said she had a lesson or something after school, then she was gone. I don't, I don't …' She started to cry again. 'I don't think I said goodbye,' she said, and Nat leaned forward to hug her again.

Rawls put his tin down on top of a gardening catalogue; it struck him as ironic that they had saved it. 'Mrs DiAngelo, did she mention what lesson she had to stay for?'

The woman shook her head. 'I should've known, I should've known,' she whispered. 'You're supposed to know when you're a mum. It's what a proper mum would do.'

Rawls glanced at Ray DiAngelo, who had his head down, staring at his belly. 'What about her friends?' he asked. 'What did they think?'

'They thought the same as us, that she didn't run off. Why would she? Over some trainers? Why would she? Why?'

'No boys, no one on the internet that she might have mentioned to her mates?'

They shook their heads, and Mrs DiAngelo looked up at him. 'I don't mean to sound rude or nothing, but shouldn't you speak to them?'

Rawls nodded. 'We will, Mrs DiAngelo, I just wanted to speak with you and your husband first.' He brushed at his legs and stood up. 'Right,' he said, 'I think we can leave you in peace, but would it be alright for us to have a look around her room first?'

Mrs DiAngelo nodded. 'First door on the right,' she said, gesturing towards the stairs. 'Don't mind the mess. I left it as it was, in case of evidence and stuff.'

'Such a good idea,' said Nat and Rawls smiled at her. It had been seven years; he wasn't sure the evidence would hold. 'Really good idea, Mrs DiAngelo, thank you,' he said.

The room had indeed been left undisturbed: the bed, unmade, had more items hanging off it than on. A grey-looking duvet, which might have once been white, hung over the edge, a pillow on the floor beside it, and two blankets had been bunched up in the corner. Pyjamas with rabbits on them lay on the floor beside the pillow and beneath these, the carpet, which might never have been vacuumed, was strewn with books, clothes, odd socks, shoes, stuffed toys, books, plates, plastic bottles, glasses and a whole lot of dust. Rawls thought it looked like an art installation. 'Tracey Emin, eat your heart out,' he mumbled.

The room darkened for a moment as Mrs DiAngelo leaned into the doorway behind them and Rawls asked where her daughter's computer was. She shrugged. 'She didn't have one. She had a mobile phone but she had that with her – at least she must have, 'cause I ain't seen it since that day she left.'

'Did she keep a diary or anything, do you know?' Nat asked.

'I ain't never seen her with one, but she was a teenager – they have secrets, things they don't talk to their mums about.'

Rawls nodded. 'I know what you mean,' he said, 'got one of those myself.'

'So you know, they comes in and you're lucky if they say hello and then they're upstairs for the rest of the night.' A tear breached her defences and slid down her cheek and she pushed it away. 'She weren't really interested in us, she just lived for her music and stuff.'

Rawls was looking out of the bedroom window into the garden beyond where a broken and rusted supermarket trolley had found its final resting place among the tall grass and bindweed; it looked like a scene from a post-apocalyptic TV show.

Without turning around, he asked her what instrument her daughter had played.

The woman laughed a little and her voice sounded tinny and shrill. She waved a hand in the air. 'Oh,' she said, 'I don't know, anything and everything. She played guitar for a while, then she had singing lessons, then she wanted to learn the drums.' Mrs DiAngelo paused for a moment, frowned then turned and shouted down the stairs, 'Ray?'

Ray DiAngelo grunted a response.

'What instruments did our Harriet play, do you know?'

'Piano? Drums? I dunno, don't you know?'

'I wouldn't ask you if I knew.' She offered Nat a weak smile and mouthed 'Men!'

'I don't remember exactly, tell them to ask her school.'

Mrs DiAngelo nodded. 'You should ask school. She had all her lessons there, so they would know – they keep records on that kind of stuff, don't they?'

'Did she only play at school?' Rawls asked.

'I, I'm not sure, do you mean like was she in a band or something?'

Rawls rubbed his forehead. 'I don't really know what I mean, just thinking aloud, but was she in a band?'

Mrs DiAngelo shook her head. 'No, not that I know of, but she never really told us much about all that. To tell you the truth, I think she was a little embarrassed by us, me and 'er dad. I mean, she would do things at school, like talent shows and that sort of stuff, never even told us.' She paused, then nodded. 'She were definitely ashamed of us.'

Nat rubbed her shoulder. 'I'm sure that's not true.'

The woman smiled and touched Nat's hand.

'Did she hang out with a different bunch after school?' Rawls asked.

'Different, what do you mean?'

'Different from her school friends. I wondered if she might have other friends outside of school.'

Mrs DiAngelo squirmed a little. 'I don't know. Like I said, she never really talked to me. I ... We didn't talk like that and now, well, now I think it's too late.' She paused for a moment, biting her lip, waiting for her voice to come back. 'I used to pray to God every night. Please find 'er, I'd say to him, please God, bring 'er back. I was a bad mum, I know I was, but if you bring 'er back, I'll do better. Tell 'er I'll do better.' She looked away, unwilling to cry again, and when she spoke it was in the smallest of voices, 'Maybe she did run off, maybe she didn't wanna come back. Maybe she 'ad enough of,' she waved her hand around the room, 'of this, of us, of everything.'

'You mustn't do this to yourself,' Nat said softly, and Rawls nodded his agreement. He was glad to have Nat with him; she had a way with people, a warmth that they were drawn to. It was something that he thought some of the longer serving officers lost over time, but then, being called a pig and bastard or scum had a way of doing that to you, he supposed. Perhaps her very newness, the thing that he had seen as a liability, would be an asset after all; perhaps he had underestimated her.

'It's a terrible thing,' Mrs DiAngelo said, 'this not knowing. It's like life 'as to go on hold. You can't move forward, not properly, you just stay put, waiting. Every time there's a knock at the door you think it might be 'er, or the police come to say they found 'er body, or someone to say that they seen 'er, something like that, you know? It's terrible, and no one seems to care. They just said she run off and that was it.' She wiped at her nose with the back of her hand. 'I miss 'er,' she said, 'even now, after all this time, I miss 'er.'

'Mrs DiAngelo,' Rawls said, 'we're going to do our best to find out what happened, you have my word on that.'

She offered him a grim smile and wiped at her wet face with the sleeve of her cardigan.

'You've been most helpful,' Rawls said. 'We might need to speak with you again, but in the meantime, you will call us if you think of anything else, won't you?'

She nodded, her teeth biting at her upper lip again, and Rawls noticed that she had made it bleed a little. Something about that almost insignificant smear of blood on her teeth made him look away, for the moment unable to see the woman in such distress. Keeping his eyes on the landing carpet, he headed back downstairs.

On the doorstep Nat hugged the woman one last time. The small crowd had gathered again along the pavement in front of the house as though they had been summoned by some sixth sense and they were watching intently, like troops lined along a hilltop.

'Keep strong,' Nat said, and Mrs DiAngelo smiled. It was weak and watery, the smile of someone who had given up hope a very long time before.

'Thank you,' she said, and Nat squeezed her hand.

Chapter 11

It was early the following morning and Rawls had decided to take the Focus. It was the first time that he had driven it and, he had decided at some point during the night, in between mind-mapping the similarities and differences between the missing girls and taking one of several trips to the toilet which he was prone to do when he had things on his mind, probably the last. On one of his many barefoot walks to the bathroom and back, he had taken his phone, opened the AutoTrader App and placed an ad: 'Sad to be selling my mint condition Ford Focus RS'. He hadn't been lying, he was sad, but he was also finally coming to his senses. Eileen had been right; the car was a folly and he had been a fool and it had to go.

Now, as he navigated his way along Kelston Road, giving the pavements an elaborately wide berth lest he kerb his

19-inch boy-racer alloys, he remembered why he had wanted the car in the first place. He loved it, that was why – he loved everything about the bloody thing. How it seemed to hunker down and grip the road as it came into a bend, how it grunted a response to the slightest feathering of the accelerator, how it looked and how it smelled. It made him feel young again, young, and somehow alive.

He indicated left at a set of traffic lights. Set on a steep hill with a sharp left turn that must make new drivers weep; to be fair, it wasn't exactly thrilling Rawls. The lights taunted him with a brief flash of amber then turned green and Rawls kangaroo-hopped his way around the corner. He flushed, convinced that all the other road users were currently laughing their heads off at his inability to handle the beast. It had to go, that was the decider. It got worse when he pulled in to the Royal United, Bath's main hospital. There was, as ever, nowhere to park, especially if you were concerned about some impatient driver slamming their door open and dinging your door with as much care as they might level against swatting a fly. He groaned, admonishing himself silently for bringing the Focus on such a perilous journey.

He had used it because he hadn't wanted to be seen. It was his disguise, like the flat cap he had donned when he left the house and the old tweed jacket that he had pulled from beneath the multitude of winter coats that hung in the cupboard under the stairs. He wanted, as he did on each of his visits to the RUH, to remain incognito. To be spotted here would have dire consequences. Not only would he lose his job, he might even find himself in front of the IPCC. He could explain till he was blue in the face that he was there because he cared, because he felt guilty, because he knew that what he had done was wrong, or even because he needed to own up in his own mind to the mistakes that had brought him here. The trouble was, Rawls knew, that would not wash. What the IPCC would see, was harassment. A senior officer harassing a suspect, and not just any suspect, but one who was in absolutely no fit state to defend himself. They would see that and, Rawls knew this too, they would have a bloody field day with it.

He circled the car parks several times before a place came free in a location that he considered suitable. He wondered briefly how people with an actual appointment managed; it was almost laughable. He reversed in, carefully checking his mirrors, stopping and starting like a little old man driving a car full of Miss Daisies. Finally, after several minutes of swearing, he managed to manoeuvre the car between the designated lines. He squeezed himself out of the driver's side without letting the door brush up against the hedge which he hoped would defend the car against the hordes of unruly brats that he imagined were primed and ready to wreak havoc on the paintwork. He pulled his cap down and feeling, as he always did, like a deviant, walked briskly back towards the main reception.

He kept his head low as he headed down the sterile halls, avoiding any kind of eye contact and, even worse, CCTV cameras. He didn't need to follow the signs; he had memorised the route. They would be moving the boy to Bristol shortly and he suspected that, much like his trip here in his new car, this would be the last time that he would see him. Once they moved him to Bristol, he figured that these surreptitious visits would probably have to cease entirely. Not because he would not want to, but because the journey would be too far and would take up too much time. This, he could do without anyone noticing; a trip to Bristol, on the other hand, would take up the best part of his morning, his absence would be conspicuous. He crossed the shiny corridor and pressed the button on the lift that would lead him to the floor marked 'Neurosurgical Unit'.

He would not go in. He never did, he couldn't, even if he wanted to, and he didn't. He would simply walk past the room, glance through the open door and make sure that he could hear the machines. That would be enough – enough to remind him, to reach into his chest and break off another little piece of his heart. The boy didn't need him. The boy might never need anything else again, except for the machine that breathed for him or the one that dripped some kind of nourishment into his wasting body, but Rawls needed him; Rawls needed that boy more than he could ever have expected.

No amount of counselling could take away the regret; he would blame himself until the day he died. It had been his fault, all of it, nothing could change that, and because of that, the boy who had once been his adversary was now his silent accuser, and his hospital room was the court, the place Rawls would come to time and time again, furtive and unseen. Here he would seek forgiveness and find nothing but his own culpability.

The boy's name was Logan Bishop and once, not so long ago, Rawls had hated him. He hated him for what he had done and, if Rawls didn't stop him, what he would continue to do. Logan had dragged a young girl, Ellie Dalmore, to the ground as she had walked alone one evening and he had brutally raped her. Ellie had been working part-time at a local Co-op and she had taken the scenic route through Alexandra Park on her way home. It had been slightly out of her way, she had told Rawls later, but the evening was still warm and the view of Bath from the park was always spectacular. Logan, seventeen years old and already well known to the authorities for a host of offences – possession, violent disorder and harassment – had seen her, and had acted on impulse. For Ellie, who was due to start university in the autumn, this should have been a normal day like all the others in that long, hot month, but Logan had robbed her of normality for the rest of her life. The ordeal had left her so broken, so utterly devastated, that her blank, staring eyes had haunted Rawls in his sleep. She was beautiful, smart and funny, with her whole life ahead of her, and, in one selfish moment, he had taken a small but vital part of that life. Rawls knew that outwardly she might seem to recover, she might pretend that time had indeed healed her, but inside, she would hold a little piece of that fear with her wherever she went. It would wake her at night, it would fizzle in the back of her head and would cloak her in terror if she found herself walking alone, and it would gnaw at her sanity the way that a monster might gnaw at the bars of a cage.

Rawls had seen that trapped look too many times before. He knew that she would never fully recover from this terrible thing; time would not completely heal this vibrant young woman's wounds. Rawls knew it and he hated it. What he hated even more, however, what kept him awake at night and turned itself over and over in his mind, was the fact that the little shit did not seem to give a damn. They never did, these boys, youths, young men, call them what you like; they had lost their empathy. They seemed, not just without remorse, but even worse, without understanding. They seemed, in his opinion, to have somehow managed to completely disassociate their behaviours from their lives, as though the two were entirely unrelated.

Ellie had offered them a good a description of her attacker. She had remembered so many of the seemingly insignificant details: the shape of his nose, his eyebrows, his eyes, even his teeth, but it hadn't been enough. When the chips had been down and she had sifted through the photo line-up, she had not been able to single him out. Not without the fear of identifying an innocent man, anyway. The trouble was, Rawls had thought, they all look the bloody same, every one of these little bastards, hoodies up and eyes down, that was their uniform, their camouflage in the landscape of the empty lives that they lived. Each one of them stared up from their photo, their faces disinterested, their eyes blank. She had tearfully put them to one side, she had shaken her head.

'I'm sorry,' she had said, wiping her nose with a tissue that Rawls had passed to her, 'I just can't say.'

Rawls had reassured her, told her there was nothing to be sorry for, better this way than accusing the wrong person. Ellie had nodded, staring up at him with those desperate, pleading eyes.

'Do you know who it was?' she had asked him, and he had glanced around as though he was checking that they could not be overheard.

'Yes,' he had said, 'I'm pretty sure that I do.'

She had blown her nose and balled the damp tissue up into her hand. 'Can you tell me which one you suspect?'

Rawls had shaken his head. 'No,' he'd said, reaching for the neat pile of photos in front of her, 'I can't tell you.' And he hadn't. Perhaps it would have been better if he had, perhaps that would have prevented what happened only a few days later. If he had told her, perhaps his life would not have been turned upside down.

Logan had crossed the road ahead of him. Rawls knew it was him straight away; it was the way he walked, with the swagger of one who believed that he was meant for greater things but without the mental acumen to do anything about it.

Rawls had found himself picking up his own pace to keep up with him. He had followed him along the pavement, past the chippie and into a small coffee shop. The door had banged shut behind him and Rawls had hesitated for only a moment before pushing it open and following the boy inside.

Rawls closed his eyes, not wanting to go there, stopping himself before it was too late.

He had lost time at the hospital – time, Rawls knew, that he could ill afford, but visiting the boy had become more than a habit; it had become a compulsion, a dangerous one according to his counsellor. In fact, his counsellor, Tobias Avery, a handsome man with a receding hairline and a broad smile, who was young enough to be his son, or at the very least his nephew, had warned him of the dangers of becoming obsessive about the boy's wellbeing. Rawls had nodded his agreement and promised to make every possible effort to curb his behaviour, but he had found the habit a hard one to break. He had visited Logan several times since, first telling Tobias his secret, but keeping subsequent visits to himself. The shame was almost too much for him to bear – it had certainly been too much for him to share, and in any case, he told himself, it wasn't hurting anyone.

It had made him late, however, and he had rushed to drop the Focus back at the lock-up before meeting Nat so that the two of them could keep their appointment with the principal at Southerton Academy, the school that Tanya had attended.

He leaned out of the Passat and spoke into the intercom. 'DS Peter Rawls,' he said, 'I have a one p.m. meeting with Mrs Foundry.'

There was a brief pause, the clicking sound of a keyboard consulting with a computer and a disembodied voice answered: 'Thank you. Please drive in and park on the right, there should be spaces in front of the astroturf pitch.'

Rawls wondered if the astroturf would make itself immediately obvious and, finding that it didn't, he pulled into a place that he hoped the school would find acceptable.

He climbed out and stretched briefly, his back popping like a damp log in fire. Nat joined him and they headed for the sign that said, 'WELCOME TO SOUTHERTON ACADEMY – ALL VISITORS MUST REPORT TO RECEPTION'.

Inside they were met by a small woman in her thirties, or perhaps forties – it was difficult to tell. She stared at them through enormous round glasses that might have been fabulous if they were being worn by someone like Yoko Ono, but on her looked as though her decision had been made with an emphasis on necessity over style.

'I've informed Mrs Foundry that you are here. She will be with you presently. Please take a seat in the reception area.' Rawls wondered if she spoke this way all the time or if it was something reserved for formal visits, a method perhaps used to relay her understanding of the gravity of the situation.

Rawls had encountered the standard school smell many times before but had never really got used to it: a mixture of teenage feet and deodorant, greasy hair and shampoo, body odour and hormones. It lingered in the air, never quite clearing, part of the fabric of the walls themselves. The sounds were the same: laughter, shouting, singing and even a piano playing from some distant music room. The endless corridors with their highly polished plastic tiles and walls full of photos and paintings, models and projects, reminded him of his own time in similar corridors, in a similar school, in a similar town but in different times.

He thought about the other three girls, Melody, Harriet and Yvette. Each one of them the kind of girl who could disappear in the system, not troubled exactly but not without problems. They had marks on their records for truancy, swearing, smoking, underage drinking and even fighting, but had also been described as 'hard-working' or 'talented' or even 'exemplary' by both school friends and teachers. Harriet was all but teacher's pet in English Lit. and Yvette had never missed a drama class either inside or outside of school hours. They had had their issues, yes, but they had not been defined by them.

'DS Rawls?' Rawls jumped. 'Oh, I'm so sorry,' a plump woman said, and Nat and Rawls stood up to greet her. She had the kind of bustling voice that would have seemed more in keeping with someone in an old-fashioned sweet shop than a headmistress. 'I'm Mrs Foundry, won't you follow me?'

With that she turned on her heels and marched back up the corridor and Rawls saw that the sweet old lady act was simply a routine. They grabbed up their bits and followed, trotting a few paces to catch up.

They passed through a maze of corridors, their passage marked in a kind of class-to-class relay by the disinterested eyes of bored adolescents. Rawls imagined that they all knew why they were there. They might not be in uniform, but they had 'police' written all over them.

Mrs Foundry stopped in front of a door with a sign that said 'Headteacher, knock and wait to be called in'. She used a swipe card to open the door and walked in, gesturing for them to take a seat.

Rawls took in the room, the filing cabinet in the corner, tissues on the desk, an open laptop, a large window that looked out on to what they would have called a quad in his day, scatters of paperwork, piles of what looked like student essays and a stuffed bear, one eye hanging off and an ear missing completely.

'This is a terrible situation,' Mrs Foundry said. 'We are, of course, deeply upset by Tanya's disappearance. The children are all terrified, as you might imagine. We're even considering a staggered end to the day because so many parents are insisting on collecting their children from school now – not willing to take the risk of them walking, you understand?'

Rawls nodded; he did understand.

'Luckily we have staff willing to adapt to the situation, just until you catch this, this ...' She trailed off, unable to find the right word. 'Well anyway, we have plenty of staff who have volunteered to help with this temporary arrangement, directing cars in the car park, making sure no one gets run over – that sort of thing. And not just teachers, everyone is pitching in: reception, the canteen staff, even the cleaners. Honestly, it's heart-warming.'

'That all sounds very sensible,' Rawls said, 'and commendable.' He waited for a moment in case the woman had anything else to add before saying, 'Mrs Foundry, what I was hoping to find out was if there was anyone in particular that Tanya was close to, anyone that she might have confided in – perhaps someone that you think we should have spoken with but haven't yet?'

The head teacher considered for a moment, staring at the bear on her desk as though he might be sharing some great wisdom with her. 'No,' she said at last, 'I honestly don't think so.'

'What about the teaching staff?' Rawls asked. 'Is there anyone that I should talk to amongst your team?'

Mrs Foundry recoiled, her head jerking back against the leather office chair as though she had been slapped. 'Are you suggesting that a member of my staff could have taken a child against her will?' She clutched her neck as though the very thought might choke her. 'I assure you, DS Rawls, my staff are all rigorously vetted. Moreover,' she narrowed her eyes at him, 'I feel compelled to point out that there have been other cases, remarkably similar ones, that you in the police have failed to resolve. My understanding is that these other cases involved different schools. To lay the blame at our door hardly seems fair.'

'Of course,' Rawls said, 'and I hope you understand that I was in no way accusing you or your staff. But I do have to ask. I wouldn't be doing my job if I didn't.'

Mrs Foundry smiled thinly and leaned forward, her hands clasped together on the desk as if she were about to embark on a sermon. 'I appreciate that you have a job to do, DS Rawls, and I apologise if I seem abrupt, but this whole ...'

she paused, staring at the bear as she searched for the right word, 'thing,' she said, unable to find one. 'This whole thing has upset the entire school. Children are being mentored, parents are terrified, the staff are simply broken-hearted. She wasn't the best pupil in the school, but she was bright and full of life.' She paused, thinking. 'It seems so out of character for her, she just wasn't the type.' Rawls thought that the woman might be about to cry.

'And there is no one here at school that you believe is behaving differently? Anything like that would be helpful,' Nat said.

Mrs Foundry stared at her as though she had not given her permission to speak then turned to Rawls. 'I assure you, DS Rawls, my staff are some of the best in Somerset, perhaps in England. I cannot stress enough how insulting I find these accusations.' She turned to Nat, her face as pious as a priest at Mass. 'And any suggestions that the school faculty might be involved is both lazy police work and libelous, I hope you understand that.'

'I'm sorry if I offended you,' Nat said, and Rawls leaned forward as though he was trying to intervene between two angry cats.

'That wasn't our intention at all,' he said, 'and we'll let you get on with your day.' He smiled with all the charm he could muster. 'But if I may, would it be alright to leave my card? Just in case you think of anything else.' Mrs Foundry nodded but made no attempt to take the card from him, and Rawls opted to leave it on the desk between them.

He stood up and Nat followed him to the door.

'You're OK to see yourselves out, aren't you?' Mrs Foundry asked.

'Yes, thank you, we'll be fine. Bye, Mrs Foundry, and thank you for your time.'

Mrs Foundry had taken her glasses off and was dabbing at her eyes with a tissue as Rawls opened the door.

He paused for a moment then stepped back into the room. 'Mrs Foundry, did you know that Tanya had a job? Cash in hand, that kind of thing?'

The head teacher stared at him. 'No, DS Rawls, I did not. Is there some reason that I should have?'

'No, not at all, I just wondered. Also, do you know whether she took any classes outside of school? Drama, singing, an instrument, help with maths or science, that kind of thing?'

'My understanding is that her parents didn't have the money required for that kind of thing,' she said, 'but there is a mentoring scheme, run by the council, to offer assistance to certain bright but disadvantaged students. Let me check our list of students being offered assistance – usually it's those wishing to take triple science – and I'll get back to you.'

'It's not something that you can do right away?' Nat asked and the woman favoured her with a withering glare.

'No,' she said, 'it is not.'

Rawls threw the keys to Nat. 'You made an impression in there,' he said, grinning.

Nat looked forlorn. 'I have no idea what I said to offend her.'

'Nothing,' Rawls said, 'she was just a funny old stick.'

'Funny old stick? That's one way of putting it.'

'Don't let it worry you,' Rawls said, 'it happens sometimes.' He headed for the passenger side of the car then added, 'You don't mind driving, do you?' It was a statement rather than a question. 'My phone's been ringing off the hook.'

They climbed in and Rawls tapped his phone, looked at the missed call list then dialled Linda Greenhill's number. She answered on the second ring.

'Sarge, how quickly can you get to the office?'

Rawls looked up and out of the window, gauging the distance. 'About fifteen minutes, ten if there's no traffic.'

'We'll assume twenty then, shall we?' Linda said.

'Twenty-five,' Nat whispered, pointing at the queue of cars ahead.

The road was backed up almost to the top of the hill. 'OK, twenty-five,' Rawls said, 'can't blame me for being optimistic. What's the rush anyway?'

'Well, you won't believe who's sat downstairs right now drinking a cup of terrible coffee with his bloody solicitor in tow.'

'I'm not much of a one for guessing games, Lin.'

'No, you never were much fun. I thought it might while away the time while you were stuck in traffic.'

'Bloody hell, Lin, tell me who's there.'

'Alright, alright, keep yer 'air on.' She was clearly enjoying the moment and Rawls thought it must be something good. Linda always got this way when something positive was about to happen – it was her way of announcing the mic drop moment.

'Too late for my hair,' he said, rubbing his head.

'The estate agent's here – Dave Alkham. I've been trying to get hold of him but his phone kept going to voicemail. I left him a couple of messages but thought we might have to go to his office to get his attention, but then, out of the blue, he shows up downstairs and says he wants to speak to you.'

'He asked for me? By name?'

'Yup, he says he'll only speak to you.'

'Did he say why?'

'No, just that he wanted to "rule himself out".' She laughed. 'Rule himself out! Don't you just love it?'

'Yeah,' Rawls said, 'love it.' He looked at Nat. 'Hang on a sec, would you, Lin? I want to put you on loudspeaker.'

He fiddled with his phone and swore, then said, 'Lin, you still there?'

Linda laughed. 'I'm here.'

'OK, thanks, I just wanted Nat to hear. We've just been talking to the head teacher at Tanya Hickock's school.'

'What was she like?'

'I don't know, evasive, didn't like the suggestion that one of her lot might have been involved.'

'Funny, that.'

'So what's this guy like?' Rawls asked. 'Our Mr Alkham?'

'Like an estate agent,' Lin said. 'Nice enough, I suppose.' She hesitated for a moment as though she was thinking, then said, 'Actually, he's kind of smarmy. And let's not ignore the fact that he has his solicitor with him, but even so, he doesn't exactly look the type, you know what I mean?'

Rawls leaned back in the seat. He wondered what the type actually looked like.

'Although I suppose he could be doing a Soham on us,' Linda added.

She was referring to the murders in 2002 of the two young girls, Holly and Jessica, in Soham, Cambridgeshire. Linda would not use the killer's name, Ian Huntley – none of them would; it was the victims that they would remember, not the bastard who took their lives. Rawls knew full well that perpetrators often tried to insert themselves into the investigation, just as Ian Huntley had. Sometimes it was the excitement, other times it was because they wanted to know what the police knew, and occasionally it was just in the hope of pointing the police in the wrong direction. Rawls knew of one case, he forgot where – Croatia maybe or Macedonia – where a serial killer was also a reporter, reporting on his own killing spree. Rawls could well imagine the kick that he must have got out of that. He wondered if something similar could be at work with this guy, inserting himself into the thick of it, armed with his solicitor, ready to manipulate or manage them; whichever came easier.

'Get him set up in room three, would you?' he asked Linda.

'Will do, Sarge, see you in a bit.'

Rawls ended the call and leaned back in his seat. Why would Alkham specifically ask to speak to him? And Linda was right – why the lawyer, straight off the bat? Why would you do that, unless you had something to hide? Or maybe he really did just want to rule himself out.

Dave Alkham had been seated with his solicitor in a small room behind a plain desk. Above them the fluorescent light hummed and lit the two of them with a pale, yellowed light. The solicitor was as one would expect, slim, greying, handsome in a rugged sort of way, tanned and wearing a suit that Rawls suspected had cost him more than his own entire wardrobe. The solicitor did not bother to look up from his notes.

'Thank you for coming in,' Rawls said as he pulled his chair up. It made a long, high-pitched scraping noise that got the solicitor's attention and Rawls flashed him a smile. 'I don't think we've met.'

The solicitor pulled his lips back into what might have been a smile of his own. 'No, we haven't,' he said, and he looked back down at his notes.

'Well, Mr ...' Rawls turned his attention to the man sitting next to him and looked down at his own notes, running his finger down them in an elaborate display, 'Mr Alkham. We're most grateful to you for coming in.'

Now it was Dave Alkham's turn to smile, and when he did it was wide and full of gleaming white teeth, like the joker in Batman. 'I thought I should. I mean, I heard the messages and I was worried,' he said.

'No need to worry, Mr Alkham. May I call you Dave?'

Alkham nodded, and Rawls continued.

'I'm DS Rawls and this is my colleague, Detective Parkinson.'

Alkham smiled at Nat, his eyes briefly tracing the curve of her face, her neck, her chest. 'If only we could have met under different circumstances.' He elongated the end of his words, accentuating each one so that it sounded like a hiss.

Nat ignored him and Rawls leaned forward, his elbows pressed into the desk, his hands cupping his chin. 'So tell me, Dave, what brings you here today?'

Alkham leaned away from Rawls; he was clearly uncomfortable having him in his personal space. He wore a racing green polo shirt with beige slacks and a tweed blazer, the outfit as carefully selected for the occasion as one might take care dressing for a wedding, or a funeral. 'Well, I was concerned when your lady officer left those messages. I mean, I'm not a suspect, am I?'

Rawls looked at Nat and laughed as though they heard this every time, 'Of course you are,' he said, 'everyone's a suspect at first.'

Dave's lips formed a smile and he glanced briefly at his solicitor, who looked up. 'DS Rawls,' he said, 'may I remind you that Mr Alkham is here of his own volition?'

Rawls nodded, his brow furrowing. 'I do apologise, Mr Alkham, you'll have to forgive us. We have an odd sense of humour here in law enforcement.' He grinned at Nat conspiratorially and she nodded briefly. 'So,' he said, leaning back, hands behind his head, 'what do you have for us?'

Dave looked uncomfortable. 'I, well, I don't have anything for you, not exactly. I just, well, I did know one of the girls who has gone missing – Harriet DiAngelo. She did her work experience in my office on Guinea Lane, we had an office there back then.'

'This would have been?'

'In 2011,' he said.

'And the agency is yours?'

Alkham nodded. 'For my sins.'

'Business going well?'

The solicitor looked up. 'And this is relevant because?'

'Because I asked,' Rawls said. Then, smiling, 'Tell me about Harriet.'

'To be honest, I didn't know her very well, just to ask how her parents were, that sort of thing. I left her in the care of a junior member of staff – I can let you have her name if you like.' He paused, glancing at Nat then back to Rawls, 'Well, if you think it would help.'

'That'd be great,' Rawls said. 'For the time being, though, let's talk about your relationship with Harriet.'

'I can't say that I had one.' He looked flustered.

'Did you find her attractive? A young girl, running around in short skirts, long socks, that sort of thing?'

Dave Alkham stared at him, his face flushed with anger.

'I most certainly did not.'

Rawls didn't like this man and the point had been a cheap one, but worth it to see the reaction.

There was a tap on the door, and they all looked up as Tess walked in. 'Would you mind if I cut in?' she said to Nat, nodding towards the door to let her know that she should leave. 'Mr Alkham,' she said, her voice soft spoken, charming almost, 'I just wanted to say how grateful we are for your time. I wonder if you would mind walking us through what you remember about Harriet and perhaps fill us in on the last time you saw her.'

Rawls felt a flush of pure anger. What the hell was she playing at? Why was she doing this? He stared at the table for a moment, trying to count to ten, trying to clear his head, trying not to stand up and walk out.

Dave Alkham was smiling at Tess, his white teeth gleaming. 'What do I remember about her?' He turned the answer into a question, he was good at that.

'Yes, if you don't mind,' Tess said.

'Well,' he said, scratching briefly at his neck, 'as I said, it was a while ago.'

'Eight years,' Tess said. 'Cast your mind back if you would, just tell us what you can.'

Rawls glanced at her, his fists clenched. She was taking over and he had already convinced himself that she thought he was about to do something unprofessional, which infuriated him. This wasn't the same as before, not by a long shot, yet she was acting as though she couldn't trust him to do his job. What made it worse was the fact that she had needed him on the case – she'd almost begged him, for God's sake – why then was she trying to undermine him now?

'I can't say that I really remember her,' Alkham said. 'But I seem to recall that she made us all laugh, quite the comedian.'

'She was funny? And attractive? Did you find her attractive?' Tess asked. Rawls turned his head to watch her.

The solicitor glanced up. He said, 'I believe we have already covered this, DI McGovern.'

'We're not in court,' Tess said, 'and no, my colleague asked,' she glanced at Rawls, 'but I'm fairly certain that your client did not give us an answer.'

Rawls smiled at him; perhaps Tess was on his side after all.

'She was pretty enough,' he said.

'Pretty enough? Enough to be what?'

Alkham glanced at his solicitor. 'She was pretty, that's all.'

'And how often did you speak to her?'

Alkham folded his arms. 'I can't say that I remember, it was a long time ago. Do you remember how many times you spoke to someone eight years ago?'

Tess looked at Rawls, who shook his head and said, 'I don't.' He smiled at Tess. 'Do you?'

Tess shook her head. 'But we're not the ones answering the questions here. So, how often, Mr Alkham?'

'I really can't remember,' he wiped at his forehead, 'but I don't recall having too many reasons to speak to her.'

Rawls stepped in. 'Did she come out with you at all? Perhaps to visit a house you had on your books, or to see how a viewing was carried out, something like that, maybe?'

'Not that I recall.' He definitely seemed flustered now.

'Mr Alkham,' Tess said, 'what if I told you that we received a tip stating that you had Harriet with you when you showed someone a house? In fact, what if I told you that we have several tips stating that you had young women with you when you carried out viewings? What would you say to that?'

Alkham sank in his chair. His lawyer leaned against him and said something that Rawls didn't catch.

Alkham had the look of a child caught with a mouthful of sweets. 'OK,' he said slowly, 'I did take our work experience girls out with me. It wasn't like you think, I just took them to see how it was done. I liked their company – they were young and full of ideas and ideals and they made me laugh. There was nothing else to it, I swear, nothing at all. I just took them out. Maybe I was showing off or, I don't know, had some grand idea about inspiring the youth – it feels stupid now. The business only participated in the work experience scheme for a few years, anyway.'

Rawls watched him for a moment. He thought Alkham might be about to cry, but the man got it together. 'Why did you stop, Mr Alkham? Was it something to do with Harriet?'

Alkham leaned forward and put his head in his hands. 'Not like you think,' he whispered. 'I liked Harriet, she was smart and funny.'

'Attractive.' It was a statement, not a question.

'Yes, she was attractive, but I never touched her, I swear; I never touched any of them. I took her with me to a house on The Circle. It was empty, and I thought she'd get a kick out of seeing the interior – it was opulent to say the least. All that wealth, it was like a different world for her.'

Rawls thought about his recent visit to her parents' home, how they had said that she was ashamed of them, and thought the man was right, it would have been a different world for her. 'Go on,' he said to Alkham.

'I showed her around and she loved it, but she was, well, unprofessional, naughty, I suppose. She kept picking things up and pretending to steal them. I thought she might actually take something if my back was turned; she was being silly, turning the TV on, that sort of thing. She even poured herself a glass of water and left the glass on the side. I didn't know what to do. I kept telling her to stop and it was as if she thought it was a game; she kept laughing and running to a different room. I shouted at her in the end and threatened to report her to her school.'

'What did she do?'

'She reminded me that I was a middle-aged man alone in an empty house with an underage girl; she asked me if I thought it was wise to report any such thing.' He looked first at Tess and then at Rawls. 'I knew I had made a terrible mistake and she knew it too. She told me that she would stop doing what she was doing and leave me alone if I gave her money.'

'She blackmailed you?'

Alkham shook his head. 'It wasn't blackmail, just a transaction. I gave her fifty pounds and told her not to come back to the office.'

'And that was it?' Rawls said.

'That was it, that was the last time I saw her.' He looked at his hands. 'It's the truth, I swear it is.'

'Do you recall the date?'

'I do, it was the tenth of October, 2011, a Monday.'

'That's very precise,' Rawls said.

'I checked my records before I came out. If you want the time, it was just after four.'

'Did you offer to drive her back to the office or take her home?'

Alkham stared at him. 'Of course not! That was the last time I wanted to be alone with that little ...' he paused, 'that girl. Anyway, I got the impression that she had somewhere else to go.'

'Why?' said Rawls.

'Why? I don't know, sometimes you just get a feeling, this was one of those times.'

'Did she say that she was going somewhere else, perhaps meeting someone?'

'No, of course not. I just, well, I just thought it, that was all.'

'And when she left, you thought it would be the last time that you would see her?'

'I hoped so.'

Rawls pursed his lips. 'Are you married, Dave?'

'Married? Yes, I am.'

'Kids?'

He shook his head. 'No, no kids, my wife – well my wife and I couldn't have children.'

Rawls went on, 'Did your wife know about all your young girls?'

The solicitor interrupted, 'I believe my client has already explained.'

Rawls raised a hand. 'Yes, yes, of course, it was all purely business. But here's the thing: we have a young girl who has disappeared without a trace, and here we have a grown man who freely admits to taking her out of a safe office environment and spending time alone with her in an empty house, where she blackmailed him.' He turned to Tess. 'I don't know about you, but I think that sounds suspicious. What do you think?'

Tess ran a hand across her face and sighed. 'It doesn't sound good to me, and there were other girls.'

Alkham glanced at his solicitor. 'There were other girls, but I have a full list of their names and the dates that they worked with us. I'm sure they will vouch for my being professional at all times.'

'Except when you took them to see how the other half live,' Rawls said.

Alkham studied the back of his hands. 'I know how this looks,' he said.

'We will need that list, Mr Alkham, and we might need to speak with your employees from that time. I take it you will be able to furnish us with that information?'

Alkham nodded vigorously. 'Oh yes, absolutely, of course, no trouble at all.'

'Also,' Tess said, 'and I know this is not going to be easy, but we are going to need you to verify your whereabouts on a couple of dates, well, four, to be precise. I wonder if you would mind having a quick look at this list and telling me what you think.'

She pushed a typed note to Alkham who waited whilst his solicitor picked it up and read it.

The solicitor said, 'This is madness. How can he possibly say what he was doing on the twentieth of July 2009?'

'When Melody Lockyer was last seen,' Tess said, looking at Alkham.

Alkham smiled, his teeth as bright as a ray of sunlight on a cloudy day. 'Actually I can. I have all of my diaries going right back to 2003, it's a silly obsession that I have.' He glanced at his solicitor. 'I like to keep records, I can't help it.'

'Are you able to give the information straight away?'

Alkham shook his head. 'It's all on my computer, at the office.'

'In that case, how would it be if we sent someone to your office later on today?' Rawls asked. 'The quicker we get the information from you, the quicker we can rule you out.'

For a moment Alkham said nothing, then, 'I think I might need a day or two.'

'Tomorrow evening then,' Rawls said, 'how's that sound?'

Alkham's solicitor nodded. 'Tomorrow evening.' He was ignoring the stare from Alkham who clearly didn't agree.

Tess brushed at the desk and Rawls knew she had heard enough – so had he, to be honest. The guy might well be hiding something but they would not find that out until they had spoken with his staff and previous work experience students.

He would have liked to have been able to hold the guy on something, but for now they had to be patient, bide their time.

Tess stood up and extended a hand to Alkham. 'Thank you for coming in, Mr Alkham, you've been really helpful.'

They stood together and watched as Dave Alkham followed his solicitor along the corridor, his suede shoes squeaking a little as he went.

Rawls turned to smile at Tess, but she was already walking away. Probably a good thing, he was tired, dog-tired as the saying went, it had been a long day.

Chapter 12

They had spent the morning in the office. Tess had barked her orders at them. 'I want bums on seats this morning, folks. I want you looking at tips, going through the case files, looking for what we've missed, what we should have seen before.' He had agreed, but reluctantly, he wanted to be out there, not stuck in the office looking at a bloody computer screen but Tess was SIO, and he wasn't in a position to argue, not yet anyway. And, as it turned out, it had been helpful, they had regrouped, coordinated and assigned tasks. They had all left feeling a little clearer on where they were heading, in his case to Radstock with Nat. Known in Roman times as the 'stockade beside the Roman road', Radstock had later become a hub for Somerset coal mining. Now, some three hundred or so years later, the place had the forlorn look of a town with little going for it except the addition of estate after estate of new homes. They parked up behind the Working Man's Club and crossed the car park to hurry through the cold drizzle to the Public Library. It was a squat little building, ugly to the point of brutal; concrete, gravel and glass all pressed together in various shades of drab, on the front though, beside the front doors, an angel spread its wings and they both paused to admire it. Radstock Library had survived the recent library cull by turning itself, with the assistance of the Town Council, into a community hub, the angel had come as result of the community's love for the place.

There were two reasons for their visit. The first was because the tech guys had traced the IP address for the social media account to that location. Eve Burgess, or whoever she really was, might hold the key to the whole case – or she might be another dead end. Either way, they needed to find her as quickly as possible. The second reason for making the trip, in what Rawls considered an extremely interesting coincidence, was that the Radstock librarian, a Miss Grace Stokes, was the one and only employee ever to leave the services of Stoney Barrow View. If this wasn't a case of serendipity, then Rawls didn't know what was.

Grace Stokes had taken a late lunch break to meet with them. She looked like someone who had partied hard in her youth and taken to a vegan diet in her mid-life. She was thin to the point of gaunt and her loose-fitting hippy pants did little to disguise her scrawny body. Rawls found that he didn't like her – he didn't know why, he just didn't. There was something about her pinched features or her dark eyes that avoided his when they spoke that he found he could not warm to.

There was no offer of tea or discussions about the weather. She took the only seat behind a large desk and pointed to a couple of grey waiting room chairs against a wall for Rawls and Nat.

'What is it that you think I can help you with?'

'A couple of things,' Rawls said, 'but to start us off, we believe you were once part of a group of people who followed a man named Berkeley Wolf.'

'Father Berkeley,' she said.

'Yes, that's him.'

'That was a long time ago.'

'I appreciate that,' Rawls smiled.

Nat leaned forward. 'Were you there for a long time?'

Grace favoured Nat with a smile. Rawls guessed this was about as warm as the woman could get. 'I was. Is that a problem?'

'No, not at all,' Nat said.

'In that case, why are you here dragging up old history? Surely you have better things to do with your time.'

Rawls said. 'We're more interested in your time after Father Berkeley died.'

The woman narrowed her eyes at him. 'After?'

Rawls nodded. 'What happened after he passed away? The place was run as a kind of sanctuary in those days, wasn't it, a sort of prelude to it becoming a retreat?'

'The Stoney Path, it was a beautiful place,' she said and her face softened as she remembered. 'My mother joined when I was barely a teenager. We had been moving around a great deal, living hand to mouth, and we were lucky to be offered the opportunity to join. People came to stay with us from all walks of life – some left after a few days or a few weeks, but some, like my mother, never left. It was a sanctuary,' she smiled weakly at Rawls, 'that is exactly the right word for it.'

Rawls, remembering his own visit there many years before, did not exactly share the sentiment, but he nodded. 'And the place carried on after he passed away?'

'Yes, until it was sold.' Grace sighed.

'There was an interim, though, a gap between his passing away and it being sold?'

She looked down at her hands, studying them for a moment. 'Yes, we tried to keep it going, but somehow, it just wasn't the same.'

'So who took over, who was in charge?'

She looked at Rawls for a moment. 'No one was in charge. We were a community; no one needed to be in charge, as you put it, because we all worked for the good of each other.'

'That sounds like an opportunity for animosity,' Rawls said. 'People must have argued from time to time.'

'People will always have their differences,' she said, 'but I left nearly five years ago and I'm wondering why you are suddenly so interested.'

'Actually,' Rawls said, 'that was what we were interested in – why you took the decision to leave, after being there for such a long time. Did you have a falling out with someone there – the new owner, perhaps?'

'Falling out?' She touched her hand to her mouth. 'No, not at all. Most of the members of Stoney Path stayed on after it was sold. I don't keep in touch with any of them, but there was no falling out.'

'And you left when the new owner, Sebastian, took over?' Rawls persisted.

She shrugged. 'I tried to stay there, to work for the new place, the retreat. Sebastian had made it clear that we were all welcome to carry on working there if we wanted to and I thought that perhaps I could be happy, but ...' She stared out at the wet road for a moment. 'It wasn't the same. Being a member of the Stoney Path felt like belonging – we felt part of something bigger than ourselves. To the outside world we were misfits and oddballs, but in our own world, well, we were family. We had occasional arguments, but overall we were all happy together. But Stoney Barrow View, this new incarnation, it just wasn't the same. I thought it felt more of a place to make money than somewhere to find peace.'

A phone rang behind her desk and she picked it up. Holding one finger up to them, she turned away as she spoke then replaced the phone and smiled at them. 'I am so sorry, but I really must rush you now. You said you had two reasons for coming – may I press you for the other?'

Nat glanced at Rawls and he leaned back in his chair. 'We wondered if you could provide us with a list of internet users on a couple of dates,' he said.

She steepled her fingers together in front of her face. 'I'm afraid that I can't do that. GDPR rules are very strict. I think you would need a warrant for that kind of information.'

Rawls nodded. 'We were hoping that you might be able to just take a look at a couple of dates.'

'No,' she snapped, and Rawls saw an angry flush in her cheeks.

'Ms Stokes,' he said, 'I do, of course, understand your reluctance to supply this information.'

She stopped him. 'No, DS Rawls, I honestly don't think that you do.' She flashed him a cold smile. 'People come here to use our computers for all sorts of reasons, but mostly because they need privacy. I am not at liberty to simply supply you with their details on a whim. I don't mind sharing my own information with you, but I have no intention of sharing that of others. You may not like that fact, but there it is. In fact, not only do I not want to, but I'm pretty sure that you know full well that I would be in breach of my terms of employment if I did. My suggestion is that you return as and when you are legally allowed to do so.'

Rawls sighed; she was right. 'Ms Stokes,' he said, 'I can't stress too much how important it is that we find out who it was that accessed your computers, but you're quite right – without a warrant we can't just come in here guns blazing and expect you to give us that information. However, I have a list of dates here ...' He passed her a sheet of paper. 'I would be extremely grateful if you could have a look at them and if you see anything about those dates that you might be able to help us with.'

She pursed her lips. 'May I ask why you want to know about them?'

'Because,' Rawls said, cautioning himself not to say too much, 'four young girls have gone missing and someone has used these computers,' he waved a hand at the two machines on the other side of the room, 'to provide information that may or may not be valuable to our enquiries. The account is set up in a false name and we really need to find the person behind it as quickly as possible.' He smiled. 'We are, of course, working on obtaining a warrant, but we were hoping that you might be able to help in the meantime.'

She ran her hand through her hair. 'Leave it with me,' she said. 'I'll see what I can do. Is that good enough for you?'

Rawls smiled. 'I'd appreciate any help you can give us.'

They picked up a long overdue lunch in the Co-op, Nat opting for a tuna salad and Rawls, the southern fried chicken wrap. Nat drove and they stopped in a lay-by, the engine running to keep them warm.

'What time did Lin agree with Mrs Solderton for tomorrow?' Rawls asked around a mouthful of chicken.

Nat covered her mouth and swallowed. 'The DI wants to see us in the morning, so Lin said we'd be there in the afternoon, around three.'

Rawls looked out of the window. Around them green hills rolled lazily towards the horizon, and a handful of cows waited patiently beneath a tree for the rain to stop. They were only a fifteen-minute drive from Bath but somehow, here amongst the shades of patchwork green that made up the landscape,

Rawls felt that he could breathe again. He realised, in that moment, without having considered it before, that he was feeling better than he had done in the past couple of months. He felt good, in fact, great, as if a weight had been lifted from his shoulders. Perhaps the therapy was working; perhaps the time off had allowed him to heal; perhaps, he thought as he swallowed the last of his wrap, he was just better off at work doing the thing that he was supposed to do.

Rachel Solderton opened the door to Rawls and Nat the following afternoon, her face stony, and ushered them into the lounge. Tiny particles of dust floated in the warm light that lit the room. Rawls watched them for a moment before he spoke. 'Mrs Solderton, thank you so much for seeing us. We know it's late.'

Mrs Solderton had expressed her anger at not being visited earlier. She had seen the press conference and had tried calling the office straight away. It had been Linda who had spoken to her and made the appointment, apologising all the while for the delay.

Now, with early dark closing in around them and the constant drizzle seeming to lend a solemnity to the proceedings, they sat in the woman's open-plan home, their wet jackets across their laps and Mrs Solderton looking both broken and furious in equal measure. Rawls found he could not fault her for either emotion.

She was a trim woman, good-looking but tired. She wore pale slacks and a tight polo neck jumper and sat with her arm resting on a cushion decorated with a brightly coloured pheasant. All the cushions in the room had either a pheasant or a fox on them and Rawls wondered briefly if they were a pro- or anti-hunt statement. It seemed of little consequence either way.

She looked at Rawls, her eyes angry, as though it was his fault that Yvette had never been found, and truth be told, Rawls probably felt the same way. 'The third of February 2015,' she said, holding his gaze, 'that's when I last saw her, around two fifteen in the afternoon.'

Rawls nodded but said nothing.

'How many times have I seen you, Detective Sergeant Rawls? Since that time, I mean.'

Rawls cleared his throat. 'I couldn't say.'

'I can,' she said, 'Eight. Eight times in four years.'

He held her gaze, 'Mrs Solderton, we have had a number of leads.'

'A number of leads.' She looked towards the dining room table on the far side of the open-plan room. 'How very reassuring. What number?'

'Sorry?'

'What number? Seven, eight, fifteen? What constitutes a number of leads?'

'I'm so sorry, I really can't go into details.' He wanted to reach out and take her hand, assure her that he would do everything in his power to find out what had happened and to make amends for what had gone on before, for not pushing harder, trying harder, working harder. Instead he said, 'As I'm sure you're aware, we're looking at three similar cases that we now believe to be linked to your daughter's disappearance.'

'The rest of us have thought that for a long time.'

'You're referring to the press?'

She laughed; it sounded hollow and desperate. 'You lot always blame the press. The press, Detective Sergeant, are doing your jobs for you; you should be thanking them.'

'We're grateful for any information, wherever it comes from.'

'God give me strength! Tell me this, Detective, do you believe they're dead? My Yvette, those other three?'

'I would like to believe that they're not ...' he looked at the floor, at the cushions, at a cat that had wandered into the room, anything to avoid looking at Mrs Solderton, 'and we're still looking at ...'

'If you say she joined a cult, I will scream,' she interrupted. 'I will, I'll just lose my shit and scream until you send the men around with the white coats and I'm locked up for my own good. Do you hear me? I will scream.'

Rawls said nothing.

Mrs Solderton turned to Nat. 'She didn't join a fucking cult,' she told her. 'She wasn't into that sort of thing. She was a material girl, she liked stuff; she wasn't some hippy with a pierced nose and dreadlocks.'

Rawls stayed quiet, he hoped Nat would too, he wanted to let the woman talk.

She crossed her arms and rubbed her hands at her elbows, comforting herself. When she spoke again her voice was hoarse, 'Do you know, I see people on TV, on the news, people who have lost children, mothers who have lost children, and I'm not sad for them; I'm jealous of them. I think to myself that they don't know how lucky they are, they know what happened, they can grieve. They know where their children are, they can take flowers to them or teddy bears or plant bulbs on their graves. What do we have?' She directed the question at Rawls as though he should have an answer. 'What do we have?' she repeated. 'Us, the parents of the missing? We don't have anything. It's hell, literally hell.'

She paused, still rubbing at her arms and now staring at her own reflection in the window. 'How do I recover? How do I move on? How do I heal? What right do I have to heal? I don't even know where my daughter is, let alone what she might be going through. Who am I to move on?' She stared at her reflection a moment longer then turned back to Rawls. 'There's no preparation for this, you know? No life lessons that you can apply when someone is ripped from your life like this. This isn't television, there won't be a resolution brought to you by baby-wipe adverts or online estate agents, there's no quick answer, no Sherlock Holmes and his powers of deduction. There's just nothing. Day after day after day of just nothing. It's purgatory.'

Nat leaned forward and rested a hand on the woman's shoulder. She smiled weakly at her and touched her fingers against Nat's. 'I must have been very wicked in a past life to deserve this,' she said. 'To have done this to Yvette.' She let her hands drop to her lap, where she wrapped them into a fist. 'There were sightings in the beginning, lots of them. We set up a Facebook page, we asked for any information at all, we asked people to share her photo, to let us know if they heard anything or saw anything.'

Nat nodded.

'But it got too much for me, there were too many for me to deal with. Some were people just messing around. They'd send photos of themselves, and they would say things like, "Am I your daughter?" or, "I just saw this girl in Asda and I think it might be your daughter", or they told me they had heard about girls being sold on the black market, like people trafficking, that sort of thing. It got too much, I couldn't take it, I just couldn't. My ex-husband was supposed to help but he couldn't deal with it either, so now a couple of my friends do it for me. They had one photo sent through, about a year ago, of a girl tied up on a bed. They sent it to your tech guys but they traced it to a couple of kids just messing around – they said they thought it would make us laugh.' She wiped at her face. 'Can you believe that? The little shits. I wanted to find them and run them over with my car at the time, see if they thought that was funny.'

'I don't blame you,' Nat said.

'I didn't, though, I didn't even press charges. I just couldn't face it, it was too much on top of everything else.' Mrs Solderton turned to Rawls. 'Why are you here, really? What are you hoping for?'

'Honestly,' Rawls said, 'we're not hoping for anything. We just wanted to do our best to reassure you.'

She made a sound that might have been laughter. 'Well, that's all fine then, I'm reassured. Reassured that you have nothing, no leads, no proper sightings, no suspects, just a load of gossip that my daughter ran off to join a cult.'

Rawls looked down, keeping quiet, wanting to let her carry on and say her piece.

'I lay in bed, you know, night after night, wondering, who has her, what are they doing to her? I ... I can hardly bear to imagine. She might have been sold, or used for, for ...' Her voice faded out as if she was unable to say what she was thinking. 'Sometimes, I hope she's dead, you know?' She ran the back of her hand across her nose. 'I think she'd be better off dead, better than the alternative.'

'Mrs Solderton,' Rawls said, 'I promise, I will do my best to find out what happened to your daughter.'

She nodded at him. 'I know you will,' she said, 'but I don't think it's going to be good enough.'

Rawls glanced around the empty room. There were no pictures on the walls, no empty cups on the side tables, no magazines on the floor. 'Do you live alone, Mrs Solderton?'

She looked around as though she hadn't considered it before. 'My other daughter, Dotty, is at uni now – she's up in Manchester doing a music degree. She tries not to come home, I think it's too much for her. It's funny, she chose to do a music degree, well, musical theatre. I was surprised – it was always Yvette's thing. I thought Dot would do fine art or illustration, something like that.'

'Yvette loved her music then?' Rawls asked.

'Oh yes,' she said. 'She was always a little performer, always singing or dancing. She would put on little plays and dance around the room. I always imagined that she would be on the stage one day. I think she thought she'd be Roxie Hart in *Chicago* or Millie in *Thoroughly Modern Millie*; she loved a musical and she played the piano – you should have heard her, utterly brilliant. I guess that was why Dotty chose to do it, perhaps in memory of her sister. In memory,' she said, 'like she's dead.' She put her face in her hands and cried into them.

After a few moments she spoke again from behind her hands. 'I'm sorry, I can't do this. I need to ask you to leave. I have a hospital appointment in the morning, I just can't … I can't.'

'Mrs Solderton, we just have a couple of questions …' Rawls tried.

She stood up, pushing at her cheeks with the palms of her hands. 'No I can't. Speak to my husband. You have his number, don't you?'

'Yes, but …'

It was no use. She had crossed the room and already had her hand on the door. 'I'm sorry,' she said again, 'I really am. I just can't.' She opened the door and they felt the cold, damp air push its way inside. 'Perhaps we can talk again, when you have more.'

Rawls kept his foot in the door. 'If I could just ask you about her boyfriend at the time …'

She stared at him. 'Jacob? You think that Jacob took her?'

'No, we don't, but we're just trying to cover every angle,' Rawls said. 'Did you know him?'

She shook her head. 'Not really. He was too old for her. We – my husband and I – we told her that, not to mention that he was off his head most of the time. But she was so strong-willed, she wouldn't hear a word against him.'

'Did you wonder about him, at the time, I mean?'

She was rubbing at her arms, cold in the night air. 'We did, but then, he was a drug addict. He couldn't have killed her then hidden her body, he wasn't clever enough.'

Rawls nodded; those had been his thoughts as well. He handed her a card. 'Mrs Solderton, if you think of anything, no matter how trivial or how many times you might have said it before, please call me.'

She pushed the card into the back pocket of her slacks before closing the door without saying goodbye.

'She's gone through a lot,' Nat said.

'Call her husband first thing in the morning, would you?' Rawls said. 'See if we can see him in the afternoon.'

Chapter 13

Friday came, as they always do, at the end of a long week that had gone by all too quickly. They were a week into this now and Rawls felt no further forward. He had woken early and left the house before Eileen or Carmen were awake so that he could take a walk along the river. He stood beside it now, his hands in his pockets, his collar pulled up against the south-westerly wind, watching seagulls in the metal-grey sky. His head felt overloaded. There were too many people and places, names and dates: the missing girls, their friends, their teachers, all jostling for position in his mind. He needed some calm, a little space to clear his head and arrange his thoughts, and as he stood there, he did his best to think of nothing. He wanted a revelation to come to him, a missing piece of the puzzle, a tiny detail so insignificant that they had all overlooked it but so huge in its importance that it would blow the case wide open. And so, he waited, watching the clouds moving, dark grey on light grey, drifting, changing shape, coming apart and reassembling themselves, their gloom broken only occasionally by the appearance of a bird.

He wanted to shout, to turn his face up to the drizzle and scream, let the frustration out, free himself of at least some of the burden; instead, he swore under his breath, over and over again, the same four-letter words, letting them mindlessly trip off his tongue. It did nothing really, his mind failing to unlock any secrets, refusing to cooperate, and so he turned, shoulders hunched, and began the half-mile or so walk to the office.

He had woken in the night, wondering what they might be missing, who they should have interviewed and who they already had spoken with. The list was long, overwhelming, unforgiving. He had tried to break it down into lots of little problems instead of one big one. He had seen the parents and that was good, but he wasn't sure it had made any difference. He wondered about Yvette's father; he hadn't managed to speak with him yet, but he could get to that. That brought him to Yvette's boyfriend, Jacob. He was a mess, and admitted to being violent towards young women, even thought it was funny, but a killer? Rawls didn't know, not yet anyway. And what about Sebastian, the new owner of Stoney Barrow View – wasn't he just a little too perfect, too squeaky clean? The place seemed nice enough, but Grace Stokes the librarian had left, hadn't she? She had managed to avoid telling them why – like a good politician, she had dodged every one of their questions on the subject. Could she have discovered a secret, something so dark and so unpleasant that after all the years of putting her life and soul into the place, she had upped sticks and left?

He paused again, the wind at his back now. Why did it feel like such a mess? Why couldn't he see the wood for the trees?

What about the headmistress? She had been hostile to the suggestion that a member of the faculty might have been involved – was she hiding something? Protecting someone? He didn't think so, and in any case, as she herself had pointed out, the missing girls had come from different schools. And then there was Alkham. Rawls didn't like him. He might have tried to spin it differently, but he was blackmailed by Harriet and he had more than one witness stating that they had seen him with young girls. Could he have something worse to hide?

His phone rang in his pocket and he fumbled for it, pulling his gloves off to answer the call.

'Rawls.' It was Nat. 'What time are you due in?'

'I'm about five minutes away. Everything alright?'

'Yes,' she sounded relieved, 'I thought you might have forgotten.'

Rawls tried to think. 'Forgotten?'

'We have that guy in.'

'Which one?'

'He owns the facilities management business,' he heard her pause and knew that she was checking her notes, 'ABC Property Maintenance.'

Rawls grimaced. This was the vehicle seen parked up on the Wells Road at around the time that Tanya Hickock had last been seen. Nat had found the details after they'd been to visit Mrs Solderton and had contacted him and made the appointment; he'd been happy to come in the following morning. Rawls glanced at his watch. 'Shit, sorry, Nat, I thought he was coming in at eleven, I'll get my skates on.'

Nat laughed. 'Don't go too mad. He's pretty chilled, I don't think he'll mind waiting.'

'Give me five,' he said, trying not to pant into the phone.

'Shall I get you a coffee?'

'You read my mind; it's bloody freezing out here.' He ended the call. He could have done without an interview straight off the bat, could have done with half an hour or so to get his head in the game. Still, it was what it was – see what today brought to the table.

Rawls made a dash for the loo, drank the coffee Nat had ready for him, popped a couple of Tic Tacs and was good to go. Nat had been correct, Mark Calver was relaxed. He had his legs crossed and a cup of tea in front of him when Rawls walked into the interview room.

'Mr Calver.' Rawls extended a hand.

The man stood: he was six foot three, maybe six-four, and broad, with a thick brown mane of hair. He had the kind of eyebrows that dominate a face, and eyes so dark that it was hard to distinguish his pupils from the iris.

They shook briefly then sat simultaneously, chairs scraping across the cold floor. Mark Calver pressed his fingertips together in front of his mouth. His nails were clean and his shirt sleeve, which poked coquettishly out of his jacket, looked expensive.

Rawls asked him if he would like another drink – tea, coffee, water?

Calver smiled at Rawls and it was surprisingly disarming. 'No, thank you so much, this one is still hot.' He shook his head. 'This is a terrible business.'

'What's that?' Rawls asked.

Mark Calver leaned forward. 'The missing girls,' he said.

'And you know why we asked you to come in?'

The man shook his head, closing his eyes. 'I'm afraid I don't.'

Rawls sat back and crossed his legs in front of him, mirroring Calver. He opened the file that he had brought in with him and pulled out a sheet of paper. 'Your vehicle,' he read the registration from the notes, 'was seen on the fourteenth of November at around four p.m., parked on Wells Road.'

'Right?' The man looked confused.

'I wonder if you would mind telling me what you were doing there?'

Calver thought for a while. 'Four, you say, and sorry, what day was that: the fourteenth?'

'It was a Thursday.'

Calver frowned. 'Do you mind if I have a quick look at my diary? I move around a fair bit during the day.' Rawls nodded and he took his phone out of his jacket pocket, pressed his thumb to it and swiped the screen a couple of times, 'Thursday the fourteenth,' he said, 'at four? I was, oh yes, I was on the Wells Road.' He handed his phone to Rawls so that he could see the screen. 'I was across the road, at the block of flats. We maintain the grounds, cut the hedges, clean the paths, that sort of thing. It's one of my regulars.'

'You're there every week?'

'Oh no, probably only monthly, perhaps less. We don't have the contract for the interior yet, that would mean being there far more often,' he smiled and tilted his head, 'but we're working on it.'

'Do you remember what time you left?'

'God,' he said, frowning, 'now you're asking. What time would I have left? Probably around four to four thirty, but that's just a guess, I wouldn't want to swear to it.'

'What did you do there that day – cut hedges, clean the path?'

He shook his head. 'To tell you the truth, I don't really do the hard work. I'm a little more management and a little less hands on; we subcontract most of that kind of work. I was there to check things over, in case I needed to get someone in.'

'You own the business then? ABC Property Maintenance?'

He nodded. 'It keeps me out of trouble.'

'And you're busy?'

Mark pointed to his phone. 'You saw my calendar,' he said, 'I'm all over the place.'

'May I ask how far your calendar goes back?'

Calver picked up his phone and swiped to open it. 'Let's see, I should have thought at least three years, that was pretty much when I started doing my appointments that way, maybe a little longer.' He frowned at the screen, then turned it again for Rawls to see. 'Five years.'

'Could I ask you to check another date for me?'

'Of course,' he said, 'fire away.'

Rawls checked his notes. 'The third of February 2015.'

Calver swiped, tapped, smiled. 'I was out of town.'

He passed the phone to Rawls who squinted at the screen. The day had been blocked out in purple; it said, 'André Rieu.'

'He's a conductor and violinist,' Calver said.

'You went to see him?' Rawls asked.

'In London. It was the trip of a lifetime, I adore him.'

'You're a musician?'

'Well I don't play the violin like he does.'

Rawls laughed. 'My daughter once tried to learn, worst eight weeks of my life.'

'I'm with you on that. I tried too but I was useless.'

'We were glad to see the end of it, I imagine you were too.'

Calver laughed. 'Not at all. I play a couple of other instruments: piano, guitar, even the drums, just never mastered the violin, but it wasn't for lack of trying.'

Rawls brought him back to the subject. 'What about further back – would you have diary records going back to say, 2011, 2012?'

'Oh God, I would, but they'd be filed in boxes in the office. I could check for you, though, by all means.'

'I'd appreciate that.' Rawls sat back in his chair, his back aching from the walk. 'Tell me about your work.'

'My work?' He smiled. 'There's not a whole lot to tell. I've been doing this – property maintenance, that is – for as long as I can remember; my wife and I run the business together. We also buy and sell houses, from auctions usually. We buy them when they look like they're going to fall apart, we do them up and sell them on. That sort of thing.'

'Blimey, sounds stressful.'

He nodded. 'It can be.'

'Do you get much time for your hobbies, for your music?'

Calver beamed. 'I do keep my hand in. I volunteer for a performing arts charity, bringing music and drama to underprivileged kids. I know it sounds cheesy, but it's life-enhancing, it really is. I've taught young people of all ages, some talented, some,' he grinned, 'less so, but all of them have brought something to my life.'

Rawls nodded. Personally, he could think of nothing he'd like to do less with his spare time. He glanced at the clock on the wall; he needed to get on. 'Mr Calver, do you mind if I showed you some photos?'

'No, of course not.' Calver reached into his pocket and took out a pair of reading glasses.

'Their names are: Melody, Harriet, Yvette, Tanya,' Rawls said as he spread the pictures across the table. 'Do any of them look familiar to at all, Mr Calver?'

Calver stared at the photos, moving them one by one, then pushed his chair back a little so that he could cross his legs. 'I honestly don't think so,' he was shaking his head. He peered at Rawls over the top of his glasses. 'These cases go all the way back to the noughties, don't they?'

'Back to 2009,' Rawls said. 'Perhaps if you take a look at Tanya's photo – she went missing in November this year, or Yvette – she disappeared in 2015.' He separated their photos from the others as he spoke.

Calver shook his head. 'I'm so sorry, I really don't think so.' He touched the photos again. 'I will check my records though, if you let me have the dates in question. I could get that information over to you quite quickly, if that would help.'

'That would be most helpful, Mr Calver, really appreciate it.'

'No trouble, you just might need to bear with me. Give me a couple of days, but I'll get them over to you as soon as I can.'

Rawls thanked him, then asked, 'How do you find your clients?'

'My clients?'

'Yes, do you advertise? Have a website, that sort of thing?'

'Oh, yes, we have online adverts, but mostly it's word of mouth.'

'Ah,' Rawls said, 'of course, and would you say that you get on with your clients?'

Calver smiled. 'Most of the time. You get the odd funny one, but mostly they're nice and I like working with people. I'd hope they say that they get on with me.'

'I'm sure,' Rawls said, then, changed the subject. 'Do you have any children?'

'Children?' Calver shook his head. 'Sadly not. People always seem to feel sorry for us when I tell them that and then they ask me why. The truth is that I don't know why, we just didn't ever get around to it and now we're too old. I don't particularly regret it, though. Do you?'

Rawls regretted mentioning earlier that he had a daughter. He shifted in his seat. 'I do, but if it's OK, I'd like to stick to the missing four.'

Calver's brows creased into a frown. 'The missing four,' he repeated, 'such a horrible way to put it.' He looked down at his hands, one hand rubbing at the other. 'It's awful that there are people amongst us willing to take young girls away from their homes, from their families.'

Rawls nodded. 'Some people think they ran away – you must have heard that on the news.'

Calver pursed his lips as though he was thinking. 'Yes, I did, but I don't think it seems likely.'

'You don't? Why's that?'

'Well,' Calver said, 'otherwise you wouldn't be tracking down cars and interviewing people.' He gave a weak smile. 'I don't know, I think I must watch too much TV, but these sort of things don't usually end well, do they? Don't they say that if you can't find them after forty-eight hours then it's probably too late?'

'That's not always been my experience,' Rawls said.

Calver took his glasses off and rubbed his eyes briefly. 'Surely you have phone records, things like that, for the last two anyway? Can't you track their phones?'

'We're working on those at the moment.'

'And witnesses, someone might have seen them.'

'Seen them?'

Calver shrugged. 'Like getting into a car or something. I thought there were cameras all over Bath.'

'There are,' Rawls agreed. 'Tell me about the afternoon of the fourteenth. Where did you go after you left Wells Road?'

'Home,' Calver said shortly.

'And can anyone corroborate this?'

'Corroborate? I don't know, I could ask my wife if she remembers.'

'That would be good,' Rawls said, 'thank you. I have to ask again though, just to be clear, you have no recollection of meeting any of these girls, not even in your volunteering work?'

Calver looked shocked. 'I don't know what you want me to say.'

'I don't want you to say anything, I just wanted to be clear. Listen, Mark, here's my thoughts about what might have happened. Just hear me out OK? Maybe someone met Tanya while they were driving from place to place, visiting customers, perhaps. Maybe Tanya confided in that person, told that person about her sad life, how she had such a tough time, and maybe, just maybe that person told her that she would be safe with them. How does that sound?'

'I resent the implication,' Mark said, his face flushed.

'As you should, it's a horrible implication. But just supposing that's what happened, things could have got out of hand. People do silly things, accidents happen. I mean, maybe this someone didn't mean to hurt her but, you know, perhaps he just got carried away.'

Calver sat up and stared at Rawls. 'This is ridiculous – you know that, don't you? You're accusing me based on, what, the fact that I might have been in the same area at the same time as one of these girls went missing?'

'As I said, I'm not accusing you,' Rawls said calmly. 'I just wanted to run it by you, see what your thoughts were on the matter.'

'I know my rights, Detective. I can leave right now if I want to.'

Rawls nodded. 'You can, and you're free to do so if you wish. I'm sorry if you feel under attack, that's not my intention. I really was just thinking aloud.'

'Well, here's what I'm thinking aloud, Detective. I'm thinking that I should get a lawyer,' Calver paused, pushing his hair back from his face, 'but I won't. I believe in living by the truth and I have nothing to hide – nothing.'

'That's good,' Rawls said. 'I know I've asked already, but would you like a drink – tea, coffee, water, a Coke?'

Calver sat slightly hunched in his chair. 'I'd love another tea, two sugars if that's OK?'

'Absolutely,' Rawls stood up. 'Bear with me, I won't be a minute.'

'I'll be waiting.' Calver smiled weakly.

Tess caught his arm as he came out. 'What are you playing at?'

'He's a complete wanker,' Rawls said.

'He may well be,but being a wanker doesn't make you a rapist or murderer. You can't convict someone just because you don't like them.'

He sighed, she had a point. Being an arsehole didn't make Calver guilty of anything.

'Just be careful,' Tess said. 'If he is our guy, we don't want to spook him.'

Nat materialised with a cup of tea for Calver and another coffee for him. He took them with thanks. 'Once more unto the breach, dear friends.'

Nat opened the door and he walked in and sat back down.

Calver seemed to have regained his composure. He took a sip of the tea and smiled. 'Can't beat a cup of tea, can you, Detective?'

'I'm a coffee man myself.' Rawls leaned back, crossing one leg over the other. 'Listen, I'm sorry. I feel like I came on a bit strong, it's just that we have to work with what we have and right now, between you and me, we don't have a great deal.'

Calver blew on his tea. 'I'm sorry to hear that, I really am.'

'Look, how would you feel about letting us take a look at your phone?'

Calver finished his tea, then put the cup down on the table in front of him. 'Is it alright for me to ask why?'

'Of course. We just think that if these girls were groomed, there would be a record of text messages, and since we don't have their phones, we have to check all suspect phones.'

'Surely you can check their phone records, see if my number comes up?'

'We can, yes, but the truth is that it takes time, obtaining the records. This helps us rule you out more quickly.'

Calver leaned forward. 'Here you go.' He put his iPhone on the table next to his cup. 'How long will you need it for?'

'A day, maybe two at the most.'

Calver considered this for a moment. 'I do need it for work.'

'We'll be as quick as we can.'

Calver pushed the phone towards him, 'I'd appreciate that.'

'Do you mind letting me have the log-in pin?' Rawls asked.

Calver took the phone back and began swiping. 'I'll do better than that,' he said, 'I'll turn the security off.' He clicked a couple more times then folded his arms and leaned back. 'Are we done?'

'Unless you want to add anything else, I think so. Till next time,' Rawls said, and Calver smiled.

'Let's hope there isn't a next time.'

'Yes, let's hope.'

Rawls shook Calver's hand. It was warm and damp and he had to resist the urge to wipe his own off afterwards. 'I'll make sure you have your phone back by Sunday, Monday at the latest.'

'Appreciate it,' Calver said.

'Nat will show you out,' Rawls said politely. 'Thank you for your time.'

Calver smiled at Nat. 'Lead the way, young lady.'

Rawls looked at the phone. There would be nothing on it – Calver had given it up too easily for it to hold anything of any use to them. He rubbed a hand across his face. It was only lunch time and already he needed a shave; a shave, a cup of decent coffee, and a break in this bloody case.

All the same, it was funny what a difference the last few days had made. He was feeling better by the day, more like his old self. He wished he could make Eileen understand, that he could tell her how great he felt, how good it was to be back at work, back in the thick of it again. Even Tess seemed to be starting to trust him, and he was surprised to see how relieved he was by that. He wondered what Tobias, his counsellor, would make of this new positive outlook and smiled at the idea of telling him. Things were starting to look up.

Chapter 14

It was a little after four in the afternoon when Carmen closed the front door, dropped her bag and kicked off her shoes. She stood for a moment and stared at her reflection in the hallway mirror. She looked OK, she thought, despite the rain. Her make-up had lived up to its waterproof claims and, although her hair hung in damp rat's tails about her face and neck, she still thought she looked acceptable. But acceptable wasn't enough. Tonight was a big night – tonight she had a date, *the* date. They were going to meet at the cinema, although – and she couldn't say this to her mother, of course – he had told her that they were not going to see a film. She bit her bottom lip; it was both exciting and scary. He had told her not to be scared, she would be fine, it would be fine.

It. She twisted a damp strand of hair. It scared her – she had told him so in their texts, and he had told her not to worry. He would take care of her, he would make sure that nothing would happen between them that she wasn't completely happy with. He had told her that she needed to know that.

She did, she told herself, of course she did; she knew that he would never hurt her. He loved her. He had told her that she was beautiful, that he thought about her in his every waking moment, that he couldn't wait to be with her, to hold her, to kiss her, to touch her. She shuddered and the feeling sent goosebumps up and down her arms.

She smiled again, biting still at her bottom lip, liking how she looked, liking the dark of her eyes, how the sinew in her neck moved when she opened and closed her mouth. She could imagine his lips at her neck. She closed her eyes, letting the anticipation wash over her, imagining it. Then she opened them again, afraid to let the image go any further, afraid of what he might expect, of how he might insist, how she might have second thoughts.

She turned away from the mirror. For the first time she doubted herself, wished she had told her mother the truth. But that was ridiculous. She could never tell her mother what she was going to do.

Her phone beeped as it found the home WiFi and she glanced down as a WhatsApp message lit up her screen.

Looking forward to seeing you.

She smiled, typed, *excited*, added two red hearts, and hit send, her heart beating so fast that she thought she might faint.

> *Can't wait to see you.*
> *Me neither.*
> *Can't stop thinking about you.*

She leaned against the wall and smiled at the phone. What had she been worried about? Everything was going to be fine.

She typed *me neither* again and wished that she could think of something better.

> *7.30, and don't be late.*
> *I won't.*

Chapter 15

The rented garage was situated in a row of brightly painted garage doors behind a grim housing estate. Weeds grew out of the cracks in the pavement, pushing lumps of concrete out as though they were no more than pebbles on a beach. In places, where the render had come away, red brickwork showed through like the work of a graffiti artist. The rain, which had remained little more than an annoying drizzle throughout the afternoon, had ramped up to a heavy downpour and Rawls watched it for a moment through the steady rhythm of the windscreen wipers before climbing out of the warmth of the Passat and running the couple of steps to the garage door.

He'd only put the ad up two days ago and already it looked like it was going to be sold; the guy had been really keen. This was good, this was what he needed, the car was one distraction too many. He had made a mistake buying it. *Buyer beware*, he thought to himself as he yanked hard on the ancient garage door-handle and pulled the rusty structure open. Buyer beware indeed, but oh, it was so beautiful, the paintwork so mint that even in the hazy light of the single bulb that dangled overhead, he could see himself reflected in the bonnet. He would be sad to see it go but it was the right thing to do, he knew that. He might not like it, but he knew it.

He smiled, remembering Tobias's face when he had told him about the car. Rawls still couldn't decide whether the man had been shocked or jealous. Jealous, Rawls suspected – that would explain why he had advised him to let it go, telling him that his compunction to buy the car had come from his own feelings of mortality – apparently common in many men of his age. Rawls had thought at the time, but managed not to say, that he could have told Tobias that himself. Wasn't that why all men bought expensive things at a certain stage in their lives? Of course, Tobias might also have told him that not all men had been through the same trauma that he had, nor had they been so damned stupid.

He looked at his watch; nearly seven and the guy had said half-seven, quarter to eight. He'd told Eileen that he would be late; she'd been on her way to Zumba and was going to be late herself. She had reminded him that Carmen was out as well, so he was, for the next couple of hours at least, a free agent.

He pressed his head into the car's leather seat, relishing the smell, the creak of the leather. He didn't love the car yet, but he really, really liked it; he sort of hoped the guy wasn't going to turn up. At least he could tell Eileen that he had tried. She couldn't hold it against him if he was trying to sell it, could she? He thought perhaps she could. It seemed she had a number of things that she could hold against him, the way things were between them at the moment. He made mistakes and Eileen remembered them.

He let his mind drift, away from his wife, away from his car, and the guy who was coming to buy it, and back to the case. He thought about Tess, how she had gatecrashed his interview with Dave Alkham, the real estate guy. He thought about how he had wanted to stand up and walk out, that old sense of stress rising up, threatening to overwhelm him at the fear of being undermined, but then, how quickly it had abated as Tess had become his ally, the two of them working together to try to figure the guy out. Dave Alkham was difficult to read. On the surface he was sleazy, making Rawls suspicious of his intentions, but beneath that perhaps the guy was just foolish, a middle-aged man trying to impress young women. Either way, Rawls wasn't ready to rule him out as a suspect. They needed more on him. Had he known any of the others? Could they place the girls with him? Could Alkham have come into the station in a misguided attempt to put them off his scent?

He leaned back in the seat and closed his eyes. Around him the sounds of the city seemed distant and vague and he cautioned himself about falling back into his old ways. He had been certain once before, that he knew who the perpetrator was, perhaps too certain; and look where that had got him. This time he needed to be careful. He pressed his hands against his cheeks then rubbed at his eyes. God, he was tired. He let his mind drift, let it go where it wanted for a while. By the time he realised where it was taking him, it was too late to stop it.

Ellie Dalmore, her face wet with tears, after she'd looked through all the photos from the line-up and been unable to pick out her rapist, Logan Bishop. She had apologised to him, as if *she* had let him down. Rawls had not known how to respond. Guilt had washed over him in a wave so huge that he thought he might drown in it. *He* had let her down in her time of need; *he* had not been able to do his job and she was apologising to *him*. He was the one who was supposed to keep the streets safe; he was the one who was supposed to catch the bad guys and protect the good; he was the one who had failed. Failed her, failed himself, failed in his job. He had gone home that night, his hands trembling, his heart racing, his palms wet with sweat. He had closed the door behind him and, without saying a word, he had taken himself upstairs to sit alone in the bedroom, the lights off and the curtains drawn. The stress of the job had been building over the past few months and Rawls had known, at that moment, that it had finally come to a head. Dealing with it was too much for him to do on his own, he had needed help.

A sudden bright light from the dashboard brought Rawls back to the present and he realised with a start that his phone was still on silent and had lit up with an incoming call. He looked at the caller ID; he didn't recognise the number.

'Rawls,' he said, swiping the green button on the screen.

'Oh, er, Mr Rawls, Peter, it's Jack. I'm, er, coming to see the car. I'm stuck in traffic, I just wanted to let you know that I was going to be a bit longer than I thought.'

Rawls glanced at the time. 'I should have warned you about Bath. It's a bloody gridlock most of the time,' he said, 'but that's fine, just give me a shout when you're close and I'll tell you how to find me.'

They said their goodbyes and Rawls put the phone back on the dash.

Carmen stood up as the bus pulled up with a sudden jolt. She waited as people collected their bags then followed them out into the cold night air. They were at the bus station and she had no choice but to disembark. She supposed that she could simply wait at the station and then catch the next bus home. She could call her mum, ask her to come and pick her up when Zumba was over, or try her dad – he might be close by, close enough to come and get her. She could do any of those things – but Carmen knew that she wouldn't.

Thanking the driver, she climbed down from the bus and crossed quickly at the lights before heading up St James's Parade. The walk would take less than five minutes and she felt a mixture of elation at her independence and apprehension at being so alone. Mostly, however, she felt excited. He'd told her how beautiful she was, how she didn't need all that make-up, how sexy he thought women without make-up were and how much he loved the natural look, which was why she had come out this evening wearing only the tiniest slick of mascara. She felt naked without it, bare and exposed without her foundation to hide under; ugly and plain without her eyebrows and eyeliner, but she would brave it, for him.

When she had first met him, the first time that she had sat beside him, his hands resting beside hers so that their hands touched just the tiniest bit, she had felt a kind of revulsion. It had washed over her like an oil slick, moist and sticky; it had curled its fingers, first around her hand, and then crept into her back and she had needed to physically control an urge to shudder. And now, here she was, walking nervously, in her favourite white Adidas trainers, with no make-up on, to meet him for a date.

The familiar smell of popcorn and chlorine hit Carmen as it always did when she walked into the cinema foyer. Thoughts came at her in a swathe of voices: her mother's, her father's, even her friends'. What would they say if they knew? What might they think? What did *she* think?

She looked around, her head spinning as though she had just climbed down from a ride. The complex was busy, loud voices and ominous laughter emerging drunkenly from the Wetherspoons, families drifting in and out of TGI Fridays and groups of teenagers moodily hanging around the coffee bar. It was exactly as it always was, a place she was familiar with, where she had always felt at home, but that suddenly felt alien to her. She was alone, loitering, twisting her trainer-clad foot around her rain-soaked parka which she had dropped on the floor against the wall. She was fiddling with her phone, swiping, typing, tapping, anything to look busy while she thought. Perhaps she should plan her escape?

Carmen scanned the kiosk; he definitely wasn't there. That settled it for her. She would leave, she didn't want to go through with it now. There was no hiding from the truth: something felt wrong. She glanced up and a woman, no more than a few feet away, smiled at her. Carmen smiled back, unsure of herself. Still smiling, the woman, who was short and thin but muscular, held her gaze. There was something wrong with that smile, the way that it didn't quite reach her eyes, the way that it didn't falter even as she continued to stare at Carmen. The smile, Carmen thought, looked as though it had been glued in place, too broad, too wide, like the smile of the Cheshire Cat in *Alice in Wonderland*.

She took out her phone and started to type a message to her dad, asking him if he could come and pick her up, then changed her mind. The woman was staring, that smile still in place as though it had been drawn on, her body blocking Carmen's only exit. She needed to hear her dad's voice more than she had ever needed it before. Carmen navigated her way to the call app. Her dad's number was saved in favour-ites and she tapped it with a finger that shook as though she had come down with a fever. She felt suddenly more afraid than she had ever felt before.

She held her breath, listening as the phone rang once, twice, three times, then her father's voice; calm, familiar,

'Hi, this is DS Peter Rawls. I can't take your call right now but please leave a message at the tone and I'll get back to you just as soon as I can.' Carmen felt her legs grow cold with terror, her stomach turned, and her mouth became suddenly very dry.

'Dad,' she whispered at the beep, 'can you come and get me from the cinema, please?' All at once she felt silly, terrified, cornered and alone. 'Please, Dad,' she said again and ended the call as the woman, her lips still pulled back in that God-awful smile, took a step towards her.

Chapter 16

Eighteen grand is a great deal of money. It all but filled the A4 envelope that the guy had brought with him.

Rawls had wanted twenty-one, that was what he had asked for in his ad, but the guy had clearly been watching *Wheeler Dealers* or *Gas Monkey Garage*. He had spent time on the ritual of buying the car, dragging it out, clearly enjoying the process.

'You're asking twenty-one, yeah?'

The guy had sucked air in over his teeth, walked back to the open bonnet, tapped something and raised an eyebrow. 'I think we need to find somewhere south of that figure,' he had said.

South? Rawls wondered what south meant – presumably, down. How far down? He thought about wisecracking himself, sucking in his own breath and saying something like,

247

'Mate, do you want it or not? The car owes me twenty-one.'
That was what they said, didn't they? The car owes me.

Instead, he said, 'Um, how far south?' He would have
happily hit himself on the head except that it would make
him look more stupid than he already did.

'Fifteen.'

'Fifteen?' Rawls had all but squawked.

'Eighteen, but that's my final offer.'

His phone had rung in his pocket; he glanced at it, saw
it was Carmen and sent it to voicemail. He'd give her a call
back as soon as they were done. The guy was offering eighteen, that would do – he could live with eighteen grand. He
pushed his phone back into his jacket and extended a hand.
He wasn't exactly over the moon but he wasn't too upset by
it either. He knew that Eileen would be pleased to see the
car go, but he would miss it. Somehow a family-sized Passat
with nearly 100,000 miles on the clock lacked the daredevil
glamour of the Focus. Still, it was what it was.

Now, driving home, his mind drifted, as it always did, back
to the case. It felt disjointed and he tried to pull it together.
What did they have?

'Four missing girls,' he said out loud, then he named
them, one after another, 'Melody, Harriet, Yvette, Tanya.'
He repeated the names as though it was a mantra, 'Melody,
Harriet, Yvette, Tanya.'

He drummed his fingers on the steering wheel. 'What's
the same?' he asked the silent car. 'What's the same and
what's different?'

The engine ignored him, humming to itself while outside, the rain started up again, blurring brake lights into splashes as red as blood through the frantic windscreen wipers. He slowed down, not wanting to soak a group of schoolgirls huddled in a bus stop outside St Hilda's Catholic School. They glared at him with an air of suspicion and distaste as he passed by, none of them grateful for his small courtesy, all of them under-dressed for the weather. They were wearing some kind of gym kit – hockey, he guessed – must have been a night match. One of them shouted something towards his car and they all laughed, except for one who was sitting alone, separate from the others.

'That's who he goes for,' Rawls said out loud, 'the girl on the end, the girl on her own.' He stopped at a set of traffic lights, the sound of the wipers making a rhythm out of the girls' names again in his head. 'Melody, Harriet, Yvette, Tanya.' That was what they had in common. They had been alone when they disappeared, heading somewhere: Melody shopping for a top to wear to a date with a boyfriend, who to this day remained nameless; Harriet on her way to school; Yvette storming out after a row; Tanya on her way home or perhaps to a secret job. Had someone, their perpetrator, known they would be alone; had they communicated that fact to him?

He sighed; it was about more than that. It was about cults and acting in plays, and playing the piano, and work experience, and cash-in-hand jobs, and young girls going through tough times. It was about all of this and probably much more besides. He thought about the estate agent, Dave Alkham. The guy had no priors but then he wouldn't; predators were careful and appearing normal was their disguise – hide in plain sight, as the saying goes. Not that Rawls had any reason to believe the man to be a predator; he hadn't done anything wrong after all. Not unless you counted his being alone with young girls who were only there to do work experience.

Rawls told himself again that the guy had no business being alone with them. So what else did he know? The guy was married, granted no children, no pets. Nothing wrong with that though, loads of people had no children and no pets. But there was something about the guy, something that kept popping up in the back of Rawls's mind. What was it that bothered him? What didn't bother him might be easier to answer. The guy had taken a young girl to an empty house, he said that he had enjoyed her company. Really? Really? But then, it wasn't against the law to take someone to a house, was it? Especially if you were an estate agent, but still, something about it left a bad taste in Rawls's mouth. It just didn't feel right. That didn't make the guy a murderer or a kidnapper though, it made him sleazy, that was all, or at least that was all until evidence was found to prove otherwise. He tried to tell himself that there was a difference between circumstantial evidence and pure speculation; he even told himself that speculation might be putting too much of a positive spin on it – fabrication might have been a better word – but nonetheless, he needed to know whether any of the other girls had worked for him. He added the thought to his mental checklist.

He moved on to the cult angle. They were odd, no getting away from it – the place was weird and more than a little bit creepy – but did he believe that the five-star wellness retreat was luring children and hiding them against their will? None of the staff seemed to be younger than thirty, and even if by some stretch of the imagination the cult had somehow continued after the sale of the property, the dots just didn't join up.

His mind took him back to the guy with the van, Calver. Now, that guy was a creep, but despite what TV dramas might have people believe, not all kidnappers are creeps who drive vans.

'Melody, Harriet, Yvette, Tanya,' he said, pulling up in front of his house. 'Where on earth are you?'

The lights were off inside the house. Carmen was at the pictures, on her big date, and Eileen was presumably still out with the Zumba gang. Perfect, he would find somewhere to hide the cash from the car sale until the morning. It felt odd having that much cash in the house and for a moment he considered the extremely slim but 'oh wouldn't that be just about perfect' chance that they might be burgled in the night. He had intended to leave it in a drawer beside his bed but then, panicking, he pulled it out and hid it in an old *National Geographic* box. The magazines that it had once held were mostly missing, and the gap they left behind was an eighteen-grand-sized hole. He jammed the notes in then took them back out again and counted once more, just to be sure. All there, all good, all over. He sighed, shoved the box back on the shelf and stood back to admire his handiwork. Perfect, nothing to see here.

The door opened and a voice called out, 'Only me.' Eileen sounded merry.

Rawls went downstairs to find her in the hall, swaying slightly. 'You didn't drive like that, did you?'

She laughed. It came out as a snort and that made her laugh again. 'Nope, left the car at the Lege,' she meant the British Legion. 'Cherry,' she snorted again, 'sorry, Sherry brought me home in her chariot.' She giggled. 'Sherry has a Range Rover.'

'Good for Sherry,' Rawls said. 'I take it the British Legion provides a wide variety of fine wines for ladies of your calibre to choose from.'

'Indeed, they do, sir,' she said, putting her hands on her hips in mock indignation. 'They offered both a Merlot and a Pinot – all the ohs.'

'Ah, those two fine favourites,' Rawls said. 'Glad they catered to your incredibly discerning palate.'

She grinned, pulling off her trainers and sitting down. 'Where's Car?' she asked.

'Not home yet, what time did you tell her?'

'Around ten,' Eileen said, 'so she's OK for a bit. Has she called you at all?'

Rawls remembered the call. Shit, how had he forgotten to call her back? He pulled his phone out of his pocket and swiped to open it; there were several missed calls, all from his voicemail. He dialled 121 and put the phone on speaker. Carmen's voice came from the phone like a ghost in a haunted house: 'Dad, Dad can you come and get me, please?'

Eileen's hand flew to her neck and Rawls felt his blood turn to ice in his veins. Something in the tone of his daughter's voice told him that she was in trouble. He dialled her number, even as Eileen reached for her phone to do the same.

It went straight to voicemail.

Nat was reading a book when her mobile rang. She had been at the point before sleep where her eyes blurred and lines merged together in a jumble of letters when it had shrieked for attention. She glanced at the caller ID then sat up in bed as if she had been caught napping at her desk.

'Gov?'

'You're awake,' Tess said, and Nat wasn't sure if it had been a question or a statement.

'Yes, I'm awake. Is, er, is everything alright?'

There was the briefest of pauses before Tess answered, 'We might have a situation that needs our immediate attention.'

Nat moved the phone to her other ear and pulled her slippers on. 'Immediate like now?' She felt silly asking – of course Tess meant now.

'Yes, now, if you're able to. Do you need a babysitter?'

Nat was mildly surprised that Tess knew she had a child at all. 'Um, no, I can ask my mum or dad to come over.'

'Good.' Tess was clearly in no mood for idle chat. 'Rawls's teenage daughter hasn't come home.'

'Rawls's daughter hasn't come home?' Nat repeated and she felt suddenly very stupid indeed.

Tess sighed as though she was talking to a small child, then she ran through the facts. Rawls's daughter, Carmen, who Nat already knew was fifteen, had left home earlier the previous evening to go to the cinema and hadn't returned. It was now just after one.

'And they can't reach her?'

'No, they've been trying to reach her all night, her phone's been turned off. We have the tech guys on it now, they're trying to trace it, but the last ping was from a mast in Bath, near the cinema where she said that she would be – nothing since then.'

'Can they trace it without it being turned on?' Nat thought she should know this but now wasn't the time to be coy.

'No,' Tess said, 'they can't.'

'And Carmen, has she ever done anything like this before?'

'No, Rawls says it's completely out of character for her.'

'Do they know anything about the boy, anything that might help?'

'No,' Tess said, 'all we know is that they met at rehearsals.'

'Do we know what she was rehearsing for?'

'Not yet,' she said. 'I'd like you to get on to that as soon as we've finished the briefing.'

'Yes, of course.'

Tess sighed. 'Nat, I have to take him off the case.'

'Rawls? Yes, I thought that you might.'

'Can I trust you?'

Nat was confused. 'Gov?'

'Not to share information with him?'

'I would never,' Nat said, although she wasn't entirely certain that this was true.

'I want you to work with DC Greenhill on social media appeals. She's already been in touch with Lola and they're working on a series of Facebook messages and Tweets, but I would like you involved too.'

Lola, Nat knew, had the somewhat vague title of Senior Project Manager. However, vague or not, Lola was an extremely competent member of staff and all the officers respected her. Nat was glad that she would be advising them on how best to manage publicity. 'Do you expect to find Carmen soon?' she asked Tess.

'Let's hope,' Tess said, 'but in the meantime, we're going to go balls out on this. I want her found as quickly as possible.'

'I'll be at the station in twenty minutes,' Nat said.

'See you then,' Tess said, and hung up.

Rawls had gone straight to the cinema complex; it was the last place that his daughter had been seen and he wanted to be the first to speak to them. He knew from experience that he should not be there; Carmen would have been classified as a missing person from the moment he had reported her not coming home and Rawls would not be allowed to investigate his own daughter's disappearance. In fact, he was fairly certain that he would be removed from the other cases as well. They were too similar, for one thing, but even if they were not thought to be connected, Rawls knew full well that he would be put on leave until further notice. What that might entail, he didn't know but if his concerns proved correct he would be excluded from all investigations, and that was something he could not bear to imagine, so he had called ahead and spoken with Brian, the manager, who was waiting for him now in the lobby.

Brian was a tall man, thin with a ridiculous waxed beard that made him look like he was auditioning for a part in *Peaky Blinders*. The complex, usually bustling with gym goers, swimmers and cinema connoisseurs, looked strange against a backdrop of empty concessions and cold white lights. Brian smiled but did not chat and Rawls thought that he looked tired; his eyes were dark and heavy, his face pale and drawn.

Rawls held his hand out to him. 'Thanks for waiting for me, I can't tell you how much I appreciate your time.'

Brian nodded then smiled. 'That's no trouble at all,' he said, and his voice was slow and deliberate as though he were compensating for something. He reached out and shook Rawls's hand; like his smile, his shake was unexpectedly firm.

'You want to see the CCTV from this evening?' Brian asked, and when Rawls nodded he added, 'May I ask why?'

'I'm so sorry, but we really can't divulge any information at the moment.' Rawls felt a sense of panic. He couldn't tell Brian why he was there – just to mention Carmen's name at that moment was beyond him. He needed to keep his head clear, keep a lid on his emotions for Carmen's sake.

Brian shrugged and smiled with teeth so yellow that they completed his *Peaky Blinders* look. 'No trouble,' he said, 'just being nosy, I guess.' He pointed to a door marked Private. 'It's all through here,' he said, and Rawls followed him into a small back office.

A burly man in a security uniform sat behind a desk cluttered with empty coffee cups and biscuit packets, and he nodded a greeting when they walked in. 'I've got it all cued up ready,' he said, 'from seven p.m., is that correct?'

'For now,' Rawls said, and for a moment he wished that Nat was with him; it was always easier when you were part of a double act. What made it worse was that time was doubly important. He closed his eyes, thinking about the file that Nat would be collating right at the moment; Carmen's details: her name and address, marks and peculiarities, her height and what she would have been wearing. She would be summed up by the details that defined her at that precise moment: time and date of her last sighting, who she had been with, what she took with her, who her friends were, whether she was in a high-risk category – it was all so impersonal. They would be trying to establish whether or not Carmen was in danger or a danger to herself; they would be running her details through various databases, preparing for a time where they might need to compare them to unidentified bodies

He realised that the burly guy was talking; he was explaining that the cameras would play at twice the normal speed.

He asked if they were ready and Rawls nodded. There were three screens, all showing the front entrance. The three of them watched intently as people bustled by, as jerky as an early black and white movie of Laurel and Hardy. Rawls narrowed his eyes, desperate to miss nothing; he leaned forward and held a hand up.

'Stop,' he said, and he tapped the monitor. 'Can you rewind a little, just a few seconds, then pause it for me?'

The burly guy did as he was asked.

Rawls's heart hammered in his chest and his legs felt weak. There, on the screen, was his beautiful daughter. There was Carmen. He steadied himself and when he managed to speak his voice was so dry that he feared he might cough. 'Can you change to normal speed now?' he asked, pressing a hand into the guy's shoulder.

He glanced at Rawls. 'Tell me when you're ready.'

'Ready,' Rawls almost whispered.

The footage rolled again – kids running about, lovers holding hands, teenagers slumping against the walls. Most of the young people there were either in couples or groups; most but not all. Carmen was alone. She paused for a moment at the entrance looking around. She pulled off her wet coat then headed off-screen. The operator paused the frame and looked up at Rawls. 'She'll be heading for the toilet,' he said. 'At least, the girls usually do,' he added in a voice that made Rawls's blood run cold. 'Perhaps they check their make-up in there.' It was a strange job when you thought about it, perfect for a peeping Tom – you were literally paid to watch people.

Rawls nodded. He had to force himself to breathe as they waited to see if Carmen would come back into frame. She did, just a little more than three minutes later. She stopped again, looking around her as though she was scanning the room for someone. Rawls felt a terrible sense of his own inability to protect her. He wanted to turn back time, to be there at that moment, to be watching her in real time, in a time when he could have helped her, could have stopped whatever had happened from happening, could have protected her.

On the screen, he saw Carmen take her phone out, saw her fiddling with it, trying to look cool as she swiped and touched the screen, furtively looking up from time to time as if she was waiting for someone. He saw her look directly at something off camera; she looked down, then up again. She touched her screen, started typing, stopped, put the phone to her ear.

She's trying to call me, Rawls thought. *She's trying to call me, oh Car. Baby, I'm so sorry, I'm so sorry.*

Brian glanced at him briefly, offering him a tight, uncomfortable smile before glancing back at the screen where a woman was now approaching Carmen. Her head was down so that the camera picked up nothing but a red baseball cap and a fuzz of brown hair. As she approached Carmen seemed to shrink against the wall as though she hoped that it would open up and she might be able to escape through it.

Rawls felt a tightness building up in the back of his throat and he swallowed back fearful tears. He wanted to reach out and into that picture, to bat the woman away, flick at her the way that one might flick at a spider or a fly. He felt his own terrible impotence at that moment, his inability to change things. He heard himself shouting at Carmen, informing her that this was the last date that she would be going on until she was either a black belt in karate or willing to carry a rucksack full of pepper-spray. Those would be the only two options – that would be his lecture when she came home, when all of this was over. That would be what he would tell her and Eileen could say what she liked, this time he would put his foot down. He would shout at her and then he would hug her, and then he might just shout at her again. Wasn't that his job? To protect her? Hadn't he promised Eileen that he would love, honour and protect them both, so help him God?

He had made that promise and now he had broken it. He had not been there and, even worse, when she had rung him, asking for his help, he had not been at the end of the phone. He had been selling a bloody car, for God's sake.

Chapter 17

Linda and Nat sat at a shared computer; they were going through a pile of tips that had already come in following a Facebook and Instagram alert. Coccia and Iles were both on the phone, Iles in conversation with a neighbourhood watch member who was certain she had seen Carmen with a bunch of teenage boys who had been breaking a fence adjacent to the park opposite her house sometime after ten that evening, and Coccia was thanking a young man who had called to say that he might have seen Carmen getting on a bus heading out of town, perhaps to Keynsham, maybe Radstock, he couldn't exactly say for sure and come to think of it, he couldn't be entirely certain that it was Carmen, it had looked a bit like her though. Other officers, drafted in to help, were also on the phones, and one stood at the printer trying to work out how to load paper into it.

The five cases were officially linked now, the similarities too many to overlook. The girls were of similar age, had similar features and had gone missing under similar circumstances. Add to that the fact that the daughter of a senior investigating officer had gone missing and it would have been inappropriate not to. Carmen's name would soon become yet another multi-agency collaboration. Her name along with the names of the other missing girls – Melody, Harriet, Yvette, Tanya – would forever be linked by the very worst of circumstances. Child Exploitation and Online Protection Centre, CEOP for short, would be informed, the National Crime Agency would have all five girls' details on their database, there would be appeals made to the public, searches at hospitals, even recent arrests would be cross-referenced. The worst would be assumed until there was proof of anything to the contrary.

It was into this hustle and bustle that Rawls made his way at a little after two in the morning. He had come straight from his trip to the cinema and he had the images on a memory stick. Brian had not questioned him when he had asked for two copies and he had offered no explanation. Tess caught him by the elbow as he stopped to read the screen over Nat's shoulder and walked him into the office that had been his only a few short hours earlier.

'Peter,' she said, 'I didn't expect to see you.'

'I came straight from the cinema.'

Tess turned on him. 'The cinema?'

He tried to ignore the tone in her voice. 'Yes, we needed the footage as quickly as possible, so I went straight there.'

'Rawls,' she said, her face incandescent with rage, 'you had no business going there.'

'No business?' Rawls repeated. 'I had every business being there, Tess.'

'You know the rules,' she said.

'I do.'

'You know that I have to put you back on leave, with immediate effect?'

'I do.'

'You need to hand everything over to DC Chivers.'

'Chivers?' Rawls felt his blood run cold. 'You're putting Chivers in charge of my daughter's case?'

Tess looked at her desk. 'I'm still SIO but we have the four other missing girls; I just need someone that I can trust on the front line looking for Carmen. He knows what he's doing.'

'But Chivers?' Rawls said, biting his tongue, furious. 'Why not Linda?'

'She doesn't have the track record.'

'Chivers only has the track record because he takes the credit for other people's work.' Rawls could barely speak with anger.

'I will be with him all the way,' Tess said, and Rawls made no attempt to hide his contempt.

'I hope you don't think that I am just going to sit on my hands and do nothing.'

'Peter, I understand, I really do, but you know the routine. You need to be at home. Carmen may try to make contact, she might even come home. You need to be there, just in case.'

Rawls would have laughed if the situation hadn't been so dire. Having Chivers and Tess leading the hunt to find his daughter filled him with dread.

'Right now,' Tess said, 'I need you to go home and be with Eileen.'

'And let that cretin take care of finding Carmen? You must be having a laugh.'

'I'm warning you, Rawls.'

'Warn away,' Rawls said, 'warn away as much as you like.' He reached for the door, 'But I'll tell you now, I'm not going home to sit on my hands.'

'Just get some rest at least,' she tried to smile, 'you look terrible.'

Rawls bit down on his lip, trying to contain the anger building up inside him. He had known that he would have to take leave, it went without saying – but putting Chivers in charge? That he had not seen coming. The man was a fool, an incompetent, an arsehole. What was Tess thinking? He stared at her, his legs shaking and his fists clenching until at last he managed to pull in a loud, shaky breath. In his mind's eye he saw himself shouting at her that she was making a big mistake, bellowing that Craig Chivers was the wrong person, that he was not ready for a case this important, screaming at her that if she thought he would stand back while that buffoon looked for his daughter she had another think coming.

He didn't, though, he just stood there, furious, holding the door handle until Tess spoke.

'Peter,' she was holding a pen in her hand and using her thumb to depress then release the button on top over and over as though she were trying to communicate with him in Morse code. 'You need to do your best to keep it together. Don't let the stress build up, not like before.' Her voice was flat, emotionless; it irritated him.

He straightened his back, thrusting his feet into the floor as if he were grounding himself. 'I'm alright,' he said, his voice shaking. He let the rage go, but only a little, then managed to smile weakly. 'Sorry. It's just …'

'I know what it is,' she said. 'Just go home, get some rest, be with Eileen. Rawls, listen, we're on it.'

He nodded. The mist in his head had passed and he felt stupid and desperate and exhausted. 'OK,' he said and pushed the handle down.

Tess stopped him. 'The footage, Peter, from the CCTV.' She held her hand out and he turned towards her, removing it from his jacket and placing the memory stick in the palm of her hand.

She touched his shoulder. 'We might all be worrying over nothing. You might get home and find her there. We're assuming the worst, that's what we do, but it might be entirely unrelated, you know that.'

He closed his eyes. 'Yeah, you're right.' He paused, his hand still on the door handle. 'Tess, will you be holding a briefing in the morning?'

'At ten a.m., yes.'

'Could I come in?'

She looked away from him for a moment. 'You might be helpful,' she said slowly, 'but you would need to understand that you are no longer part of active enquiries.'

He nodded. 'It's just so important, in this early stage, that we consolidate, get all the facts straight. It will save time in the long run.'

'OK, be here at ten,' she relented, 'but this will be the last time that I can involve you – you know that, don't you?'

'I do,' he said, 'and thank you.'

The house was quiet when he walked in. He felt more tired than he ever had in his life before. Eileen came out of the kitchen, her face pale and desperate. He wanted to wrap her in his arms, but she nodded a greeting and turned towards the stairs.

'I think I need to get some sleep,' she said, 'I can't think straight.'

He knew how she felt. His body was all but vibrating from exhaustion, his eyes felt dry and he found it difficult to concentrate and, when he spoke, he could hear the slur in his speech. He followed her into the dark, and they sat on the bed together. The room felt too hot, airless, like it was swallowing him. He touched her hands and she turned to face him, tears wet on her cheeks.

'I don't know what to do,' he said – because he didn't.

'Me neither,' Eileen whispered back.

'We should sleep, you're right,' he said. 'Have you been out all night?'

'Jo drove me around. She got someone to drop my car back as well, in case we needed it.'

Rawls prickled at the name. Jo and Eileen had been friends for years and Rawls had never really understood why. She was the kind of woman who managed to make everyone else around her feel somehow inferior. She was also extremely wealthy, and although Rawls did not begrudge her that, the manner in which she managed to flaunt it at every opportunity drove him close to crazy. On the other hand, she had been on the doorstep within minutes of Eileen's call and had held her in her arms in a way that even Rawls had not been able to. 'Where did you go?' he asked her.

'We didn't know what to do so we just drove around for a while and then we stopped and just walked around. We went everywhere I could think of.' He could hear the desperation in her voice.

'And you called her friends?'

'As many as I could, some didn't answer.'

'Did they know who this guy was? The one she was meeting?'

She turned to him, her face a grey silhouette in the shadows. 'The ones I spoke to, none of them know who this boy was. She hadn't mentioned it, that's what they said, that she hadn't mentioned a date. Who the hell is he? Oh, Pete, I should have checked, should have asked for more information. I didn't think. He might be ...' She broke off, sobbing, and he pulled her to him.

'You weren't to know.'

'But I should have, I should have.'

He let her cry, his hand rubbing her back.

She spoke into his shoulder, 'Are they looking for him?'

'They're looking at everything,' he said.

She started crying again. 'I don't know what I'm supposed to do, Pete. I keep thinking about the other girls. Is she now one of them now, is she the fifth girl?' Her voice caught in her throat. 'Will she be missing forever, like them?'

Rawls looked away, a lump in his own throat making it impossible to answer her. He tried to visualise himself in his day job: Detective Sergeant Rawls, finder of lost children, investigator of violent crimes. What would he say to this woman? What would his advice be as she sat sobbing in the dark? Go to bed, get some rest, let us look for your daughter? Of course he would – it came out easy, almost casually. 'You go home, put your feet up, watch some telly, let us take care of finding her.' God, he wondered, what kind of people could sleep with their daughter missing, what kind of people even went to bed with their daughter missing?

'You have to sleep,' he heard Eileen say as if she had read his mind. 'We both do. We've got to keep our strength up. We have to find her, Pete, you and me.'

He kept his hand pressed to her back, he could feel her trembling against it. After a while he realised that she was drifting into a fitful sleep and he lowered her to the bed where he lay down beside her, his arm across her waist.

He climbed out of bed little more than a couple of hours later, the room still dark, rain beating against the windows. Beside him the bed was empty; Eileen must have woken while he'd been asleep.

Across the hall, Carmen's bedroom door was ajar, and a band of warm light fell across the carpet. His heart did a double take in his chest. Could Carmen be home? If it was Carmen, she wasn't going to hear the last of this. He would literally go bonkers, then he would hug her and hug her and make her promise never to do that to them again. He heard the words in his mind, heard Carmen saying sorry, heard Eileen telling her that sorry wasn't enough, telling her to listen to her father, that they had been beside themselves, that she needed to understand exactly what they had gone through. In his mind he heard all of this almost as clearly as if it had been real; he pushed the door and looked inside.

Eileen sat on the bed, her back slumped, her hands folded and empty in her lap; crying silently. She looked at Rawls as he walked in and her pleading expression was almost too much for him.

He crossed the room and sat down beside her, resting an arm on her shoulders. They didn't speak but instead sat that way for several minutes, both of them crying, both of them powerless to do anything else.

'You didn't manage to tell me what happened after you left last night,' Eileen said eventually.

'I went to the cinema.'

She frowned. 'To look for Car?'

He shrugged. 'To look for her and to get a look at the CCTV footage before they put me on leave.'

'Are you off the other cases, then?'

'I'm on leave for the time being.'

'Who's in charge of looking for Carmen?'

'Tess is SIO but Chivers is doing the legwork,' he said, hiding his doubts at the man's capability.

'What did you get from the cinema? Did you see her? Did you see him? This boyfriend, oh God, Pete, did you see him?'

Rawls rubbed at his tired eyes then leaned back and looked at the ceiling as he spoke, unwilling to meet his wife's eyes. 'I saw Carmen,' he said.

'So, she's OK?'

He looked at her briefly. 'She was fine when she was there, but there was no boyfriend.'

She stared him. 'I don't understand. He took her, didn't he? This boy – who else?'

He closed his eyes and described Carmen waiting, the woman heading towards her, touching her arm.

'Touching her arm or taking it?' Eileen asked, holding her hand to her throat.

It was a good question. 'I think she took Carmen's wrist.'

'Then?'

'They talked for about a minute, a little less actually, then Carmen put her hand to her mouth as though she was upset.'

'Upset?' Rawls saw a tremble in her chin, but she got it back under control. 'Like she was going to cry?'

Rawls shook his head. 'I couldn't tell, the footage isn't brilliant.'

'Did she leave with this woman?'

Rawls nodded. 'They walked off together; the woman had her arm around her.'

Eileen covered her face and closed her eyes; he heard her breathing behind her fingers, slow and rhythmic as if she was trying to get herself under control. 'What happens now?' she asked.

'Now I'm pretty certain they'll arrange a search. There'll be a press conference, we'll be invited. They'll appeal for witnesses, urge the public to come forward, ask anyone if they recognise the woman, that sort of thing.'

'Peter?'

Rawls looked at his hands; he knew what she was about to ask.

'Peter, look at me.'

He looked up.

'Do you think she was targeted because of who you are, because of your involvement? Do you think that's why she was taken?'

He took her hand. 'I don't know, hon. To be honest, we don't even know that the other four are linked.'

'But?'

'But I think they are.'

She picked up a jumper from the end of the bed and held it up to her face. 'And Carmen?'

'Maybe.'

'Oh God,' her voice cracked. 'Oh Pete, say no. Say no way, they're entirely different, say anything but maybe. Please.'

Rawls stared out of the window. 'I wish I could.'

They sat that way for a while, Rawls watching rain trickle down the window and Eileen smelling her daughter's jumper. It was as though they were in mourning, as though they had lost her already.

Rawls roused himself. 'Listen, I'm going to go in to the office, one last time, for the morning briefing.'

'I thought you were off the case?'

'I am, but I'm going in to go through what I have so far.'

Eileen closed her eyes.

'You'll be OK? I mean, Jo will be here soon, won't she?' Eileen nodded, and he kissed her. 'I'll be as quick as I can.'

Chapter 18

There was a peculiar feeling in the office that morning. To an outsider, it would look as though nothing was wrong. People were going about their mornings, hunched over monitors, others on their phones, some turning pages in folders; all of them looked busy. It was like the old saying, '*Look busy, Jesus is coming*,' but to Rawls it felt as though they had replaced the word Jesus with Rawls: *Look busy, Rawls is Coming*. Most said nothing as he passed, keeping their eyes down and avoiding contact, but a couple of them nodded or frowned; one PC, a girl Rawls recognised but could not actually name, briefly touched his shoulder and he felt a wash of gratitude at the gesture. He knew they would be dedicating every spare moment to helping him now. Nothing cut an officer of the law deeper than knowing that one of their own had been hurt. It moved Rawls in a way that he had not expected.

Tess, Nat and the rest of the group were waiting for him in the conference room; he had called ahead to let them know what time he would be in and to check that it was still OK. Tess had said that they would share what they could.

The group had grown since he last met with them. Tess had freed up a few more bods, it seemed, when the missing girl was one of their own. Rawls wasn't going to complain; now was not the time for moral theatrics. He felt a surge of emotion as they turned to greet him, a kind of camaraderie written across their faces. Nat leaned forward as though to stand but Tess was already moving.

'Rawls,' she said, gripping his elbow and guiding him to a chair with the skill of a practised Tango partner, 'you look bloody awful.'

Rawls managed to smile. He had needed someone to break the tension and he felt grateful to her. 'Sorry,' he said, 'no time for make-up.'

Tess tried to smile then nodded at Nat. 'Let's catch Rawls up on where we are now and then let him give us a debrief on the earlier cases. This should help us determine how best to proceed. In the meantime, I'll grab him a coffee.' She clacked her way across the tiled floor and Rawls noticed the exchanged glances around the room. Tess was making Rawls coffee – bloody hell, who knew that she knew where the kitchen was? She returned minutes later and put a cup in front of him before addressing the room. 'As you all know, our missing girl is Carmen Rawls, DS Rawls's daughter. In light of this it has been decided that DS Rawls is not best placed to lead the investigation.'

Rawls tried to look positive. 'For my benefit as well as the case,' he said.

Tess glanced across the room at Chivers and Rawls felt his stomach clench. 'DC Chivers and I have reviewed the CCTV footage and we are certain that Carmen has not gone missing of her own volition. However, we are not yet entirely convinced that this case is linked to the older ones.'

Chivers nodded his agreement as though he had given Tess permission to speak. Rawls kept his eyes down, making notes on a crumpled notepad; he wanted to argue but was afraid of what he might say.

Tess seemed not to notice. She turned to Nat. 'So, Nat, what have you got so far?'

'We're applying for phone records,' Nat said, 'and, just to be certain, we've notified hospitals and local constabularies.'

'What about CCTV around the cinema, are we working on that yet?'

Nat looked at a couple of uniform. 'We're heading off this morning,' the taller of the two said. He was bald and probably in his fifties. Rawls liked guys like him; they stayed on the beat because they felt that was where they could make the most difference. They were usually salt of the earth coppers, the good guys who were in it for the right reasons. Looking at this one, Rawls saw no reason to think he might be any different. Rawls tried to focus on this, tried to use it to calm himself.

Nat went on, 'We're also hoping to get CCTV from all the car parks. If someone drove off with her, we should be able to find them and hopefully get the vehicle reg to run through ANPR.'

Tess thanked her then said, 'Peter, do you want to give us the rundown on where you were at on the older cases?'

Rawls cleared his throat, he felt like he had something caught there. 'I think it would be worth re-evaluating the links between all five girls,' he said.

Tess tapped her pen against her lips but said nothing. Beside her Chivers had folded his arms above his belly. 'Care to elaborate?' he said.

Rawls tried not to look at him, seeing that fat smirking face might make him do something he would regret. 'We have five girls, all aged between fifteen and seventeen.'

Chivers leaned forward. 'The other four were sixteen and seventeen. Carmen is the anomaly here, she is fifteen, she doesn't fit with the pattern.'

Rawls bit his lip. 'Then there is the similarity in their appearance.'

It was Tess who challenged him this time. 'Rawls, you said yourself that they all look similar when they are this age.'

'Also, Chivers added, 'the timescales are all wrong. There were long gaps between the first four girls' disappearances, weren't there?'

Rawls pulled in a long breath, trying to calm himself before he answered. 'Yes, there were, I grant you that.'

Chivers nodded to himself as if to confirm that he was always correct. 'A minimum of three years between each, four between Yvette in Tanya if I'm not mistaken.'

Rawls felt himself crumple. 'You're not mistaken.'

'But you want us to believe that the perpetrator suddenly changed his method of operation at the last minute? Why?'

'Perhaps he targeted me?' Rawls said with no conviction; he had only just joined the team and this seemed unlikely even to him.

Chivers frowned as if he was considering this. 'Alright, let's assume that it's the same guy, it still doesn't clear up the issue with the profile.'

Rawls looked at Tess. 'The profile?'

Tess nodded. 'On the earlier girls, we have the offender profile now.' She looked at Chivers who pulled a report out and spread it in front of him.

'Came over this morning, mate. The suggestion is that if the four earlier cases are linked, and it is still just an if, then we are looking for a white male, between twenty-five and thirty-five years of age, probably unemployed which allows him to live a transitory life giving him time to stalk his victims. He is likely to have acted alone.' He put the report down, took off his glasses and laid them on top of it. 'Your Carmen was taken by a woman,' he said as if he needed to remind Rawls.

Rawls adjusted himself in his seat and addressed his comments to Tess; he thought that if he so much as looked at Chivers he might lose his shit. 'Tess, this profile is wrong. It must have been prepared before I came on board, I haven't had any input into it. The guy could be simply self-employed which would have given him the time to stalk them; he might have taken others which might explain the timescales, he might have—'

Tess held a hand up. 'Rawls we have to trust the data and you have to trust us to do our jobs.'

Rawls felt panic in his chest, he could barely breathe. 'The others were taken without a single eye-witness. They were all alone when they disappeared, they could have been taken by a woman, it would be less likely to be noticed by a casual passer-by and the girls all—'

'Rawls,' Chivers stood up, 'mate, I want to find Carmen as much as you do. You know me, I get results.'

Rawls couldn't argue, Chivers did get results, on paper anyway, what nobody was saying was that he also always had someone else with him, someone else guiding him. He was being single-minded. Rawls thought he might even be trying to prove him wrong. How could he find Carmen that way? If he refused to listen, refused to see what was in front of his fat face? He looked at Linda Greenhill. 'Lin, what do you think?'

Linda glanced at Tess. 'I think Craig's right, Pete, I think the cases might not be as closely linked as you see them.'

Rawls looked around the room, no one met his eye. He was suddenly very alone. Shit, they weren't listening to him and even worse, they should be further ahead than this, speed was of the essence in this kind of situation. Right now the last sighting of his daughter had been at a little past seven on Friday evening and they were sat around arguing about a bloody perp's profile. They should be doing more, for God's sake, way more, way more. He closed his eyes and counted to ten. Somewhere in the room he could hear Tess talking about finding the missing boyfriend: who was he? Why had he not appeared at the cinema? Who was the woman? Were they connected? He let her voice wash over him, unable to concentrate, unable to take it in. He knew that he needed to let the anger go. It was pointless, he couldn't alienate them now, no matter how inept he thought they were. He heard Tess dismiss the group and was vaguely aware of them leaving, filing past him with a hand on his shoulder or a touch on his arm. They thought he was losing it, they would all be talking about him later, how he couldn't let it go, how he wouldn't trust the evidence. They would probably all feel grateful for him not being around, he would be a hindrance after all.

The door closed and he realised that only Nat and Tess were still in the room with him.

Tess said, 'Are you OK, Peter?'

'I'm fine, just tired,' he lied.

'I know you're unhappy having Chivers on Carmen's case.'

Rawls stared at her for a few seconds. 'No, it's fine, honestly, I'm just tired.'

She studied him for a moment. 'And you know this is the last time that I can let you in? You are now officially to stand down. Do you understand?'

He nodded – there was little point in arguing. They weren't going to find her, he knew that. He would just have to find Carmen himself.

Rawls left the station and turned right on to the A36, heading past the new trading estates; drab but somehow enticing in the misty air. On his left the old railway arches, red brick in sharp contrast to Bath's usual oolitic limestone, seemed to watch him with sullen disinterest as he passed. He had intended to drive straight home but his head was still spinning. He was tired and emotional, feeling the stress of Carmen's disappearance almost as though it was a physical object. He arrived home a little after one – he had been driving for well over an hour, maybe longer.

'Peter?' Eileen's voice was shrill as she emerged from the kitchen.

He kissed her briefly then, seeing Jo over her shoulder, nodded a greeting.

'Have you checked your phone?' Eileen asked.

He patted his coat. 'I think it's in the car.'

'Tess rang. She's been trying to reach you – she said that you left them a couple of hours ago. There's going to be a search this afternoon.'

Rawls ignored the implied question. 'What time?'

'Two. You need to get changed. I've got our walking boots and coats out already.' Eileen pointed to the front door where a pile of coats, boots and hats waited for them like an invitation to a hiking party.

Jo asked if he wanted a coffee and he thanked her as he walked up the stairs.

'I've made you a sandwich as well,' Eileen shouted after him, her voice urgent. 'Hurry, Pete, we don't want to be late.'

A small crowd had gathered in the car park not far from Royal Victoria Park. They huddled together chatting in small groups; to Rawls they looked the way a crowd must have looked in the days when they still hanged people at the scene of their crimes, excited and expectant.

He thought about the four missing girls. Two days ago they had been his first priority; today they were little more than a memory. Today he had one focus, one priority: Carmen. If she had been taken, there was still time to find her. It might be too late to find the others, but not for Carmen, not yet.

He looked around, searching the crowd, looking for Tess, Nat or Chivers. He couldn't see them and he intended to do his best to keep it that way. Tess had been clear that he was to leave things to them, to keep out of the investigation; she hadn't been rude but she had been firm about the point. Now, seeing two young girls that he recognised from school visits for parents' evenings and school plays, Rawls headed towards them.

He greeted them and they both looked sombre. 'You're Carmen's dad, aren't you?' the taller of the two asked him after he had introduced himself.

'I am,' he said, 'are you friends of hers?' It was funny, Rawls thought, how you knew less and less about your children as they grew into adolescence. It wasn't that they were secretive or that you were uninterested; it was simply that they found lives of their own.

'We're in Carmen's tutor group,' the tall girl said, 'but not in many of her classes.'

The short one took over. 'We're in drama class with her as well.'

Rawls paused. 'Drama? At school, you mean?'

They nodded together, 'And after.'

'After, what do you mean?'

They looked at each other briefly. 'Oh, for the play. We know her from rehearsals, that's all. We really liked her, you know?'

Rawls felt the past tense in her sentence like a punch in the gut. Liked, not like. Shit, they all thought she was dead already; they'd all given up on her.

'What play is this, then?' he asked, feeling again that tug of distance between him and his daughter who had grown more and more independent by the day.

'We're doing *Pygmalion*.'

He remembered then and nodded. 'Oh yes, of course. I think she mentioned a boy – do you know who that might have been? Did she mention a boyfriend or look like she was interested in anyone in particular?'

They looked at each other, shaking their heads simultaneously. 'No, sorry, like we said, we didn't really know her that well.'

'But we could let you know if we think of anything.'

Rawls smiled. 'That would be great.' He handed them a card and watched them walking away.

Later, when it was all over, they regrouped back at the car park. Rawls was exhausted. They'd walked for what felt like miles; people had looked in sheds, beneath bushes, behind and inside wheelie bins; they had knocked on doors and handed out flyers. A drone had been sent up ahead of the crowd and its whining engine had been their constant companion throughout the afternoon, marking their progress as it zig-zagged in tight formation around the parks close to the cinema.

Every bone in Rawls's body ached, his head throbbed, and his feet felt as though someone had taken a baton to them. He spotted Eileen and Jo at the edge of the park; Jo holding Eileen's arm as though she was afraid that her friend might collapse to the ground at any moment. They were hugging a group of women, each one pausing to hold Eileen's hand. Rawls felt his heart might break. How had they come to this? His daughter had homework to do, they had a holiday booked for the summer, his wife went to Zumba for God's sake – this sort of thing couldn't happen to them. He jogged a few paces, his feet screaming at him to stop, and joined the group.

Jo greeted him with a thin, tight smile and Rawls thought he saw a glimmer of accusation. 'You didn't find the others', that smile said, 'and now look at what's happened. This is all on you.'

Eileen hugged him. It was warm and desperate and for the time being, it held no resentment, just exhaustion, and despair perhaps, but not anger, not blame – not yet.

'Oh, Pete,' she said into his chest.

Rawls held her, feeling the tiny convulsions of grief pulsing through her body. He pulled her in tightly as though the very act of holding her might help to steady them. He could hardly bear it. Jo was right: this was on him. He should have found the others; he had to find Carmen.

He kissed the top of her head and her hair smelled of apples and chemicals.

Across the road, he saw Tess talking to Nat; Tess raised a hand towards him then made a dismissing motion. The movement was somehow both irritated and caring, and Rawls wished, once more, that he could read her better. She made an exasperated face at him. 'Go home,' she mouthed, 'rest.'

He nodded back. She was right, he did need rest, they both did. In his arms, Eileen felt small and feeble, as though someone had filled her clothes with loosely packed flour. 'Let's get you home,' he said, and she complied, holding on to him the way that a small, tired child might hold its parent's hand after a long day at the park.

They walked back in silence, down Royal Avenue and towards Queen Square where he had left the car. The tree-lined road, usually so elegant in its Georgian formality, seemed somehow to leer in at them, as though the trees wished, not to protect them, but, instead, to hinder them by obscuring their view.

Jo walked beside them, and Rawls was, as usual, irritated by her presence. It wasn't that he didn't appreciate her being there, but then again, perhaps it was. Jo was like a shadow in their relationship lately, an unwelcome third wheel – unwelcome by Rawls anyway. He didn't like Jo. He couldn't help it, she was just a little too testy and spiteful and, even worse, too quick to crack open a bottle of wine to help them to 'de-stress' after a long day, or a long week, or a long Zumba class, or pretty much a long whatever. The way that Rawls saw it, if Jo could label something as 'long', she could use it as an opportunity to open another bottle.

Eileen looked up at Rawls; her face was pale and dark shadows pooled beneath her bloodshot eyes. 'Do you think anything came out of it?' she asked. 'Do you have any idea of what to do next?'

Rawls felt the desperation in her question and he wished, not for the first time, that he had more to offer. He had never felt so helpless in his life.

They were walking again, and the sun was doing its best to break free of the grey. The puddles on the pavement glinted with harsh white light, and the three of them had to squint a little against the sudden brightness. As they walked, Rawls found himself searching the face of every passing pedestrian and scanning every car. It was something he had done many times before but never with such attention to detail. He wasn't sure what it was that he hoped to see in these people as they went about their daily business: signs of guilt maybe? His daughter in disguise? One of the other girls, grown up now, a member of a cult?

'Peter?' Eileen pressed him, jolting him back to himself. 'Do you think anything has come out of the search?'

Rawls hesitated. He knew that a great deal would have come out of the morning's search, much of which would need to be considered and discussed so that they could form a plan. He also knew that the guys from CEOP would be putting their two pennies' worth in and he wished that he could be there to hear it.

But the search had been fruitful for him as well. Walking and talking had a surprising way of relaxing people, getting them to open up to him, to remember. He had spoken to friends of all five of the girls, people just wanting to help; he'd spoken with teachers, with friends of their parents; he'd had chats with people who thought they might have seen something or who had theories on what had happened. Some thought they had run away from home, others that they had been taken and held hostage; most that they did not expect them to be found alive. He would not say this to Eileen.

She was watching him. 'Well?'

He shook his head. 'Not yet.'

He looked, first at his wife and then at Jo, who raised an eyebrow. 'A lot of people were talking about that cult again,' she said.

'It's not a cult any more, Jo,' Rawls corrected her, 'it's a retreat, for rich people.'

Jo gave him an acid stare. She and her husband, Nathan, were rich people and they were also the kind of rich people who would go to a retreat. Jo had, in fact, gone away on many a mission to find her true self: to Devon, Pembrokeshire, even India a couple of years ago, and Rawls was pretty certain that she would be right at home in a place like Stoney Barrow View.

'Peter,' she said, suddenly earnest, 'it might call itself a retreat but it's not. It's strange and, before you ask, yes, I have been there. Nathan and I went there for a bank holiday weekend. It was a mess – they were having some sort of landscaping done on the land adjacent to the property and there were excavators everywhere. We were so angry that we wrote to the owner,' she turned to Eileen, 'do you remember?'

'Yes, didn't they fob you off?'

Jo nodded. 'They did, they told me that the land adjacent to them was not their responsibility and suggested I contact their neighbours. I mean, honestly, as if I should be the one sorting their issues for them! The letter we got back was outright aggressive – you'd have thought that we were the ones in the wrong. They all but told me to mind my own business!'

She looked as though she had forgotten the reason they were there, that Eileen and Rawls were hunting for their daughter. 'Of course I took it up with them,' she went on, full throttle now. 'I told them that if you're going to run a place of healing in Bath of all places, you really must make every effort to make it the best that it can be. You simply cannot have a building site right next door to you. I visited the Thermae Bath Spa when it opened – when was that? 2006? 2007?' She shook her head. 'Doesn't matter, but that place knew how to look after their guests and they would never have tolerated a mess like that. At the very least it should have been screened off. For heaven's sake, Bath has been healing people since the Romans, and even before that the bloody locals were popping their offerings into the waters for Sulis to heal them! It's not like we don't have a reputation to keep up.'

Rawls imagined the letter that she and Nathan would have sent, full of self-righteous indignation about how important their lives were and how much income they had lost as a direct result of having to look at the muddy mess without a proper screen. He might have laughed if the circumstances had been different.

'They flatly refused to reimburse us, let alone compensate us. Honestly, I was furious. The owner was just hideous.' Jo walked on for a moment, looking off into the distance. 'What was his name? I can't quite remember.'

'Sebastian?' Rawls suggested.

He thought about his recent visit, the landscaping that he'd noticed. He'd also thought that it should be screened off, that it was a mess. 'When was this, Jo?'

She considered, counting on her fingers. 'Two, maybe three years ago now; I can ask Nathan when I speak to him.'

Rawls was thinking about the excavators he'd seen when he had visited Stoney Barrow with Nat. Sebastian had told them then that the people who owned the adjacent land were putting in some kind of lake. Could they still be working on the same thing, after all these years?

Jo was saying that she would call Nathan as soon as she could. He was flying in from somewhere, Rawls hadn't heard where, but would be home soon.

'Do you want me to come in?' Jo was holding Eileen's hand.

'No, we're OK. Thanks so much for today,' Eileen hugged her, 'you are my rock.'

Rawls thanked Jo and unlocked the front door. Rock was one word for her – he could think of a couple of others.

Their bedroom might have been taken from the pages of a magazine: antique white walls, a fern on a stand, a dressing table, wardrobe and bed in a French style that Rawls had often joked would not have been out of place in the Palace of Versailles. Lace curtains hung listlessly in the windows, still as a burial shroud in the airless room.

Eileen had fallen into a fitful and restless sleep a few minutes after they had climbed wearily into bed, and Rawls took comfort in the sound of her breathing. He looked at his phone: just after ten p.m. He wondered if it was too late to call Tess. He unlocked it and swiped the screen, his finger hovering briefly over her number. He had titled her contact *Ma'am* and, feeling suddenly churlish, he pressed the details button and changed it to *Tess*. Somehow, sarcasm had lost its charm.

He saved the changes then slipped quietly out of bed, pausing for a moment at the door to listen to his wife. She snored gently then whimpered briefly, like a child having a nightmare, and he closed his eyes as though doing so might block out the sound, then turned and headed, barefoot, along the corridor.

Rawls needed to work.

Nat answered on the second ring. 'I knew you'd be calling,' she said.

'Creature of habit, I guess,' Rawls said. 'I can't sleep, Nat, I've got to do something.'

'We're on it right now,' Nat said. 'I'm still at the office, we all are.'

When Rawls spoke his voice was little more than a whisper, 'I can't tell you how grateful I am.'

'We're going to do everything we can,' Nat said. 'Tess calls it clearing the ground beneath our feet.'

Rawls smiled despite himself; he could almost hear Tess saying it. He asked about what they were focusing on and Nat filled him in. They exchanged ideas, then he said, 'Are you looking at the retreat at all?'

There was a pause before Nat answered. 'It's not high on the list. Tess seems to think that it's a dead end.'

Rawls rubbed the base of his back. 'I thought you might say that. In that case, do you think you could do me a favour? Can you dig around and see if you can find out who sold Stoney Barrow View?'

'The land or the retreat?'

'Both,' he said. He remembered their first trip out. It seemed like a million years ago now. 'Thanks for helping, Nat,' he said, 'I really appreciate it.'

He cut the call and slid down the cold hallway wall to the floor beneath him. He cried into his knees, the muffled sound like an animal caught in a trap. He cried until he heard his wife at the top of the stairs.

'Pete, come to bed,' she said, her voice almost a plea, 'please.'

He did, and they both cried, holding on to each other like passengers on a sinking ship, until they fell asleep at last.

In the morning, Eileen made them both breakfast. Rawls had wanted to rush off, but she had insisted and now he was glad. Sitting with her at the table, a bowl of steaming porridge in front of each of them, he felt a quiet sense of calm.

'She's not dead,' Eileen said, looking into her coffee.

Rawls struggled for a response.

'Peter, we have to find her. She's not dead. I'd know if she was. I know she's alive, I feel it, I feel her.' Eileen looked at him with an urgency that seemed to reach across the table and grab him, but her voice was calm and almost conversational. Rawls guessed they had done all their crying the night before.

'OK,' he said, 'then it's my job to find her.'

Eileen nodded. 'I'm going to stop drinking,' she said.

Rawls said nothing.

'I know you know,' she said. 'I know you look in the recycling; you pretend you're all dismayed at how much rubbish we create but I know you're counting.'

He made a sound as though he was going to argue but his heart wasn't in it; this was no time for lying. Eileen had been drinking too much, he knew that, he just hadn't known what to do about it. Now, however, with Carmen missing, it didn't feel like the right time to have the conversation. He took a sip of his tea and looked at his wife.

'I'm going to stop right now,' she said, and a single tear cut a line down her cheek. She looked up at Rawls, her eyes desperate for him to believe her, as though her not drinking might be the penance she had to do to get her daughter back, as though perhaps God would look down on her and declare her worthy of the return of her child if only she could leave the Merlot alone.

Rawls licked his lips and nodded. 'Good,' he said, because he had nothing else. He took a mouthful of his porridge and it stuck briefly in the back of his throat as he tried to swallow it. He stretched his hand across the table and took his wife's. 'I do love you,' he said.

'I know you do,' she said, and they sat in silence, holding hands.

'Is Jo coming over this morning?' Rawls asked a few minutes later.

Eileen paused and looked up from the dishwasher, a cup in her hand. She stared at Rawls for a moment before a weak smile cracked itself across her face. 'God, I hope not.'

'Oh, I thought she was supporting you.' Rawls pronounced 'supporting' as though it was a rude word.

Eileen put the cup in the dishwasher. 'So does she,' she said. 'Pete, I just want to be left alone for a bit, I don't know how to tell her.'

He considered this for a moment. He understood because he too wanted to be alone – it helped him think, plan, work things out – but Eileen, he wasn't so sure that she should be. She had flat out refused to have a support officer in the house, and he had agreed to that only because she had Jo. 'Babe,' he said taking her elbow and pulling her away from the dishwasher, 'I can't leave you here alone. I just can't. If it's not Jo then it has to be a liaison officer.'

She stared at him for what felt like the longest time. Her eyes were wide and held a little note of crazy in them again, her hair was pulled back into a loose ponytail and strands of wiry curls fell around her neck and across her face. She looked exactly what she was: a woman on the brink. He could see that she was going to argue with him, to tell him that she was fine, she needed to think, or rest or to clean the house, but even as she opened her mouth to say it, she closed it again and sighed.

'Fine,' she said, 'I'll text her and tell her to come over when she's dropped the kids off.'

Her face crumpled. Rawls knew why, he felt the same urge to cry. It was the idea of dropping the kids off: so simple, a daily chore, an annoyance, a trek through queues of traffic, battling drivers who couldn't drive, shouting at roundabouts, trying to speak to sullen children who stared out of the window with as little interest in you as they would have in a maths exam, of pausing in traffic and quickly signing homework books, of arranging collection points and remembering after-school activities. It was hideous and stressful, but in that moment, Rawls knew that, like him, Eileen would give just about anything to say those words, 'I'm just dropping Carmen off, see you in a bit.' He wrapped his arms around her and kissed her warm neck. She was breathing heavily, and he realised with a sudden wash of sadness that her breath smelled of alcohol.

Chapter 19

In a distinct contrast to the Georgian splendour of the city centre, the concrete monstrosity that was home to Bath Constabulary was bleak and foreboding. Nat often thought that the architect had perhaps been given a brief that started with the words 'make it ugly', and if so, she mused, he or she had succeeded. Bath didn't have a proper nick, all arrests still had to go to Keynsham for processing but the nondescript building just off the A36 served as office space for them. Inside smelled of detergent and polish, deodorant and stale air; it was the kind of place that nobody chose to come to unless they absolutely had to and the building itself seemed petulant and sulky, unhappy with its lot. She brushed past the green felt boards pinned with notices, calling out hello to a couple of uniforms, and grabbed a quick tea. Then, with the sound of her trainers squeaking along the polished floor making themselves into an odd tune in her head, she tapped on the door to DI Tess McGovern's office. It was funny, she thought, as she waited, that only a few days ago, ten at the most, she had been terrified off Tess. The DI had fixed her with a gaze that bored beneath the surface, that felt intrusive, probing. The reality had, so far, proven to be somewhat less unpleasant. Tess was terse and to the point – some might say blunt and almost rude at times – but mostly, Nat had come to realise, she was simply driven to get the job done. She was short on words and occasionally on explanation, but that, Nat was beginning to understand, was because to Tess, time was of the essence. Nat had found that she liked it. She liked being given an instruction and simply getting on with it, no questions, no arguments. Nat not only knew her place in the pecking order but was happy with it.

This morning was different, though. The door to Tess's office was opened by Chivers. Tess was on the phone and she held a finger up to signal that she would not be long. Nat took a seat and Chivers sat himself on the edge of the desk facing her.

She pulled out a notebook, trying to ignore Chivers who was pretending to look at something on his phone. God, he made her uncomfortable. She wondered what he would make of the conversations that she'd had with Rawls the night before, and for a moment she feared that they might somehow already know. Perhaps that was why she was here, perhaps it was just to give her a warning or to take her off the case.

Tess smiled, made a gesture to demonstrate that the person on the other end of the phone wouldn't stop talking and then showed them five fingers. Chivers nodded, moved himself from the corner of the desk and took a chair opposite Nat's.

Nat stared at her notepad and thought back to the night before, to the conversation with Rawls. She had told him that Tess and Chivers had come up with two initial objectives. The first was to find out who the woman was in the CCTV, the one seen walking out of the cinema with Carmen. They had talked for some time about the woman's demeanour, and how she seemed so rehearsed, as if that had not been her first time. Rawls had asked her about the rest of the CCTV footage that they had gathered so far and she had filled him on what they now knew about Carmen's movements; how the woman had turned right out of the cinema, passing Bath College, where she had headed towards Kingsmead. Rawls thought that would be a good place to leave the car and Nat had agreed, and she'd told him that they were working on getting traffic camera data in an attempt to locate the vehicle and its movement and that she would let him know what they found. Even then she'd wondered what on earth she thought she was playing at. Now, in the cold light of day, she realised just how stupid she had been.

She all but cringed now at the memory. Her conversation with Rawls had worried her all through the night, waking her with the sound of her own voice in her mind, the sound of her giving information to Rawls that she had had absolutely no business sharing with him. Dear God, if Tess found out . . .

Chivers clapped his hands together, making her jump. 'Wakey, wakey,' he said.

Nat flushed. 'Sorry, I was just thinking.'

'Ooh,' said Chivers, 'careful now, we wouldn't want you to strain yourself.' He grinned as if to demonstrate that it was a joke, letting her know that she was overly sensitive if she thought otherwise. He continued, 'I need you to fill me in on the past couple of days. I'll need a report by lunchtime, everything you and Rawls discussed on the case so far.'

Tess had ended the call and Nat looked at her. 'I thought our focus was on finding Carmen?'

'It is,' Chivers said before Tess could respond, 'but we still have four other missing girls. Also, I'd like you to look into Carmen's social media a little more, see what you can dig up. Who did she speak to, what about this boyfriend?'

Nat glanced at Tess again. She didn't like taking orders from Chivers, but Tess nodded agreement.

'Rawls wanted me to take a look at the retreat,' she said, choosing her words carefully, 'you know, find out who owns the place, have a look at them in more detail.'

'There's nothing more to be gleaned from that place for the time being,' Chivers said, 'and in case you had forgotten, Rawls is on leave.' He gave her a mocking smile then strode from the room as though it had been a parting shot, a reminder that he was in charge now in case she forgot where her allegiance should lie.

Tess ignored her questioning look. 'Go through the socials for now,' she said, 'and fill DC Chivers in when you're done.'

'Will do,' Nat said.

'Nat, before you go, can I ask you something?' Tess said.

Nat nodded but said nothing.

Tess drummed her fingers absently against her mouth for a moment and then said, 'The guy from CEOP ... he's asked us to consider Rawls as a suspect.'

Nat laughed disbelievingly. 'Rawls? That's, well, that's ridiculous!'

Tess nodded. 'I thought so too, but it's not beyond the realms of possibility.'

'What are they suggesting? That Rawls abducted his own daughter? Or that he's hurt her in some way? It's insane – why would he do it now? With all the focus from the other four cases on him already, it doesn't make sense.'

Tess nodded again. 'Unless he was using the other cases to hide behind. If you look at it that way, it would be the perfect time for her to disappear. He could use them as cover.'

'Still,' Nat said, 'it makes no sense to me, ma'am.'

Tess stared at Nat, clicking her pen a couple of times. 'Either way,' she said, 'it's standard procedure – start from those closest and work outwards.'

'Yes,' Nat said, 'but this is Rawls, he would never ...'

'Never is a long time,' Tess said. She rubbed her temples. 'Nat, keep it in the back of your mind, will you? I know you're in contact with him,' she held a hand up to save Nat from arguing, 'but you must be careful. He has some issues. You know why he was signed off before this case, don't you?'

Nat shook her head. 'I knew that he'd been stressed at work.'

'Well yes, that's true, but it was a little more than that. This is between us, Nat, OK? It can't go beyond these walls.'

'Of course.'

'Rawls came close to having a complete breakdown. It affected his judgement, people didn't want to work with him.'

'Oh,' said Nat, 'that makes more sense.'

'It didn't come out of nowhere,' Tess said. 'It followed on from a rape case Rawls was investigating – the victim was a young woman called Ellie Dalmore. He thought they had a watertight case; all he needed was for her to ID the guy in a photo line-up.'

'She wasn't able to?'

Tess shook her head. 'Rawls blamed himself. He didn't have enough physical evidence on the guy so he wasn't prosecuted. Rawls took it to heart. He felt that he had let Ellie down, it drove him crazy with guilt.'

'Poor Rawls,' Nat said.

'It gets worse,' Tess said. 'The girl's father took it badly too. He knew that Rawls thought the guy was guilty and he followed him to a coffee shop. There was some sort of altercation and her father – Logan Bishop his name was – hit him with a hammer that he'd brought with him, damn near killed him, left Logan in hospital in a coma he's unlikely to ever come out of.'

Nat looked appalled. 'I had no idea.'

Tess shrugged. 'Rawls blamed himself for that as well. He thought that if he'd put Logan away it wouldn't have happened, it sent him off the deep-end for a while. He's never been able to forgive himself.'

'For something that was out of his control?'

Tess nodded. 'Exactly.'

Rawls and Nat had arranged to meet at the Garrick's Head. The pub was rumoured to be the most haunted in Bath. Situated next door to the Theatre Royal, it had provided sustenance to many a sophisticated punter through the years and had the honour of being the starting point of Bath's famous ghost walks. This afternoon it felt quiet, with only a handful of drinkers sitting at the scattered tables. It was a tourist spot, not somewhere that they would be likely to be seen – it wasn't the usual haunt of off-duty coppers.

Rawls walked in and, seeing no sign of Nat, took a table at the back wall. It was an old habit, sitting where you could see the entire room. He glanced at his watch. Nat was late but only by ten minutes; he was grateful that she had agreed to come at all. He felt desperate. They were well into the final hours of the first forty-eight and he was afraid. Time was fast running out and the stress of not knowing was mounting. He needed to know what was going on, if there had been any movement. His hands shook a little as he took a sip of his Coke. He wasn't sure how long he could hang on.

The door opened and Nat walked in and crossed the room to join him.

'What can I get you?' he asked.

Nat tried to smile but her face was solemn; she looked extremely tired. 'Would you be offended if I bought my own?' she asked him. 'It's just ...'

Rawls finished the sentence for her. 'It's just that you're not supposed to be talking to me.'

She nodded, reddening.

She came back with a glass of water and a bag of crisps. 'Lunch,' she said, sitting down, her eyes on the crisps. 'This is off the record, OK?' She looked up at Rawls with a gaze that somehow managed to be both trusting and suspicious in equal measure.

Rawls nodded. 'Start with what I've missed this afternoon, would you?'

Nat looked down at her glass and ran a finger down the side so that it left a line in the condensation. She drew in a breath, then let out a sigh.

'Tess has added me to the list of suspects in Carmen's disappearance, hasn't she?' Rawls said.

She looked up at him briefly, then back to the glass. 'Yes.'

'You know that's standard procedure? You start from the middle and work your way out, it's just a tick-box exercise,' he said.

She nodded. 'I know, it's just ... I mean ...'

'You're concerned that you could be colluding with a suspect by talking to me?'

'I *am* colluding with a suspect.'

Rawls looked out of the window. The wet road glistened and people in scarves and hats sat beneath canopies at the bar opposite, drinking coffees and warming themselves next to outdoor heaters. It was about as British a scene as one could get.

'It's fine if you'd rather not,' he said, 'I would totally understand.'

Nat looked up at him, her eyes dark and intense. 'I have to speak to you, Rawls.' She lowered her voice to little more than a whisper, 'I know I'm a newbie, but, well, the truth is, I don't think that Tess and Chivers are going to find her. I think it has to be you, and I think I have to help you. For Carmen's sake.'

He smiled at her. 'I cannot tell you how grateful I am for that. It means a great deal to me, it really does.'

She rubbed at her eyes with the heel of her hands. 'God, I hope no one sees me.'

'Then let's make it quick,' Rawls said.

Nat seemed to wrestle with her conscience a moment longer before she spoke. 'Tess has me going through Carmen's social media accounts.'

'Anything on the boyfriend?'

'Not yet, and, as you know, without her phone we're limited.'

'What about pinging her phone? Seeing if it's recorded on any masts – any joy on that?'

She shook her head. 'It's turned off. Has been since about five minutes after she rang you.'

Rawls screwed his eyes shut and rubbed his face. 'Shit,' he said, 'it's like we're standing still.'

'Chivers is on it with the phone company as well.' Nat put her hand briefly over his. 'Carmen is our number one priority at the moment – you do know that, don't you?' She picked up a coaster and began weaving it through her fingers.

Rawls reached across the table and took it from her. 'I'm going to find her,' he said.

Nat nodded.

'I'm going to find her and bring her home.'

She nodded again.

'In the meantime, I can't thank you enough for sticking by me.'

She bit her lips nervously. 'Tess told me what happened,' she said, 'with Logan Bishop.'

Rawls felt his face flush. 'I'd rather not talk about it,' he said, 'not now. I have enough on my plate for the time being.'

They said their goodbyes and Nat hugged him briefly. He had waited, his arms at his sides, afraid that if he embraced her it would ignite the fuse of emotions that he was trying so hard to suppress. He feared he might cry or scream, he wasn't able to tell which, and so he had simply waited, grateful for the warmth but unable to reciprocate. Afterwards he took her hand and patted it briefly, then thanked her one last time and turned to head back in the direction of his car.

All around him the busy streets of Bath reminded him of the loneliness of his plight. People were going about their business, their lives unaffected, oblivious to his pain, and he had to resist an urge to shout out or to stop someone just to tell them, to let them know that his daughter was missing – she was missing, dammit, and why did no one seem to care?

In the safety of his car he allowed himself a moment to catch his breath, thinking he might be about to cry again, but his tears seemed frozen. He sat in the artificial brightness of the underground car park, then started up the car and drove out of town. As he drove he thought about Carmen, his only child, wondering where she was, who she was with, whether she was asleep or awake, whether she was comfortable. His mind tried to take him where he didn't want it to go, tried to show him Carmen hurt, perhaps even ... He shook his head. He couldn't let his feelings cloud his thoughts; it wouldn't help, it was dangerous to even consider. She would be OK, of course she would. She was his daughter, she would be fine – bad things happened to other people. Didn't they? Then why had this happened? How had some bitch taken their daughter right out from under their noses? And who was this woman anyway? Someone from school? A teacher perhaps, or the mother of one of her friends, or a lunch supervisor. Or perhaps it was this elusive boyfriend's mother – maybe she'd come to collect Carmen, to bring her to him, then they'd been in an accident – could it be as simple as that? Could they have gone off the road, the car lying in a ditch, unseen?

Thoughts jostled for a place in his mind, ideas coming at him like video clips in a movie. He slammed the steering wheel with the palm of his hand and shouted at the empty road ahead until finally the tears came and he had to pull over into a muddy lay-by. Beside him a rusted gate rested on wet grass and a lone magpie called angrily down from the skeleton of a tree barely visible against a blanket of grey mist. At any other time it would have been starkly beautiful, the sort of image that Eileen would have snapped a photo of to put on Instagram, but not now – now he slammed his hand on the wheel again, hard enough for it to hurt. 'Fuck,' he said, at first softly, and then, 'fuck, fuck, fuck,' the words punctuating each blow until he was beating out a sort of desperate cathartic rhythm. By the time it passed he found himself exhausted, his throat and head aching and his hands throbbing.

The phone rang in his hand as he picked it up and it made him jump; the caller ID told him that it was Eileen.

'Peter?' Eileen's voice sounded strained, 'Where are you?'

'I'm on my way home,' he said, avoiding the question.

'There's a guy here to see you.'

'A guy?' Rawls was cautious, 'What guy?'

'DC Chivers.'

Rawls felt his heart rate quicken. 'Chivers? What does he want?'

'Apparently he needs to interview you about Carmen.'

'Eileen,' Rawls said, 'tell him I'll meet him at the station, OK?'

Eileen started to cry. 'Why the station, Pete? Why can't you talk in front of me? Where are you? Why would they want to speak to you?'

'It's standard procedure, hon, that's all.' Rawls didn't think this was going to be just standard procedure, though. Chivers would have something to prove.

Rawls pulled up behind the station and killed the engine. Sucking in a long breath, he was surprised to see that his hands were shaking. Tess's car was already there but he didn't know what car Chivers would be in, so he had no idea if he was back already or not. He glanced at his reflection in the rear-view mirror; he looked exhausted.

'Rawls,' Chivers rapped his wedding ring against the car window, 'you can do your make-up later.'

Rawls jumped and tried to smile, then climbed out and they headed into the building together.

Chivers put him in an office with a desk and two chairs and nothing else, then left to get them both a coffee. Rawls had asked for Tess to be present but Chivers had declined: 'She told me to go ahead,' he said.

He sat down opposite Rawls and smiled warmly. 'How's Eileen?' he asked.

'You know how she is,' Rawls said, 'you were just there, at my house.'

'I meant how is she handling this?'

'How do you think?'

'I should imagine it's a strain?'

Rawls stared at him for a moment. 'You imagine it's a strain?'

'I can't even begin to guess what she's going through.'

Rawls looked down at his hands. 'She's in an awful state.'

'Well, it's an awful situation. Not knowing where your daughter is.'

'It is.'

'When was the last time that you saw her?'

Rawls looked up. 'Thursday evening.'

'So you didn't see her Friday morning at all??'

'No, I left the house early before she or Eileen were up.'

'And how were things generally?'

Rawls realised that Chivers had already spoken with Eileen. 'Things have been a little tense,' he said.

'Tense?' Chivers smiled with the corners of his mouth, and Rawls saw that he was enjoying this. 'How so?'

'You have kids,' Rawls said.

'We're not talking about my kids,' Chivers let the smile fade, 'we're talking about your daughter. Sorry, your *step*-daughter.' The smile was back.

Rawls balled his hands into two tight fists. *Step-daughter* – was this arsehole going there, was he really? He bit down on his tongue, forcing himself not to respond; now was neither the time nor the place.

Chivers was watching him, his eyes like little black stones. 'Now please, if you don't mind, could I ask you to explain what you mean by tense?'

Rawls felt the first surge of panic. They couldn't really suspect him, could they? 'We had had a family discussion about ten days before.'

'Discussion or argument?'

'An argument, for God's sake. Craig, you know I have nothing to do with this.'

Craig Chivers stared at him for a full thirty seconds. 'We know nothing until we have established the facts. I think you taught me that,' he smiled broadly, 'didn't you?'

'We had an argument.'

'You know I'm going to need more than that.'

'Carmen had skipped school, she'd done it a couple of times.'

'You read her the riot act?'

Rawls shook his head. 'No, it didn't go that far.'

'But she was still upset about it the following week?'

'She's a teenager,' Rawls said.

'Yes,' Chivers said, 'young and impetuous. They don't always act rationally, do they?'

Rawls leaned back and closed his eyes. 'She didn't run away if that's what you're thinking.'

'I'm not,' Chivers said, and it only took Rawls a moment to realise what the man was saying.

'You think I did something to her?'

'Did you?'

Rawls was incredulous. They were actually considering him as a suspect, he couldn't quite believe it.

'The last few months can't have been easy.'

Rawls was too angry to respond.

'You've had a great deal on your plate.' Chivers opened a folder. 'You were off work for ...' He pretended to look through the notes.

'Two months,' Rawls said.

Chivers held his finger on a printed sheet. 'Yes,' he said as though the question had been part of a maths test, 'that's right, two months. That's a long time. You must have been under tremendous pressure.'

'I kept myself busy.' Rawls sounded petulant, even to himself.

'How?'

'I have bonsai trees.'

'I did not know that,' Chivers said. 'Bonsai, eh? You don't look like the kind of guy I would have pictured doing that.'

'Well there you are.'

'Here we are,' Chivers agreed. 'Any other hobbies to,' he winked at Rawls, 'keep you out of trouble?'

Rawls folded his arms. He'd had enough of this; he wanted to be out looking for Carmen, not wasting time with this prick. 'I have no idea what you're driving at, Craig, but whatever it is, you have it all wrong.'

'Do I?' Chivers looked down and smiled at the table. 'Eileen seems to feel differently.'

'Eileen? What's Eileen said?'

Chivers shook his head. 'You know I can't tell you that. Let's just say that she mentioned that you hadn't been yourself recently.'

'I honestly don't know what you mean.' Rawls felt a sudden cold wave of fear run through him. 'I had nothing to do with Carmen's disappearance,'

Chivers folded his arms over his belly, leaning back and pursing his lips. 'Your daughter was last seen at,' he consulted his notes, 'seven fifteen, is that right?'

'Leaving with an unknown woman,' Rawls said.

'Unknown to us,' Chivers said.

'What are you suggesting?'

'I'm not suggesting anything, I'm just stating a fact; the woman is unknown to us.'

'For fuck's sake,' Rawls said, 'come on, Craig, you know that I don't know this woman.'

Chivers nodded. 'I know you say that you don't, but things tend to happen around you, Peter.'

Rawls looked up at the ceiling. Things did happen around him; he was like a shit magnet. 'Craig, I don't know this woman. I had nothing to do with Carmen's disappearance, I just want to find her.'

'It just seems so convenient.'

'What does?'

'Well, you rush in to view the CCTV before we do, you get the proof that it wasn't you, all nice and tidy, don't you think?'

'Because I want to find my daughter.'

'So you said.' Chivers rifled through his paperwork again. 'Where were you on the night that she disappeared? Around, let's say for argument's sake, around seven fifteen?'

'Selling my car,' Rawls said.

'Selling your car,' Chivers smiled broadly, 'you have to admit that it all seems very convenient.'

'It's convenient because it's true, Craig. Come on, what's this all about? You know me, you know I'm not involved.'

'I know,' Chivers said, 'that you keep saying that you're not involved, but in my experience – let's face it, in your experience too – what people say and what turns out to be the truth are very often two completely different things – and what are the statistics?' He paused, pretending to think. 'Oh yes, murders carried out by family members are fifty percent higher than those with no obvious suspect.'

Rawls stared at him. 'Are you saying that my daughter has been murdered? Is that what you're telling me?'

Craig leaned back. 'No, Peter, I'm not, I'm merely sharing a statistic.'

'You're a prick, you know that?'

Chivers chuckled. 'Maybe so, but at least I know where my children are.'

Rawls stood up suddenly, the seat scraping across the floor as he did so. He saw Chivers lean back instinctively, ready for the assault, and, just in time, Rawls saw the flicker of a smile on the man's face; this was exactly what he had wanted. Rawls forced himself to sit back down again, his breath coming in angry bursts. He still wanted to grab this fat waste of space around his throat but he knew, even in his fury, that it would do no good. It was exactly what Chivers wanted him to do. He closed his eyes and counted to ten, then rested his elbows on the table and allowed his head to drop into his hands. He felt more tired than he could remember feeling in his life before.

'Craig,' he said, speaking through his fingers, 'we can go around in circles with this as many times as you want, but the truth is exactly as I've told you. Carmen had intended to meet some boy, and instead was picked up by a woman. It seems to me that if I was running this investigation, I would be trying to establish who they might be, who the boyfriend was, who the woman was. Instead, you're in here wasting time, trying to figure out how to put this on me.'

The interview had lasted for more than an hour – an hour that Rawls could have spent looking for his daughter, an hour of Chivers trying to trip him up, trying to catch him out, an hour in which Rawls had grown to hate the man even more than he had previously. He said as much to Nat on the drive back home.

'I cannot believe they're holding my car,' he said as she started the engine.

'It's just procedure,' Nat said.

'No, it's not,' Rawls said, but he knew it was. He suspected that he would have done the same if the tables were turned.

'What did you tell me? Don't let him get under your skin?' Nat said, glancing to her right before pulling into the queue for the roundabout beneath the arches. 'Maybe you need to take your own advice.'

'Easier said than done,' Rawls said. Beside him the river slid by like a great brown serpent and, beyond its banks, Bath waited indifferently, its own dreaming spires, like those of its Oxford cousin, staring down, unmoved by his plight. Seagulls argued with each other overhead, their wings spread so wide that they looked like dinosaurs against the hard grey sky.

'How's Eileen?' Nat asked.

Rawls thought for a moment. 'She's ... well, she's awful. I think maybe she blames me.'

'I'm sure she doesn't.'

'I should have answered my phone.'

'Everyone misses a call now and then.'

Rawls sighed. 'I didn't miss it, I ignored it.'

Nat flicked the indicator and waited for her turn, 'Shit, Rawls, you must feel awful.'

Rawls looked back out at the grey sky; the seagulls had gone. 'Yes, and what makes everything worse is that we're living under a spotlight. It feels as though everyone is watching us.'

Nat took a gap in the traffic, the wheels spinning a little on the damp tarmac. She looked over at him briefly. 'And you're certain that she wouldn't have run off?'

'She's not the type,' Rawls said.

Nat frowned. 'I know what you mean, but even so, the woman she left with, could she have been part of her plan, the boyfriend's mother or something?'

'I don't think so,' Rawls said, 'but what might make sense is that there could be two of them, a man and a woman.'

'Oh my God, Rawls – that *would* make sense.'

Rawls nodded. 'It would, but where does it leave us? We still don't know for sure that all the disappearances are connected.'

Nat drew up outside his house and stared at Rawls as though she was trying to see what was going on in his mind. 'Sarge, they have to be connected. I've been thinking about it non-stop.' She stared out at the street as though she was trying to get her thoughts in order. 'I know DC Chivers gave you a hard time, but he doesn't believe you're involved any more than I do. Everyone agrees that the cases are all linked.'

He looked out of the window up towards the house. 'Even Carmen?'

'Tess seems to think so.'

'Does she think Carmen was targeted, because of me?'

Nat shrugged. 'We're keeping all lines of enquiry open at the moment. Also,' she glanced across at him, 'I've mentioned this to Tess already, but we didn't check the times after Carmen left. I mean, I just kept thinking, she left with that woman at quarter past seven, but you said she had arranged to meet this guy at seven thirty, right?'

Rawls nodded.

Nat went on, 'What if this guy, this boyfriend, showed up after, at the time they had agreed?'

'Nat, you're right,' Rawls said. 'He could have turned up at seven thirty. I didn't get the guy at the cinema to go on with the CCTV because I thought we had her – I didn't look beyond the woman. I've been assuming that she's our perp. What if she's not? What if she's someone else, unrelated even? I mean, what if he, the guy, the boyfriend, that she was supposed to meet, showed up later?'

'Linda's on it already,' Nat said.

Rawls could have hugged Nat. Linda was good, she would be thorough.

'But I thought of someone else who might be able to help too,' Nat said. 'Do you need to go in?'

'I should do really, but Eileen has a friend with her – why?'

'Well, I know the couple who run the little convenience shop over the road from the cinema, Mr and Mrs Patel. I've been going there since I was tiny and they're good friends with my parents. They've been robbed a couple of times so now they have CCTV all over the place. If anyone went past them, they'll have it on their cameras.'

'Have you mentioned it to Tess or Craig?'

Nat shook her head. 'No, I only thought of them this morning, while you were having your chat with Craig.'

'And have you perhaps already spoken to Mr and Mrs Patel?'

'I may have had a quick chat with them.'

'And are you suggesting that we might need to pop over to their shop and pick up some bread, perhaps a bottle of milk?'

'Well, I wouldn't want you guys to run out.'

Fifteen minutes later they pulled into the car park at the back of Patel's Convenience, 'Open 7 to 7', the sign read, 'Car park for customers only'. They climbed out and headed around the front. 'What's this guy's name again?' Rawls asked.

'Maz Patel,' Nat said. 'He's really nice.'

She pulled the door open and from somewhere inside an electronic bell sounded. A tall, thin man with a long beard and small round glasses smiled at them from behind the counter. Behind him a large monitor was angled so that he could see it from his seat. The screen was split into six different images, each of them with an angle of the shop, the storeroom or the two doors, front and back.

'Mr Patel,' Nat said, 'this is Detective Sergeant Rawls.'

Mr Patel smiled widely, revealing a set of teeth that must have cost more than most people's cars. 'Natalie,' he said, 'where you been the last few days? Too busy to come see me?' He looked at Rawls and his smile slipped away suddenly, as though someone had pulled a switch. He came around to the front of the counter to join them and took both of Rawls's hands in his own thin but warm ones. 'Detective Rawls,' he said, 'I cannot tell you how sorry I am for what has happened to you and your family.'

Rawls flushed, touched by the man's empathy. 'Thank you.'

'The search revealed nothing?' the man asked, shaking his head as though he had answered the question for himself. 'She will come back to you, I think, God willing.' He squeezed Rawls's hand briefly, then turned towards the back of the shop, gesturing to them to follow.

They headed through a small storeroom that took them into a small living area beyond. A large red sofa sat in one corner, a chair beside it and a door to the right which led to what appeared to be a kitchenette. In front of the sofa was another monitor, this one at least 42 inches. Beneath it a DVR buzzed noisily in the otherwise quiet space.

Rawls nodded at the DVR. 'How much data does that hold, Mr Patel?'

He frowned. 'It depends on how much it picks up. The cameras that we have at the front of the shop only last a day or so; too much coming and going.'

Rawls felt his heart sink; two days – they'd get nothing. They were wasting precious time.

Mr Patel leaned down to pick up a remote control. 'But I saved the day, I think.'

Rawls looked at him quizzically. 'You saved the day?'

'After I saw what happened, I said to my wife, "They might want to see this for the investigation," so I saved it, just in case. I saw it on the news, about your daughter, and

I thought maybe they walked past here, maybe we can show the police.'

'You've seen our guys already, haven't you, Mr Patel?' Nat asked, and he nodded.

'Did you show it to them?'

'I tried to, but they just took an SD card away. They didn't let me show them. But I saved a copy, like I told you on the phone.'

'Can we see the video?' Rawls asked.

'Yes, of course.' Mr Patel held up a finger. 'I hope you will forgive me, but my wife and I have been looking too, and we want to show you something.' He pointed the remote at the screen and pressed a button so that it lit up.

Rawls and Nat watched the monitor. People came and went, holding umbrellas against the rain, their faces pale in the wintry light. Children held on to parents, babies cried in pushchairs while mothers talked on mobile phones. Rawls was beginning to think that this was a complete waste of time when Mr Patel said, 'Look here,'

They leaned into the screen to where he was pointing.

'Do you see?' he said, and Rawls nodded.

'Oh shit,' said Nat.

A woman had come into view; according to the CCTV clock it was twelve minutes past seven. The woman wore a red baseball cap, tufts of wet hair sticking out from either side.

Mr Patel paused the image. 'It's her, isn't it? The one on the news?'

'I think so,' Rawls said. 'Can you slow it down?'

'Yes, but first, watch this.'

Mr Patel pressed the play button again and the screen came to life. The woman glanced at her watch then looked up; the image quality was good enough to make out her face but not her features. She was looking at someone and appeared to nod.

Mr Patel paused it again, rewound a couple of seconds and pointed to a man just in camera. 'This is who she is nodding at,' he said, clearly pleased with his sleuthing skills. 'Watch now.'

The man on the screen nodded back then made a shooing motion with his hand.

'He is sending her on her way,' Mr Patel said, 'he is telling the woman what to do.'

Rawls walked over to the screen, staring at the man. He couldn't see his face because he had his back to the camera, added to which, he was wearing a baseball cap.

He looked at Nat. 'What do you think?'

'Could be anyone.'

'He doesn't seem familiar?'

Nat took a step closer. 'Not yet,' she said.

Rawls wanted to scream. How could they have so much yet still have so little?

Mr Patel touched his shoulder, and pressed a memory stick into his hand. 'I think that you will find her,' he said gently. 'I hope this will help.'

Chapter 20

The house was quiet when he unlocked the door. He leaned into the lounge and was surprised to see that Jo wasn't at her sentry post.

'Eileen?' he called out.

He turned to head upstairs then stopped as she said his name. Eileen was standing in the kitchen doorway.

'Where's Jo?' he asked. 'I thought you agreed that she would stay with you.'

'I sent her home, she had stuff that she needed to do,' Eileen's voice hitched, 'you know, family stuff.'

He went towards her, but she held her hand up. 'Don't you fucking touch me.'

He stopped in his tracks. 'Eileen, what's this all about?'

'What's this all about? Do you have to ask?' There was a fury blazing in her eyes that Rawls was almost glad to see. Even anger was better than the exhausted, broken woman she had become since Carmen's disappearance.

'I don't know what you're on about,' he said.

'Really?' she shouted. 'You have no idea why I'm upset? Let's have a little think about it, shall we? Let's start with why I just had to sit through half an hour of questions about the disappearance of my daughter. After that we can ask ourselves why you couldn't talk to the man in our home, with me present, why you needed to meet him at the office. And why the fuck would they be interviewing either of us if we haven't done anything wrong?'

'I told you already, it was just procedure.' Rawls tried to reach for her again, but she pulled away.

'Don't give me that just procedure bullshit! You've been gone for hours – are you telling me they did that for nothing? They just interviewed you for the fun of it? Not because they needed to find out what you might know?'

Rawls stared at her. 'Perhaps if you had been more supportive when you spoke to Chivers it wouldn't have taken so long. Perhaps I could have been out looking for our missing daughter.'

She turned away from him, her shoulders hunched. 'Not our daughter,' she said, her voice little more than a whisper, 'my daughter, Peter, my daughter.'

For a moment Rawls just stared at the back of her head, incredulous. Had she just ignited that fuse, the one that fat twat had tried to light a few hours earlier? Rawls loved his wife, he always had, but he adored his daughter, her daughter, Carmen. He had done since the moment they had met. The very first time.

It should have been a straightforward situation. He was a beat cop then, in uniform and on the streets, back in the day when they still had enough coppers to be on the streets. He had been on patrol with Skin; so nicknamed because of his shaven head which made him look like a skinhead. Skin was a stickler for doing things by the book. Rawls had been, somewhat reluctantly, in awe of him. The guy had pretty much memorised the *Police Operational Handbook* – he could literally quote at will: 'Section 1.3,' he would say, 'Managing Crime Scenes.'

It had been this very clearly defined code of conduct that had made Rawls's behaviour that day all the more out of character, not to mention insane. They had gone to a house where there had been a report of a disturbance. They were greeted by a tall man in the scumbag's uniform of the day: dark blue tracksuit trousers that had never been anywhere near a track, dirty white trainers and a baseball cap, no doubt intended to keep cameras off the owner's face rather than to protect it from the sun.

'Fuck's sake,' the tall man had said by way of a greeting. 'What do you want?'

'Sorry to disturb you, sir,' Skin had said, no doubt running section 7.3 'Breach of Peace' through his memory banks as he spoke, 'we've had reports of shouting coming from these premises.'

Behind the man, the house looked as though a fight might have recently ensued. The floor was covered in clothes, a chair had been overturned, and a coffee cup lay on its side, its contents spreading around it like a dirty brown halo.

'Are you alone, sir?' Skin had asked. He had his hand on his baton. 'We rack off on my command and only if we need to,' he had said before they went in and Rawls, who was well aware of the correct protocol when it came to releasing your baton, had nodded. *You can bloody rack off too*, he had thought to himself, but he had said nothing.

'Yeah,' the man fiddled with his crotch.

'May we come in?'

'Why?'

'Just to have a chat.' Skin had glanced around, 'I imagine that the last thing you want is to have us two hanging around your doorstep any longer than we need to – can't be good for business.' He had winked at the man then, like they were old buddies.

They had followed Skin into the lounge where the smell of cannabis hung in the air like a grubby net curtain. Skin had glanced at Rawls who had his hand on his baton; he thought he'd heard someone on the stairs. Skin made a face that told him to relax, then turned to the man. 'We're only here about the domestic, mate, just wanted to make sure that everyone was OK.'

The man dropped on to a sofa. 'This is harassment, you know. Who even called you? Bet it was that bitch over the road, she's always up in my face.' He coughed and spat into a cup. 'And before you ask, no, you ain't having a sniff round, not 'less you got a warrant.'

Skin had looked at him, his face serene, smiling. 'Mate, let's not dick around. You know I don't need one, I know I don't need one, and we both know that my mate, PC Rawls here, is going to have a look around. So, just to be clear, is there anyone else in the house?'

Rawls had heard the noise again, the faintest of creaks on the stairs, barely perceptible. The hairs on the back of his neck had perked up and his back prickled in anticipation. He looked at Skin who had not heard it and was still chatting with the guy, smiling down at him as though they were best buddies for life. Rawls inched his way to the door that led to a dirty hallway, where he would be able to see the stairs that would take him to the kitchen and the back door. He moved slowly, making no sound, unnoticed by either Skin or the tracksuited arsehole with his hand in his pants. He craned his neck, millimetre by millimetre, bracing himself for a wallop around the head or a sudden punch in the face, but nothing came. Another noise came to him from the stairs; he risked a proper look this time, his head tilted, his hand on his baton, his body tensed, ready.

There, at the foot of the stairs, was a woman: she was tall, her eyes wide and afraid, her face beautiful except for the red mark beneath one eye that suggested she might have had a fall into a cupboard door, a common issue in domestic disturbance cases apparently, or, and Rawls had suspected this more likely, a good hard punch in the face. She was frozen in place, her beautiful eyes pleading, her long red hair held back loosely with a pink and white checked scrunchy, her shorts so short that her long legs seemed to go on forever.

In her arms she held two things: the first, and this was the reason that Rawls should have stopped her, was an extremely large and healthy cannabis plant, its leaves green and lush like something out of an exotic rain forest; the second was a sleeping child, a baby in fact, no more than four or five months. Clad only in a nappy and pink T-shirt, the baby had chubby little legs that hung down over her mother's arm like two fat sausages. The woman smiled at him briefly then turned and ran out of the back door, her phone dropping to the linoleum behind her. Rawls stared at the woman for what seemed a lifetime before she disappeared and then he crossed the room and picked the phone up. He would find her and give it back to her later.

Looking back on the moment, he would tell Eileen that he had considered calling out to Skin, that he fully intended to stop her and her bloody cannabis plant, but she laughed him off. 'Fibber,' she would say and he would sigh – he was a fibber, that was true. He had never had any intention of stopping her or baby Carmen, who would shortly become the apple of his eye; they had been the love of his life from that very moment. The trouble had been, Rawls thought, that he was never entirely certain that his wife felt the same way about him.

Looking at her now, her face an older, but no less beautiful, replica of the one he had first seen at the foot of those stairs, he found he had no idea what to say. Eventually he found his voice. 'You don't mean that, Eileen, I know you don't.'

'Peter,' she said, 'they've been through the house. They searched Carmen's room, pulled everything apart, they took ...' she broke off for a moment, holding her hand across her mouth as if to stop herself from crying, 'they took stuff, her jumper, her shoes, her nightie. Why would they want her nightie, Peter?'

'I ...' he stopped himself. 'They're just doing their jobs, Eileen.'

She glared at him. 'They suspect you, don't they?'

'I imagine they suspect both of us, Eileen.' His voice was cold, sharp, merciless.

She grabbed at a glass set upside down beside the sink and threw it across the room, 'Us? You bastard. Not us, *you*. They suspect *you*. How could you fucking do this to me?'

'To you?' Rawls felt the pressure reach boiling point. 'Fuck me, Eileen, this isn't about you – this is about Carmen.'

'Don't you dare,' she screamed at him, her face so close that he could smell the wine and cigarettes that lingered on her breath, 'don't you fucking dare! You're the one swanning around getting yourself suspended, you're the one obstructing their fucking enquiries; I'm the one stuck here not knowing what to do. I'm the one left here alone.'

She turned to go back into the kitchen and he followed her and grabbed her wrist, swinging her around to face him. 'Alone?' he shouted. 'You're never alone, not so long as you have a bottle of fucking Merlot to keep you company.'

'Don't you fucking judge me.' She slammed both hands into his chest, pushing him back on his heels. 'I'm sick of you looking down your nose at me, sick to the back teeth.'

Rawls slammed his fist against a cupboard, the shelf of glasses above him shaking with the force of it. 'And I'm sick of seeing you in this state,' he bellowed.

Eileen ignored him, turning her back and reaching for a glass from the shelf. 'I need to drink,' she said from between gritted teeth, 'to live with a fuck-up like you.'

Rawls grabbed at her hand and snatched the glass from her, throwing it across the room and shattering it against the far wall. 'You don't need a fucking drink,' he said, surprised by his own fury.

Eileen spun round. 'I hate you,' she screamed, her voice breaking with tears, 'Peter, I hate you, I hate you!' She grabbed another glass and threw it across the room as he had done, where it shattered in a spray of tiny crystal shards. 'There,' she screamed, a shrill, broken scream that ripped through the air and sliced into his mind. Rawls thought he would never forget that sound. It was like nothing he had heard before, the sound of a woman breaking, tearing apart from the inside out. She reached for another glass and Rawls grabbed her hand. 'Let go of me!' she shrieked at him.

He held her hand and pulled her in tight towards him, her heart pounding against his chest.

She beat her free hand against his shoulder, punching it weakly. 'Let me go!' she screamed into him.

Rawls held his wife until the rage faded, then he loosened his grip on her arm, 'I'm so sorry,' he said.

She pulled away from him. 'We have to find her.' She looked up at him, her face swollen from crying, her teeth stained with red wine. 'You can't keep going off on your own. You have to let me help, we have to do this together.'

Rawls looked down at the shattered glass on the floor. She was right, he was doing it again, cutting her out and taking things on alone. 'OK,' he said, 'you're right, where do you want to start?'

She pushed her fingers through her hair, trying to collect herself. 'I don't suppose you have a photo of her, do you, the woman who took Carmen?'

'Actually I can do better than that,' he said, recalling the extra memory stick of the cinema footage that was still in his jacket. 'I have the video.'

They loaded it on to his laptop and Rawls touched her hand, his face a brief question mark as she moved the mouse to play it.

She glanced at him. 'I'm OK,' she said, 'I have to be, for Carmen's sake.'

She pressed play and they stared at the screen, watching as the now familiar (to Rawls, anyway) scene played out in front of them.

They watched through to the end and then again, Eileen pausing every now and then, leaning closer to the screen, then moving it on again. At last she turned to him.

'Pete,' she said, her eyes feverish, 'I think I recognise her.'

Rawls stared at her. 'Really? Who is it?'

She looked at him and he could see panic in her eyes. 'I can't remember.' She grabbed his arm, squeezing it so tightly in her frustration that it hurt. 'I can't quite place her, but I really do recognise her, Pete, I just can't think where from.' She hit her forehead with the palm of her hand as though the action might free the thought. She pressed play again and watched the figures on the screen playing out their hideous scene one more time, then she turned to Rawls. 'Maybe I've seen her at school or somewhere like that.'

'Have you tried Facebook? Maybe she's a friend on there?'

Eileen's fingers moved across her phone as she scanned photos searching for the woman that she was so certain they had met before, but there was no trace of her.

It was getting late and the argument had left them both exhausted.

'We're getting nowhere for now,' Rawls said. He felt almost giddy from exhaustion and, looking at Eileen, suspected that she must feel the same. 'Let's have something to eat then try to get some sleep.'

Eileen drew breath to protest, but he could see that her heart wasn't in it. She headed for the kitchen, there was some soup in the cupboard. 'Put some toast on, would you?' she asked him. They ate in silence and then made their way upstairs.

Chapter 21

Carmen opened her eyes, her head swam and for a moment she thought that she must be blind – either that or her eyes were covered, such was the intensity of the blackness that surrounded her. She rubbed at her eyes then tried again, but the darkness refused to budge. She was becoming aware of the smell now; damp and ripe, like vegetation beside a stagnant pool. In contrast to the blackness, which was wet and thick, this smell seemed almost sharp, as though, under different circumstances, it might irritate the senses. Terrible thoughts came to her then, images from a film she had watched only a few weeks before. It had been a horror film, she forgot the name, but even as her mind reached for it, she understood that right at that moment, the name of the film was the least of her concerns. There had been a creature in it, a terrible being that seemed half-girl, half-spider, which had crawled its way across the floor, its body jerking and its bones cracking as it moved. In her mind's eye Carmen saw this creature now, imagined it dragging its way across the damp floor, its belly brushing the wet concrete, its eyes, huge and bulging, peering at her through the impenetrable darkness as it edged ever closer to her. She clamped her hand to her mouth as if to stifle a scream.

The dull ache in her head had become a screeching white light of pain and she pressed her hands to it. Without warning her stomach lurched and she threw up violently on to the ground beside her, the new smell of vomit overwhelming all others in what her distant and agonised brain was already beginning to think of as her prison. The violence of her sudden retching brought her into a kneeling position, and she hung her head between her outstretched arms, her stomach convulsing, her head screaming in agony and her stomach pitching in waves as though it was desperate to rid itself of some hideous poison.

How long had she been here? She had vague memories: someone pouring water into her mouth, someone rubbing her back, someone pulling her hair back from her face. She had drifted in and out of consciousness, drinking, sleeping, drinking and sleeping. She was hungry now, despite her stomach protesting, and thirsty. How long had she been here, in the darkness?

She managed a weak sob, 'help, please, help,' then grabbed at her dry throat, the effort hurting more than she could have imagined. Something brushed across the back of her neck, a flutter, like a moth or a butterfly, or a spider. She screamed aloud, ignoring the pain, and hit the back of her neck, slapping at it in frantic motions intended to either remove or kill the creature. The smell of her own vomit mingled with that terrible stench of rotting vegetation forced Carmen to her feet and she stood, her hands groping for purchase, on legs so weak that she feared she might pitch forward and fall into the inky blackness. A fresh wave of pain filled her head and she grabbed at it, clutching it as though she feared it might fall off. Like a person in a blindfold, she held her arms outstretched ahead of her. 'To the left, to the left,' a voice in her mind cried out, and she thought back to her sixth birthday party when they had played 'pin the tail to the donkey'. Everyone had taken a turn to be blindfolded while the rest cheered them on, guiding them, 'You're warm, you're cold, you're boiling hot.' Carmen had not wanted to take a turn. She had been terrified by the whole affair and had run screaming from the room after no more than a couple of seconds, the blindfold still in place. She had torn at the hateful thing, hitting at her own head like a child possessed, and locked herself in the bathroom, sobbing wildly. Carmen suppressed a terrible urge to do just that now, to bolt, like a horse that has been stung by a wasp, to lunge forward, into the darkness, into the unknown.

She took another step, her weak legs trembling, threatening to let go, her head a blinding white light of pure and undiluted pain. Then her face felt the brush of something else against her cheek. She screamed, her voice echoing in her sound chamber prison; it seemed almost to reverberate, bouncing back at her, screaming back at her.

She told herself that it was her mind playing tricks and the voice in her head agreed. 'Just a spider's web,' the voice reassured her, 'just a web, like walking down the back path in the morning on the way to school, just a stray strand of spider's web.'

Yes, that was it, of course. She pushed forward gingerly, another step, her hands feeling the darkness, her fingers moving of their own accord, groping at the dark as though it were a solid presence. Two more of those terrifying steps into the abyss and her hands did feel something solid. Cold, damp and smooth. She stopped still, listening to her own breathing, and the ragged sound of tiny gasps wheezing in and out of her chest sounded almost alien to her, as though they were coming from someone else. She froze, holding her breath; was there someone else in there with her? Like in the movies? Someone wearing one of those masks that let you see in the dark. Perhaps they were watching her, smiling with filthy, jagged teeth, waiting for her to feel her way to them, to reach her hand out, to touch, oh dear God, to touch them, him, her, it.

'Stop it,' a voice shouted, and she realised that it was her own, 'just fucking stop it. Stop it now.' With her hands pressed against the wall she began searching, moving them systematically up and down, up as high as she could reach, down all the way to the floor. Up and down, she moved around the circumference and then, just as her tired body told her to stop and take a rest, she felt it, a light switch. Carmen drew in a deep breath then covered her eyes the way that a new swimmer might cover their nose the moment before they jump into a swimming pool. She brought her hand back up to the switch, swore loudly into the darkness, and then she pressed it.

Rawls had managed a few fitful hours of sleep. Easing himself out of bed so as not to disturb Eileen, he crept downstairs and made himself a coffee and headed into the dining room. Pulling his laptop towards him, he switched it on and opened a browser, then typed in the web address for Stoney Barrow View on his laptop.

His screen filled with their slick modern website. Photos of lush green Somerset countryside scrolled effortlessly across the homepage; text boxes slid across these images and bold square buttons invited him to click for more information. The site offered spa days, digital detoxes, lunch with an award-winning chef, that sort of thing. He found a page titled 'Our History' and read through the text. The house had once belonged to a famous antiquarian and vicar, Sir David Thomas Edwin. Edwin, it seemed, had carried out many of the early archaeological investigations in the area and had been responsible for protecting the locations from further damage from what he had referred to as 'the ignorant locals'. Rawls read quickly, scanning the blah, blah, blah and hoping for a nugget of interest. He found it near the end: 'The property passed into the tender loving care of a direct ancestor of Sir Edwin' who had passed ownership to his nephew. Rawls read on. The subsequent owner had wished to remain anonymous. The property was loved, but with its museum of curiosities, multiple rooms and sprawling grounds, the owner felt most strongly that it should be a place accessible to everyone rather than being a private home, and for that reason it was entrusted by sale to the current owner, one Sebastian Greaves.

He opened another tab, typed in 'estate inherited Edwin' and there, at the bottom of the first page on the website for a tiny local weekly paper, he found the information he had been looking for.

His heart thudding, he rushed upstairs to the bedroom and gently shook Eileen awake. 'We need to take a drive,' he said.

She looked up at him with bleary eyes, her face creased. 'What are you on about? Where to?'

'The retreat,' he said. 'I'll explain on the way.'

They left the house about fifteen minutes later. It was barely five a.m. and the street was dark and quiet. Rawls found himself doubting his decision almost as soon as they had pulled on to the road. What if he was wrong? What if the information he had uncovered was just a coincidence?

They pulled up at traffic lights on their way through Bear Flat and Eileen said, 'So, are you going to tell me what you found on the internet?'

He nodded. He hadn't had time to explain as they'd thrown their clothes on and raced for the door. Suddenly he doubted his conviction: the link seemed minor, tentative. 'You know the weird account, the one that kicked all of the retreat stuff off?'

'Eve Burgess?'

'Yes. Well, I was looking at the website for the retreat again. I read the history page, and it said that a guy called Sir David Thomas Edwin had owned the place. When he passed away it went to his nephew, and was then inherited in turn by another relative who sold the place to the current owners.'

'OK,' she said.

'Well, I did some more digging around. The nephew, the one who first inherited it, we already know, but we know him as Berkeley Wolf. I don't know how I missed it, Berkeley Wolf's real name was Francis Burgess – he changed it by deed poll when he started his Stoney Path cult.'

'And you think that this Eve Burgess might be a daughter or a relative?'

Rawls nodded. 'I think she was his daughter. She inherited the place when he died, but her real name is Amanda Burgess. Eve was her mother – she died when Amanda was very young, seven or eight – Berkeley Wolf was her father.'

Eileen's hand went to her mouth. 'Oh my God, so the retreat is involved?'

'No, I don't think so,' Rawls said. 'That's where we've been going wrong. We've been focused on the retreat, trying to draw a link, but there isn't one, not any more. The cult was big in the Nineties, maybe even as late as 2005 or 2006, but not now. We know that it's staffed by people who were part of the original group, but I think that's probably simply because they had nowhere else to go. Most of them were loners or people who had severed ties with their families. They'd found a new family in the Stoney Path – that's a hard habit to break. I think it runs deep, that kind of indoctrination; people find it difficult to pull away.'

'I don't know,' Eileen said. 'I don't get it, but then, I'm not exactly the type of person to join a cult.'

The idea of Eileen being told what to do by some jumped-up prophet almost made Rawls laugh. 'No,' he said, 'you're not.' He squeezed her hand. 'You're too tough for that.'

She turned away from him. 'I don't feel tough right now. I think I'd follow anyone who told me what to do, if I thought they might know how to find her.'

Rawls wanted to tell Eileen to follow him, that he would find Carmen, that he would make it all right again. Instead he said, 'You're tougher than you think.'

She dabbed at her eyes. 'Maybe this is worse, though. I mean, I could almost handle imagining that she had been taken away to join some bloody cult, but if that wasn't why that woman took her, then what do you think she wanted with Carmen? Why take her?'

He shook his head; he didn't want to answer that. It was too much to think about. Carmen had been missing for more than forty-eight hours now; the stats weren't good when you got to that point. He couldn't bear to think about it himself; he certainly wasn't going to burden Eileen with it.

'Alright,' Eileen said, 'do you think that she acted alone?'

He let out a long sigh. 'I don't think so.' He glanced at her, 'You know you couldn't get hold of me yesterday, after the meeting?'

Eileen said nothing.

'I went to speak to this couple. They run a convenience store, just opposite the cinema. I shouldn't have been there, but, Nat, well, Nat knows the owners and they had made a copy of their CCTV footage for her, for me.'

Eileen was watching him but she didn't respond.

'The thing is, we know, and the police know, that she didn't act alone. This guy ...'

'Guy?'

'There was a man as well, not with her exactly but outside the shop. He seemed to have been communicating with her, nodding you know? Almost like he was telling her what to do.' He described the CCTV footage, the man in the baseball cap, his back to the camera.

Eileen had her hand to her throat. 'Oh my God, could that be the person she was going to meet?'

'I don't know,' he was shaking his head, 'it's driving me nuts.'

'Did he look old, young, well dressed?'

'He didn't look young and, yes, well dressed but in a middle-aged man kind of way.'

She brought her hands to her head. 'Oh my God, Pete, was she being groomed? Oh my God, she was, wasn't she? Someone was grooming her, and we didn't see it.'

He grabbed her hand and held it for a moment. 'We don't know that.'

'I do – you might not, but I do. God, how could we, us, you a policeman, how could we have missed it?' She turned to Rawls, her eyes wild. 'Peter, she was always trying to hide her phone, not wanting us to know who she was texting, we should have stopped her, she must have been texting him. Him – oh God, I should have made her show me her phone, this is my fault. It's all my fault, I—'

'Eileen, stop. We don't know anything; you're making assumptions.'

She pulled her hand away. 'Why didn't you tell me before?'

He pursed his lips. 'Honestly? I don't know why. I only found out last night, and there was so much going on …' He glanced at her briefly, 'I'm sorry.'

Eileen held a hand up towards him. 'You knew there was a man and you manage to not tell me? For God's sake, Peter, all fucking night I've been focused on this woman and now there's a man, some guy outside the shop, and you don't know who he is either?'

'No, I don't know who he is, but something about him – his stance maybe, or his shape, his clothes – I don't know, but something was familiar.'

'What happened to the footage? You said they made you a copy.'

'I've still got it. It's back at the house.'

'Oh, Pete,' she sounded as though she was talking to a small child, telling him off. She was quiet for a while, her hands clenched tight in her lap, and when she looked at him again, her face was exhausted. 'I just can't believe you didn't tell me.'

He didn't want to look at her. His eyes were brimming and he didn't want her to see him crying again, to know that he was weak. He needed her to believe in him, for now anyway. 'I know,' he said, 'and I feel like an idiot.'

'You are an idiot.' She glanced out the window. 'You said you recognised him, the guy in the video – do you think that maybe you saw this guy at the retreat, at Stoney Barrow View? As a guest, maybe, or a member of staff?'

'I don't think so,' he said, 'but my mind keeps turning it over and over. The trouble was that the image quality was so bad and it was from such a long way away.'

She swore softly. 'I wish you'd told me.'

'I know, and I should have, but I think … I think that I didn't want to scare you.'

'Pete, I don't think I can get any more frightened than I am already.' The silence stretched out before she spoke again. 'OK, let's put the accusations aside for the time being, focus on what we know.'

Rawls nodded.

'Here's my question,' Eileen went on. 'All we really know is that some guy nodded to this woman outside a shop. Is there any chance that it could be unrelated?'

'It could be, I think that's another reason that I kept it to myself,' Rawls spaced his words, thinking as he spoke, 'but as we're being honest, now that I'm saying it out loud, I really don't think so.'

'Right then, let's assume they're together. We know that this woman, Amanda Burgess, owned this place before, even though it's now owned by this other guy, this Sebastian, right?'

He nodded.

'But you couldn't put the retreat aside, even before you knew that?'

He nodded again.

'So tell me why – tell me what you had before that kept pulling you in that direction. What was it about the place that you just couldn't let go of?'

Rawls pursed his lips and thought for a few seconds. 'Because so much pointed that way.'

'Pretend that I know nothing about all of this.'

'OK, let's start with Melody. She went missing in 2009. She'd been to the retreat – only once according to her mum – she was in a talent show up there; apparently quite a few schools from the area would go there because it was a fairly central venue. Then there's Harriet, she went missing in 2012. She took part in talent shows; I couldn't tell if she'd ever been there for one, but it's a link.'

'Is this the girl you told me about? The one who had blackmailed her work experience boss? She had a bit of a rotten family life?'

'Yeah, that's the one, she wasn't perfect but ...'

'You don't think that her work experience boss might have, you know, done this to other girls? Maybe he did something to them, maybe they all worked for him at some point.'

'Yup, I have thought that,' Rawls admitted. 'The guy's repulsive, a real snide.'

'The kind of person who might do this?'

He breathed out slowly. 'Yeah, I suppose.'

Eileen had her hands against her face, rubbing at her. 'What if we're heading off in the wrong direction? What if it's someone else? This work experience boss or, I don't know, someone completely unrelated to the retreat. What if Amanda Burgess is just trying to insert herself into your investigations – didn't you once tell me that people do that all the time? Maybe she just has a grudge against the place.'

She was right. People did – they got caught up in the excitement, or they wanted to be on TV, or they had a psychic dream, or they were involved and they got some kind of sick thrill in toying with the investigation. 'They do,' he agreed, not wishing to elaborate.

'So, what if it's not got anything to do with this retreat?' Eileen persisted. 'What if we're just going off on some big fat wild goose chase?'

Rawls was silent. What would he say anyway? Tell her that he had a hunch and, come what may, he had no choice but to follow it? He couldn't see that washing with Eileen.

Eileen waited, and when he said nothing she sighed and said, 'OK, who was next? Yvette?'

Rawls pulled his mind back. 'Yvette, yes,' he said, 'but this is why it's so frustrating. They went to different schools, there were so many years between them and there's so little to link them. In these cases, the perpetrator is seldom a stranger; it's nearly always someone they know: an uncle, a brother, a friend of the family, a teacher.'

'Peter.' Her voice made him jump; she grabbed his arm and squeezed so tightly that it hurt. 'A teacher – Carmen was rehearsing for *Pygmalion* and,' her grip on his arm tightened, 'her drama teacher, the same guy who taught her piano, he called me.'

'He called you? When? Why didn't you say?'

'I forgot. He rang yesterday while you were out. It seemed like nothing at the time – so many people have called to wish us well, to say how sorry they are, offer help, that kind of thing. But now that I think about it, this call was weird. He asked me if Carmen would be in for rehearsals. I told him no and he asked if she was alright.'

'What did you say?'

'I don't remember. I was so surprised that he didn't know – I mean, it had been all over the news – but I said something like I hoped she was too and I put the phone down.'

'What was his name?'

'Mark.'

'And have you met him?'

'No, he's been filling in. I think he only does this part-time, I'm sure that's what Carmen said; he was covering while her usual teacher was on maternity leave.'

'What does he do for a day job?'

Eileen considered the question, her face contorted into a frown. 'I don't know!' she said, her voice tight and high-pitched.

Rawls thought she might start crying out of sheer frustration. 'Carmen might have told me, I don't remember.'

'When did her old teacher go on maternity leave?'

'At the end of last term, so about six months ago.'

Six months. Rawls tried to ask himself the same questions that he would if he were talking to a parent of a missing child. Was there anyone new in her life? Did you notice any changes in her behaviour? Carmen had started with a new piano teacher six months ago. She had lost all interest in school, from the outside at least, but she had never missed a piano lesson and she did seem to be practising much more at home. Eileen had been excited that she seemed to have turned a corner with it, doing it for herself, and they never needed to nag her to practise in the evenings.

Rawls felt his blood run cold. 'Do you know his surname?'

She thought for a moment. 'I don't know. Shit, I should know, Carmen did tell me.'

'Could it be Calver? Does that sound familiar?' He was leading his witness, he knew that, but it was out before he could stop it. He thought about what would happen if she said yes, now she remembered, it was Calver. Then he would have no choice – he would have to call Tess, admit that he had had him and he had let him go; he would have to admit that he had failed yet again. In that brief moment he saw himself telling Tess, telling her how stupid he felt, he should have known, should have seen something, come up with something, and he saw Tess telling him that it wasn't his fault but that she was grateful for the information and he should do nothing from there on out, he should wait for them, let them do their jobs. He saw it slowing things down when speed was of the essence. Carmen had been gone for three days now. The chances of finding her alive were diminishing by the hour, by the minute; he could not take the risk, would not take the risk. Passing this to Tess would take time, and time was something they were fast running out of.

He turned to Eileen and she was shaking her head. 'I don't remember, it could be.'

He wanted to shake her, ask again, shout at her, was the guy's name Mark Calver? Was it? Was it? He tried to keep his voice calm, no point frightening her, 'Is his number on your phone? Can I have a look at it?' If it was, he had Mark's number on his own phone; they could compare the two.

She shook her head again. 'That was the other strange thing, he rang on a private number.'

'You mean, withheld?'

'I guess, yes, it just said private.' Eileen had taken her phone out of her bag and was checking her call log.

'OK, listen, what did he say? Exactly, try to remember word for word.'

'I ...' she paused, 'I don't recall his exact words. He said ...' She looked out of the window. 'Wait, OK, he said, he said, "Is that Mrs Rawls?" I told him it was, then he said, "I was just wondering if Carmen, your daughter, would be at rehearsals today. She's usually here by now."' She looked at Rawls. 'I think I said that she wouldn't be there but I was so choked up about it that I couldn't get him off the phone fast enough.'

Rawls gripped the steering wheel; he didn't want Eileen to see the panic on his face. 'What time was this?' he asked her, his eyes fixed on the road ahead.

'Around eleven, maybe a little later.'

Rawls touched her knee. 'We're going to find her.' He glanced in the rear-view mirror then indicated left at a roundabout, slowing only enough to make the turn; he felt a growing sense of urgency, a need to hurry. He glanced at Eileen. She sat rigid, one hand holding her phone, the other gripping the side of her seat. He knew what would be going through her mind, the same thing that went through any parent's mind in the same position. She would be imagining the absolute worst and he couldn't let her go there, it was too dangerous, they needed to stay calm. 'Let's not get ahead of ourselves, hon, we can't be sure. It could be nothing and we could be taking it all out of context.'

'I'm trying, Pete, but I keep seeing her, you know, seeing her tied up, or crying or screaming.'

He grabbed her hand which had gone to her mouth again and pulled it to his own so that he could kiss her fingertips. 'Shh,' he said, 'don't do this to yourself. I need you, hon.'

She pulled her hand away. 'OK, OK, you're right.' She pulled in a long, jagged breath and held it for a second before letting it out slowly. 'Is he – her piano teacher – is he involved with this retreat?'

'I don't know,' Rawls said. 'I'll get Nat to look into it.'

'And in the meantime?'

'In the meantime, we stick to what we're doing; we head to the retreat and see where that leads us.'

Eileen wrapped her arms around herself, pulling her cardigan tight, then turned away and the car was quiet again save for the clacking of the windscreen wipers.

Rawls's phone buzzed in the centre console and he turned briefly to glance at the screen. It was a text; the sender's details had flashed briefly across the top: 'Ms Stokes'. He picked it up and waited for the screen to open. Ms Stokes, Ms Stokes, who was Ms Stokes? The head teacher? No, the librarian, Ms Stokes, former member of the Stoney Path and now librarian at Radstock Public Library and community hub.

The room had filled with blinding light as Carmen flicked the switch. It felt like a million needles being stuck into her eyes all at once. She turned the switch off. She couldn't make sense of it. She'd been locked in the dark, her head ached like nothing she had ever experienced before, the room smelt of old food and body odour and something else – something that Carmen did not want to think about. Copper. No, not copper.

She covered her eyes, then reached for the switch again. This time the light filtered through her fingers in alternating patterns of light and dark. She felt like a child hiding or playing peep-bo, and the same terrible thought came to her again. When she took her hands away would someone be there? Would someone be watching her, their eyes protected by some type of infrared goggles, like the ones used by the military? Would their face be obscured by a mask?

Carmen opened her hands enough to let in the tiniest crack of light, enough to hurt but not with the same excruciating agony as before. She peered through the gap, her back still pressed to the wall, her legs shaking beneath her.

She pulled her hands away, forcing herself to look around her, to take in the room, to check for anyone else. She stopped herself – not just anyone else, it had been a woman.

His wife.

Carmen remembered the car, parked haphazardly on the side of the road. She remembered that she had considered pulling free from the woman's grip, running up the road, screaming for help. But she hadn't; the woman had been so firm, so strong as she had taken Carmen by the elbow and pushed her inside. The woman had started the engine then frowned; she had turned to Carmen and her face had been calm. 'Do you mind if I lean over you, my dear?' she had asked. 'It's just that your door isn't quite shut right, it does that sometimes.'

Carmen remembered pressing herself back into the seat to allow the woman to reach across her. What had her name been? Amelia? Ashleigh? Abigail? Esme? No, not Esme, it began with an A, definitely an A. Alice? Angela? Maybe, maybe Angela. Whatever her name was, she had leaned over Carmen and given the door handle a brief tug and then, as Carmen was distracted, the woman had jabbed something into her upper thigh. The feeling had been sharp and intensely painful, like a bee sting or a vaccination. It had burned like the touch of a hot coal and Carmen recalled grabbing at the spot with her hand. She had gasped and the woman had continued to smile at her.

'Shhh,' the woman said, 'just relax, it's OK.'

Carmen had relaxed; she had had no other choice. The world had swirled around her; the interior of the car, a blue car she had thought vaguely, had begun to shimmer. She tried to open the door but it had been dead-locked, and her hands had been so weak anyway that they had done little more than brush past the handle. 'Locked me in,' she had said to the woman and the woman had smiled kindly, her face distorting in Carmen's drugged field of vision.

'For your own good,' she had said, and Carmen had heard nothing else. She had slipped into a sleep so deep that anyone looking into the car might well have been forgiven for thinking that she was drunk. Drunk, or dead.

She let her hands fall apart now, screwing up her eyes briefly, blinking into the brightness. She was in a room, a storage room, she thought. The light switch had brought an old fluorescent bulb to life; it lit up a bare brick wall, the bricks almost grey with dust. Propped against the wall, and equally dusty, lay an old wooden frame that might once have housed a shop window. Wires hung haphazardly from the ceiling like the tendrils of some hideous creature, and, in the far corner, a bag of festering rubbish had been left propped against a rusted metal bin.

*

Eileen held her hand out, palm up. 'Let me look,' she said, 'you drive.'

'It's from the woman at the library,' Rawls said.

'The one who left the cult?' She was tapping at his phone; she never had been able to get the hang of it.

Rawls wanted to scream at her to hurry up when he saw a lay-by and pulled over, reaching to take the phone back from her.

'What does it say?' She was leaning over to see the screen.

Rawls read out loud: 'Dear Mr Rawls, sorry to send this so early but I saw you on the news and wanted to say how sorry I am for what has happened.' He paused, scrolling through the message.

Eileen stared at the message and said, 'She's written *War and Peace*.'

Rawls nodded, scanning for key words. 'She says that she saw the CCTV footage on the news, the image of the man at the shop,' he glanced at Eileen, 'I hadn't realised they had released it already.'

'Read the message, Pete.' Eileen covered her eyes with her hands as though she was afraid to see for herself.

Rawls read on: 'She says that she would like to meet with me because she has more to tell me; she says she's sorry for being so difficult when I met with her.' He scrolled again, the woman really had written *War and Peace*. 'There's a link; she says to have a look at the photo, she says that she hopes that it will make things clearer.'

He clicked on the link and the phone went blank save for a white screen that told him that his phone was not registered on a network.

He swore loudly and almost threw the phone at Eileen as he slammed the car back on to the road. 'No signal.'

Eileen held the phone out in front of her, moving it from time to time as though it might find a glimmer of signal if she pressed it to the front windscreen or up against the roof of the car.

'Try refreshing,' Rawls said even as she was pressing the little circular icon.

'Nothing.' Her voice sounded strained as though she might scream or cry, or both. Rawls felt the same, and who could blame them? In the last three days they had been through more than most people had to deal with in their entire lives.

'Signal,' Eileen screamed and then she repeated the word as though it was some kind of mantra, 'signal, signal, signal.'

Rawls pulled over as far as he could into the hedgerow. The Facebook link was opening; it was a business page. Eileen turned the screen towards him and it took him a moment to register what he was looking at. The photo was small and the faces were made even smaller by the number of people in the picture. It was a production of some sort; the cast were all in full costume, luxurious Edwardian dresses and overcoats with top hats. The picture had been titled 'My Fair Lady 2017', and standing on either side were 'our director and his lovely wife'. The librarian had written a caption above the photo: 'The lady in the photo is Amanda Burgess, Eve Burgess was her mother.'

Eileen's hand flew to her throat. 'That's the woman; I knew that I knew her. She was at rehearsals when I picked Carmen up.' She was pulling the image with her fingers, enlarging the woman's face as she spoke.

'What about the man, on the other side?' Eileen fiddled with the image until they were looking at him, at his tight camel-shit coloured jeans and his tweed blazer with matching cap. The guy had thick eyebrows and a broad jaw, handsome, Rawls supposed, in a GI Joe kind of way. It was the guy with the van, the man he had interviewed only three days before: Mark Calver.

'Shit,' he said. 'She must have kept her maiden name; Amanda Burgess is actually Amanda Calver. They're a fucking team.'

'Do you mean …?' Eileen's brow had creased into almost perfect straight lines. 'Do you mean like Fred and Rosemary West?'

Rawls ran his tongue over his teeth, his mouth suddenly dry. 'God, I hope not, but everything points to them in this together. He must have known all the girls, every one of them. They were all in a play up at the retreat or he taught them drama or the piano or some other instrument at one time or another, it's the only thing that makes sense.'

Eileen pointed to the screen. 'It says here that they hold a play or a concert at the same place every year, it's a tradition.' She turned to Rawls, 'Peter, is this the retreat? In the background, is it Stoney Barrow View?'

He nodded. 'Definitely, no question about it.'

'So we're right. That's where she is, Pete, she's at the retreat.'

He shook his head, and Eileen grabbed his arm. 'It must be, it makes sense.'

'Except that Amanda Burgess doesn't own the place any more.'

Eileen stared at him. 'Then where is she?'

'I don't know, but I think she's nearby.'

'Why?' she asked, her voice shrill.

'Because ...' he paused, wondering what he was going to say, 'the place is so important to them. I'm pretty sure they met there. This Amanda woman, she grew up in the cult, we know that. Her father was the founder, she spent most of her life there and I'll bet my wages that they met there, probably when they were very young. I imagine that he was part of it too. That sort of life, well, you just don't know what it might do to a person, especially if you've never really known anything different. I think they might have Carmen nearby, but not there, not at the retreat – they've sold that now, but I'm willing to bet you they kept part of the land.'

He glanced at his sat nav; they were only a few minutes away. Something in his mind had just fallen into place – the land adjacent to the property, where the excavators were.

Eileen was asking him, 'This Mark Calver guy, didn't you say that he owned some kind of property maintenance company?'

'He does, he said that he was a joint owner with his wife. ABC Property Maintenance, I think he said.'

Eileen looked at him. 'ABC. Amanda Burgess Calver?'

Rawls closed his eyes briefly. 'Could be.'

'And the fourth girl, Tanya, didn't they say on the news that she had a cleaning job? I'm sure they were asking for anyone with information about it to contact them.'

Rawls swore under his breath. 'That was who was giving her a lift, and that was why his van was parked up on the side of the road. He was waiting for her, Mark Calver, he was waiting for her to come to him – she thought she was going to clean one of the places that they looked after.'

'Pete, we need to call Tess or Nat.'

He nodded. 'We will, but let me get this clear in my own head first, OK?'

She frowned at him.

'Please, Eileen, right now it's all just pieces of a puzzle; let me just put them in place first.'

She nodded but said nothing so he went on, 'When I went up there with Nat, we noticed building machinery – they were putting in a lake or something, just like Jo mentioned when she went there.'

'That was a few years ago,' Eileen said.

'Exactly. What if they still own part of the estate?'

'Do you think they live there?'

'No, I shouldn't think so,' he said. 'Nat was going to look into all of that.' He accelerated a little too quickly to beat a lorry at a T-junction in the road, 'but she hasn't mentioned anything yet, although I'm fairly sure that Calver said he lived in Bath.'

'They could have two places,' Eileen suggested. 'They might have a weekend bolthole – they would have made a packet selling the retreat – or they could use it for storing equipment, cheaper than renting somewhere in town.'

Rawls nodded. They could do, that made a lot of sense.

'I still think we should tell Tess now.'

Rawls checked the navigation and slowed for a turning. 'Let's just see what we can see when get there, OK?'

'If we told them, though, couldn't they go and have a look, search the place, that sort of thing?' Eileen persisted.

'Not without a search warrant and that takes time,' he said, 'and I would bet my bottom dollar on Tess telling us that there isn't sufficient evidence to request one.'

'But it's all there,' Eileen said. 'What more would they need?'

'At the moment it's just circumstantial,' Rawls said. 'We've nothing concrete yet, nothing definite.'

Carmen took the room in, moving her eyes slowly from one item to another. There was an old poster in a frame on the floor beside the bin and, as her eyes adjusted to the glare, she realised that what she had first mistaken for more dust, was actually an airbrushed image of the sea. 'Weston-Super-Mare' had been written across the top, and at the bottom, just below a glamorous woman in a red bathing suit and wide-brimmed hat, she could see the rest of the legend, 'escape with us'.

She became aware then of the silence. The darkness had been bad enough and the visions that her imagination had conjured up of spiders and snakes and rats had all but rendered her paralysed with fear, but the silence was something altogether different. It made her feel alone and vulnerable. She thought that that silence, given enough time, would be enough to drive her insane.

She wanted to cry out, to plead for help, to beg for someone, anyone, to come and get her, but she could not, would not, because to do so would mean breaking the silence and whoever had brought her there might hear her. She held her breath instead, straining her ears to listen for even the softest of sounds: a footstep on the floor above, the cough of a person on the road in the distance, the sound of a car, anything to let her know that she wasn't alone, that the world was still out there, living, walking, breathing.

How long she stood that way she didn't know, but her back ached and her legs had started to quiver when the sounds came to her.

The sound of someone moving above, footsteps on a wooden floor, a tinny sound, something being rested on the floor. A sloshing sound, like someone throwing out a bucket of water.

Carmen held her hand over her mouth, afraid of crying out, afraid even of breathing.

The footsteps stamped above her then paused, and there was another sound, something familiar, a scratch, sudden and sharp. It took Carmen a moment to register the sound of a match being struck. That was when the smell first came to her.

Smoke, acrid and dirty, the kind of smoke that comes from a firelighter. The kind of smoke that hurts your eyes and clogs up your throat. She heard it then, the fire burning somewhere above her.

The rain had subsided, and a cold wind had taken its place when Rawls pulled into the small gravel lay-by that Eileen had pointed to. Ahead of them, no more than a hundred or so metres along the road, was the entrance to Stoney Barrow View. Beyond that, and not too far in the distance, was the reason they had pulled over: a streak of blue and white smoke cut a line across the sky from between the dark shadows of trees.

They got out of the car to look, and Eileen grabbed his arm, her fingers digging into the flesh. 'There's an old railway shed out that way – we've walked there, do you remember? When Carmen was little, I made you bring us out here for a picnic. You didn't want to come because it was too far out, do you remember?'

He did remember and his mind took him back to the place with a moment of perfect clarity. The building was both beautiful and scary, like something from a horror film. The crumbling walls had been pockmarked by BB gunshot, silver nitrous oxide canisters had been scattered around the floors, graffiti covered the walls – mostly just tags, but some that made insightful and highly intellectual statements like 'Jamie is a dick' and 'welcome to the asylum, it's your home now'.

'Are you certain?' he asked. 'Over there?'

She nodded, her fingers still biting into his arm. 'Yes, and do you remember the trapdoor? We laughed because it looked like the kind of place that was perfect for a doomsday prepper.'

'Or a hostage,' Rawls said, the memory of that warm summer's day growing clearer by the minute.

He looked once more at the pillar of smoke on the horizon and then turned to his wife. 'Get in the car!' he shouted, already running towards it. 'We have to get there.'

Eileen was opening the passenger door. 'That's right at the far end of the grounds of the retreat, isn't it?'

'Yes, I'm pretty sure it is.' Rawls pulled on to the empty road and headed towards the plume of smoke. They could be there in little more than a couple of minutes – that was if he could remember how to get to it, the lanes had a habit of all looking the same around here. He thought he would cross that bridge when he got to it; their first and more immediate issue was the steam that their damp bodies had produced, the windscreen clouding with a mist so sudden and complete that it was almost as though someone had pulled a wet curtain across it.

He swore loudly and asked Eileen to check his jacket pocket on the back seat for paper napkins; he remembered shoving a handful in the last time he'd been bought a coffee.

Eileen leaned around and grabbed it, and as she did so, the note he'd jotted down with the details of the Ford Focus fell out of the inside pocket. He saw an accusatory look cloud her features. 'You should have answered your damn phone,' the look said, 'you should have been home, not dicking about selling a car that you hadn't even told me about.'

Guilt spread through him like a drug from a dirty needle and he thought that she might hit him, but her face cleared, and she handed him a bundle of white napkins. She took a bunch for herself and, with the fan blasting air so loudly that it mercifully prevented any conversation, they wiped desperately at the steamy glass.

'Just drive,' Eileen said, 'I'll keep wiping.'

He went as fast as he could, keeping the dirty smear of smoke ahead of him, letting it guide him, like the pillar of fire in Exodus. The closer they got, the less it looked like a biblical manifestation of God and more like a streak of paint left by a sloppy, or drunk, artist; filthy and pungent, it spoke of old tyres and burning metal. Rawls was certain that this was no ordinary bonfire. He felt a growing sense of panic; time, he knew, was running out.

'Turn right here,' Eileen shouted in a voice so shrill that it sent a new surge of terror through his head. 'Look,' she was pointing to a public footpath sign, 'I can see the smoke over there; this looks as though it would lead you straight to it.'

Rawls parked the car on the side of the road. Next to the sign that Eileen had picked out was another, this one less rusted, more recent; the sign read: 'Private Property, Entry is Forbidden'. He scrambled over the wet stile and started running into the trees.

Eileen was following behind him and he shouted back over his shoulder, 'Call Tess, give her our exact coordinates – you can get them off the navigation – tell her to hurry. If Carmen is in there,' and God knew he hoped that she wasn't, 'we're going to need an ambulance.'

Eileen said nothing but he saw the look on her face, and it told him that she understood. 'Go,' she shouted at him, and she ran back the way she had come.

The ground was thick and muddy beneath his feet, but the wind had continued to clear the clouds and the rain was mercilessly absent. Wet vegetation brushed his legs and arms, and the sagging boughs of overhead branches caught his face, slowing his passage. The smell of the smoke was strong now, and something about it drove him forward. A terrible feeling of panic was creeping through him, a sense that something was happening, something more than a bonfire at six thirty on a wet morning – something bad. His rational mind tried to tell him that it was probably just some kid getting Instagram likes for burning a stolen motorcycle, or some arsehole fly-tipping an old bed and a pile of old tyres, but his instinct told him something different – he had to get to that fire, come what may – and it was his instinct that he intended to heed.

Now he was deep in the trees and the path ahead of him widened into one that was big enough for a vehicle to get through. Further up, no more than a hundred feet or so, the road split into two and Rawls felt a sense of despair creep over him; he had no idea which path to take. For a moment he found himself rooted to the spot, his head spinning, his heart a tractor ploughing treacle. From somewhere nearby a crow called out, followed in short order by a volley of furious replies. The sound of them made him shiver.

Above him a canopy of trees and thick smoke blocked out the sky and he looked around wildly, trying to determine where the source of the fire must be. His sense of direction was lost without a view of the horizon to guide him and everything seemed to slow down. The sound of the fire, which had been little more than a background hum only seconds before, now seemed almost deafening; it rumbled and roared with an intensity that was both hypnotising and terrifying. The sound should have led him to the fire but it did the opposite: it seemed omnipresent, like a low bass sound, from everywhere and nowhere all at once.

'What now?' he said aloud, turning in a wide circle, his trainers, now soaked through, trying to pull him into the thick mud. 'Which way?'

A bed had been made for Carmen. Nothing special, just a mattress, a sheet, pillows, a duvet. It was all neat, all clean. Next to the bed, Carmen saw now, was a portable toilet and a jug and bowl, the kind you saw in period dramas. For a moment she was taken by the attention to detail; she was touched, almost. The woman, it seemed, had made an effort, but then again she had also ditched her in the dark with the spiders and was now about to burn her to a crisp like a rat in a hole.

Carmen had been holding her breath, trying to keep the smoke out, trying to keep the clean air in. She let it go in a long and frantic whoosh then drew in another, this one filled with soot and smoke. She ran for the duvet on the bed, stripping the cover and wrapping it around her mouth like a Bedouin nomad. It blocked out some of the smoke but made it difficult to breathe.

She dropped to the floor, certain that she had read or heard or been told, sometime in her life, that during a fire the air is cleaner lower down. She crawled on to the mattress, tucking herself up against the wall. A small bottle of water had been left for her and she poured some into her eyes, gasping as it flushed them, relishing the temporary relief. She had to stay calm, she had to think. There must be a way out. Above her she thought the fire must be in full swing and she felt a terrible fear that the ceiling would cave in and crush her beneath it.

Scanning the room, she tried to find anything that she might climb under in the event of the ceiling falling through. Her mind tried to show her images of herself, her hair on fire, her clothes melting on to her skin, her eyes red and streaming. She pushed them away, focusing instead on the space around her. Struggling to stay calm, she tried to remember the sum required to calculate the volume of air in the room. Something in her mind told her this was a pointless exercise – it tried to stop her, to make her lose her concentration, to drive her into a panic – but she ignored it.

'I need height, width and length,' she said into the duvet cover around her mouth. 'So, let's guess that the room is, say, two metres high.'

She cried out in fright as something exploded with a soft pop in the room above. She imagined a frame buckling in the heat or a window caving in or perhaps even an old deodorant tin exploding.

'And the width is about ...' she was trying to ignore the small puffs of smoke that were trickling in, like thin, grey, baby snakes, through the cracks in the ceiling, 'about three metres, no, let's say four.' Her mind raced; she couldn't recall her estimated wall height and she tried again, scanning the walls around her. 'Two metres high, three metres long and, and ...' She couldn't finish. Above her the fire cackled its dry laughter and there was another tremendous crack like the sound of a car backfiring. Carmen gave in to the panic and started to scream. She would scream until she ran out of air or until her throat was destroyed, whichever came the sooner, but she would not die quietly in this horrible dark place. She would not go down without a fight.

Rawls ran wildly towards the burning building. Breathing heavily and with his heart pounding in his chest, he took a moment to consider the best route. Frozen for a moment, he saw that flames were forking out of the windows, their red and yellow tongues licking at the walls. He strained his ears against the crashing sound of the fire and he thought – no, he was sure – that he heard a voice, faint but definite: 'Help me! I'm inside, please!'

His heart seemed to pause in its task of jackhammering itself out of his chest and he forgot to breathe. The voice, oh dear God in heaven, could it be? Was it Carmen?

'Pleeeeaase!'

Adrenaline pushed him forward, providing him with the power he needed to navigate the branches, roots and brambles that bit at his legs and threatened to trip him.

'Carmen,' he screamed as he neared the building and he now remembered that it was part of the old railway line. It was a squat brick shed, most likely used for storage rather than as any kind of station; Rawls was pretty sure that the nearest station would have been Radstock or Frome. They would have held all kinds of equipment there, but what was racing through his mind was flammables. Would they have been cleared? He thought they would, but he couldn't be certain.

The fire had engulfed the top half of the building and flames rolled around the carcass, first orange, then yellow, then black. Rawls thought that no one could survive being inside that building, and panic rose in his throat like a wave of nausea.

'Carmen,' he bellowed into the flames, 'Carmen!'

'Help me.'

He froze, listening. The sound had not come from the building, not exactly; it had come from below, and he remembered the trapdoor. Thank God, she was in the cellar, he still had time.

An enormous crash came from the crumbling construction and Rawls saw a beam fall to the ground inside, setting off a new wave of flames.

'Carmen,' he screamed again, his voice hysterical, 'Carmen, answer me, damn it!'

His eyes and nose felt as though the heat had already burned them to a crisp and his mouth was so dry that he feared that if he tried to swallow it might send him into a coughing fit so overpowering that he might never recover.

He opened his mouth, readied himself to shout, and heard the voice again. It was faint beneath the bass boom of the fire, but he heard it, nonetheless.

He spun around frantically, turning back to the building in time to see one of the remaining windows crack and then collapse in a shower of broken glass. The trapdoor was in there and there was no way to get to it now.

'Carmen,' he croaked, 'Carmen, is that you?'

'Underground,' came the response, 'undergroooouuund.'

'Stand back,' he screamed through the cracks. 'Stand back, OK, away from the smoke.'

He heard a response but couldn't make out the words. 'Stand back!' he screamed one last time and brought his foot down as hard as he could.

He felt the surface shake and he brought his heel down a second time. This time the shake was followed by a loud but unmistakable crack and the ground beneath his feet gave way to splintering wood and falling sand. From beneath him he heard a brief scream and then a sound that he would remember for the rest of his life, a sound that filled his heart with joy and heartbreak in equal parts.

'Dad?'

Rawls fell to his knees, pulling at broken splinters of wood and shouting, 'Carmen, it's me, can you get to me? Can you get ...'

A face appeared below him, Carmen's face, and he cried out with the joy of seeing her. He lay down flat, his arms thrust through the gap. 'Grab my hands,' he shouted, but even as he did, he realised that she wasn't tall enough; he couldn't reach her.

Eileen dropped the phone into her jacket pocket. Tess had been calm, cold even. She had told Eileen that all three emergency services were already on the way, the fire had been reported. She had told her to stay in the car, to wait for help, to try to stay calm. She had told Eileen that under absolutely no circumstances whatsoever should either Eileen or Rawls enter that building. Eileen had cut the call and now, as she clambered back over the stile, with the smell of smoke choking her and a feeling of panic intensifying in her chest, she could hear the sirens wailing from somewhere in the distance. *Coming for us*, she thought, *coming for Carmen*.

A knot of bare roots had tangled beneath the stile and Eileen lost her footing as she tried to step over it. Falling to the ground, she heard the sound of air leaving her lungs first and only felt the pain in her leg a moment later. Twisting her body to get a better look at the widening dark patch on her jeans, she first assumed that she had landed in a puddle deeper than it first appeared, but then, as the pain seemed to grow rather than subside, her mind distantly informed her that it wasn't mud, but blood. She pulled at her trouser leg, lifting it up to reveal a gash in the dark black material and, behind it, where she should have seen pale smooth skin, she saw the open mouth of a wound that had gone so deep that it revealed the soft yellow fat beneath the skin's surface and, below that, the pale white bone of her shin. She grabbed suddenly at the edges of the wound and tried to push them together as though they were an especially unpleasant three-dimensional puzzle. Her vision swam as her mind tried to shut her down, but she bit her lip hard enough to bring blood until it cleared.

The distant sound of the fire had grown to a steady roar and every now and then she could hear the distant voice of someone, she assumed Rawls, shouting to someone else. She needed to get up, to get to him, to help him to free Carmen, or whoever was in the building, but the combination of the pain and the sight of the open wound had left her weak and afraid to move.

Clinging to consciousness, Eileen allowed herself a brief scream and then bit down hard on her lip again, forcing herself to stop. Tearing her scarf from her neck and wrapping the wound with it as tightly as the pain would allow, she tried to push herself up. In the distance there was a sound like something exploding and she could hear Peter above the din, shouting at someone. That got her moving. Her baby was in there, she knew it, she had no doubt now.

'Please God,' Eileen whispered into the cold air, 'please, not in that building, not my Carmen.'

She pulled herself up, screaming into the damp air as a bolt of pain, white-hot and like nothing she had felt before, tore through her leg. Ahead of her the fire crackled and vaguely, through the din, she thought she heard voices; Carmen perhaps, crying out.

She closed her eyes, bit down on her bottom lip and let adrenaline push her forward.

'Dad, I'm scared.'

The pale, soot-blackened and exhausted face of his daughter stared up at him from what Rawls thought must have been some kind of underground storage in the long distant past. The building that had once covered it had all but rotted away, leaving just the one room which was burning with a savage hunger that seemed all consuming and impossible to oppose. The tiny shotgun line of flames that was devouring what was left of the floor was creeping ever closer to him and Rawls feared that they had seconds rather than minutes to escape its hungry passage.

'You need to grab my hand,' he shouted to her.

'Dad, I can't, I can't,' she screamed back, her voice high and hysterical. 'I can't, I'm scared.'

Rawls stretched his knees out behind him, one hand grabbing on to an overturned tree trunk for purchase, the other stretched into the ground beneath him. 'Try,' he screamed, and his own voice seemed to his ears to be as close to hysteria as his daughter's was. 'Please, baby, please try.'

Carmen stood on her toes, her hands reaching up towards him like a fanatic in a fit of religious ecstasy. Their fingers touched briefly, and even as they did, Rawls knew it was pointless, they would never be able to hold on to each other.

He pushed himself up, his eyes frantically searching for anything – a rope, a log, a chain – that he could lower down into the hole for his daughter to use. Anything to get her out before the fire reached flashpoint and everything in its vicinity exploded like a pine cone on a barbecue.

The woods remained stubbornly empty; there was nothing he could use. He ran back to the edge, 'Carmen, do you hear me?'

'Yes, I hear you. Daddy, the flames are coming in.'

He pulled his jumper off and wrapped it around his face. 'Carmen, I've got to climb in.'

'No, Dad, the flames, they're coming in.'

He looked into the hole, smoke burning his eyes and searing the back of his throat. All around him the fire crackled as it consumed the crumbling walls. He closed his eyes. 'Stand back,' he shouted again, and then jumped.

Carmen ran to him as he fell. She wrapped her arms around him and cried. Rawls hugged her briefly then pushed her back.

'Is there a door?'

'Over there,' Carmen pointed to the wall where the flames were now a bright, hungry orange. 'We can't go through it, Dad, we'll burn.'

Rawls knew she was right. He stared around, searching for something, anything that they could use to escape. It was becoming difficult to breathe, difficult to think, difficult to hear. 'Get down on to your knees,' he shouted at her. For a moment she looked confused and he made a gesture with his arm, she dropped down and he followed.

They crouch-walked across the floor as the flames made their way into the room, forming a dirty orange arc between the wall and the ceiling. Rawls glanced at it briefly in horror; if the ceiling came down they might well be crushed by it. It wouldn't be long, he knew, before the arc became a wall of flames. Black smoke billowed like smoke signals into the grey sky above.

The fire had sent out little sentinels of flames that were tasting the wooden floor and, finding it good, had begun to gorge themselves on it, racing towards the two of them. Rawls gauged that they had less than a couple of minutes before they too would be consumed. He grabbed Carmen's arm and pointed to the hole that the fire had made in the wall. Beyond it a flight of stone steps led upwards, flames licking the wooden panelling on either side.

Carmen shook her head and tried to pull away.

He nodded and pointed but she shook her head again, holding her hand over the duvet cover that she had wrapped around her mouth.

'We have to,' Rawls shouted into her ear, 'it's our only hope.'

She tried to pull away from him, but he grabbed her arm. 'On three, you stand and you run with me, head down, arms tucked in, OK?'

'Dad, I can't,' Carmen was trembling, her body almost convulsing, 'I can't go through it.'

He tried to pull her but she resisted, her feet planted; even in the dark Rawls could see the terror in her eyes. He looked around, desperate, hoping for a plan, a way to get his daughter moving. 'I'll carry you.'

She pulled back, panic making her curl her lip. 'No, I don't want to go up there, the fire ...'

'The fire is going to kill us if we don't move.' His lungs were burning, speech was becoming more and more difficult, his throat was constricting and his brain felt fuzzy, unable to focus.

There was a loud crack from the staircase, closely followed by a scream. Eileen.

Carmen ran forward. 'Mum?'

'Carmen,' Eileen's voice rose above the flames, 'Carmen, I'm coming.'

'No,' Rawls shouted back, 'stay where you are, don't come down.'

Eileen's shadow filled the stairwell and Carmen grabbed Rawls's hand frantically. 'Don't let her come down, the fire ...'

The flames were everywhere now – the walls, the debris on the floor, the poster advertising rail trips to Weston-Super-Mare – and the smoke made it almost impossible to breathe. Rawls felt his mind swimming, his vision doubling and re-doubling. He was aware from some distant part of his mind that Carmen was pulling at him, the yank hard enough to make him take a step forward. She screamed something to her mother, Rawls could barely hear her, then she turned to him.

'Move,' she shouted, and he felt propelled by her determination. The two of them made their way through the wall of flames and into the light of the stairwell beyond.

They fell back on the hard ground. In front of them the skeleton that had been a building groaned beneath the weight of the fire that had almost reduced it to nothing more than a few blackened timbers and spits of outlying flames. Carmen rolled on to her side and vomited into the mud. Rawls, coughing himself, tried to put an arm around her but found he barely had the strength to lift it.

From both somewhere and nowhere, he heard his wife's voice and he looked up to see Eileen, laughing and crying as she fell to her knees in front of Carmen, pushing her daughter's hair away from her soot-covered face as if to confirm that it really was her. Carmen tried to speak but her words were lost to coughing and she bent over and heaved a couple more times.

Rawls pushed himself up and looked back at the burning building. It seemed to be folding in on itself and he thought that it would probably die back to nothing more than a few smouldering heaps within the next few minutes. He reached over and put his arms around Carmen and Eileen, kissing one and then the other on their heads over and over again.

Behind them the building gave one last wretched sigh and the last of the frame collapsed beneath the dying flames.

Eileen looked at Rawls. 'Thank God,' she said. 'Thank you, God.' She turned her face towards the sky and from somewhere in the distance the sounds of emergency services filled the air as though God himself had answered her. 'It's over,' she said to Rawls, but he shook his head.

'Not yet,' he said, and the sound of people running towards them from the road stopped him from saying any more.

Chapter 22

Rawls stood in the doorway. He hated hospitals, the way they smelled, the harsh lights that seemed, despite their brightness, to do nothing to drive out the murky feel of the place. He hated doctors speaking in quiet voices and nurses scowling at him as he passed; he hated the smell of cabbage cooking and people so pale and thin that he marvelled at them being able to walk unaided; he hated long, impersonal corridors and windows that looked out on to sad gardens where nobody ever seemed to sit. He hated all of these things, but what he hated more than anything was the fact that Carmen was here right now. Carmen, who had been through so much, had to be left alone in a metal bed in this bleak place.

She was sleeping when he walked into her room, her back to him, her breathing steady. Every now and then she would make a tiny noise in the back of her throat; it was a sound that he had heard her make a thousand times before, a sound that she always made when something bad had happened: a fall from a bike, a fight at school, being kidnapped from the cinema.

'Carmen,' he whispered, crossing the room and pressing a hand on to her back. 'Car, I need to talk to you.'

Carmen moaned a little in her sleep and he touched her again. 'Car, we've got to talk.'

Carmen rolled slowly towards him. 'Dad,' she said, 'Daddy.' Her face was bruised in more places than he could count, her hands and lower arms had been bandaged and there were stitches above her left eye. She looked at him with eyes that were shot through with bright red veins and he thought that she looked like an extra from a vampire movie. 'Dad, I'm sorry,' she said.

He leaned down and kissed her cheek. It felt too hot somehow, as though the fire had left a permanent mark in her DNA. 'Babe,' he felt himself crying, 'you have nothing to say sorry for; nothing at all.'

Tears spilled down her pale face and dampened the pillow beneath her; in them Rawls could see flecks of soot like the ones that he was still wiping from his own eyes. He didn't want to do this. He didn't want to quiz her now, not now, not here. He opened his mouth to speak and then found that he couldn't, and he closed it again.

As though she had read his mind, Carmen said, 'I couldn't tell you, Dad. You're a policeman.' She started to say something else but her voice cracked, and she broke into a coughing fit.

Rawls reached for the glass of water beside her bed and held the straw to her lips. He waited for the coughing to subside before he lowered himself on to the bed beside her. It made an unhappy scraping sound under his weight. 'OK, tell me now, as your dad, not a policeman.'

She turned her face away from him and he waited as she stared at the blue curtains that provided the only privacy in the room.

'We're on our own,' Rawls said. 'Car, I need to know about Mark, your piano teacher. I need to know how he fits into all of this.'

'I, we ... well, he said that he liked me, he said that I was ...' she looked away, embarrassed, 'I was beautiful, and it sounds stupid but I thought I liked him.'

Rawls cringed at the word beautiful; he had told himself that he wouldn't but it happened before he could stop it.

A look of hurt flashed across his daughter's face. 'I knew you would do that, Dad.' She looked away, 'I knew you would judge me.'

Rawls touched her arm; it seemed the only place that he could touch her that wasn't either bruised or covered in some kind of dressing. 'I'm not judging you, darling, it's him.'

She tried to smile. 'Isn't that the same thing?'

Rawls sighed. 'No, it isn't the same at all. You weren't to blame, he is. Whatever went on, he was to blame.'

She looked at him, a flash of hurt anger in her eyes that made them come alive. 'Nothing happened, Dad. We were just texting.'

She looked away and Rawls knew that she was not telling him the truth. He nodded but didn't speak. He didn't want to imagine what those texts might have said, nor did he want them to become part of the evidence against this man, or for his daughter to have to go through the indignity of having to explain it all to him, or even worse, to a court. It hurt him to even imagine it, but he knew that it was too late now, and he rested his hand on top of her small bandaged one.

Carmen was watching his face intently, 'I thought ...' she pulled her hand out of his, 'I thought he loved me.'

Rawls felt a terrible sadness for her. He had been young once himself, young and naive. His sadness was replaced quickly with a sense of black anger. The guy had played Carmen – had he done the same to all of them? Had he done this over and over? Would they find more missing girls, groomed by him? He thought they probably would. 'Carmen,' he said softly, 'I need to ask you some questions, is that OK?'

She turned away from him again, staring at the blue curtains. 'OK,' she said, and her voice was little more than a whisper.

Rawls reached into his pocket and pulled out a folded piece of pale green paper. He had found it in her bedroom when he had gone home to pick up their clothes. Tess had offered to send someone but Rawls had declined. He had needed the quiet, and as he had sat on his daughter's bed, crying softly into his hands, he had noticed the paper lying next to the waste paper basket. It hadn't been the paper that had caught his eye, but two words written on it, 'Stoney Barrow'. He had picked it up and opened it, drying his eyes with the back of his hand. On the front it read, in a fancy font, Baskerville or something similar, *'In celebration of our long relationship with Stoney Barrow View Retreat and Resort, The Mark Calver Players invite you to our annual event: My Fair Lady.'*

Below, in a smaller, less exotic font, *'Join us for an evening of fabulous food and stunning entertainment!'*

Rawls had turned it over in his hands, hating the feeling of the paper. It was as if all the evils of the past few days had somehow infested it. On the inside cover in extremely small font was a long list of the cast and technical team and Rawls had scanned it quickly.

Now, he laid the folded sheet on the bed beside Carmen. She looked at him, her eyes frowning, uncertain.

'The play,' she said. 'I don't understand.'

'Is that where you met him?'

She turned away. 'No, I met him at school. He was covering for Miss Haltrow while she was on leave, he mentioned the play and, well, I wanted to, you know, to …'

'Shh,' he said, 'you don't need to explain.'

She raised her eyes to his briefly then looked away again, and he reached out and put his hand on her arm. Beneath it he could feel her trembling and he knew that she was crying again. He waited for her to settle before he spoke.

'Car,' he said softly, 'why did you go with Amanda? What did she say to you? Had you met her before?'

Carmen hesitated. 'I didn't know her, but I knew who she was.'

'You knew she was his wife?' Rawls tried not to allow emotion to seep into his voice.

'She told me to come with her. She said that if I didn't, she would tell you, she would tell everyone.' Carmen covered her face with a bandaged hand. 'I'm so sorry, Dad.' She tried to smile. 'I thought he loved me, I thought I was the only one. His only one.' She turned away and Rawls made no effort to stop her. 'I remember her talking to me, in the car. I couldn't speak because she injected me with something that made me pass out, but I remember her telling me that I wasn't the only one – he'd done it with other girls too.'

Rawls felt a prickle of anger in the base of his spine. 'Other girls?'

'Yes, Amanda said that he … he had done it with others over the years, that I was just one of many.' She broke off sobbing now and Rawls reached for her. In the back of his mind the prickle of anger was growing into a full-blown rage. Many young girls … the thought made his blood run cold.

Carmen wiped at her face. 'When's mum coming to see me?'

Rawls glanced at his watch. 'Any minute now. She had to have her leg stitched but she'll be here in a bit. She's going to be with you when they interview you.'

'Not you?'

Rawls shook his head. 'They want Mum there.'

'Will they be cross with me?'

'Cross with you? No, of course not.'

'I'm sorry, Daddy, I didn't mean to cause all of this.'

Rawls turned her to face him. 'Listen to me. You didn't cause anything and you have nothing to apologise for.'

He wrapped his arms around her and, as he did, a terrible thought came to him.

He knew with absolute certainty that he intended to find Mark Calver and, when he did, he was going to kill him.

Chapter 23

Nat rang the doorbell. Rawls had spoken to her outside Carmen's room at the Royal United Hospital. That had been a little over forty-five minutes ago. She had asked him how Carmen was, and he had told her that she was as well as could be expected.

'You'll be present during her interview?' Rawls had asked, and she'd shaken her head.

'They've allocated a specialist case officer and, of course Eileen will be present.'

Rawls had thanked her for the information and turned to leave.

'Sarge, where are you going?'

'I'm not Sarge at the moment.' Rawls's voice had sounded flat, as though he was talking from a different universe.

'Rawls, then, where are you going?'

'I won't be long,' he said. 'Just look after my girls, OK?'

She had watched him leave, her sense of dread growing with every step he took. 'Rawls, what should I say to Ma'am?' she called after him.

'Tell her whatever you like.' Rawls rounded a corner and disappeared from sight.

'Rawls, don't do anything daft, OK?' Nat said to herself, although she knew that doing something daft was exactly what he intended to do.

'You're going to find him, aren't you?' she said, still talking to herself. 'What on earth are you playing at?'

Nat knew that Tess and Chivers were heading to the Bath home shared by Mark and Amanda Calver – they would be there any minute, but Nat was suddenly sure that they would find it empty. She knew where Rawls was headed, and she was equally certain that he would find the Calvers there. She realised that if she was going to stop Rawls from making the biggest mistake of his life, she would have to be quick. She couldn't tell Tess; the DI would order her to stand down.

Nat left the hospital as soon as Eileen had been wheeled around from her ward.

'Where is he?' Eileen had asked.

'I'm going to find him,' she'd said, and Eileen had squeezed her hand.

'Be careful,' Eileen said, and Nat had nodded. 'I'll do my best.'

Now she stood on the doorstep of a converted barn. The place was in darkness except for a light somewhere behind the mahogany front door. She had remembered the story that Rawls had told her about the time that he'd gone in search of a missing young man – the 'shit job', Rawls had called it. He had told her that he'd visited an old barn – the milking parlour, Rawls had called it – on the far side of the property, tucked out of sight from the main house. The place had been derelict, but they had agreed at the time that they should have the place checked out. That had been before Carmen's abduction, before Rawls had been put on leave, before everything had gone a little mad. Before, she realised now with a sense of overwhelming regret, she had forgotten.

There was a rustle behind the door as though someone was trying to see who was on the doorstep and, in that moment, Nat was aware of how exposed she was, and alone. She had expected to find Rawls here, she had no weapon and the only person in the world who knew that she was here at all was Eileen, and she wasn't sure that Eileen even knew where she was exactly.

'Mr Calver,' she bent and spoke into the letter box, 'my name is Detective Natalie Parkinson. I wonder if I might come inside, I have a couple of questions to ask you.'

The door opened and a handsome man looked out at her. He was dressed casually in the same skinny jeans he'd been wearing when they'd watched him on the CCTV cameras at Mr Patel's shop, salmon pink and turned up to reveal his ankles.

'Detective Parkinson' he said, 'have you bought my phone back?'

'Your phone?' She wracked her brain, trying to remember, oh yes, Rawls had taken it during their interview, 'um, no sorry, I think it's still in evidence.'

He smiled. 'Well no bother, it was only my work phone. Do come in.' He stood aside and extended an arm, pressing himself against the wall so that Nat had to brush against him as she passed and, as he closed the door behind her, she had the sense that she had just stepped into a lair. She glanced around looking for Rawls; he was nowhere in sight.

'May I take your coat?' the man said from behind her and she shook her head.

'That won't be necessary,' she said, 'this shouldn't take long.' She was growing increasingly aware of the sheer stupidity of her actions. She should have gone back to the car, called for back-up, tried Rawls again; anything but blunder into a house alone with a wanted criminal. What the hell did she think she was doing?

'Would you like tea? I've just boiled the kettle.'

'That would be lovely, thank you,' she said. 'White with two sugars.'

He smiled at her and walked across the open-plan room, his moccasin-clad feet making almost no sound on the black and white Italian tiled floor. 'Are you alone?'

'Alone?' she echoed. 'Oh no, my partner is on his way.' She hoped the lie sounded believable. She glanced up at the mezzanine floor above. The rooms up there were in darkness, the house was silent. Where the hell was Rawls?

Calver walked into the immaculate kitchen. It was sparsely decorated, the walls white, the cupboards and countertops black. It looked like a bachelor's pad rather than the holiday home of a married couple.

Calver saw her looking. 'We only come here on weekends, but I'm sure that you know that already.' He stood with his back to the kettle, steam rising behind him like a volcano.

Nat hadn't planned this far ahead. She had imagined herself getting here just in time to stop Rawls from doing something stupid, something that he would regret, but now, instead, it was Nat who was regretting her mistake – she was the one who needed to be rescued.

'Mr Calver, I assume that you are aware of the fire on your property earlier today?'

He turned his back and took two white porcelain mugs from the cupboard. 'No, I'm not. Was that back in Bath?'

'No, it was here, near the retreat,' Nat said. 'You didn't see the smoke or hear the fire engines?'

He kept his back to her. 'I can't say that I did, but then, I didn't get up till late.' He glanced at her briefly, 'You don't mind a mug, do you?'

'I ...' She wasn't sure what to say. This was surreal, they were playing a game that she had no possible way of winning. She tried to stay calm. 'I'm happy as it comes,' she said.

He lifted the kettle and poured water into the two mugs. 'But seriously, I was completely unaware of a fire. When did it happen?'

Nat felt hot. She pulled her jacket off and laid it on one of the tall stools at the counter. 'Early this morning, in an old railway lock-up.'

He turned to face her. 'Oh, I know where you mean now. I can't remember, did you want milk?'

'Yes, please.'

He opened the fridge, took out a bottle and poured a little into both cups.

'You were saying that you knew the outbuilding.'

He sighed. 'I do, of course, but ...' He screwed the lid back on to the milk before putting it back in the fridge. 'Sorry about the milk,' he said, passing a cup to Nat. 'It's soya – my wife insists – but it does separate a bit.'

He opened a drawer and she felt herself stiffen, imagining him pulling out a knife.

Calver caught the look on her face and smiled. 'Teaspoon?' he said, holding one up. 'To stir your tea?'

She thanked him and took it.

He stirred his own, watching her above the steam. 'We rarely have anything to do with that side of the land.'

'That side?'

'Where the storage shed is, where you say the fire was – that's on the "to be dealt with" list. This is an enormous estate. We sold a chunk of it off to the retreat, as I'm sure you know, but the land, well, that's all ours and there's just so much of it.'

'I see.' Nat wondered how far she should go with this questioning. She wasn't supposed to be there, after all.

He ran a hand across his mouth. 'Was anyone hurt? In the fire, I mean. We have kids in there sometimes; they have parties there, I imagine. You know what kids are like,' he gave her a knowing wink.

'No, no one was hurt,' Nat said, 'but the building was destroyed.'

He seemed to hesitate for a moment before speaking again. 'And there was definitely no one inside?'

Nat smiled. 'No,' she said, 'luckily not.'

'Well,' he looked down and brushed at his jeans, 'that's a relief. As for the building, it'll be a bit of an admin headache, I imagine, but probably for the best. We would have ended up demolishing it anyway.' He lifted his eyes like a librarian peeking over reading glasses. 'You said you had a couple of questions, Detective.'

Rawls had kept himself low to the ground, his back humped, his head down. He had skirted the small lawned garden using the large rhododendron bushes at the outer perimeter for cover; the rest, he had discovered, lit up like a bloody prison if you stepped in front of the many PIR lights. Holding his breath and crouching in the shadows, he looked into the kitchen, watching the interaction between Nat and Calver. Nat wasn't supposed to be here. He had explicitly asked her to stay at the hospital and instead she had hotfooted it straight over to the bloody lion's den. He'd heard her car pull into the gravel driveway and had slipped into the shadows, then as she'd climbed out, Rawls had made his way around the back. He risked another glance over the top: they were still talking, and Calver had his back to him. Rawls hoped that Nat would keep Calver occupied long enough for him to make the dash across the lawn and into the shadows of the corner of the house.

The sprint across the grass had left him breathless. He leaned against a wall, scanning the awnings for security lights, but it seemed there were none here. His breath was coming in small, frantic gasps and his back ached; he made a promise to whichever god ruled over his lungs that once this was all over he would get healthy: eat green stuff, swap beer for water, whip up a stir fry instead of ordering a takeaway, that sort of thing – whatever they needed if they would just let him breathe again. Come to think of it, he might even call his counsellor. Boy, did they have stuff to catch up on.

It had all come to Rawls while he waited at the hospital. The place had been too important for Mark and Amanda Calver to let go of, but it hadn't been the retreat that they remembered; it had been the makeshift tents in the woods, the old buildings with their dirty curtains for doors. It had been those wild days of their youth that they still sought to recreate. They had inherited a stately home, an estate with hundreds of acres. They were property developers, they bought and sold houses, they did them up and sold them on. The old milking parlour which had once been home to the revered Father Berkeley would have been ripe for developing, but this time they were doing up the place for themselves. They could go there on weekends, to the place that had always been their home.

He felt for the door handle, his eyes scanning the garden for movement in the shadows. The door was locked, and he pressed his ear to it to listen. It was silent, dead silent. He closed his eyes as though the very act of seeing might diminish any sounds and he stayed that way for several long seconds listening for Nat inside, wondering what to do.

It was time, he realised, to call Tess, to tell her what was going on and ask for her help. Nat had come to find him, she had come alone, she had clearly told no one or they would have been with her. She had done this to protect him and he had led her straight into danger.

He pulled his phone from his pocket and found Tess's number.

Mark padded across the tiles and Nat followed. Her arms had broken out in goosebumps and she rubbed absently at them. It had been a really long day and it was showing no signs of letting up any time soon. She felt suddenly almost too tired to walk.

They stood by the window looking out and Calver turned to her. 'You wanted to ask me a question?'

'Yes,' her voice sounded distant, her words slurring as though she was drunk; her eyes felt glazed and heavy.

Calver steered her back towards the kitchen, and she rested her free hand on the countertop.

'Are you alright, Detective?' he asked and, as she looked at him, he seemed to separate and divide. Briefly he became three, then two. 'Detective?'

'I feel …' she licked her lips, her mouth was dry and unresponsive, 'I feel giddy.' She fell back against the stool, vomit rising in the back of her throat, an explosion of pain behind her eyes, a tightness in her chest.

Mark leaned over her and brushed a stray hair from her face. 'Shh,' he whispered, 'just go to sleep.'

Nat stared at him but although she had heard him, his words were somehow alien to her. It was like listening to a voice on a badly tuned radio, distant and separate. 'I feel giddy,' she said again as her eyes glazed over and Mark took the mug from her hand and wrapped an arm around her waist. He held her with ease as her legs gave way beneath her and he lowered her slowly to the ground.

'Shh,' he whispered into her ear, 'this won't take long.'

Rawls heard the blow to his skull just a fraction of a second before he felt it. He had no doubt that it was meant to knock him out, but he was equally certain that it had failed. He spun on his heels, surprisingly nimble for a man with a bad back and perhaps now a minor concussion. His lungs seemed to close in on themselves and he drew in a long, ragged breath. 'You,' he said to the woman standing in front of him, 'you.'

Amanda Calver smiled. 'Me,' she said, and she raised the hammer to hit him again.

In that moment, time seemed to slow down. He had time to see her hand with the hammer in it, the arc of descent that her hand would make as it came towards him and the steps that he would need to take if he was to avoid the inevitable blow. He clenched his fist. Knowing that she would expect him to step backwards, to protect himself and to try to avoid the blow, he took a step towards her, narrowing the gap and putting himself almost up against her. The wound from his head was bleeding profusely but he raised his fist and aimed it straight at the woman's temple.

The punch went wide, glancing off and to the side of her head as she stepped back. She flailed at him with the hammer again and this time he felt the pain as it hit his upturned hand. Rawls stared at the hand for a moment; a depression had appeared in the back of it where the bone inside had broken in two. He looked up just in time to see that she had brought the hammer up again. She swung wildly at him, like a woman trying to hack her way through a bramble bush, and Rawls, his eyes fixed on hers with a kind of tunnel vision, saw that she had every intention of killing him.

She grasped at the handle with two hands, pulling the hammer back over her shoulder.

Rawls bent down, ignoring the explosion in his head and the one in his hand, as he let out a guttural howl and ran at her like a bull. He felt the hammer slam into his chest, then brought his head forward in a violent jerk and heard the sickening crack as it made contact with her nose, For a moment she stared at him, her eyes registering a mixture of disbelief and anger before they glazed over and her body fell limp against him.

He stood up, wincing at the familiar popping sounds coming from his spine, and that was when he noticed the smell.

*

Nat felt herself slide to the ground. Barely able to think, her vision blurred, she bit down on her tongue hard enough to draw blood, not wanting to lose consciousness. Mark had his back to her; he was washing her cup. 'Hiding evidence,' she thought crazily, 'he's trying to hide whatever he put in my tea.' She wanted to get up, to run from the place, escape this madman, but she didn't think that she could move. She might be conscious, but she had no control over her limbs; they felt as though her bones had been removed.

This is how he does it, she thought wildly. *She lures them, they drug them and then he kills them.* She hadn't wanted to imagine what else he might do to them before that; it was too much for her to handle.

Mark, his back still turned, opened a cupboard and rifled around inside. He was humming to himself as he pulled out a roll of plastic bags, unravelled one and tore it off. He put the roll back inside the cupboard and turned towards her, the remaining bag in his hand. She realised with terrible clarity that he intended to put it over her head. She could see him in her mind's eye, pulling it down, sealing it around her neck, perhaps using tape or just the drawstrings that hung like tiny yellow snakes from the open mouth of the bag. She tried to stand up but her legs stubbornly refused; she tried to push herself away using her arms, but they too remained out of her control. Even her voice, when she tried to scream, would not work, and she was powerless to do anything but stare at the man as he crossed the room, a small smile playing at the corners of his mouth.

'This won't hurt a bit,' he said, bending down.

Nat tried to scream again, but now, as the drug continued its war on her body, even her mouth seemed alien to her. At that moment she wished that she had passed out but, as he brought the white bag down over her head and the strangely familiar lemon scent filled her senses, she realised that she hadn't been supposed to. He wanted her awake, had probably wanted all of them awake; that was the reason that he did it, that was his kick, knowing that they knew what was happening and knowing that they were powerless to stop it. This was the control that he needed, this was his pleasure.

She heard tape being pulled off a roll from somewhere that was both close by and a million miles away. In her mind she begged him to stop, she pleaded, she screamed, but she also knew that he wouldn't. He couldn't.

She felt the tape around her neck, and she tried to hold her breath as though that might save her oxygen. She tried to clench the muscles in her neck – she had read somewhere that escape artists did this with their hands when they were tied; it was something about the clenched muscles making the limbs ever so slightly bigger. In Nat's case it made no difference because her muscles still stubbornly refused to respond. *Please*, she tried to say but her mouth would not work, *please*, she thought one last time and then, mercifully, she fainted.

Rawls forced himself up, biting down on the scream that the pain in his back was trying to force out of him. On the ground beneath him, the woman lay motionless. He felt for a pulse and was relieved to feel one, faint but definite. He stared at the woman, his mind racing through scenarios. Why had she tried to kill him? Why hadn't they just left – what were they waiting for? None of it made sense.

Behind him the smell of burning grew stronger: the basement was alight. That was why they were still here, his mind told him: they were hiding evidence, and that was probably why they had burned the storage shed as well. Rawls didn't want to imagine what they might have had in there. There was nothing he could do about it now; smoke was billowing out of the cracks in the door and it would only be a matter of time before the main house caught too. He could faintly hear the sound of Mark Calver's voice. He held his breath listening for Nat, and with a growing sense of alarm, realised that he could no longer hear her at all.

Reaching down, he grasped the handle of the hammer, which was so slick with his own blood that at first it slid from his hand. He grabbed at it again and stuffed the handle into his shirt so that he could pull himself to a standing position. Limping towards the bifold doors, he wondered wildly if they would be hammer-resistant. He hoped not – they might be the only chance he had of getting in.

Pressing his back to the wall, he reached into his pocket and felt for his phone. Opening it, he opened the camera and changed the mode to selfie, held it up in front of him and moved it slightly to the right. The kitchen came into view, at first blurry and difficult to see. Rawls touched the screen, forced the image to focus and gasped.

Mark Calver was sitting on the floor, his back to Rawls, and in front of him, lying on the floor, was Natalie.

Rawls grabbed inside his shirt for the hammer and felt his phone fall to the ground. There was no time to pick it up. He swung the hammer high above his head, ready to break the door, and was about to bring it down when he noticed the handle. Calver still had his back to him, and Rawls assessed whether he had time to try it. He decided that he did and reached for it with a speed that he had not known he still possessed. At first it seemed to do nothing, resisting his touch before sliding open in front of him.

Mark turned just in time to see Rawls throw the hammer, but not quickly enough to move out of its way. It caught him on the side of his face, and he screamed with pain. Rawls was on him then, bellowing with fury. He threw Mark to the ground, feeling the now familiar sensation of a body making contact with a hard surface. Mark sat up, spat blood and laughed. Rawls tried to pull him up, but his broken hand sent a shock of pain through his arm that made him cry out and Calver took the opportunity to scramble to his feet and run from the room.

Rawls turned to Nat, praying aloud that she was still alive.

Afterwards, Rawls would wonder if he had even considered chasing after Mark Calver. The choice, Rawls knew, would have been between saving Nat's life or catching Calver, and he was pretty certain that the idea of leaving her had not even crossed his mind. He grabbed at Nat, pushing his fingers into the bag, tearing at it frantically. The plastic stretched against his grip for what seemed an eternity before finally giving way and he ripped wildly at it with his nails as he pulled it from her face.

Beneath the kitchen lights, Nat's face was blue; a faint line of white seemed to have been drawn around her lips in a hideous outline and a string of vomit drooled from her mouth. Rawls scooped at with his fingers, clearing her airway before clamping his mouth over hers.

In the back of his mind he heard the Bee Gees singing 'Staying Alive' as he parted her lips and blew into them. Again and again, he forced his breath into her lungs as the faint but distinct sound of sirens filled the room.

How long he stayed that way, he didn't know, but he didn't stop when he heard the police banging on the front door, he didn't stop when he heard them breaking it in, he didn't even stop when the paramedics came into the room and told him to get out of the way. They pulled him away from her, and Rawls saw a swarm of green uniforms taking his place. Exhausted, he fell back, staring down at them the way that a wandering spirit might stare down at its own body on a hospital bed.

'Is she OK?' he was asking everyone and no one. 'Is she OK?' His voice was rising in a panic and even as it did, he was aware that he was crying. A paramedic stood up from the group and signalled to a uniformed officer who was standing at a distance. Outside the PIR light had come on and Rawls saw more green scrubs in the garden. They circled the woman lying on the ground and in his mind's eye, Rawls saw again the terrible unnatural angle of her head, the blood encircling it like the devil's version of a halo. He saw the look on her face, a look of shock and surprise as she had fallen, and he heard again that awful sound of something, he hoped not her neck, breaking beneath him.

He leaned back against the wall, the sounds of the emergency service personnel all around him. Red and blue lights flickered on and off, reflected against the white walls, and he felt a wave of relief. It was over, Tess had sent the cavalry.

Chapter 24

It took Rawls nearly nine months before he was able to talk to Amanda Calver. She'd been detained under the Mental Health Act, and he thought it might have been easier to arrange an appointment to visit the queen. He found himself strangely nervous as he waited for her to arrive.

The room was oppressively hot. No windows had been opened despite the early June heatwave that had caught the country by surprise once again, bringing the railways to a standstill and melting tarmac on garage forecourts, and Rawls was sweating profusely in his black chinos and long-sleeved checked shirt. He had lost more than a few kilograms during the intervening months. They had been difficult; his suspension had led to his resignation and his marriage had gone in a similar direction.

Eileen had found herself unable to forgive him. The car, she said, had been more than a betrayal; it had been a symbol of their separate lives, their inability to talk, their drifting apart. The break-up had not been bitter or acrimonious; the exact opposite, in fact, congenial and agreeable. Rawls had packed a bag, collected his iPhone charger and hugged both his wife and daughter goodbye. He had gone, first, to a Premier Inn and then, once circumstances allowed, to a small new-build on the outskirts of what had been a sleepy ex-coal mining village and was now described as an 'up and coming' location. There, he had settled into life on his own. He had bought a dog, a black Labrador, and then another to keep the first company when he was out. He had made friends with his neighbours and learned to take his own bags with him when he visited the local Co-op. Rawls had carved a lonely but somehow satisfying life for himself.

He knew, as they all did, that life would change soon. The bodies of the girls had been found. Their deaths had not been unexpected, not by a long shot, but that had made them none the less devastating. Rawls had been kept informed by Nat, who during the course of the investigation had blossomed into an excellent detective and Rawls was certain would be in line for a detective sergeant role in the not too distant future.

Forensics on the first three girls, Melody, Harriet and Yvette, had been difficult but not impossible. Their bodies had been buried deep, nearly eight feet down. They had been covered with a muddy silt and had gone unnoticed in the constant evolution of the nature pond at the very edge of the estate, where it bordered with the retreat at Stoney Barrow View. Rawls had thought it a horrible irony that a place so tranquil and beautiful had hidden such a dark and terrible secret.

The pathologist had not been able to determine whether or not the first three girls had been raped but, he had informed Tess and Nat, who had told Rawls, he couldn't be entirely sure due to the state of decomposition. They had been drugged, this he could confirm, and toxicology reports had also confirmed that the drug, a tranquiliser, found in the girls was identical to the one used on both Carmen and Nat. Cause of death was also difficult to say for certain for Melody, Harriet and Yvette, but a post-mortem carried out on Tanya, who had died within days of her abduction, had concluded, from the presence of petechial haemorrhaging – small red spots in her eyes and lungs – that death had been caused by traumatic asphyxia: suffocation to the lay person. All four of the girls had been buried, if you could call it that – disposed of, was the term that Tess had used – with plastic bags covering their faces. Nat's lips had trembled as she had told Rawls about the bags and he understood why. They were all similar to the one that he had ripped from Nat's own face, not too many months previously.

The bags, it seemed, had been carefully chosen; they had tie handles and were opaque. It was assumed that this had allowed Calver to watch as the girls had struggled for those few terrible minutes before they had finally died. All the girls had indications of tranquilisers in their systems, one that was readily available on prescription and provided in both oral and injectable forms. It had come as no surprise to anyone that the prescriptions for these drugs had been made out to a Mrs Amanda Calver. She had facilitated and covered for her husband for more than ten years.

Rawls had attended each of the funerals; Carmen had come with him, but Eileen had not. They had sat silently at the back, where they could remain unnoticed, Carmen's thin hand clasped in his. They had not spoken during the services, nor had they on the way home; they had simply been there. Rawls had thought, on more than one occasion, that they had gone there to atone for their own sins: he to be forgiven for not stopping this soon enough and she for surviving when these other girls had not. Rawls thought that his daughter's survival would be the cross she would carry for the rest of her life.

The bodies had been uncovered exactly where Amanda Calver had told them to look. The lake. The one that she had been digging or, to be more precise, the lake that ABC Property Maintenance had been digging for the past decade. She had done as she had been told: dug holes where she had been instructed and filled them when she had been instructed. This, the psychiatrist's notes informed Rawls, had been her go-to behaviour for a great many years.

Calver had manipulated his wife, using her in a manner that most people would have found impossible to comprehend; she had been his accomplice, his assistant, his enabler. Calver did more than control her, he owned her. She had been declared 'unfit to stand trial' and her case would be considered instead by a 'trial of the facts', a law that protected those that the court considered unfit to plead. In this type of trial, the courts would determine the facts against Amanda and sentence her accordingly. Rawls hadn't been sure that anyone, least of all Amanda Calver, could claim to know the facts, and he suspected that they never really would. So, when Amanda had asked to speak with him, he had had his misgivings at first but these had quickly given way to curiosity. He had to know, perhaps not the facts, but at the very least the reasons.

He wanted to know why she had acted as she had. Along with everyone else, he had been surprised when she had informed her doctors that it was Rawls and Rawls alone that she would confide in.

The hoops that he had needed to jump through had been plentiful and Rawls was the first to admit that there had been many an occasion when he had wanted nothing more than to wash his hands of the affair, to move on with his life and start afresh. However, it had been Carmen who had survived when the others had not. Carmen who would live with the mental scars of her ordeal for many years to come. Carmen who would doubt every decision she made, who would be afraid to trust, who would be afraid of the dark, of fire, of God knows what else that might trigger her memory.

It was Carmen's face that he held now in his mind as Amanda Calver crossed the room, clad in a grey sweatshirt and leggings, and took a seat in front of him.

She perched like a bird, her hands clasped in her lap, her lips compressed so tightly that they had lost their colour altogether, and her eyes cast down.

'Hello, Sergeant Rawls,' she said without looking up.

'Hello, Amanda,' Rawls said. 'Call me Peter or Rawls or Mr Rawls if you like, but I'm not in the service any more.'

Her eyes flicked briefly towards him; they held his own for a few moments and then dropped again. She nodded, 'Mr Rawls.'

Rawls opened his mouth to speak but she held a hand up briefly to stop him. 'Have you caught him yet?' she asked, her voice little more than a whisper.

Rawls assumed that she meant her husband. 'No, not yet, they're working on it. He was all over the news for a while but we've had nothing so far … Did you know that others have come forward?'

'Others?'

'Other girls, making accusations against him.'

She looked over his shoulder, at the metal bars that were encased by more metal bars. 'I didn't, but I thought there would be more.' Her voice drifted off as though she had forgotten what they were talking about and she clasped her hands together in front of her, like a woman in prayer. 'This is a terrible thing,' she said, then she looked at him and smiled weakly, her dry lips parting to show two missing teeth. Rawls saw that her lips were bleeding a little. It gave her the look of a woman on her death bed and he found that he had to look away.

'What happened?' he said, touching his own teeth.

She shrugged. 'They don't have much time for kiddie killers in here.'

Rawls crossed his legs – it was easier since the weight loss. 'But you're not a kiddie killer, are you?'

Her eyes flashed. 'Haven't you read my statement?'

'I have,' Rawls said, 'but I assumed that was what you wanted to see me about, to retract it perhaps.'

She sat back against the hard plastic of the chair. 'I killed them,' she said and held her hand up when she saw Rawls about to protest. 'I killed them just as much as if I had put the bag over their heads myself.'

'How do you know that's how he did it?' Rawls asked.

She looked away again, staring out of the cage that held her. 'Because I did it.'

'You mean you saw him do it?' Rawls pushed her. 'You saw him, and I think that you were so afraid that you did nothing. Isn't that the truth?'

She shook her head and her lip trembled. 'I saw nothing,' she said, turning her head and closing her eyes like a toddler refusing food.

Rawls touched her hand briefly. 'Why didn't you report him?'

She looked at him, her face genuinely baffled. 'Report him? He was my husband; how could I report him?'

'For what he did, for what he made you part of.'

'It wasn't his fault,' she said, and for a moment, Rawls thought that her eyes had sharpened a little.

'Then who?' he asked. 'Whose fault was it?'

She leaned back in her chair, pushing herself as far away from Rawls as she could get. She looked at him through narrowed, distrustful eyes, 'I told you already,' she said, 'mine.'

Rawls moved in his seat, unfolding his long legs so that he could stretch them a little. He wished that he had an Ibuprofen; despite the time that had passed, the scar on the back of his head still throbbed when he was stressed. He was stressed now, and his head was pounding as though his brain might explode.

'No,' he said, 'not yours, we both know that.' He waited a moment, hoping that she might fill in the silence, but she pursed her lips as though she needed to lock the words away.

He sighed. 'OK then, tell me about your father.'

She kept her lips pursed, her eyes darting around the room as though she was looking for a means of escape.

Rawls pressed his hand to his forehead and closed his eyes; his head really did hurt like a bastard. He stood up and went to the cooler where he poured them both a plastic cupful of water. He drank his down, then filled it again before sitting back down and placing hers in front of her.

'Ready?' he said, trying to sound light. 'Good, let's begin.' He tried to look at her but she kept her eyes away from him. 'Feel free to correct me if I get anything wrong, won't you?'

She ignored him and he wondered if she was even listening.

'You lost your mother in a car crash when you were only around seven or eight, that's correct, isn't it?' He waited in case she might respond but she stayed quiet. 'You were sent to live with your father, Francis Burgess, or did you call him Father Berkeley?'

She shook her head. 'I called him Father,' she said in a voice little more than a whisper, 'everyone else called him Father Berkeley.'

'Were there many of you back then?' Rawls asked. 'When you first went to live with him?'

'No, not at first, just a couple of families.'

'He had changed his name, though?'

'He changed it officially when he inherited the manor house.' Amanda closed her eyes as she spoke.

'Stoney Barrow View?'

She kept her eyes shut but nodded.

'So, you went to live with your father and two other families at Stoney Barrow View? Where did you live? When I visited, there were more than two families and no one living in the house.'

'We were in the house at first, until I was about nine or ten,' she said and she opened her eyes and stared at the bars as she spoke, 'but the place was freezing and dangerous while it was being done up. Father was becoming famous, not just in Bath.' She smiled, still proud of his memory. 'He was on the radio and TV all over England, talking about the importance of clean living.'

'Clean living?' Rawls queried. His memories of the hell-hole that he had visited were of anything but cleanliness.

'Clean food, clean minds, clean hearts,' Amanda elaborated.

'People were handing over their salaries to him,' Rawls said, 'and as far as I could tell, they were living in muddy tents covered in shit.'

'To build a better world,' she snapped.

And to line his pockets, Rawls thought but did not say.

'We only lived in the tents for a couple of years.'

Rawls thought that a couple of days would have been too much for him. 'After that you all moved into the big house?'

She nodded. 'It was so beautiful, you should have seen it back in those days.'

'And Mark, when did he arrive?'

She folded her arms, either for protection or to close herself off, and looked away again.

'As far as we can tell,' Rawls continued, 'Mark's parents joined the group when he was twelve, so that would have made you, what? Eight?'

'Nine,' she corrected him, 'almost ten.'

'OK, but still young, and impressionable.' She said nothing so he went on, 'Things were tough on the Stoney Path, weren't they?'

She glared at him. 'Of course they were, building a better future is never easy.'

'And Father Berkeley wasn't exactly a doting father figure, was he?'

She stared at the wall.

'He liked the ladies, didn't he?'

'He had a mission,' she said.

'From God, no less,' Rawls agreed.

She bent her head. 'From God, yes, but from all of us as well; we needed him, his guidance, his love.'

'Did he have a special lady friend? Someone you could call a mother?'

'He had many lady friends, they were all my mother.'

'That doesn't sound very loving,' Rawls said. 'I mean, it can't have been easy.'

A single tear had forced its way out over her eyelids. 'I had plenty of love,' she said.

'But none from a mother, no mother to guide you, or to confide in, perhaps to talk to about your new boyfriend? About Mark?'

She stared at him. 'Mark was so strong, not like the others. They all cried when they were separated from their parents, but not Mark, he was strong, strong enough for all of us.'

Rawls cocked his head. 'You were separated from your parents?'

She looked at him as though he was a little mad. 'We had to be. They had to work, to earn money and to help with the restorations; we were distractions to them. In the wild you don't see animals having to look after their young once they're able to feed themselves, do you? And we're meant to be superior to them, yet we cling to our parents long after we are capable of bearing children of our own.'

Rawls wanted to respond but found he couldn't.

'Mark protected me,' she said, 'from the others. They could be boisterous at times, and Father Berkeley believed that rules would hinder our growth as people, so there was nothing to …' she hesitated for a moment, 'to curb them,' she said at last.

'Curb them?' Rawls asked and she looked up at him almost coquettishly.

'The boys,' she said, 'curb their advances.'

Rawls shuddered, imagining a place where children ran wild, acting as they saw fit, doing what they wanted, when they wanted. 'You didn't have to help with the restorations?'

'Of course, but we didn't have to work constantly,' she looked at him earnestly, 'we weren't in prison.'

Rawls thought about the lives these children must have led, left to their own devices, no one to nurture them, no one to call them in at bedtime or to help them with their homework; he felt sad even now. 'What about school, though? How did you all manage that?'

She smiled. 'We were home-schooled, Mr Rawls. Father Berkeley and a couple of the other older members taught us.'

Rawls rubbed his forehead. *Of course he did*, he thought to himself, *of course he bloody did.*

Amanda suddenly laughed out loud. 'I remember the plays we put on for him, he loved drama, it was his passion. Every year, without fail, we would put on a big production. At first it was just us but, once the house had been officially turned into a retreat, he would bring in other drama groups from the area. We did the same play every year.'

Rawls smiled. '*Pygmalion*,' he said; it wasn't a question.

She smiled brightly, covering her missing teeth with the back of her hand. 'Yes, *Pygmalion*, Father Berkeley loved that play. After a while, when he was too old to manage it all himself, Mark took over. He was so talented, he could sing and dance and play the piano, my father loved him.' Her voice hung in the air for a moment. 'Mark was supposed to take over the group when Father Berkeley passed away, that was why he gave me to him, so that we could run it together.'

Rawls was taken aback. 'Gave you to him?'

She screwed her eyes up and nodded. 'As his woman. Men can have many women, but they have one main woman, to look after them, see to their needs, that was the way of the Stoney Path.'

How convenient, Rawls thought, having one woman to see to your needs. 'And that was what you did for Mark?'

She looked down at her bony hands for a moment and when she looked up, she seemed almost serene. 'Of course I did, Mr Rawls, that was my job. It's the job of all of the women who follow the Stoney Path.'

'No matter what *their* needs might be?'

She looked away. 'It wasn't our place to judge.'

'Did they all know?' he asked, his voice so low that he wasn't certain that she would be able to hear him. 'The women at the retreat, did they know what was going on?'

She shrugged. 'You would need to ask them yourself.'

Rawls felt an anger in his chest. Was this possible, could the entire place have known? Could their adherence to a doctrine written by a guy who had been dead for nearly fifteen years really have been enough to ignore what Mark was doing? A thought struck him, 'Did your father have similar needs to Mark?'

She looked away. 'No, he didn't. Mark had needs that were … different from the rest of us.' She bent her head as her eyes brimmed with tears.

'You knew what he was doing?'

'He …' she bit her lip, 'he liked young girls.'

'Liked them?' Rawls was incredulous. 'Liked them? He killed them.' She shook her head, but he persisted, 'Yes, he did, and you knew it, Amanda. You knew it but you chose to ignore it.'

Amanda's shoulders hitched as she cried silently into her hands.

'He told me that he'd let them leave, and made it look as though they had run away.'

'And you're trying to tell me that you believed that?' Rawls was incredulous. 'You're trying to tell me that you believed that he was just going to let them go?'

She bent her head, allowing it to bang against the cold tabletop. 'Not trying, I did believe that. I really did.' She lifted her head and locked her swollen eyes on his furious ones. 'You have to understand, Mr Rawls, I knew that whatever he did, I belonged to him, it was never my place to question him.' She lifted her head again and covered her face as she spoke, peering through parted fingers so that she looked like a woman making the sign of the evil eye, 'I had to believe that, or I'd have gone mad.'

'But you buried the bodies.'

She looked away. 'I buried things for him, yes, that's true.'

'You're trying to tell me that you didn't know that they were bodies?'

'I ...' she looked at her hands, spreading her fingers wide, 'I didn't ask.'

'Don't ask, don't tell,' Rawls said, and Amanda nodded.

'Something like that.'

'I need to know why you took them, how he chose them. I need to know why he chose my daughter, my Carmen.'

Amanda winced as though the name hurt her somehow. 'She was pretty, they were all pretty.'

Rawls gritted his teeth. 'They were pretty? He chose them because they were pretty?' He had raised his voice enough for the nurse, stationed outside the door, to look up. 'You're as bad as he is,' Rawls said, his voice trembling, 'you two deserved each other.'

He stood up suddenly. 'I don't know why I came here. I don't know what I thought you would tell me but you're mad,' he said, tapping at his temple, 'you're stark raving mad.'

He turned to leave but stopped as she cried out, 'Wait, Mr Rawls, please just wait. I saw one girl, what he had done to her. I think you're right, I did go a little bit mad. She was just lying there, and I knew she was dead.' She looked at Rawls, 'She had this bag over her head and ...' she bit her lip hard enough to break the skin, 'he had drawn a face on the bag, like a kid's drawing, eyes and eyelashes and big red lips. She had blood all over her blouse, and it was ...' she gasped, 'inside the bag. I think her nose had been bleeding.'

'When was this?'

She closed her eyes and put her hands to her mouth. 'God forgive me,' she said, 'it was the fourth girl.'

'Tanya Hickock,' Rawls said.

'Yes, Tanya, it was after she had gone missing. I went into the basement. I wasn't supposed to, but I did. I saw he had left the key on the sideboard and I just did it, on the spur of the moment, I crept down the stairs and I unlocked the door.' She ran her tongue across her bleeding lips. 'I was like Bluebeard's wife, Mr Rawls. I had seen what my husband could do, was doing, but Bluebeard's wife was innocent, and I am not. I was part of it. I was his accomplice; you could say his unwilling accomplice maybe, but what difference does that make? I'm as guilty as he is.'

She let out a noise that Rawls interpreted as a sob. 'You just kept quiet and went along with him after that?'

'Of course, I kept quiet. I tried to block it from my mind.' She wiped at her mouth absently with the back of her hand, seeming not to notice the smear of blood that it left behind.

Rawls stared at her. 'But you saved Carmen, why?'

'Carmen, I knew she was next. He had sent her a text to arrange the date. He wouldn't normally have gone for another girl, not so quickly, not straight away.'

'He usually left it a few years.'

She nodded. 'Till the right one came along.'

'Why did he change? Why take Carmen so quickly?'

She shrugged. 'My guess is that he knew he was running out of time. He just wanted one more before the net closed in.'

Rawls stared at her, incredulous. She was so casual about it, as if she had helped him to put a bet on a horse at the races.

'Did you always pick the girls up for him?'

'Yes, he said that they would trust me. He was right, they always did. I could tell them anything: that I was collecting them because their mother was ill, that school had sent me, that they should go with me or I would tell their parents – or with Tanya, I had parked up on the side of the road, she thought I was taking her to work.'

'So it was you parked in the van, not Mark?'

She smiled, her cracked lips now red with blood. 'Of course it was me, he never did his own dirty work. The girls never questioned me, never argued, they were like lambs to the slaughter.' She looked away, pushing at her cheeks with the back of her hand.

He studied her, her grey hair screwed up in unbrushed lumps around her face, her swollen eyes, red-rimmed and desperate, her pale skin pulled tightly over her bony face, her cracked lips bleeding into her teeth, she looked for all the world as though she had been in captivity herself, and Rawls supposed that she had.

'Mr Rawls, did you wonder why I wanted to speak to you?'

'I assumed you wanted to clear your conscience.'

'Yes,' she closed her eyes, 'but also to explain. I tried to save Carmen. I need you to know that. I tried to hide her.'

Rawls felt his head swim, was she really going to try to exonerate herself now? Was she going to try to explain away her part in this?

'I just couldn't take it any more. It was too much, Mark was out of control, I was terrified. I had to try to stop him so I hid Carmen away. I hoped that he had forgotten about the storage shed, I put her there, just till I could work out what to do. I couldn't think straight.'

Rawls hadn't seen this coming. He said, 'I don't understand, why did you light the fire, you must have known it would kill her.'

It took a second or two – to Rawls it felt like a lifetime – before she answered him.

'I didn't, Mark did. He knew that I had betrayed him, and he was furious because I wouldn't tell him where Carmen was. But he was certain that you, the police, were coming for him. He had taken stuff, from the girls, you know?'

'Trophies?'

She nodded. 'I guess that's what you could call them. Anyway, he said that he had to get rid of them. He'd been hiding them in the basement at the barn but he remembered the old shed and took them there. He told me that he covered the place in fire-lighting fluid and just threw a match in.' She gave Rawls a look so sincere that he almost felt sorry for her. 'I don't think he knew that your daughter was down in the basement. I don't think he meant to kill her.'

Not then, maybe, Rawls thought.

'I saw the smoke and knew what had happened, that was why I rang 999.'

There had been a number of calls to 999 and Rawls had been surprised to discover that one of them had come from the Calvers' home.

'Are we nearly done?' Amanda asked him. 'I need to take my medication at six – is it six?' Her voice suddenly sounded distant and he could see that she was exhausted; he felt the same way and his headache was making him feel sick. At least, he thought it was the headache.

He glanced at his watch and sighed. He didn't think he could take much more of this woman and her excuses. 'Do you know where Mark might be?'

She shook her head, her eyes shut tight. 'I really don't.'

'Would you tell me if you did?'

He thought she might take a moment to consider before answering, but she didn't.

'No,' she said, 'probably not.'

Rawls tried to resist it, but he couldn't help feeling sorry for the woman. She seemed to be almost collapsing before his eyes. It was as though first her face, and then her body, were sinking below some unseen murky surface. It was like watching someone drown in slow motion.

She searched his face as though she were trying to read him. 'For what it's worth,' she said, 'I am sorry for my part in all of this.'

Rawls found he had no response. He could not, would not, exonerate her, tell her that it was alright, that she was not to blame. She *was* to blame: she had had a choice and she had chosen to defend the man, to cover for him, to help him. Rawls could not tell her that it was all going to be OK. He touched her shoulder briefly; it felt brittle beneath his palm, as though it might break if he squeezed too hard. He picked up his coat and rubbed at his aching temples. 'Thank you for seeing me.'

She turned away and Rawls walked across the room, nodding to the nurse on the other side of the door to let him out.

He shivered as he walked out of the building. It was a warm evening, but the prison had been hot inside and he felt cold now in his shirt sleeves. He hadn't expected the debriefing with Amanda's doctors to take so long, and he was tired and hungry. He stood for a moment, looking at the high walls that surrounded the car park. Shepton Mallet prison was nearly four hundred years old and Rawls knew that it had seen its fair share of misery. From incarceration to hanging, the place had played host to more miserable souls than Rawls cared to imagine. As he stood in the cool night air, he felt as though the building itself might somehow be watching him, its sad history lingering somehow in the very fabric of the walls and in the windows that stared down like eyes, cruel and remorseless for all eternity.

From somewhere came the crack of a twig and he spun around to see a shape, black against the white of a lamp, watching him from across the small courtyard. He called out and the thing moved, its tail swishing as it climbed over the wall. A cat, he laughed at himself, bloody fool. He rubbed at his arms, at the goosebumps that had risen there, and turned to the car park where his car waited alone in the shadow of an ancient oak. He would be glad to leave this place.

His phone vibrated in his pocket and he pulled it out, unlocked it, and then read the message that had appeared on the screen.

For a moment he stood perfectly still, his feet rooted to the spot. A cold sweat had broken out on his forehead and he felt as though every hair on his body was standing on end. He turned, moving slowly, almost unable to breathe, the sound of his heart hammering in his head. He forced himself to look once more at the brooding edifice behind him, staring back at him, cold and pitiless. He was aware of every single sound: the growling of evening traffic beyond the prison walls, the sharp beeping of a pedestrian crossing, even, somewhere in the night sky, a plane droning its way towards Bristol Airport. To his left the small courtyard sat silent, lit only by a small decorative lamp which made ghost shadows out of the squat shrubs that hunkered there. Beyond that the only other light fell across the great wooden doors which had been closed so deftly behind him.

He took a step, and the sound of it seemed to echo against the stone walls, torturously loud in the quiet of the night. Forcing himself, he took another and found that he wanted to bolt for the safety of his car, expecting, at every step, a blow to his head or a voice in the dark. Unable to resist, he ran the final few steps and stopped briefly to examine the back seat before unlocking the door and climbing inside.

He slammed his fist against the lock button and blew out a long, trembling breath. Outside the cold moon made malignant shadows out of all that it touched, and it was all Rawls could do to force his trembling hand to open his phone and read the message for a second time.

How's my wife, Peter?

Acknowledgements

I genuinely thought that someone was playing an elaborate joke on me when I listened to a voicemail from a gentleman named Luigi Bonomi some two years ago now. His message suggested that I might like to call him back with reference to my entry in the *Daily Mail* Penguin Random House First Novel Competition and, needless to say, I did so fairly swiftly. If it was a joke, it's been an incredibly good one. Luigi, thank you, you will probably never really know just how much that call meant to me. While we're on that subject, Selina Walker, Fern Britton, Sandra Parsons and Rebecca Millar, I cannot properly express just how grateful I am for your collective faith in *The Fifth Girl*, thank you so much for pulling my novel out of the pile and giving me this opportunity.

Georgia Fancett

Sonny Marr, my editor who is always, always right (and I will hear nothing to the contrary). Thank you from the bottom of my heart for the effort you put into this book and for making it so much better than the one that I thought I was going to write. What's it like being so blinking brilliant?

Sarah Bance, my copy-editor, thank you for your keen eye and for saving my blushes over such minor issues as which day of the week it is.

Elizabeth Garner, my Oxford Creative Writing tutor, your kindness, support and inspiration has meant so much to me over the years. Thank you.

From Wiltshire CID, Detective Sergeant Ian Magrath, I am indebted to you for your time and advice. Also, to the Avon & Somerset Police Citizen's Academy team, I hope you can forgive my mistakes.

Sylwia, thank you for loaning me your girls, Amelia and Esme, who did their level best, along with Hardy and Jack, to teach me a little bit about how teenagers communicate, although I still don't fully understand what a Snapchat *streak* is.

I would also like to let Lou Morrish know just how grateful I am to her for her advice, pep talks and support but, most of all, for becoming my very good friend. Lou, you are a diamond!

Thank you also to my mum who rang me and suggested that I '*give this competition in the paper a try*' and to my dad who taught me, above all, that 6 X 7 is 42, always.

To my gang: Calico, Hero, Hardy, Atti, Chris and Pip, thanks for the support and encouragement, you all make me so very proud.

Lastly to Ben, my husband, my love and my rock. Thank you for listening, reading, supporting and improving this book. This really is for you.

About the Author

Georgia Fancett's debut novel *The Fifth Girl* won the Penguin Random House First Novel Competition in partnership with the *Daily Mail*. She lives and writes from her home in Bath in North East Somerset with her husband, children and dogs.